A 21st Century Copernicus Effect

by

Will Disdale

Grosvenor House
Publishing Limited

Will Disdale is hereby identified as author of this work in accordance with Section 77 of the Copyright, Designs and Patents Act 1988

This book is published by
Grosvenor House Publishing Ltd
28-30 High Street, Guildford, Surrey, GU1 3EL.
www.grosvenorhousepublishing.co.uk

A CIP record for this book
is available from the British Library

ISBN 978-1-908596-82-6

Acknowledgments

I'd like to thank everybody I have spoken with over the years about the big unanswered questions and anomalies we notice in these lives. I thank my mother, father and brother for providing a very pleasant the home life and upbringing as well as acting as a sounding board for my questions of life on more than one occasion! To all my friends in Wokingham England, to my uni friends all over the world, to everybody I met while travelling in Australia and to all the Palmersport Crew in Bedford, you have inspired me and I thank you all graciously.

Acknowledgement is also made to people I've never met, wise minds who have left their mark on time. Your words have inspired me and given me confidence that other people have realised what I believe I've realised.

Author Background

This is Will Disdale's first book, and it was written over the three years between November 2008 and September 2011. At the time of publication Will is 31 years old and is self-employed working as a motor racing instructor.

Will's educational background lies in engineering and science and he holds a bachelors degree in Automotive Engineering and a PhD in Computational Mathematics. After completing the PhD in 2007 he lived in Sydney for a year working and travelling where he was pulled onto a more spiritual journey of curiosity and soul searching. Upon arrival back into England the journey continued and gave him the conviction he needed to complete this book.

Author Forward

What's your opinion of the current human systems that are presently shaping our children's tomorrow? Really think about it: the money and finance systems, the legal and corporate systems, the education systems and the political systems? Do you think the next generation will thank the previous for their systematic inheritance and the consequential impacts on their lifestyles and cultures? Or do you think we could build a better world? I would like you to bear this question in mind as you read this book

Nicolaus Copernicus was an astronomer who lived in the late 15th and early 16th century. In 1543, on his deathbed, his controversial studies of the heavens were published, putting forward his assertion that the apparent movement of the sun across the skies was in fact due to an effect caused by the movement of the earth about a stationary sun. The authority at the time, namely the church, thought the idea ludicrous, as it flew in the face of observation and went against the scripture that said the Earth was the stationary centre of the heavens. If the Earth was moving, as Copernicus had postulated, then the people would be able to feel its movements, surely. Also if the Earth was moving it would cause the oceans to slop about the Earth in a non-orderly fashion. Copernicus was obviously wrong in the eyes of authority, and was criticised for being a heretic (heretic is defined as anyone that does not conform to an established attitude, doctrine or principle.) and a fraud.

It wasn't until almost one hundred years later, after astronomers like Johannes Kepler and Galileo Galilei had researched further with advancing theories of gravity and inertia and using tools like telescopes that Copernicus' model was seen to be more likely throughout the scientific community than the church's. It was the start of modern physics as we know it today, and these names are esteemed as being the fathers of that science. Even still however the old ideas died hard, for the church chastised Galileo for supporting Copernicanism and the last eight years of Galileo's life were served under house arrest after he was found guilty in 1634 "vehemently suspect of heresy".

Knowing what you do now about the solar system would you have preferred to go against the establishment in your knowing the truth and faced charges of heresy, or would you have dropped your assertions for an easy life? Can you imagine what the likes of Copernicus and Galileo must have felt as they were branded heretics?

How times change. Today, the Copernican model of a central sun and orbiting planets is a given. It is the model we teach our children, it is the model that explains the tides, the seasons and the eclipses. It's blindingly obvious you say now... with hindsight.

But: a word of caution here, lest we not get too confident, for while it is believed true that we do know more about the movements of our solar system and now our galaxy, we are still going through a Copernicus Effect in the 21st century with regards to other issues. What those issues are, I will leave to your intellect, but I will tell you this: it's my assertion that the heretics of yesteryear are today disguised as anything that will discredit them; "crackpots", "cranks", "frauds", "con-men", "conspiracy theorists" and even "terrorists" and "criminals", and that's only if they're lucky enough not to wind up "committing suicide" before people know about them. As history has shown; to ignore these modern day heretics in their entirety will usually be at the peril of the truth. It also begs a question as to our modern day authority, whether you believe it to be a government, or a church or a secret banking fraternity, and why they are so hesitant to evolve. Why do they consistently stand in the way of human idea progression?

A 21st Century Copernicus Effect is a completely fictitious story, because of the freedom it gave me in pulling in the reader's imagination along the way. Einstein said that imagination is more important than knowledge; why do you think he said that? My own interpretation is that knowledge is germinated in the imagination from an initial seed of information, so the quality of one's knowledge depends on the quality of the seed and the quality of the imagination of the observer. Hence; imagination is more important than knowledge, for one can't have knowledge without imagination. What's more, what we call our 'understanding' is our association to the knowledge we have grown, i.e. where the seed came from and how the knowledge grew

Today however, we teach our children to "stop day dreaming" and "pay attention", "come into the real world" etc... We can all picture the smile disappearing from a child's face as they start paying attention, the eye brows dropping and the lips pursing as they concentrate on the outside world again. I think there's something quite dark about that; like our own imagination and being-ness is somehow considered fake and illusory compared to the real world beyond us that we observe through our senses. Well, I do not concur. *We* are the reality. The collective world beyond us is merely a mirror of what we have created for ourselves and quantum science is starting to agree. If we want to change the world we live in we need to change the way we think about it; problems cannot be solved with the same consciousness that created them, another Einstein quote there.

Conflict in the world is a result of conflict in the collective mind of humanity and the sooner we realise that, the sooner we can give peace a chance. At the moment we are all parts of a whole that think as we were trained to do- to accept histories and facts the way they're taught to us and not to ask questions about them. Well, our questions are like roads that eventually navigate to towns, cities and cultures of grander concepts. Which concepts have we arrived at today? How did we get here? Are there better concepts we could travel to? Well give us a map you say! You have a map. It's called intuition; I'd dust it off and start listening to it. ☺

Enjoy the story...

Will Disdale, 2011

"Therefore I would not have it unknown to his holiness, that the only thing which induced me to look for another way of reckoning the movements of the heavenly bodies was that I knew that mathematicians by no means agree in the investigations thereof."

Nicolaus Copernicus, Scientist (1473 – 1543)

Prologue:

Siberian Foothills:
March 10th 1978:

Some scientists say there are as many as eleven dimensions. Some people say there are an infinite amount, however on Earth as humans we see four; up/down, left/right, forward/backward and time. We live on a space-time continuum we say.

One man living on that fabric of time and space was called Igor Popovic. A recluse, but a genius, Popovic spent most of his days working in his secluded laboratory high in the Siberian foothills. In privacy, he'd designed and built a portal that lead to many of these said 'extra' dimensions.

Over the last few weeks, Popovic had become a private inter-dimensional traveller and had used the portal to visit the dimensions many times before today, but this time his portal experience was different. He received information about a looming future Earth and it looked bleak. Visions of a planetary nuclear holocaust scared him to his core.

The avoidance of the future catastrophe lay in the mind of man and for that, his portal was the key of enlightenment, but *his* invention was before its time and would eventually become suppressed by the rulers of the world.

For now, his own portal needed to be destroyed along with his own knowledge, and early one morning in March his secluded research station in the Siberian foothills exploded in a ball of flames. The portal had intentionally exploded, taking with it the knowledge of its own existence, and also taking Igor Popovic's life.

The post-portal timeline was now literally hidden from the mainstream view of the planet along with the knowledge of the other dimensions. But for anyone who knew about the portal and the explosion, the hidden passage of time would for all intents and purposes become reality.

* * * * * * *

1: You're Retired

1

"Do not hire a man who does your work for money, but him who does it for love of it."
Henry David Thoreau, Philosopher and Transcendentalist (1817 – 1862)

1.1 –

Hidden Timeline, Thirty years later:

March 11th 2008:

Jack looked up at him while they were still walking on the pavement, his bright brown eyes, beaming. They were holding hands and Jack spoke, 'Why do we have to cross the road Daddy? There's a car coming.' His little voice seemed to echo.

Callison responded, looking down at his young son, Jack, 'We have to, Jack. We're having steak for dinner. Mommy needs the best steaks from the butcher.'

As father and son crossed the road, Callison felt the uneasy feeling come over him. It was happening again. He didn't want to go into the butcher's but he was propelled forward and into the dark building. The man serving behind the glass counter seemed sinister, and glared at them as they walked in. Their turn came and the man behind the counter asked what they wanted.

He gave the man his order.

As the serving assistant was bending down to get some meat out of the glass counter, he spoke quietly at first. 'Watch out for your son.'

'Pardon?' Callison said.

'Watch out for your son.' the butcher said with louder words.

'Pardon?' It was hard to hear.

'Watch out for your son….' He said louder still and gestured out side to the street with his eyes, but spoke no more.

Callison couldn't move: stuck in his place. No matter how much effort he put in, his legs would not carry him outside.

The loud screech of rubber on tarmac outside the shop deafened him as he cried in agony. Jack had been run over again.

Things went quiet all too soon and his circumstance changed. He was having another nightmare. The wind picked up, and the clouds were overcast as he walked up to an old rickety house. Jack and the butcher shop were nowhere to be experienced anymore, the dream seemingly changing unconsciously. The windows of the old house in front of him were open and the frames flapped in the driving winds. A statue standing on one leg pointed towards the front door. The front door was ajar, and creaked open as he entered the derelict house. He was in the hallway, stairs on the right and a room on the left. He was always guided left into the room where writing on the wall above the fireplace confronted him. As soon as he tried to read it however, it vanished in front of his eyes.

Suddenly a deafening noise screeched through him again, but it wasn't rubber on road this time.

The noise continued as Callison Trebla stirred from his nightmare. He woke up into his bedroom again. The alarm was going off which meant it was 6.30am. *It was just a dream*, thought Callison with relief as he lay awake in bed not wanting to relive the memory, but he found it hard not to.

He had been sweating again and at sixty-five years old, he was not the man he had been in his prime. Had he the mental capacity to stay positive, he might be mistaken for a younger man, but the years showed. He was bald but for a surround of grey hair, that sat on top of his weathered face. Callison's eyes screamed out for meaning to this bad dream and to life at large. A grey moustache wilted over his mouth and his unshaven cheeks bore the same silvery hairs.

Callison leaned over to stop the alarm. Not once had he found an alarm he liked the sound of, or maybe he just didn't want to wake up and face the coming day. He pressed the 'snooze' button, which gave him 5 more minutes before another wail. Today would be a different day. It would be his last day at work before retirement.

On Callison's right side lay Eleanor, his wife of 35 years. She was facing away from Callison, but rolled over to face him. Her warm eyes opened out of 30 years of habit, but she was still asleep, 'What time is it dear?'

Callison told her, 'Half past six.'

'Have you pressed snooze, or did you turn it off?'

'Snooze.'

Eleanor drifted back to sleep, as Callison lay awake with his eyes closed, thinking about the forthcoming day.

The five minutes of 'snooze' time had seemed like five seconds, before the alarm woke him from his slumber again. This time he silenced the alarm for another twenty-four hours before slowly levering himself out of bed. Age was holding him in its grasp and as he moved to stand up, his knees and back ached. He pressed his hands into the small of his back for support as he walked slowly towards the door and soon got used to being awake again. His mind was the next thing to slowly start waking up, but that would take longer for him to realise; *Cigarette and tea* he unconsciously thought.

His red dressing gown was hanging up on the back of the bedroom door. He picked it off and threw it round him, tying up its cord round his waist as he walked over to a pair of trousers draped over a chair near his bed. He reached into one of the pockets and pulled two cigarettes out of yesterday's packet.

Eleanor, now partially awake from the alarm clock's revenge, half leaned up. She spoke softly and sleepily, 'Those things will kill you, you know.'

His voice gave away he was a smoker, 'We're all going to die Ellie,' Callison croaked as he walked towards the bedroom door, 'one more won't hurt.' He knew he was kidding himself, but over the years had come to live with his lie.

Eleanor sighed and slipped back out of conscious thought as Callison descended the stairs and made his way to the kitchen. Having his cup of tea and cigarette on the back patio had become his unconscious ritual so much that he didn't even realise the process was happening at all. As the kettle took its time to boil, he rested against the kitchen sideboard and gazed at the floor. *My last day of work* he mused, as he ran his hands over his grey stubbled cheeks and moustache, *What am I going to do with my time?*

His thoughts turned to retirement, his last day of work ever and what he was going to do today. He was a scientist, researching the possibility of time travel for Quanta Research Laboratories and was under strict instruction and contractual obligation, to give up all research upon retirement. His computer at work held some of the most classified secrets in the country, as did his laboratory. He thought to himself as the kettle started to boil and made up his mind what he would do today. *I'm too close to give it all up now*, he painfully thought, *stuff the consequences. I'm doing it.* It was that choice along with many others that kick-started Callison's eventful journey into the mystic. The kettle started to whistle loudly as the water reached temperature and Callison snapped out of his thoughts.

He walked out of the kitchen and through the back door that lead out to the patio area of his garden. He put his tea down on the ornamental metal garden table and pulled one of the heavy metal chairs of the garden set from underneath. He sat down wrapping his dressing gown tighter around him and crossing one leg over the other to retain warmth. He lit his first cigarette, pulling the ashtray towards him, and took in the refreshing morning.

It had not long turned light and there was a subtle mist hanging in the garden along with dew formation on the grass.

The turn of spring had officially begun, but the morning was still cold and his exposed head felt the chill; the tea was warming him though as he sat and smoked. The smoke from his cigarette seemed thicker as he exhaled into the cold crisp air. His mind fell back to its habitual processes and he thought about the nightmare he had just endured.

Nightmares about Jack were common for Callison, even though it had been 28 years since his death. The day stuck in Callison's mind as surely as Excalibur in the stone; the 23rd October 1980. He had been taking his young son, Jack with him to buy some beef steaks for a barbeque that he and Eleanor were holding to celebrate someone's promotion at Callison's work. The irony of the whole incident was that Callison was expecting the promotion but didn't get it, and was reticent about holding the barbeque at all. Jack was knocked down by a car outside the butchers in the high street, and died in Callison's arms only soon after his fifth birthday.

The car concerned carried the number plate, BLIS4ME, which Callison thought was a cruel divine irony. The unfortunate driver stopped, and a tearful Callison had to look the driver in the face, as the driver also cried with regret. The phone calls to family, the sleepless nights and the agonising regret still all haunted Callison's mind.

After the accident, Eleanor was doing the washing up when she got the dreaded phone call and she said she could feel Jack's spirit in the kitchen with her. It was talk like this that gave Callison goose bumps and he never really wanted to talk about it openly due to an unconscious, but programmed fear of death.

The accompanying house in his recurring dream confused him also. He didn't know what the writing ever said on the wall, but he felt he would find out one day.

His thoughts drifted back to his cigarette; it had come to an end. He snapped out of his automatic thought process and his awareness was brought back to reality with a big swig of tea. The hit of hot tea on a cold morning is what Callison called living; the cigarette excuse merely gave him the means. Onto cigarette number two. By the time this one was smoked, his tea would be finished.

As his second cigarette burned, he sat and tuned into the morning symphony of birdcalls. There was a particular bird that called at this time and its tune was short and high-pitched, but had character. Listening to all the birds' individual calls being projected and answered was a sound that Callison found peaceful, and again, the cigarette provided the means. He and Eleanor would be moving out soon and making home in their new cottage. Callison would be sad to leave these birds; it was as if he had formed a bond with them.

His second cigarette neared the end and he took his self-synchronised last gulp of tea before stubbing his second cigarette out in the ashtray. He put in the effort required to stand, his knees creaking like an old crane as he raised his body from the chair, ready to face the day.

1.2 –

It was eight o'clock in the morning. Callison had shaved and showered and looked respectable, but he still had a looming inside-anxiousness about the coming day. His moustache had perked up and a strong aroma of spicy aftershave lingered in the car.

Callison turned the ignition key and the engine broke into life as if it had never slept. His ride was a powerful German saloon. It was still his new car that carried with it a sense of excitement about the drive to work. It didn't have many miles on the clock, and had a black leather interior. *A wonderful place to be,* thought Callison as he turned the heaters on to their high setting and inserted a CD into the slot. It was a CD that his wife, Eleanor had given to him and he'd promised to listen to it to sooth his troubled, but genius mind. It was composed of tranquil instrumental tracks performed by no one he'd heard of before.

The music started and with an infrared key fob, Callison fired a shot over his shoulder to open the large automatic garage door. The shutter whirred into life, and when it reached sufficient height, Callison reversed the car out of the garage and three-point-turned in the roomy gravel drive way. Another click of the key fob, and the garage closed. He turned left out of his drive and joined the morning commute to the sound of stress dissolving tunes.

He had on a yellow shirt with his ID security card hanging on a cord around his neck, and navy blue jeans. He kept his suit jacket in his office, which he used for the occasional meeting or interview. His suit jacket would be coming home with him today.

The small country roads fanned out into larger roads, which eventually led to the motorway. His drive took him from his small village in the countryside into the small conurbation of Justanother Town. It normally took him about 20 minutes, and today he was making good time. He exited the large roundabout that led on to the motorway. Callison's foot hit the floor and he punched the large sedan up to 80 mph. The feeling of power under his right foot made Callison feel powerful himself and as he blasted up the slip lane, he smiled at the car's performance. However, the motorway was revealed: thick, but steadily moving traffic. He eased off the accelerator. *Bloody traffic.* He turned up the CD player's volume.

Callison was seeing out his last day of work. He thought he should be happy, but he was terrified. For thirty years he'd worked as a scientist for the same company: Quanta Research Laboratories. It was a research corporation owned by a wealthy syndicate of investors. The syndicate owned all of the rights for the scientific breakthroughs the scientists were making. These breakthroughs related to the nature and make up of space and time and because of this, all employees had to sign confidentiality agreements. In the past they had barred Callison from releasing technical papers about time-travel. It was just one more reason why Callison had not really enjoyed working there, but it was his life, his second home. Without it he would be lost. No structure, no tasks, nothing to do; nothing to do, but think. And it was the *thinking* part that terrified him.

He lit a cigarette and then clicked the electric window down a notch, filling the interior with a wind noise that echoed through the car. Puffing away at 70 miles per hour he sat and listened to the CD. Track six finished and track seven started. The introduction was comprised of panpipes. No singing accompanied the sound. Callison found it spellbinding. It was one of those melodies that emoted memories of sunny days gone by. He thought of Jack again. He thought about being young again. The song came to an end after only two and a half minutes. *The good ones are always short lasting*, he thought, as he started it again, tapping his fingers on the steering wheel to the rhythm.

His motorway exit soon beckoned. The cigarette smell in the car had been blasted out the open window along with the cigarette. Using his indicator, but half cutting up another road user, he darted through the middle of two cars travelling in the inside lane of asphalt. The off-ramp dropped down and led to a roundabout under the motorway, where a small traffic queue had formed. Callison waited before turning right; he was on the home stretch now. A two-mile south bound trip on a dual carriageway into the north of Justanother Town. The song came to a close for a third time and Callison started it for a fourth. As he drove, wedged into the traffic flow, he picked the CD box up from the passenger seat. He wanted to know what the song was called. "Track 7: Bliss" *Strange name for a song*, he thought.

His place of work approached on the left hand side. A large silver and light blue logo of a nucleus and three electron orbits hovered above the business name: Quanta Research Laboratories Incorporated. Callison drove into the main entrance.

His car rolled to a stop at the security gate, where two cars in front of him were waiting for clearance from a security guard to drive in. They were taking longer than necessary Callison thought. The car in front of Callison was a red Ford estate. The personalised number plate read: 'BLISS4U'. *Strange.* Callison picked up the CD again. Track 7: Bliss. He'd never seen that number plate in all the years he'd driven in to work. He didn't know what to make of it apart from coincidence. That's when the significance of the number plate hit home. His memory cast directly back to Jack's death, and the number plate of the car, 'BLIS4ME'. *What are the chances?* he thought. He zoned out in the horror of his own mind's incoming information.

The barrier rose, and the red Ford drove into the complex. The barrier came down again as Callison unconsciously drove forward. He was still stunned, and forgot completely to open his window. The security guard gave a light knock on the glass and Callison snapped out of his trance. He clicked the button of his electric windows and they whirred down. Callison held out his security clearance card, whilst not really concentrating.

The card was on a spring-loaded yoyo type device that attached to a shoelace style cord around his neck. It meant the card could be swiped easily at all the swipe zones without bending down close to the numerous card-readers. The security guard scanned the card with a bar code reader, and as usual it took a few seconds to process. He often talked to the workers, 'How are you today Dr Trebla. Security pass is on its last day I see.'

'Yes I'm retiring today.' Callison muttered into the air in front of him.

'Bliss for you! Congratulations! I'm going to miss seeing this car come up the road. It is nice!'

'Well, yes I've worked very hard for it.' The barriers went up and Callison wanted to drive through.

The guard wanted to chat some more, while continuing to scope the car, 'Yeah, my cousin has one of these. They're amazing on a racing circuit.'

Callison wasn't in the mood for talking, and was getting blunt, 'I wouldn't know', came an impatient, *let me drive off now.*

The guard sensed his snappiness and let him go, 'Ok, Dr Trebla, you have a good day now. See you.'

Callison's car lurched forward, but stopped suddenly a few metres later. Callison spoke out of the window over his shoulder to the guard, 'Why did you say, "bliss for you"?'

The guard was confused and automatically defensive. 'What do you mean?'

'You said: "bliss for you" when I said I was retiring, why those words?'

The guard shrugged, becoming relaxed but confused, 'I don't know why I said it like that.' It was a phrase he'd never used before.

Callison shook his head. *Weird.* 'Doesn't matter.' He hit the electric 'window up' switch and drove into the complex, thinking he'd witnessed a bizarre coincidence. Little did he know it was how the universe nudged people into choices they had been avoiding making.

About a hundred yards after the security post was a second fortifying failsafe. No security cards needed here, just a camera. Callison's time in the corporation meant he knew that this camera was equipped with the latest face and car number plate recognition software on the market. He had heard it had cost one hundred thousand pounds to install. *They take their security too seriously*, Callison thought. As he approached the camera he knew that his face was being tracked with mathematical precision. He pulled a face to try to fool the machine. He held the face all the way up to the camera, but the car cruised on past without any laser interceptions.

One of the perks of being in one company for thirty years meant that you had a reserved parking bay. Callison's was right next to the entrance, which was a godsend on rainy days, but today it was dry and remarkably bright. Callison hopped out of the car and locked the door. *Let's get this day over with*, he thought as he walked intrepidly into the building, swipe card at the ready.

1.3 –

Callison's office was situated in the old wing. He had visited the coffee shop en- route to get a frothy cappuccino, before finally reaching his room. It was about half way down a long thin corridor, containing offices on one side, and laboratories on the other. The new wing of the Quanta Corporation, which is where the modern Quanta did its business, was a lot more up-market. Quanta's customers were wealthy and usually unknown for legal reasons. The modern wing of Quanta comprised client meeting rooms, function rooms and new swanky offices. Callison liked being away from the humdrum of commerce. It was all about the science for him.

The door to his office had frosted glass in the top half with his name etched into the frosting:

Dr Callison E. Trebla
Principal Research Scientist
Space-Time Effects Division

He unlocked the door with his electronic swipe card and walked in. *My last day here,* he thought nervously.

His office was stately in nature. He put the caffeine drink on his desk and looked around the room. The old wing was nearly fifty years old, and still carried the 60's vibe. His office had deep oak shelves that ran around the walls, housing books and reports, shelves and filing cabinets. The walls were painted in a sludge coloured beige that Callison hated. Oak floorboards covered the floor apart from the area in front of his desk where a red rug lay trapped under a sturdy looking desk. Behind his desk was a large room-length window that looked out onto the Quantum Physics car park and let the shallow rays of the early morning sunshine stream into the office.

Papers lay strewn haphazardly on his desk next to his computer. His work was not tidy and people would often comment on the unique filing system he employed, but the response from Callison would always be the same: 'I know where everything is. Do not touch please!'

A piece of work lay open on his desk. It was an internal Quanta paper that Callison and an ex co-worker called Peter Montague had written, and was open on a page showing a photo of Callison and Peter standing in front of a large round metal doughnut mounted in a spider web of metal frame work. The device became known as the Trebla Eye and was an as of yet unproven portal, that would one day open up the possibility of time travel.

Callison looked at the photo, and reminisced about his co-worker. Peter had qualified for a redundancy package four years earlier as part of a Quanta restructuring programme and he had taken it gleefully. Peter had left Quanta, vowing to Callison to invent a method to magnetise steam but Callison hadn't spoken to Peter since, so never knew if he'd managed it. He still had his number though and wanted to give him a call to 'catch up' but that was a stupid reason to call, or so he habitually and negatively thought.

Since Peter's departure, three more people had all been assigned to work under Callison, to learn the project and carry on the time travel research after Callison's retirement. None of them knew the project like Callison though, and Quanta knew it.

Callison had been interested time-travel concepts from a young age, and when the opportunity arose with Quanta to research the field he jumped at the chance. That was twenty years ago.

The Trebla Eye was similar in operation to the CERN particle-collider that consisted of a twenty-five mile tunnel underground that swept through 360 degrees to make a continuous loop. Sub-atomic particles were accelerated up to near light-speed inside the endless tube by the use of powerful electro-magnets placed at intervals along the tube. CERN's interest was in smashing these particles into each other and observing the 'crash' in the hope that new smaller particles could be witnessed.

The Trebla Eye didn't smash particles into each other but used the concept to accelerate Quanta patented mono-atomic iron powder up to speeds in excess of light-speed. The theory, written by an unknown author for legal reasons was that when particles of matter, iron particles in this case, reached light speed inside the circular tube it would induce a tear in the fabric of space-time in the middle of the circle and open up the zero-point-field. This tear in the zero-point-field would become a walk-through style portal by which time could be theoretically accessed.

The latest prototype of the invention was standing up in the laboratory opposite his office and consisted of a small circular tunnel that wrapped back on itself making a two-metre diameter that stood upright in a two and a half metre high frame with six large electro-magnets accelerating the mono-atomic iron around its circular internal peripheral tunnel. Due to an inner and outer electro-magnet, the iron was suspended on the centre line inside the tunnel, touching no surfaces, meaning no friction. Air resistance was negated by the creation of a vacuum inside the circular duct. With careful power supply to the six hefty accelerating electro-magnets, light speed iron was nearly a reality.

It hadn't happened yet, however. The device had propelled the iron powder to speeds of 0.89C, that is, 89% light-speed, before the temperature of the equipment reached its working allowable limit, even with an absolute-zero liquid nitrogen coolant. During the run they had witnessed the start of the tear in space-time in a strange rippling light effect appearing at speeds above 0.5C, which grew in size in the middle of the two-metre wide portal as the speed was increased further. This showed Callison, and Quanta, that something was on the verge of revealing itself; they just needed to find some more speed to find out what it was.

Callison sat behind his desk and put the piece of work on top of another pile of papers. He turned his computer on and it whirred into life. As it took a few moments to boot up, he sipped his cappuccino while nostalgically looking around his office again. This had been his office for nearly 15 years. *My last day here*, he thought again. It felt scary.

He started to go through his emails; nothing of substance in his inbox, just a few farewell retirement messages and some mundane messages detailing Quanta's exit procedure. He had to hand in all company credit cards, company security cards and sign the declaration of secrecy, again.

About 20 minutes had passed when there was a loud and abrupt knock at his door.

'Come in.' Callison said clearly.

The door opened and in bounded Heinrich Muller. In his late fifties, he stood 6 feet and 6 inches, had a wide frame and a booming voice. He had been Callison's superior at Quanta for the last six years. 'Morning Callison!' His voice boomed through the office. It had impact, but lacked sincerity.

'Good morning Heinrich.' said Callison.

'Last day today then, it sure won't be the same without you!' Heinrich said.

Callison didn't care much for Heinrich. Heinrich had come to prominence at Quanta in the early eighties after a much-publicised lawsuit he had won against an ex-Quanta researcher called Richard Coffman. Muller was accused by Coffman of having plagiarised an early form of string-theory; then at the forefront of scientific endeavour, and published it with Quanta as his own. The lawyer working Muller's case was supplied by Quanta at huge cost to drag the trial out, thus forcing the financially weak Richard Coffman to bail out. Callison had never forgotten that.

He spoke back to his boss, 'I'll miss it for sure, but *go* I must!' he joked, 'I can finally start living my life!' He didn't really know what he meant, but didn't want Heinrich thinking that he was resentful. Not today. He needed his enemies close.

Heinrich continued, his voice echoing through Callison's ears, 'Listen Callison, we are having a bit of a bash over in the new wing for your retirement, will you come by for about eleven o'clock this morning? Nothing too extravagant, just some farewell speeches, you're the longest serving scientist here, it would be rude not to give you a flamboyant send off!'

Flamboyant? Callison questioned. *You must be joking*. Callison didn't want a send off. He came across surprised and excited, 'Oh, ok I'll be there. Hope you haven't got anything untoward planned. I'm sixty-five, not twenty-five you know!'

Heinrich laughed, 'No, just tea and cakes Callison. Just tea and cakes.'

'In which case, I'll be there.'

'What are your plans for the rest of the day?' Heinrich enquired.

'I'm just working on this handover document for the rest of today; just dotting i's and crossing t's, nothing major. Then packing my retirement stuff up.' He added, 'What room is the retirement bash going to be in?'

Heinrich was apologetic, 'Sorry, room B4.329. See you there.' He had some more to say before he left, 'Oh also, could you leave some space in your schedule to come and see me before you leave today? You can take me through the handover document again, and I can get your autograph on some forms and things. About three pm?'

'Yeah ok.' Callison said grudgingly.

'Great. See you at eleven in B4.329.' With that he turned and walked out of the office closing the door behind him. His shoes clumped up the corridor getting quieter and quieter.

That will be an afternoon task I don't want to do, Callison thought. Heinrich was having exactly the same thought.

1.4 –

It was 11:00 am as Heinrich Muller started his speech. Callison was wearily smiling next to him in front of about thirty employees in a function room in the new wing. Someone had sent a group email invitation round the offices, which had attracted people Callison didn't really know. *An hour off work usually creates a crowd* Callison thought. He didn't like the attention.

'Well Callison, what can I say, you've been the longest serving Quanta employee. It will surely be sad to see you go.' Heinrich Muller smiled and started to applaud. The other onlookers applauded also. After the false praise had died down Heinrich continued his speech, his bounding unrelenting voice holding the room. The stage was his, as usual.

'I remember my first day here, almost thirty years ago. Callison was working on our then infamous theoretical string theories, and zero point field research that made Quanta what it is today....'

His words disappeared into the ether as Callison's mind started to wander. He started to think about how he was going to smuggle the equipment required to continue time travel research as a solo 'basement' researcher. He really only had a need for the experimental data, which he could smuggle out of the building on a CD, and the magnetic acceleration units that would get the patented iron powder up to speeds nearing the speed of light. He already had about half a kilogram of the patented mono atomic iron powder in bags at home. His mind was brought back to his retirement ceremony abruptly when he noticed the silence in the room. Heinrich had asked him a question.

Heinrich repeated, 'Earth to Callison! You feel these guys can get time travel all wrapped up in the next few years?' He pointed to a group of six researchers that were taking up the reigns of the research after Callison's departure.

Callison automatically humoured them, 'Sorry. Oh, yes of course these guys can get it done. I shall expect to see your progress on the news!' The eager eyed, but naive researchers believed him. Callison knew that should they have a breakthrough, it would be used for military purposes first and foremost, as the law dictated. It would never appear on the evening news. Heinrich's voice continued.

'Yes, I'm confident in these researchers also, and I'm glad they have your blessing Callison. Anyway, it leaves me to say thank you for all the time and dedication you have put into our research over the years, and we all wish you a happy and peaceful retirement.' The audience again applauded, as Heinrich and Callison shook hands.

'Now we have put out some pots of tea and coffee. Please feel free to help yourselves. There are also some cakes and other bits out, so please eat them. They'll be thrown out otherwise!' He ended with a serious tone. 'But we'll be back to work in about 30 minutes people, we don't pay you to have fun.'

Callison hated the whole charade. *Time to keep up appearances,* Callison thought as he went about chatting to the people in the room.

The whole send off lasted about forty-five minutes, and he was glad when it was over. It was just before lunch, and on his way back from his retirement celebrations Callison stopped by the storage department.

All store related matters had to be dealt with by the storage officer, a skinny guy on the other side of a hatch style window. Callison asked for six cardboard boxes and after six signatures on six contracts relating to what he can and can't do with the boxes, they were his. *It's bureaucracy gone mad*, he thought to himself as he walked away. He knew he was going to be breaking some of the contracts he'd just signed. He felt a rush of fear, but kept his cool.

He walked back down the main corridor of the old wing; boxes in hand and his pulse racing. Instead of turning left and into his office, he turned right and into his research laboratory. The laboratories were quite long but narrow and Callison's lab space had sideboards running down each side, full of research material, equipment, data and books. His baby was in the middle of the laboratory looking like a large Ferris wheel. He smiled every time he saw it, and today was no exception.

The latest prototype of The Trebla Eye stood there in all its glory. The round tube, whose internals would house the monatomic iron powder, had six magnetic accelerators equally spaced around its periphery. It was held upright by a larger square structure that had a sturdy base. The square outer structure also carried wires that supplied power to the strong electro-magnets and cooling ducts carrying liquid nitrogen to the parts that needed to be cooled.

His attention was drawn back to the task at hand. Under one of the shelves running the length of the lab, lay thirty 'spare' electro-magnetic accelerating units. Callison knew that Quanta's records only showed twenty-four magnetic units due to an ordering calamity when the units were fabricated. Due to the way in which Quanta acquired funding, the need for profit and proper business acumen was lacking. He'd stayed quiet about the over-order for just a day as this.

It was going to be quiet for the next half hour as most people in his building would be on their lunch breaks. Callison took the boxes he'd acquired from stores and started to place a valuable electro magnet into each box. The magnets were self-contained units in themselves. All Callison would need to do is supply power to them, and fit them to his version of the Eye. Everything else needed to replicate the Eye could be manufactured either by him, or by local fabrication houses. Beads of sweat dripped down his forehead as he boxed the accelerating units up, as much from the exertion than from the fear of being caught in the act. His pulse still raced.

He took the electro-magnets, boxed, into his office across the corridor. There he covered the magnets under 'sentimental' lab jackets, papers, pictures, and anything else he could find that would constitute his retirement belongings. Five boxes were full, however there was one more box that revealed a magnet. He needed something else to cover it, but couldn't think what could do the job. He spied his suit jacket hanging up on his door. *Eureka.* That would be coming home with him also today. He laid the jacket, folded in half over the last magnet. *Would this work?* He crossed his fingers and picked up the first two boxes.

He carried the boxes, two by two out to the car park. The boot of his large sedan just about held the six boxes. They were positioned upright, and from looking into the boot they looked like six innocent boxes of retirement belongings. *Perfect*, he thought.

One afternoon to go, then I'm Scot free he thought to himself. He got nervous and lit a cigarette, standing by the exit to finish it. His mind cast back to the strange coincidence at the security entrance this morning. He was still none the wiser as to what to make of it.

1.5 –

Five o'clock had seemed like an eternity away. The meeting with Heinrich in the afternoon had been more awkward than either of them had expected. Heinrich knew that Callison was taking most of the project knowledge but remained upbeat. Callison knew he was breaking all the laws in the book, so became overly helpful. Neither of them had let their true colours shine through, which created an invisible barrier of awkwardness.

Callison signed the secrecy documents, and Heinrich bore witness to his signatures as per security protocol. Heinrich read out the security and legal spiel from a form, which verged on threatening. He told Callison he now had no power within Quanta, and could not go round telling people about anything that he had seen or been witness to in his thirty years of employment with the company. He also pompously reminded Callison about Quanta's successful legal history.

His last interaction with his difficult boss went surprisingly well. It was nothing more special than the typical 'good luck then, good luck to yourself' conversation, but it was more natural than all the rest of their meeting. It made Callison almost sad that they would not meet again and made him feel like he might need his nemesis to spur him on, but the thoughts vanished quickly.

As he started his car almost a retired man, his awareness centred upon his contraband cargo sitting in the boot. With his pulse just under the red line, he slowly reversed out of his spot. He hoped they would not search him on his way out of the building. *They never have done before*, he thought, but he had a sneaky feeling that they could.

As he neared the security gates to the Quanta complex there was an unusually long queue of cars waiting for the barrier to swing up; the agony was going to be longer than estimated. He was so conscious of what he was carrying on board, that he forgot to put the radio on. *Normally the radio would be on*. He turned it on. His heart was pounding a lot faster than the cars in the queue were moving. He read the number plate of the car in front. It was a regular one. *I'm going mad now!* He was impatient. *Come on hurry up!* The cars slowly crept towards their evening of freedom.

A different shift was now on duty and this guard looked authoritarian in stature. He stood about three cars ahead scanning people off the premises.

After what felt like an eternity, it came to Callison's turn. The barrier came down in front of him and he clicked the 'window-down' button as he rolled to a stop next to the guard. Callison no longer had an electronic card. The security guard, none the wiser, had his weapon aimed and ready.

'Err... yep, it's my last day today I'm retiring, so I don't have a card anymore.' Callison explained.

The guard stood back from the car and radioed the query through to someone else. 'Yeah, can I check the status of…' he leaned in to Callison, and off-radio asked, 'What's your name?'

He told him.

'…Callison Trebla, he says he's retiring today?' His name echoed into the Quanta radio network. There were a few moments of radio silence. The guard paced listening for a voice back. Callison's heart raced, until a crackly voice spoke back through the device. 'Yes, he has been given clearance already, let him go.'

Callison felt a wave of relief fill his bones.

'Ok off you go. Good luck!' said the guard.

'Yep, cheers, thanks.' He didn't really know what to say.

The barrier was raised and Callison drove on through. He turned right out of the complex, and disappeared towards the motorway. The sound of the engine exhaust roared as he left the complex. He'd done it; he had the material to recreate the Eye at home. *Time Travel will be up to me now*, Callison thought. He smiled, before starting to laugh.

1.6 –

It was by now quite late in the evening. Heinrich Muller was still at work, sat down in the Quanta security office after giving the security guard an unscheduled cigarette break. A security CD lay on the desk in front of him. A few moments passed, before Heinrich leant forward and inserted it into the computer. He watched Callison steal the electro magnets earlier in the day.

Before doing anything, his mind moved to the investors of the project, the hands that fed. They were the most reliable investors that Quanta had, and they had been with Quanta almost since the founding of the business. They were rich aristocrats and influential characters from the power dynasties, for which any sum of money was merely a flick of a pen away. Over their time working together, Heinrich got the impression that they were waiting for something like the Eye; it was like all their funding had been in case of miraculous breakthroughs like this. It was as if the Eye project was more important than the entirety of the inventions their partnership had fostered before. Or maybe that's just what it felt like to Heinrich. The security guard entered the room after his cigarette, and Heinrich ejected the CD, taking it away with him.

Back in his modern office in the new wing of Quanta, the totally frosted glass walls gave Heinrich privacy from the passing eyes walking the corridor outside. The investors of the Eye advised that they be informed of any developments on the project, no matter what, and they demanded that discretion and secrecy be of utmost importance; Callison didn't even know he was working for them. Heinrich picked up the phone and punched in a secure number. He waited while the phone rang, before speaking, 'Hello, it's Heinrich, could I speak with Harold?' It was a code name.

After a few moments, a deep but assured voice spoke back down the phone, 'Hello Heinrich,' he spoke slowly, 'what news?'

'There has been a development on the Eye project.' said Heinrich.

'Well, do tell.' said the voice, sounding interested.

* * * * * * *

2: Living the Dream

"A dream you dream alone is only a dream.
A dream you dream together, that's reality."
John Lennon, Songwriter and Musician (1940 – 1980)

2.1 –
Hidden Timeline:
April 14th 2008:

A month had passed since Callison's retirement and today, he and Eleanor were moving into their mysterious retirement cottage. It was about an hour's drive from their old house and was situated in a small village about 2 miles inland of the English Channel. The welcomed change of scenery filled both Callison and Eleanor with an air of hope and freedom.

From the moment he first saw the property on the Internet, Callison felt that this cottage was meant to be. 'An act of crazy destiny…' Callison often said to Eleanor while talking about the coincidence. A few months previously, while still working for Quanta, Callison and Eleanor sat on the Internet looking at different retirement properties and not liking any of them. The ones they did like were too expensive and the ones they could afford were not to their liking. The frustrating search prompted Callison, out of bloody mindedness but also out of unconscious intuition, to type in to an internet search engine: "Where is our perfect house?" The search returned millions of results, the top one being a cottage on the south coast of England, being sold by a company called Destiny Real Estate. The pair were awed at the suitability of the dwelling. The price was right, the location was right. The fateful process slightly unnerved both of them.

Upon viewing the house in person Callison was even more dumbfounded, as to his astonishment it had played host to the setting of the recurring dream he had been having.

The dream included a statue of a man pointing towards the cottage. The statue stood on one leg and rested the other on something rectangular. The dream always included the front door, which was always ajar. The cottage in the dream was derelict, as if neglected for years and the exterior walls and surrounding land was overgrown with foliage. The windows were broken and the shutters flapped in the wind. In the dream he walked through the open front door that led into a hallway: stairs on the right: lounge through a door on the left. In the lounge was a fireplace with white writing on the wall above it, but every time he tried to read the writing, it disappeared. After some moments of confusion he would wake up back in his bedroom.

During the physical viewing, Callison had hoped something would be written above the fireplace, thus putting his dream to rest. But he was let down; there was nothing but a layer of paint on the wall, and the dream still confused him. But every cloud had a silver lining; the cottage had a basement, which was accessed by a door under the stairs, near the kitchen and at the end of the entrance hall. His dream had never included the basement, but he required one nonetheless.

2.2 –

Eleanor was inside the hallway of the new cottage, directing the removal workers as they carried in furniture and belongings. Eleanor was the organised one that got things done. Callison, despite all his degrees and doctorates, could not get things done like Eleanor. He helped.

Age had been kinder to Eleanor than it had been to Callison, and she looked 10 years younger than the sixty-three she had lived. Her eyes were a deep hazel colour, and harboured nothing but honesty and love. She was greying slightly, but dyed her shoulder length hair brown. Despite not having another child since Jack, she held less resentment and accepted the loss better than her husband.

'Put the dining table in the room next to the kitchen.' she said with a smile to the workers, who had already been issued with two cups of tea each. She had a list of belongings that had been packed onto the lorry, and was ticking each one off, as and when they entered the cottage.

All she had trusted to Callison was opening the mail, and a statement from the bank had arrived. Callison walked out of the new kitchen with a piece of paper flailing in his hand. He leaned up against the basement door, 'Our statements say we've made payments to 'Argos catalogue,' he was confused, 'have we bought anything from them?' Callison handed her the statement, and she scanned down it like a hawk would its prey.

'No, we haven't bought anything that I can think of from Argos.' Eleanor said, confused also.

'I'll sort it,' said Callison, confidently. He shook his head, 'there must be a mistake here.'

Eleanor continued supervising the move.

Callison stood on the front lawn of his new retirement cottage, pacing around while on the phone. The statement was still in his hand and he wore his reading glasses. He'd unknowingly worked the call into an argument, as if exercising his 'ills' with the world would make a difference. The large yellow removal lorry was parked on the street and the removal company's workers were busy up and down the garden path, within earshot. The wardrobe they were carrying in suddenly made a bang as one of the doors fell open. No damage, but Callison pulled the phone away from his ear and shouted. 'Be careful with that wardrobe! It is very valuable!' The removal workers acknowledged him and continued with more care as Callison continued his call.

...'I don't understand it, I haven't made those purchases! What would a sixty-five year old man need with a Nintendo what-ever-you-call-it?!'...

He paced before replying.

...'Then reimburse what was taken!'...

He was quiet for a while, still pacing the lawn flat.

...'If a robber came in to your bank dressed as Mr X, Y or Z, and held you up at gun point, would you say to your customers' "we thought Mr X, Y or Z took it all – Mr X, Y or Z, you'll have to pay for it" or would you get your insurance to pay it?'...

He waited again, while flattening the grass some more.

...'Why is it different?! Your system has the flaw, not my identity! Look I'm me! I've always been me, and I'll continue to be me! I have not had my identity stolen!! Your 'system' obviously has loopholes that have been exploited!'...

His face was turning red from the frustration. The colour spread to the bald crown between his grey hairs. His replies got louder in volume.

...'I *am* careful with my bank statements! I'm *always* careful with them...' He looked at the sky, making a gnarling frustrated sound. Eleanor had heard him building up his frustration, and approached him. She knew that his bark was louder than his bite.

...'So you're saying my credit card will have to be replaced. Well what if I want to make a purchase with it today?!'...

...'Yes, that's what I thought. I can't. Well screw you! I want to cancel all business agreements with your company. Good day to you!!'

One of the workers cheered quietly.

Callison tipped his head forward and looked for the 'hang-up' button over his glasses. Just as he was about to hit it, Eleanor jumped in.

'Here, let me speak with them dear, you go and calm down.' Eleanor took the phone. 'Hi it's his wife, Eleanor Trebla here. Sorry about that, he's just...' she started climbing out of the hole. 'Well, he's stressed at the moment. We are moving house today. What seems to be the problem?' She walked inside.

One of the removal workers overheard the conversation and made a comment. 'What ever happened to "the customer's always right" eh?' He was a young looking guy with an earring and a broad northern accent. He gestured a laugh.

Callison was still fuming. 'More like "the customer's always fucked!"' He lit a cigarette, and sat down on some of the garden furniture that was waiting to be carried to the garden.

The worker laughed at Callison's remark. 'Too true, mind if I smoke with you there?'

'Go ahead,' said Callison, 'it's a free country.'

'Is it?' said the worker, hinting the question.

Callison stared at him, remaining quiet.

'My name's Danny.' The removal worker said, trying to break Callison's mood.

'Callison.' He nodded back.

The worker lit up also. 'Yeah, banks.' He was trying to start a conversation, 'They make a bucket load of profit, but can't help out the little guys.'

'I'm not a little guy, I'm their customer!' His face was still a peachy red colour.

The worker didn't seem to be phased by Callison's anger. 'You'd have been treated differently if you had millions in your account.'

'Yeah, don't I know it. Where's the logic in that?'

'No logic at all mate; it's like celebrities getting free gear, when they have enough money to buy it anyway. The peasants like us have to work for it!'

A brief silence ensued as they both concentrated on their cigarettes.

'I just wish we could go back to cash, like the good old days.' said Callison.

'Big brother wouldn't want that. They want to be able to track you at every transaction... *For our safety*.' he added sarcastically.

Callison heard, but imparted his opinions anyway. 'It is all about fear these days Danny. We end up living in fear of the corporations and the governments, but it's the corporations and the governments that should fear us, the consumer and the voter!'

The worker agreed before changing the subject, 'There's some interesting looking metalwork in the truck. A large tubular circle shaped object, and some other bits and pieces. What are they used for?'

Callison had been manufacturing pieces of the Eye for a month in the large garden shed of his old house. He didn't give anything away. 'It's a science experiment.'

'What sort of science?' the worker probed.

Callison thought, 'Clever science.'

'Not giving much away there!'

'You ask too many questions!' he said, cagily.

He was saved when the removal company leader, an overweight short guy, shouted over to the worker, 'Hey Danny, you gonna do some work today or are you too busy talking?'

'Oh well, guess I'll never know!' The worker flicked his cigarette out onto the road and got back to work.

Callison called, 'When you get to the 'science equipment', give me a shout. That stuff can't be chucked around like the wardrobe you almost broke.'

2.3 –

The basement lay underneath the lounge area of the cottage. Quite spacious, it would provide Callison some working space for the Time Travel research. The basement had a light, which was adequate for the basement, but the stairs were only dimly lit by an under rated bulb. At the bottom of the stairs a wall wrapped around left and into the basement itself. The room was in good condition, and needed no work doing to it. It had a distinctive earthy, wooden smell and all of the bricks of the sidewalls were painted black.

'Up a bit... Left a bit... Down a bit' called Callison as the Trebla Eye was manoeuvred down the basement steps by the workers. The large structure had been split into three separate components, the Eye part, and the sturdy square holding structure, which had been spilt into its two respective halves. They bolted together again like a large Meccano set. Each of the three parts was heavy and needed two workers to carry each of them.

'What exactly is this contraption anyway?' asked one of the workers, as he grunted and wheezed down the stairs.

Danny piped up, holding the other end. 'Science experiment right?' He looked back up the stairs at Callison as if to get more of an answer than before. It was short in coming.

'Yes. A science experiment,' replied Callison. 'Now keep concentrating, we need to get it round the corner at the bottom, and into the basement. I can take it from there.'

After a few commands and the worker's efforts, the three pieces of the Eye were leaned up against the walls of the basement. The workers went back upstairs to get more 'standard' furniture into the cottage.

In Callison's car lay a selection of plastic carry boxes full of circuitry, devices, magnets, CDs and his research. It took about half an hour to get all the extra bits down into the basement, but he'd done it without too much outside interest. He stood in the basement with all his extra time travel kit in a collection on the floor in the corner. He mentally weighed up and assessed where everything was going to go. The basement was perfect in proportion, deep enough to house the eight-foot high square holding structure and still leave another foot before the roof, wide enough to be able to walk round the structure and work on it from the back and front and long enough to install some workbenches and shelves to store all the spares, data, books, papers, results, tools and any other equipment time-travel required. A computer would run all the necessary programs and algorithms for the electro-magnets and serve as the display screen for the Chronogrammatic Control Unit or CCU as it had been abbreviated to. He guessed it would take about a week to assemble and be ready to hunt for the extra speed needed to puncture the space-time continuum. But sometimes life doesn't necessarily deliver one's plans in quite the way expected.

He hung a clock on the staircase-side wall of the basement. *Have to keep time*, Callison thought as he offered the clock up to the wall. He was interrupted by one of the workers poking his head round the corner.

It was Danny, who clocked Callison immediately and seemed apologetic, 'Oh, sorry mate, I thought no one was down here,' said the removal worker, 'I saw the light was on and was just coming to turn it off.' The look on Danny's face said he wasn't.

Callison looked back at the worker while holding the clock in place with one arm against the wall, 'No need, I'm down here,' said Callison somewhat startled, 'but I was just about to finish up, so I'll turn it off. Thank you.'

'Ok.' Danny seemed to hesitate before nodding and retreating up the stairs again.

Callison finished hanging the clock thinking about the exchange. He would need to keep the door locked, and maybe get a better door and lock system. His thoughts developed into wondering about hiding the door to the basement completely with some elaborate shelving that could double as a spy movie style secret entrance.

The newly hung timepiece was adjusted to say the time: 3.30pm. Callison packed his tools back into their respective area of the basement floor and turned the light off before ascending the stairs to help with the move again. Paranoia took over as he reached the top of the stairs and emerged into the hallway; there were footsteps and furniture noises coming from upstairs but none of the workers were in eyeshot. He pulled the small key out from his pocket and locked the door behind him.

2.4 –

The removal company left the Treblas new house about an hour ago; they'd done a good job and received an equally nice tip.

It had just turned five pm and while Callison sat in front of the TV watching some motor racing in the lounge, Eleanor was writing her daily memoirs at the dining room table in the next room. She had written her memoirs everyday for nearly thirty years. Every day had an entry; it was like a document of her life, a document that presently took up two large boxes. Callison had often asked her why she bothered writing her memoirs at all; 'No-one ever reads them.' he'd say to her. It was a statement that puzzled Eleanor also, because she didn't know the reason she wrote them. She guessed it was some kind of obsessive-compulsive disorder, because she had started the memoirs after Jack died, and couldn't find a reason to stop. But as with everything, there was a reason that she wrote, even if she didn't know it yet. She was writing about Callison's bank rage earlier in the day, when the telephone started to ring. She walked into the kitchen to answer it.

The motor racing on the TV completed its allotted time and the station started to air advertisements. He got up from the couch and walked to the bay window that looked out over the front garden and picturesque street they now lived on. An unlit cigarette hung from his lower lip as he contemplated. *The new view*, he thought. His front lawn was short and green and looked neat as it ran up to some knee-high bushes that divided his property from the pathway that tracked the road. Eleanor emerged from the dining room behind him.

'It's been all go today!' she exclaimed. Callison was startled and spun around, 'You'll be pleased to know the bankcard got sorted in the end. That was them on the phone.' said Eleanor, 'I had *some hole* to climb out of after your attempt at diplomacy!' she chuckled as she approached him.

'Thank you. What would I do without you?' He gave her a kiss and smiled; slightly embarrassed that he'd got so worked up over it, 'What have the little Hitlers done about it?'

She explained, 'Well, they said they would reimburse us for one thousand five hundred, but we have to destroy our cards. It'll be about 5 days before our new ones arrive.' She was positive, 'We kind of killed two birds with one stone, I gave them the new address as well.'

He replied downbeat, 'Still means we're put out for it though doesn't it. It shouldn't be like that Ellie, should it?'

She knew how to comfort him without belittling his contempt for the system and Callison had always felt it was one of the reasons why their relationship had stayed strong over the years. 'No it shouldn't but we just need to keep going,' She put her arm round him, 'there are greedy people out there, but that's just their way. We either choose to let it affect us or we choose to get on with life.'

'I guess you're right,' he said, 'it just pains me that's all.' He embraced Ellie back, and kissed her on the top of her head.

'What pains you?' she asked, resting her head on Callison's shoulder.

He was puzzled but spoke his mind, 'It looks like the greedy people win in life, and it doesn't seem fair.'

Eleanor had no reply, but thought about it. The brief silence between them allowed the TV to butt in and the news had started. Callison contemplated aloud with sarcasm, 'Oh, let me guess; war, economy, corruption, murder, global warming and sport?'

She joked back as they finished their embrace, 'You cynic!'

The pair watched as fact and fiction merged. A story had broken about the economy.

'See? Told you the economy would be on the menu!' Callison affirmed.

His wife laughed to humour him, but the story was presented with fear, and Eleanor felt it, 'Callison, this is quite serious.'

Callison resented the broadcast, 'It's a pantomime! Stock exchanges are like the collective egos of the world, built on confidence,' he added, 'or lack of confidence.' he gestured with his arms implicating the story unfolding in front of them. Eleanor had no reply and continued to pay attention to the TV news broadcast. Callison watched also, but thought of it as drivel and was about to go for his cigarette, when another story hooked his attention.

Towards the end of the news report, the news anchor's toned lightened, "And now on to a story about a rather strange scientific breakthrough. A group of scientists in Europe have managed to magnetise water. Here's Nick Collins with the report."

Callison's chin dropped as he watched the unfolding story. His friend, Peter Montague was on the TV announcing the process, which could be used to extract drinking water from thin air. The technology intrigued the scientific community as to what else it could be used for. *Well I'll be,* thought Callison, Peter looked well. The news story finished almost as soon as it had started.

'I knew that man they interviewed!' exclaimed Callison, 'I used to work with him!'

'It's a small world,' said his wife, smiling, 'you should give him a call.'

Callison was hesitant, 'No, I'd have nothing to say, I'm just glad he did what he said he was going to do.' An unconscious part of him did want to call, but he would need one further prompt, and it was just around the corner.

'I'm going for a smoke anyway,' he said as he made his way towards the French doors in the dining room that led to the new back garden. He paused before he got there, and turned, 'How would you like a fish and chip dinner tonight? We can try the local seafood.'

'That would be a wonderful idea.' Eleanor replied.

2.5 –

He only came to the village to get a fish and chip supper, but he would leave with much more. He could have walked in, but his automotive habit got the better of him. As he drove he thought about his old friend Peter Montague, seeing him on the news had been weird; it felt like even though they hadn't met in years they still knew each other.

The village was small and quaint. *Retirement here might be just what I need* thought Callison as he parked in an angled parking space on the main strip of the village. *Free parking after five.* It was half past. He smiled to himself and locked the car with the electronic key fob to explore his new locale. There was about half an hour of light left in the day and a few other people milled up and down the street completely unaware as to their newest villager.

The main strip was about two hundred yards long and contained a selection of small shops, providing the townsfolk with essentials only; a convenience store, a pub, some bookshops, cafés and a hotel were dotted about the street, mingling in with residential dwellings. The buildings lining the strip were built long ago, still having an old Tudor feel to them. The pointed roofs and wooden eaves gave Callison the impression he could be in the 1600's, but the rush hour traffic gave away the actual date. Trees lined the pavement on either side of the road, giving the street a natural, earthy feel.

As Callison strolled the pavement, a number of small cobbled alleyways branched like capillaries off the main street. Too small for cars, they led up fairly thin walkways where the eaves of the roofs on either side almost met each other overhead. There were shops hidden down the small annexed streets, mainly jewellers and small accessory type shops from what he saw. A few people were perusing at their leisure and in no real hurry, he wandered up one out of unconscious curiosity.

The cobbled alley led past a couple of quiet coffee shops and emerged into a quaint square cobbled courtyard, where there were a selection of small shops and restaurants dotted around its periphery.

Of all the luck, Callison thought to himself. He'd found a fish and chip shop. Something else instantaneously grabbed his attention. Callison froze. *It can't be,* he thought.

It was a statue, but this was no ordinary statue; it was the statue that Callison had seen in his dreams about the cottage. He continued to amble towards it, his gaze transfixed on the bronze piece. It was of a man pointing, and wearing a triangular hat that reminded Callison of a pirate's hat. The statue stood on one leg, resting his other leg on an object in front of him. Callison felt sick. He stood, as a few people wandered on by paying no attention to him or the bronze character.

Seeing this was too much of a coincidence to be normal, especially after having just seen Peter Montague on the news. All he thought he knew about the ways of the world and life, physics and science, started to crumble. Science had been his sense of reality, the wall upon which he leaned his existence; science could not explain these seemingly unlinked events. He moved in closer still.

A bronze plaque read:

Lord Admiral Pickering
1644 - 1687
Died in battle here on the misty morning of November 2nd, 1687 fending off King Charles's Men for helping slaves escape the shores of England.
Erected in 1974 by The Village Mayor, Jonathan T. Phelps

What the hell? thought Callison. *I've never even known of this man. How could I have dreamt it?* The sick feeling worsened as he realised that the second of November, the date Admiral Pickering died, was indeed Callison's own birth date. He became unsure of his whole experience, *this couldn't be true*, he thought, *someone must be setting me up!* He looked around, but life was passing by as usual for everyone else around him.

The statue of Lord Admiral Pickering was bearded; aristocratically attired in smart looking clothes, and had socks pulled up to just below the knees. Callison tried to work out in which direction his house lay in from here and the statue pointed in that direction. *Just like the dream.* The object that he rested his raised leg on was a treasure chest. *Just like the dream.* The lid bowed over and there was a big keyhole on the front of the chest.

His sickness turned into dizziness. Gripped with curiosity and intrigue he investigated and walked off in the direction the statue pointed. He'd forgotten all about the fish and chips. The courtyard closed up again into another small alley leading away from the statue and between the buildings again. It led out to a road running adjacent to the road he'd parked on. This road was quieter and ran past a park just opposite. Over the road, a small wall separated the opposite pavement from the green park. The wall opened up into a semi circle and a vacant bench called him over. *Cigarette time.*

He wandered across the road and took a seat on the empty bench. He pulled a cigarette out of his packet and without concentrating on what he was doing, he lit the smoke. Callison drew in the fumes as he sat staring at the floor. He was happy to be off his feet, but his mind raced. He drew another hit. *What the hell is going on here?* Wondering what to make of it turned him upside down. The coincidences in his life were getting out of hand. He remembered the BLISS4U number plate he saw a month ago at Quanta, he thought about the precognitive cottage dream and seeing Peter Montague on the news, but this; dreaming something as narrowed down and as particular as the statue of a man that Callison had never heard of. *That was freaky.* It was about to get freakier.

Another man walked along the pavement wearing a cream coloured suit with a matching cream top hat, and Callison subconsciously thought it out of place, but didn't really notice him; his conscious mind was too preoccupied with the statue. The cream suited man came to sit down at the other end of the bench to Callison. He nodded an acknowledgement but didn't say anything, resting his hat on his knees and placing his briefcase down on the floor next to him. Callison had forgotten the man already.

'Beautiful day isn't it?' said the man in the cream suit. Nothing. He leaned closer, 'I say it's a beautiful day isn't it.' He had a slight accent and seemed to not be from around here.

Callison pulled his head up, 'What?' came a dazed response. His mind was in another galaxy.

'I said, it's a beautiful day.' said the man in the suit.

Callison looked at the man. He was younger than Callison, about thirty and had distinctive emerald green eyes embedded into a thin face. 'Oh yeah. It is.' Callison replied, vaguely nodding. He continued smoking.

The mysterious man nodded and looked ahead again. He took his hat from his knees and put it down on the bench between them. A few cars and a lorry buzzed past.

The man leaned towards him and spoke again, 'You look like you've seen a ghost, are you alright?'

Callison was still not listening to him properly, 'What? No, it's nothing... I mean... it's ok.'

The man enquired, 'Have the coincidences started yet? The dreams?'

If the man didn't have Callison's full attention before, he did now, 'What did you say?'

The man repeated himself, 'Have the coincidences started yet? Have you started to remember certain dreams?'

Callison heard him right the first time, 'Yeah, that's what I thought you said.' He became overwhelmed, and faced the floor with his head in his hands, speaking mainly to himself, 'What is going on?' He panicked, 'No, this can't be happening!' He pulled his head up, 'You're not real are you. You must be a figment of my imagination, I must be going mad, I must be hearing things, seeing things.' He touched the man's arm. He was real.

The man explained, 'I'm as real as I think real is. I've been practising lucid dreaming and interpretations for the past 20 years now, and I give talks on consciousness all around the world, and so will you one day.'

Callison enquired pessimistically, 'Lucid dreaming, what's that?' He felt inferior.

'Lucid dreaming is where the dreamer consciously wakes up within a dream, but doesn't leave the dream state. You can explore, talk to other lucid dreamers, talk to people that are dreaming unconsciously.' He was enthusiastic, 'There's lots of valuable information to be had in the dream realm.'

'What sort of information?' Callison said genuinely and slowly becoming more interested, 'What should I read into a dream about a statue then? The statue never says anything to me in the dream, he just points at my house.'

'Does your house have an open or closed front door?'

He thought, 'The door is normally ajar.'

The man explained, 'An open door is a sign that you are exploring yourself more. Opening your field of consciousness so to speak. A house in a dream represents the self.'

Callison backed down, 'Oh, ok.' It strangely made sense. He asked another, 'What about writing that moves and morphs and is impossible to read?'

The man nodded slowly, 'That would suggest to me that there is information waiting to come into your life. Coincidences are part of the wake up process if you choose them to be and trigger the mind to fire difference synapses to open other avenues of understanding to you. Go with the flow, for they often lead down the most meaningful avenues of life.'

Callison was interested, but couldn't bring himself to believe this crazy man blindly. That would change.

'Do you read?'

Callison was lost, 'Erm, yes?'

'I have a book to give to you.' said the man on the other end of the bench, who turned around to his briefcase on the floor.

'A book?' Callison said with a confused expression, 'For me?'

He held the book out, 'Yes, all about dreams. It's just a pocket book, I hope you find it useful.' The young man with the emerald green eyes smiled proudly as he handed the book to Callison.

Callison took the small book, but didn't know what to say. His day was turning into one surreal experience. 'Thanks.' He flicked through some of the pages before asking the obvious. 'How did you know I was experiencing coincidences?'

The man looked like he was getting ready to leave, 'It the first sign of waking up.'

'What do you mean waking up? I am already awake?' questioned Callison.

The mysterious man rested his briefcase on his lap, and put his hat back on, before looking around at the street scene in front of them. 'This life you see around you? It's just a collective hologram experience bowl, created by the thoughts and emotions of its observers. It's one of many collective dreams called dimensions of perception, but you've been hoodwinked to believe this dimension is all there is.' The man stood up again ready to leave. 'I have to be off now. Read the book; it might just help your situation.'

Callison pleaded, 'Please, don't go, I need more answers.'

The man held his gaze for a moment, before answering, 'Answers are the fruits of questions, my friend; you don't need more answers, you need more questions. You'll figure it out, I know you will.'

Callison was quiet for just a moment, 'But…' It was too late. The man had started to walk. He looked down at the small book of dream interpretation in his hands pondering why it had been given to him and by whom.

As he flicked the pages, he noticed something. He couldn't believe he'd not seen it when he flicked through the pages earlier. There was a hand-written message in black ink just inside the front page of the book and it was addressed to someone called Callison. *It couldn't be*, he thought:

Dear Callison,

One day you will realise who I am, and we will amaze about it. The portal has already changed the world. You don't need the patented iron. Magnetised steam will work best. Beware the black suits.

Good luck, and I'll see you in time, my friend.

Callison continued to hold the book open. His chin dropped in amazement and wonder. The strange man had laid weight to his claims. Callison looked back to call the man, but he was gone already. He looked back to check the message. *How did this man know I was inventing something? How did he know about the patented iron? What has my invention done to the world?*

He thought about the rest of the note, *Magnetised Steam?* As soon as he'd had the thought, another one popped in to his field of consciousness, he exclaimed aloud in disbelief, 'Peter Montague!'

* * * * * * *

3: Basket Case

"Judge a man more by his questions than by his answers."
Voltaire, Philosopher and Writer (1694 – 1778)

3.1 –
Hidden Timeline:
May 15th 2008:

Two months had passed since Callison's retirement and he and Eleanor had been living in their retirement cottage for the last month.

Receiving the message from the man on the bench had completely kicked the time-travel project onto a new heading. The message had said to use magnetised steam; well Callison finally called up his old colleague, Peter Montague and learnt that magnetised steam could be created with the right equipment, which Peter himself supplied.

Last night, the magnetised steam had its first test run in Callison's modified Eye. It had reached 0.90C on its very first run, with very little temperature concern; a huge bound forward from Quanta's 0.89C running at dangerously high temperatures. The steam had seemed to be the key. This afternoon he would examine the data from last night's test run, and if it looked glitch-free he would go for it; light-speed, and was quietly confident about the new Eye's capability to get there. The excitement lurked deep in the bellows of his stomach, but it had to wait. For now, his mind was on… well, his mind.

The dream book that the enigmatic man on the bench had given to him was interesting to say the least. It made Callison think that he had some deep emotional baggage within him and wanted to get at it, but knew he was scared about what he might find if he looked.

He'd agreed to see a psychiatrist to help him search his subconscious, but also because he wanted to know he wasn't going crazy. He thought his cottage, the dream, seeing Peter Montague on the news and his cream suited friend were somehow interconnected in order to lead him to his success with the travel-machine project, and in scientific circles that sort of thought meant you weren't a scientist, you were downright crazy.

Eleanor was the one who had actually suggested to him to see a psychiatrist. Betty, a friend of Eleanor's had seen one after a messy divorce and it had helped her gather her life back together and move on. Eleanor's hope was that it could work for her husband and his woes also. As he prepared to walk out of the front door, she had hope for him. 'Good luck!' she called down the hallway from the kitchen as Callison picked the umbrella out of the rack by the door.

Callison took a sharp breath and wearily smiled back down the hallway, 'Thanks.'

'I love you!' she added.

'I love you too my darling, I'll see you soon.' he said solemnly. He closed the front door behind him and walked out into the rain, not yet knowing that what he'd just said to his wife would be his last words to her in this dimension.

The psychiatrist was a twenty-minute drive from his cottage and it was raining as he stood on the pavement of Wattle Lane waiting outside the shrink's premises. While holding the umbrella between his head and his shoulder, he lit his last cigarette. His white moustache had little life to it and his green criss-crossed shirt had started to get wet due to the slight breeze blowing the rain under the umbrella. The sign on the wall next to the gate read: Psychiatric Therapy Services Ltd. *What if I've gone mad* he wondered in fright, as he stood and smoked.

He smoked his last cigarette right down past the ink mark to the point where it was burning his lips as he pulled, before extinguishing it. Fear had him in its hand. The old metal gate to the psychiatrist's creaked as the latest new patient swung it open. Its pitch changed, as it swung closed behind him.

3.2 –

Further down Wattle Lane, sitting in a blue Ford Focus, two men in black suits watched Callison walk in to the psychiatrist's building. The one sitting in the driving seat pulled out a mobile phone and dialled a number, it answered, 'Hi it's me. He just walked into a building on Wattle Lane.' He waited, and then spoke again. 'Ok then, we'll sit and wait for visual.' He hung up the phone, and spoke to his colleague, 'We wait.'

His colleague asked, 'He doesn't exactly look dangerous.'

'We were told to ask no questions. I don't plan on doing so.' He turned the radio on again, 'Now, keep your eyes peeled.'

3.3 –

A small pathway led from the creaky gate to the front door through a simple garden made with neat gravel and low maintenance plants. The white building had two large bay windows to either side of a covered porch, which concealed the heavy looking blue front door. There was a sign on the front door that ushered all visitors to the reception desk situated in the first room on the right and Callison pushed the door slightly. It was not locked.

He shook his umbrella dry before entering, and left it in an umbrella rack just inside the porch. While doing so, there was something blocking its way. In a fit of frustration, he pushed harder until the umbrella lodged into the rack. *Stupid fucking rack.* He was far from calm. He used the large brass doorknob to push the door all the way open. Inside he found himself in a large and wide hallway with some dark wood polished stairs on the right side. The floors were polished wood also, but were semi-covered with a Persian themed mat, and the ceilings were so high that they made him feel strangely small. He pushed the front door closed again and wiped his feet on the welcome mat just inside.

He walked into the room on the right and approached the reception desk that was situated just inside next to the bay style window over looking half of the front garden. There were about fifteen seats arranged around the room's periphery with calming abstract art on the walls. A middle aged brunette receptionist sat behind the counter-style reception desk. Her computer was tucked under the counter facing away from the clients and she seemed friendly and welcoming.

'Hello, how can I help you?' She smiled and looked up at Callison from her chair.

He rested his forearms on the desk and spoke down to the receptionist gingerly. 'err... My name is Callison Trebla, I'm here to see Dr Smith?'

The receptionist looked in the respective doctor's diary and saw his entry: 11.00am: Dr Callison Trebla.

'Ok Dr Trebla, if you'd like to take a seat,' She gestured with her arm to the waiting room, 'I'll tell Dr Smith you are here.'

Callison walked over to take a seat in the waiting room and smiled slightly, nearly acknowledging the other two people in the waiting room; *they no doubt had their own life dramas,* he thought. He looked at the magazine rack and thumbed through the magazines on offer. There was nothing he really wanted to read, but the literary eye candy meant he could ignore the other two people waiting to be seen.

After a few minutes, the psychiatrist, Dr Smith walked into the waiting room.

Callison looked like he was engrossed in the magazine article, but he was actually deep in thought about time travel and his afternoon ahead. Callison didn't see the psychiatrist, or hear him.

'Callison Trebla?' Dr Smith said aloud, speaking to all three of the people in the waiting room. A few moments passed.

Dr Smith looked at his information. Callison's date of birth gave him away; he was the only person in the waiting room with silvery white hair. Dr Smith moved in closer, 'Dr. Trebla?'

Callison whipped his head up from the magazine and came out of his trance, 'Sorry,' he smiled apologetically, 'I was miles away.'

The psychiatrist's office was the mirror image of the reception room across the hallway. As he walked in, he spotted the stereotypical shrink's couch straight away, it being next to the large bay window that overlooked the other half of the front garden. The rain had stopped but the windows still had rainwater on them creating a yellow aura in the room as the sun shone through the droplets and into the bright spacious office. Dr Smith ushered Callison to take a seat on the couch and lie back, which Callison did, his heart racing.

Dr Smith closed the door, and went to look at the paperwork on his desk. Behind his desk were extensive layers of mahogany bookshelves full of books on psyche and psychiatry. There were some pieces of art on the left wall, which looked like a continuation of the artwork in the waiting room. On the right wall were some certificates of Dr Smith's qualifications, of which it seemed he had quite a collection.

Callison's psychiatrist seemed restrained but carried himself with confidence. He was about the same age as Callison and had dark grey hair with a short grey beard. The blue shirt and white chino slacks he wore clashed with the lime green tie he had on, but the man had the eccentricity to carry the look. He stood up and walked over to the couch to hold out a clipboard. Lowering his head to look over a pair of half-moon style glasses he spoke, 'Before we start Callison, could you please pop your signature on here?'

'And what am I signing here?' Callison enquired, taking the clipboard and sitting up again.

'It's the law relating to confidentiality during this hour's session. I've signed it and you have to sign it also.' The professional was friendly.

Callison scribbled a mark on the form wondering what the law *actually was*, before handing it back to the mind doctor. The psychiatrist took it back to his desk and sat down. The desk had on it a small tube light on a ninety-degree bracket over his work area. He put the paper work to one side, 'Please get yourself comfortable Callison, lean back.'

Callison lay back, but he was in more of a reclined sitting position than fully horizontal.

The psychiatrist's first question was open-ended, 'So Callison, what do you think you're here for?'

Callison paused for thought, before answering, 'I thought *you* were supposed to figure *that* out.'

Dr Smith looked back at Callison, 'Callison, *I* cannot fix you,' He paused, and then lightened, 'you fix yourself. *My* job is to lead a conversation to get you to talk with yourself, so you can work out why you're feeling the way you are.'

Callison replied thinking it *was* the psychiatrist's job, 'Oh, then couldn't I do that myself?'

'Yes, you could.'

'Then why do people like you exist? To make a buck?' Callison had resentment in his tone, but regretted it as soon as he'd open his mouth. He recoiled.

The response from Dr Smith was calm, 'When *I* lead your thoughts you step outside your usual thought-pattern and learn about yourself.' The psychiatrist's tone was friendly. He added, 'If it reassures you, we are not the most expensive psychiatric health unit out there. Not by a long shot,' he clarified, 'you could be paying ten times what you have if you'd have hunted around. I don't want to take your money, I do this because I feel like I'm helping society in some way, but if I did this for free, I wouldn't be able to provide for myself and my family.'

At least you have a family Callison thought to himself, but felt guilty of even thinking the thought; deep down Callison still had suppressed memories, festering in the pits of his awareness. He was genuinely confused as to why he was here,

'Ok, look; I'm here because my wife said it might help me. I don't want to be here. I don't want to feel the way I do and I certainly don't want you to belittle me. I have had 65 years of life experience. I am an intelligent person that shouldn't *need* to be here.'

'So why *are* you here?'

Callison wondered, before preparing to let off steam, 'You want the truth?'

'I want to know what you *think* the truth is.' said the psychiatrist with genuine interest.

Callison leaned forward on the couch to sit up facing the psychiatrist again, 'Because I hate myself! I hate the stupid world! I hate the fools who fall into line and accept life as being this wonderful thing. I hate the evangelical pursuit of money by corporations that judge themselves more important than human life. I hate seeing war, crime, poverty and negativity on the news every night. I hate the driver of the car that killed my son. I hate the fact that I'm scared to go to bed at night because I know I'm going to have another *fucked* up dream about the day my son got run over.' Callison added, 'is that material enough for you?'

Dr Smith took notes, remaining silent.

Callison went on, 'There's more,' he paused, 'I cannot fathom how life can be so cruel. I cannot fathom how life can be so superficial. I cannot fathom the host of dreams I have. I cannot fathom *why* we dream. I cannot fathom coincidence, I am a scientist, and I should be able to answer these questions. Sometimes I wonder whether I should end it all and take my own life, the only reason I don't is because I couldn't *bear* to leave my wife, Eleanor, alone in this circus we call Planet Earth.' He flopped back in the seat crossing his arms. The tears were building in him and he breathed heavily.

Dr Smith remained quiet and after some time raised his eyebrows, 'Finished?'

Callison thought. A short pause ensued, before Callison gestured a small nod, 'Uh huh, yeah. I guess.'

'Ok Callison, you mentioned your wife; she must be a positive factor in your life? Tell me about her.'

Callison was laid back on the couch and spoke to the air in front of him, 'My *wife* is not my problem; she is my saviour. Why should I talk about *her*?'

Dr Smith explained, 'Callison, I think you have been devoting your mental energy toward the negative aspects of your life. I'm not saying you've had an easy life, but by spending time talking about the positive things, it will make you feel more confident talking about your fears later on. We still have fifty-five minutes.' He paused, 'Now, let's talk about your wife; for instance, how did you meet?'

A small smile tried to break through as Callison thought nostalgically. He answered after a few seconds, 'Three Pennies.'

Dr Smith questioned, 'Three pennies?'

'Well, a car accident really, that's how I met my wife.' Callison shook his head slightly with disbelief, 'It was thirty-eight years ago, in 1970; I was sitting in my car, waiting at some traffic lights on Penny Wright Avenue.' He paused to explain, 'The first penny.' before continuing, 'The second penny came when the radio started to play 'Penny Lane' by the Beatles. It had just come on the radio when all of a sudden, Wham!' Callison drove his fist into the palm of his other hand, 'It was Eleanor driving her mother's Ford Cortina; she had run into the back of me!' Callison enjoyed talking about good memories, 'We got out and inspected the damage. Eleanor said to me that she was coming to a stop, when some coins on her dashboard started to slide off and she tried to grab them. By the time her eyes were back on the road she had run into the back of me. And the only coin that had fallen off her dashboard in the end was a penny.' He paused for a moment as he came back to the room, '*Three pennies*. I don't know if it meant anything, but I've thought about it ever since, and my wife and I joke about it sometimes.' Callison thought to himself about the three pennies coincidence in the light of the coincidences he was now having. *Was the coincidence designed, or was it chance?* He let the psychiatrist talk again.

Dr Smith was humbly astonished, 'Very intriguing, so what happened after that? When did you think you wanted to spend the rest of your life with her?' the psychiatrist probed.

Callison started to relax, 'Pretty much as soon as I saw her I knew she would be my wife. It was hard to say why I thought that. She had the glint in her eye I guess, and she was worried that her mother would never forgive her for the damage.' Callison clarified, and smiled, 'My mother in law was strict and *very* set in her ways.'

'Mothers in law usually are...' added Dr Smith with humour.

A faint smile appeared on Callison's face. 'Eleanor started to cry after the crash; so I helped her to get her car fixed that day. The damage was not extensive but it took half a months salary to get it fixed. I still to this day have not figured out why I offered to pay for it. Anyway, I asked her to go to the pictures with me that evening, and she said yes. It's just the way it turned out to be.'

'Well that's a *charming* story.' He paused. 'Do you *still* love your wife?'

A tear started to roll down Callison's cheek. He found it hard to say, 'I...I... love her with all my heart. I love her more than she knows.' He closed his eyes and let his emotion run. His stubborn ego stood aside and he felt scared crying in front of another man, but he couldn't hold it back, he was besotted with Eleanor, 'She... she has been through all of the pain I have, but she keeps going. We've spoken on and off about our son's death and I don't know if she's holding back or she just deals with things differently from me. But yes, I love her. I love her so much.' He continued to cry.

Dr Smith stood up and passed a tissue box to his upset patient. He couldn't help but be moved, but he remained professional, 'I think you should talk to her about it,' he stated, 'I'm not *telling* you to; it's your choice, but it may help.' He went to go and sit down at his desk again, leaving Callison the box.

'I can't do it. I will end up crying like a baby again.' said Callison, 'She can't see me cry like this, I have to be strong for her.' Callison's eyes were still watery, but the tissues helped absorb the tears.

'Do you think you're being strong for her by *not* crying?' Dr Smith asked.

Callison was confused; the social conditioning firmly in his psyche, 'Well... yes?'

Dr Smith sat with his elbows on the desk interlocking his fingers. He phrased his sentence carefully, 'Well I think you should talk to your wife about it. You never know, you might not breakdown. But if you do it will only help and she won't see you as weak for it.' He nodded his head slightly, 'It sounds like your wife loves you. In fact I'm *sure* she does, so don't be afraid to show her your emotions.'

Callison's response was blunt but not resentful, 'We'll see.'

'Just take it on board that's all. Don't pressure yourself; it's important that you don't feel pressured.'

3.4 –

Callison and the psychiatrist had been building a good rapport. They'd discussed his retirement, and his resulting extra time and Dr Smith had suggested some thought exercises to practice when he felt his mind wandering into the dark. They also discussed some more of Callison's woes and the psychiatrist empathised, and told Callison to breath deeply ten times when he felt his anger coming on.

The psychiatrist decided to home in on what he thought was the major contributing factor to Callison's feelings. He knew it would be hard for Callison and used tact, 'Now I noticed you said something quite subconsciously earlier, when you were talking about how much you loved your wife,' he looked at his notes, 'you said that you've "spoken on and off about your son's death".'

Callison nodded.

'Well it's as if you unconsciously know your son's death is the reason you are feeling this way.' He came from a different angle, 'Now I'm not saying it's not the reason, but what did you do after your son passed away? Did you have any psychiatric assistance afterward?'

Callison mused and subtly shook his head, 'No, I couldn't bear the stigma of seeing a psychiatrist back then. It was like conceding defeat. And everyone looks at you strange if you need a quack.' He acknowledged his slang, 'Sorry.'

Dr Smith accepted it, 'It's ok, I'm used to it.' he smiled, before tentatively moving the subject on, 'Do you think you accepted your feelings of loss *well*?'

Callison shrugged and conceded, 'Probably not…' he paused, feeling a well up of tears coming on, '…but it's hard…' he couldn't think of what to say next and half a lifetimes worth of pent up tears threatened to breach.

The psychiatrist continued, 'Try and relax. Remember to breathe.'

Callison followed orders and composed himself as the tears abated, waiting within.

'If you don't mind,' said Dr Smith, 'I'm going to require you to do some work now. I need for you to give your account of what you felt like when your son died in as much detail as you can. Do you think you can do that?' His tone was as calm as he could make it without being patronising.

Callison lay back on the couch and closed his eyes, before instantly seeing Jack, and opened them again, in fright, 'I don't know if I can do this.' came a scared voice.

'I know it's not easy Callison, but you need to face what is causing you sorrow if you want to get rid of the pain.'

He knew he had to let go, somewhere inside him. He tried the best he could, but he was still fighting fear and tears. He kept his eyes open this time, but transfixed his gaze onto one of the paintings that hung on the psychiatrist's far wall. He started to slowly and painfully recall, 'Well… I was holding hands with

Jack as we walked on the pavement. As we walked, the butcher's was over to the left, on the other side of the road...' he stammered, not being able to explain without sharp intakes of breath, tears and fright. He paused for a moment to gather his thoughts as the tears rolled down the weathered skin of his cheeks, 'it... was... quite busy on the pavement. Jack was talking as he usually did, asking questions of absolutely everything...' He started to cry and laugh at the same time, blaming and talking to himself, 'Why didn't I *see* him run?' his explanation stalled again while the emotion of fear tried to strangle him.

The psychiatrist helped him along gently, 'Keep going, remember to talk about how you felt as well.'

* * * * * * *

4: Jack's Early Checkout

"Men fear death as children fear to go into the dark; and as that natural fear in children is increased by tales, so is the other."
Francis Bacon, Scientist and Philosopher (1561 – 1626)

4.1 –
Flashback:
Hidden Timeline:
October 23rd 1980:

His Dad said that they needed to go to the butcher's. Jack wasn't entirely sure what a butcher was, but he was happy to be sitting in the car with his Dad. He was sitting on his 'Booster-Boy' in the front passenger seat of the car. *The important seat*, he thought. As the world outside the window whizzed past, he felt happy. 'I like going fast Daddy!' He looked towards his Dad, who was doing the driving.

His Dad smiled back at him. He jerked the accelerator, jolting them back and forward. Jack laughed. His dad was being funny.

They had parked in a large multi level car park, which Jack found to be very dark, 'It's a very dark in here Daddy.'

His Dad agreed, 'Yes it is! There are lots of cars in here. It's busy today!' They found a parking space and got out of the car.

Jack held Daddy's hand as they walked away from the car. There was a nasty smell as they walked, 'Daddy, it smells in here!' he said.

His dad smiled back down at him. They waited outside a door that had numbers on the wall next to it. Jack counted them and his Dad was pleased with him. Jack was proud that he could count. The door opened up from the middle; both parts of it disappearing into the walls. 'Where did the doors go Daddy?'

'They are hiding in the walls Jack!'

His dad knew everything. They walked in. The room was small, and someone else walked into the room with them. The room had numbers on the wall inside as well. As the doors came back from out of the walls, Jack knew they had been hiding from everyone, 'There they are again!' His Dad would like to know that.

A strange sensation came over him. He felt his tummy move up for a moment, but the feeling went away again. There was a strange whirring noise. As they stayed in the room, the numbers on the wall lit up. Jack tried to touch the numbers, but Daddy wouldn't let him. 'They are for the grown-ups to push.' He didn't really understand why, but his Dad knew best. They hadn't been in the room for long, when his tummy moved again. He didn't know why, 'Daddy my tummy is moving!'

'That's because your body wants to keep moving down, but the lift is stopping, it's Newton's first law!' Jack didn't know what Newton was, but he was happy with the answer.

The doors opened up sideways, and the view had changed. It was lighter, and there were cars moving fast left and right. As they walked out Jack thought he could see the door hiding from them. He put his head close up to the doors, 'I can see them Daddy.'

Daddy needed to go somewhere, and held Jack's hand, 'Come on, we need to get to the butcher before he closes.'

They were walking on squares. Jack tried to keep his feet inside the squares as they walked. There were lots of people. They were all taller than Jack, and all looked to be very busy, rushing about everywhere. They didn't have a lot of time to talk to each other, and seemed like they couldn't even see each other.

A girl walked past holding a bit of string with a big red round shape at the end. The red shape floated in the air. Jack was mesmerised, and pointed at the girl, 'What's that Daddy?'

'That's a balloon. It floats because it's lighter than air. We have to wait here now Jack. Keep hold of Daddy's hand.'

'Can I have one Daddy?'

'I don't know where she got it from Jack. If we see a man selling them you can have one.' said Daddy. Jack hoped they would see a man selling them and looked for one. They waited on a step next to the part where cars whizzed past. Daddy was assessing the cars. The girl with the red balloon walked away from them, but Jack kept staring at her.

They walked across the part where the cars go, and up another step on the other side. Jack held Daddy's hand tightly.

'This is the butcher. Come on Jack. We're going to get some steaks for Mummy!' Jack was excited about going to the butcher.

The butcher's shop smelt funny. 'It smells in here!' He held his nose like the grown-ups did when they didn't like the smell of something. A few people smiled at him. His Daddy told him they wouldn't be here for long and to wait for Daddy.

Out of the doorway, and across the street, Jack could see the balloon girl again, 'Daddy it's the balloon again!' Daddy was talking with the man behind the glass.

Jack ran out of the door, to the balloon girl like his life depended on it. He jumped down the step, before a loud noise caught his attention. Something knocked him out of his body. Then everything went quiet.

* * * * * * * *

3: Basket Case Continued...

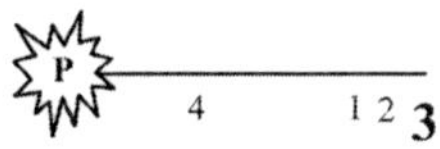

3.5 –
Hidden Timeline:
May 15th 2008:

Dr Smith was comforting, 'Well done. I think you've recalled enough now, remember it's doing you good to recall these memories. It will help you to move on. It might feel painful now, but its better to face your feelings and thoughts than hide from them.' He was also touched by the account, but years in the trade had partially immunised him from feeling the emotions of his clients.

Callison added to his account, the tracks of his tears now drying, with more confidence and ease than when he started, 'It didn't help when my wife said that she could sense Jack in the kitchen at home before she got the dreaded call. Talk of ghosts and things is just wrong and scary. Why would any one think that?'

'Well, it's only as scary as you make it up to be after all, death is a natural process.' the psychiatrist said.

Callison slowly moved out of his fear and into intrigue. It was 11.50 and the psychiatrist asked if there were anything else troubling him. They still had ten minutes. Callison spoke with some uncertainty, 'There was another thing you might be able to shed your light on Dr Smith? It's up your alley.'

The psychiatrist was willing, 'I'll certainly try.'

'Dreams, coincidences...' he hesitated, '... and destiny?'

Dr Smith recoiled to sit back on his chair and reflected the question. Callison sat on the couch facing his psychiatrist. 'They say that studying dreams, coincidences and destiny is like opening Pandora's box, did you know that?'

'No.' *You do the talking.*

He clarified, 'Well it is in Psychiatric circles. It's called Pandora's box because it provides many insights and ideas, but ultimately leads to no answer, and an answer is what people search for.'

Callison wasn't in the mood to stop now. He remembered what the man on the bench told him about the questions being just as important as the answers, and had searched the Internet ever since looking for anything to do with coincidences. 'Tell me what you know about synchronicity.'

The psychiatrist obliged, 'I think it was a term coined to describe separate events that seem linked.' He exemplified, 'Like for example, a song coming on the radio as the listener thinks of it. It was a research topic by Carl Jung I believe. He was into the whole existentialism thing.' He seemed knowledgeable.

'Yeah, that's what I have found out. Well, why isn't this mainstream? I have lived in science circles all my life, and I've never even heard of synchronicity!'

The psychiatrist again explained, 'It's not mainstream for want of trying. The orthodox scientific community never really saw this as *science*; they saw it as *coincidence*.' Dr Smith paused. 'On the other hand the research has always been there; you may not have ever looked for it before. Answers can only come after questions.'

The doctor of mind had used the same phrase as the man on the bench. *Questions come first and answers second.* He conceded on coincidences, 'Ok, what about dreams then? What does your expertise have to say about dreams?'

'Not really my speciality,' the psychiatrist answered, 'there are people who think dreams have meaning, and want to look into that, but I never have felt the need. I don't dream much.'

He continued with his symptoms, 'Well I've been dreaming a lot recently. I've had this one dream many times about my cottage, which I have been reliably informed is an indicator that I'm dreaming about myself. I dreamt it first many years ago and I've now retired and am living in the cottage I have dreamt about! I'm convinced the cottage, or the dream, have hidden meanings, but I don't know what they are!' He refrained from talking about his time travel breakthrough, seeing Peter Montague on the news, the BLISS4ME number plate or Admiral Pickering and the strange man on the bench.

'Well, I don't know...' said Dr Smith, who was openly curious, 'It does make you wonder what goes on without our knowing.'

Go on willed Callison hoping for some insight.

'I guess you'll just have to figure this one out on your own. It might mean something, it might not, but if you worry about it too much you'll miss out on the positive aspects of life.' It was a valid point, but Callison yearned for answers.

The session ended bang on twelve o'clock. It ended with niceties and a civil handshake but Callison hadn't made a repeat appointment. He walked out of the big front door in the hallway into the outside air where the sun was shining through the clouds, and the ground was dry again. He forced his umbrella from the rack outside the front door and walked back down the garden path feeling decidedly light on his feet. The gate creaked closed as he left.

3.6 –

The main agent spoke on the phone, 'Yeah, he's leaving now.' A pause ensued as his orders were relayed.

'Affirmative.' he said in response, and hung up. 'We follow but don't approach.' he told his sidekick.

The blue Ford Focus rumbled into life.

* * * * * * *

5: The First Time Traveller

"Time goes you say? Ah, no! Alas, time stays. We go!"
Henry Austin Dobson, Poet and Essayist (1840 – 1921)

5.1 –
Hidden Timeline:
15th May 2008:

Driving away from the psychiatrist, Callison reflected. It had been better than expected; he still felt sorrow for Jack, but he felt more confident, as if he knew the therapy had done something positive to him. The part of his mind that generated thought had been probed and thoughts seemed to flow more freely. He was undecided if he'd tell Eleanor it had brought him to tears.

He remembered suddenly as he drove that he needed cigarettes and pulled into a local convenience store that he'd never been into before. *They must sell them*, he thought.

He joined the back of a short queue and watched as the other people slowly got served. The shopkeeper seemed to know the 'regulars' and spoke with them about other people, and how they'd been getting on. She was about the same age as Callison and looked eccentric with a brilliantly white perm and too much make up on.

'Twenty Bensons please.' he said, when it came to his turn.

She smiled a bit more than Callison was comfortable with, before she reached around behind her to get the cigarettes off the shelf.

'That will be five pounds ninety-five dear.' said the cashier.

He noted warmth in her voice. There was also a slight accent that was hard to place, but she was easy to understand.

Callison handed her a ten-pound note and got his change. He was just about to walk away when another woman entered the shop. She was of roughly the same age as them, and seemingly knew the teller. She was loud.

'Oh, look at this one Glad, beautiful glow to him!' she exclaimed, as she pointed at Callison.

Glad, or presumably Gladys, the shop assistant agreed, 'Yes, I thought that when I saw him too!'

Callison was hit for six, 'Erm... What do you mean?' He spoke to both of them.

The woman behind the counter answered, 'We mean you aura dear, you're glowing bright blue!'

He questioned himself as we all do, 'Oh. That's good?' Just as he said it, a bright red thought of fear radiated out of his crown and created a red patch in his aura.

'Ooh, did you see that Glad?' said the visitor.

'Certainly did!' came the response.

The loud shopper explained in a friendly manner, 'We saw your thought leave your head, it's in your aura now!'

Get out of here; they're weird, Callison instinctively thought, 'Oh... ok... well... don't really know what you're talking about, but thanks, see you later!' With that, he made a quick exit out to his car.

These bizarre events were beginning to annoy Callison. He had not been witness to the subject of auras in sixty-five years, until now; right when he's questioning his own belief system. *Why now?* he thought. It felt like he was losing his mind, until he thought about the Trebla Eye being a result of the strange chain of events. *Time travel must be my destiny*, he thought to himself. The time travel line of thought led him to hope and happier feelings.

His belief system was starting to change, unlike his habits; he pulled a cigarette out of the new packet, and lit it up before getting into his car and driving back home to see his wife. Or so he thought.

He parked on his driveway and waited for a bit before turning the engine off. He wanted to ask the ladies in the shop some questions, but his defence mechanism had kicked in; flight. It was a quarter to one in the afternoon and it had just started raining again. The thoughts about the shop passed, as he realised the engine was still running and he was still in the car. *Stuff it. Not going to go back and ask now.* He turned the engine off and hopped out.

The Ford Focus up the street killed its engine also, but the two men remained in the vehicle continuing their stake out.

Callison opened the front door and called to Ellie, 'Ellie! I'm back.' He went to put his umbrella back in the stand, but there was no response in the house. He called again, 'Ellie!' Still no response. *Strange.* He poked his head into the lounge, to no avail then walked into the kitchen. There was a note on the sideboard that read:

Gone with Betty to Home Wares exhibition at last minute.

Hope your session went well.

I'll be back around 6pm. There's some microwave pies in the fridge for you.

Love, E x

Oh well, I have work to do anyway. He flicked the kettle on and it started its boiling process.

He leaned on the kitchen sideboard and smiled as his thoughts turned once more to the Eye standing up in the room below. Despite his woes, he was still buzzing with enthusiasm about the adapted idea and last night's Eye run. His mind was overpowered by the perceived enormity of what he was going to do this afternoon; he was going to go for it. *Light-Speed here we come.*

Last night he had used only 0.893 of a gram of the magnetised steam to get to 0.9C. The amount was calculated from theoretical equations he himself had formulated. A little quantum matter goes a long way. It had been calculated that the quantum energy inside the atoms of a cup of tea, if utilised efficiently, could provide enough energy to boil all of the world's oceans. Nagasaki and Hiroshima had witnessed the devastating energy of just two atoms. If the light barrier was anything like the sound barrier, Callison thought, a large push would be required to 'punch through' so-to-speak.

The kettle came to the boil, and Callison made the cup of tea. He took a cigarette out of his packet, and then put his dinner in the microwave. It would be ready in one cigarette's time.

5.2 –

The scientist descended the last step and made the turn at the bottom of the staircase. Having a time portal in his basement was like having a new car, but a million times more awe-inspiring; every time he saw the Eye he would marvel at it standing strong in the middle of the basement. *Good afternoon my darling,* Callison thought as he cordially approached with a mug of tea. The clock on the basement wall read half past one.

The Eye, including the square holding structure stood eight feet high and heavy durable steel gave it its posture. The portal part looked like a giant doughnut caught in the middle of a spider's web. Buried in the portal's round periphery was the hollow tunnel containing the new magnetised steam, not that the internal tunnel could be seen anymore, hidden beneath cooling ducts, wires, and electrical measuring devices all feeding back to the computer. The six large electromagnets could be easily placed and were equally spaced on the round doughnut. It was a walk through portal and on numerous occasions Callison had walked through imagining he was taking the *first small steps for man.* He had even built a step up to the portal's entrance to facilitate entry into the portal.

Callison put his tea down and prepared for a run. *Computer on.* The computer buzzed into life, and automatically supplied power to the Eye. Some check lights on the portal's systems illuminated as the equipment was powered up. Callison put on his white lab coat out of 30 years of habit.

Log in and password. *Always have to be careful about security.* He keyed it in: J – A – C – K. Anyone that knew him would have guessed the same word. He accessed the correct programmes on the computer and opened up the CCU control panel window. It was available to him on the screen, and he could control everything from the computer.

First of all he analysed last night's run for any strange anomalies in the test data, but all looked perfect. He was ready.

System check. The system check comprised a complete check of all joinable connectors, nuts, bolts, gaskets and seals. The computer did a check of the pressures and electrical circuits and he undertook a physical check with his trustworthy own eyes. *All systems checked and ready to go.*

Phase one of the start up was to initiate the inner and outer magnets. These magnets, were different in function from the magnets that would eventually accelerate the magnetised steam to light speed. They ran around the entire periphery of the tube in which the magnetised steam flowed. The inner magnet ran around the inside radius of the tubular tunnel, while the outer magnet ran around the outside radius, and it was these magnets that would hold the steam on the centre line inside of the circular tunnel. Callison played with the mouse, and clicked what he needed to click, a low hum reverberated around the basement as the inner and outer magnets were powered up. He was nervously excited.

Next on the start-up procedure list was to create the vacuum inside the internal tunnel and introduce the magnetised steam. At the bottom of the round doughnut there were two small valves, one was much like a car tyre's inlet valve, by which the steam entered the internal tunnel, and the other acted as an outlet by which a powerful suction pump would suck 99.9% of the atoms out. Of course, the suction had to be completed before the steam was introduced.

He connected a pipe to the outlet valve, and started the suction pump. The CCU fed back to him figures displaying the internal vacuum of the tunnel. It took about 5 minutes before it came to an end.

He disconnected the suction pump from the Eye and connected the steam introduction pipe. This was connected to an ominous looking black box containing essentially a small reservoir of water and a heating element. As the water boiled off, the steam produced was fed through Peter Montague's own combination of electrolysers and bar magnets. The magnetised steam then left the black box via a thin rubber hose, which led into the Eye's inlet valve. Due to the vacuum, the steam was sucked into the internals of the Eye. She was filling up, the inner and outer magnets holding the steam and spacing it evenly around the tunnel on the centre line.

After about 5 minutes, the pre-calculated 0.893 grams of the tub water had boiled off and entered the Eye. The inner and outer magnets had to be turned on before the introduction of the steam, so that none of the steam had a chance to condense on the internals of the tunnel wall. *That's it.* He turned the black box off and disconnected the pipe from the inlet valve. He visualised the steam now suspended inside the tunnel. All systems still looked fine on the monitor. He opened another window on his computer monitor to display the current steam distribution within the Eye and again all systems reported no abnormalities.

The steam had to be kept as evenly distributed as possible especially at the higher speeds. Any matter accentuation or concentration while travelling quickly would act like a mass on a wheel, and put the Eye into a state of imbalance.

He took a swig of his now lukewarm cup of tea. *Ok, lets see how fast we can get this stuff moving.* The computer monitor showed that the distribution was perfect, and a read out in the top left corner of the screen read 0.00C.

Power was supplied carefully and equally to the 6 large electro-magnets, that began accelerating the magnetised steam around the Eye. Callison held a round twistable dial by which he could tell the CCU to increase or decrease the power going to the magnets, thus controlling the speed of the tunnel matter.

He slowly turned the dial clockwise and just millivolts were supplied to the main accelerating electro-magnets initially. The software on the computer ensured that the power was regulated in such as way as to not favour one electro-magnet more than any of the others due to the imbalance issue. The steam slowly started its rotation around the internal tunnel of the Eye. He checked the distribution again. *Distribution still good.*

The CCU read 0.01C as the matter continued to accelerate. The equipment ran a lot quieter using steam for some reason. There was the noise from the inner and outer electro magnets, which sounded like a low constant bass and the accelerating magnets provided the melody, increasing in pitch and volume as more power was fed to them. The CCU displayed the steam speed as 0.15C after ten minutes of acceleration. *15% down, 85% to go*, he thought. He continued to twist the dial and watched the distribution window on the screen intently as the steam slowly accelerated to 0.23C.

His excitement was interrupted by the sound of the doorbell above.

Callison stopped observing the screen momentarily. He knew Eleanor was out with Betty. *Strange. I'm not expecting anyone.* He decided to ignore it. *They'll go away.* He concentrated on the read outs from the computer again. The doorbell went again about a minute later. *Would you give up already!* He was frustrated and carried on observing the computer's information.

Suddenly a loud crash was heard above. Callison froze. It sounded like the door being forced open and his heart began to race. There were footsteps in the hallway above him.

5.3 –

'It's down here.' Callison heard the voice echo down the basement steps. The basement door was closed, but unlocked.

Callison saw the light fall down and illuminate the bottom of the stairs as it creaked open. Shadows were on their way down the steps.

They know I'm here! Callison was panicking, but had completely frozen. Had he a more aggressive nature, he might have thought about taking a large implement and dealing a crushing blow. He remained, stuck on the spot in a similar way to his dreams about Jack. His legs were immobilised and his eyes were fixed on the bottom of the stairs, his heart racing.

The Eye maintained a steady 0.23C, quietly waiting to be accelerated to its target speed. Callison had forgotten it was even going.

At the bottom of the staircase two men walked in wearing black suits. *The message*. Callison got nervous.

'My, my, we've been a naughty boy, haven't we?' said the taller one.

His face was familiar. Callison tried to remember his name, 'You're the removal worker!' He racked his brains, 'What was your name…' he wagged his index finger as he thought, 'Danny! That's it! Danny! You knew what the equipment did all along!'

The tall suited agent replied, 'Good memory old man, I'm impressed! I *was* the removal worker, but my name isn't *Danny*.' He smiled at his colleague, who remained silent smiling. Both of them looked menacing and had cold looks in their eyes. 'Danny' explained further, 'I wasn't lying. Would you believe me if I told you I still don't know what that contraption is? Looks better than it did when I moved it down here though you lazy bastard!'

Callison was scared witless, 'W... What do you want from me?' he asked with a quaver in his voice.

The other shorter agent replied, 'Well that's up to the boss.'

'The boss?' said Callison, wondering who was pulling the strings.

The ex-removal worker, Danny pulled out a mobile telephone from his inside jacket pocket and held the phone up to show Callison. 'The boss,' he said. He seemed to be superior to the shorter one. The boss was on speed dial and the taller agent paced the end wall of the basement next to the steps as he spoke, 'Yeah, hi it's me. Looks like we're ready to rock and roll down here?' The agent walked over to the corner of the basement, and seemed to talk to the wall, 'Hi, can you see us, you're watching basement TV!' He laughed, waiting for his orders over the phone, 'Ok, we'll hold him until you arrive.' He switched the phone off and put it back in his pocket before turning to face Callison. 'Now we wait.' he smiled.

'You've been s... spying on me?' Callison was heartbroken. The Eye was still humming behind him, idling at a steady 0.23C. It had a good view of the basement proceedings.

'The *boss* has been spying on you. I'm not sure what this invention does, but it sure is valuable!' He laughed callously, while his companion smiled.

Callison tried to spoil their party, 'Yeah? What if I break it now? All it would take would be one...'

He stopped talking as they both pulled out guns and aimed them at Callison, 'Don't do anything stupid now,' said the taller agent, 'the boss will be here soon.'

These guys were serious; he was trapped. He tried to reason, 'Look, I need to make sure this equipment is maintaining itself. I am just going to monitor the computer, if the equipment becomes unstable, we could all be dead.' He thought about sabotaging the Eye, but couldn't bring himself to kill his baby.

'Ok, but don't touch anything until the boss arrives.'

'How long will that be?' he enquired.

'Not long.' They still had their guns drawn, and looked happy with themselves.

'How much are you being paid to do this?' Callison asked.

'Enough.' came the characterless response.

He guessed they needed him alive for when the boss arrived, 'How do you sleep at night? You're the bastards here, not me. Do you know that?' The answer surprised Callison.

'We work for Queen and Country and we're proud to enforce the security of this great nation.'

He couldn't believe his ears, 'Who trained you to say that?!...'

'Whatever, I'm not arguing,' said the agent bluntly, 'you're a threat to the nation; we're managing the threat. Shut the fuck up.' The response lacked any semblance of emotion.

They were right. *The oppressor and the slave.* Callison thought to himself, and replied out of reaction rather than bravery. 'The idea of dividing land into countries is manmade, England is an idea in our heads, it's a label, not a fixed thing of reality! You do realise that?'

The suits missed his meaning and in their brainwashed frustration they restored their power with threat, 'Look just shut up old man, you're starting to really piss me off.' His cold grey eyes lacked any kind of soul and he turned to face his shorter accomplice, 'Get some chairs from upstairs.' He faced Callison again, 'May as well get comfortable.' he said, smiling like he didn't care about any of it.

The three of them sat down in silence. Guns drawn. Callison's mind was racing. *What if Eleanor came home to find this shit going on? What if she was dead already?* The fear started to strangle him. He could see the eye was still maintaining 0.23C and he hoped it would remain in that steady state.

5.4 –

It took about ten minutes for the boss to arrive and it was the longest ten minutes of Callison's life. He had maintained his gaze at the steam distribution window on the monitor for the duration.

Footsteps were heard on the hallway above them.

'Sounds like the boss has arrived.' said the shorter agent. He called up the stairs, 'We're down here.'

A voice boomed down the stairs, as the footsteps got louder, 'I know where it is, I bugged the house you moron!'

Callison knew that voice.

The footsteps stopped and Heinrich Muller strolled slowly and confidently round the corner of the stairs and entered the fray wearing a long black jacket over his suit, and black leather gloves. He was now the tallest man in the basement; his cold smile faked. His voice was quiet and controlled, 'Callison. Nice to see you again, it's been a while. How is retirement treating you?'

He felt only confusion, 'You!?' Callison exclaimed.

'You didn't think you'd actually get *away* with it did you?' he calmly said, towering over the people in the room.

'Why?!' Callison was confused, 'Why would you do this?'

Heinrich ignored him and listened to the Eye whirring quietly behind Callison; he glanced at the screen to see it was operating at 0.23C. 'It's running now isn't it? You're 23% of the way. It's quieter, why is it quieter?!'

Callison thought. *You're never going to believe this but there was this man I met on a bench…* He remained muted.

'Ok, be like that,' said Heinrich, 'we've just come to take back what is rightfully ours, we'll find out why it's quieter in the labs. We are well within the law here, you are the criminal, let us remind ourselves of that!'

Callison launched verbally, 'It's mine! It's my ideas that have created this, it's mine, not yours!' Both agents pointed their guns at him again and he quietened.

Heinrich spoke to the shorter agent, giving him a bit of paper, 'Get that front door fixed. It's a fucking mess. Ring these people. They'll come and do it. Then you stay on lookout for third parties.'

'Yes sir.' The agent disappeared up the basement steps.

Sir? Callison puzzled to himself.

Heinrich smiled and pulled a piece of paper from inside his jacket, 'The law...' he looked at his one remaining agent, '...so we're all clear.' He slowly and clearly quoted from the paper as he paced the basement, his voice boomed, 'I… signed by one Dr Callison Trebla, acknowledge that any research or knowledge gained while working at Quanta Research Laboratories Incorporated is now under sole ownership of the Company, and I… signed by one Dr Callison Trebla, in accordance with the laws in place as of the 11 March 2008, promise to relinquish any commercial property, intellectual or otherwise.' He paused, looking at the grey-haired scientist as his words hung in the air.

'I had to sign that! If I didn't I'd have been arrested!' He glared at the agent who posed as the removal worker, 'Just another example of the little guy getting fucked… Eh *Danny*?' The agent laughed, but kept his weapon aimed.

'The military needs it first Callison, you know the national security laws and you broke them! You stole the electromagnets from us!' Heinrich boomed.

Callison's tone was quiet and controlled, 'I just wanted to help people. Time travel could reshape people's lives.' He added, 'That is, if it's *not* discovered by a multinational company who would put profit above benefit.' He walked over to the computer to keep an eye on the steam distribution; *still perfect*. Even in the given situation he felt proud that his machine was behaving itself. 'Anyway, I've cracked it, and there's nothing you can do to take that truth away. An invention is the inventor's forever, no matter who claims it as their own.' His chest was hurting him, but he didn't let on.

Heinrich was angry, 'We CAN take everything away from you! And we WILL if you don't cooperate!' Callison said nothing. 'You know Callison, all it would take would be a few phone calls and a large publicly viewed law suit, and you'll be laughed out of science.' His tone was threatening, 'We both know I have a good track record in the courtrooms, so start paying attention!'

Heinrich changed the subject as he walked over to the rear wall of the basement. He felt a seemingly random shiver fly down his back, like a ghost had walked on his grave. He'd been trained not to dwell upon it and calmly he carried on, 'How is the Eye performing that quietly Callison? We saw your little 'live show' last night.' He reached up to the brickwork about seven feet up the wall and, using a fist-sized magnet retrieved a metallic object from a tiny-drilled hole.

'What is that?! Is that the camera?!' Callison said with surprise.

His old boss turned around, and plucked the small camera from the magnet, 'Its technical name, Callison is the X1120 GSW4, the 4th prototype of pinhole camera technology.' The device he held up was about 10mm long. 'Didn't even know it was here did you? It's been broadcasting continuously on loop. It downloads the information to us, then resets its memory and keeps recording.' He smiled, as he realised the device had done its job. 'We put another one in your laboratory back in your good old days of *legal research*!' he shouted.

Callison had given up. He shrugged.

Heinrich continued again, 'So I asked you, how is the time-machine operating that quietly?'

The suited sidekick exclaimed, 'Time-machine!?'

Heinrich didn't answer him, but stared him quiet. He looked back at Callison.

'Well Callison? Are you going to show and tell?'

Callison was nervous, but remained stubborn and sarcastic, 'You're its owners, Quanta, you should know!'

Heinrich reached into his coat pocket, pulled out a gun and cocked it. He aimed it at Callison's head, 'Ramp it up.'

5.5 –

I'm a sell-out. I'm powerless. I'm weak. He was stood at the computer, and slowly started to increase the speed of the Eye. Heinrich and the lone agent looked on. *This is my invention! I hate Quanta! I hate Heinrich!* he thought. The Eye started to increase in pitch as the magnets drew more and more power.

Not completely in the dark on the topic, Heinrich looked at the distribution display on the screen, 'This iron distribution is perfect. Why is it like that?'

Why should I tell you? Oh yeah, you're going to kill me. He still didn't say how he'd come up with the fix; he doubted they'd believe him anyway. 'I decided to use magnetic steam instead of your patented iron dust, and it just works better than the iron.' He thought more and the words fell out before he could rein them in, 'So in actual fact, this makes your legal ground quite rocky.'

Heinrich gestured towards his gun, 'My ground is just perfect thanks.'

Callison didn't answer.

The computer screen showed the speed: 0.46C. Callison had started; he may as well tell them all about it, 'You'll soon begin to see a white spark of light emerge from the portal's dead centre. It appears at 0.5C, and then grows larger as the speed approaches light-speed.' Heinrich and the agent glanced back and forth between the speed dial on the screen and the portal itself. The whirring hum continued to noticeably increase its pitch.

0.47C... Nothing... 0.48C... Nothing... 0.49C... Nothing... 0.50C... Something.

A small white spark of light appeared in the centre of the portal, glimmering like a distant star. Heinrich had seen examples of this phenomenon back at Quanta, but not since Callison had left; Callison *was* the project. He was enthralled to see the effect again. The agent was completely blown away by it. 'What is that!' the layman exclaimed.

Callison felt duty bound to explain, 'It's light being bent back into coherence. Normally we see seven colours, or a mixture of them but the fast moving steam plasma flow has pulled the light towards itself. We are literally tearing open time and space.' The agent gave a blank look.

Callison was checking gauges, pressures and distribution while slowly increasing speed. 0.60C... to 0.70C... to 0.80C... The gun-toting pair watched as the white speck grew into a shimmering white sheet of light growing in size and stretching towards the periphery of the doughnut. The white shimmering portal was bright, and threw out white light, casting three silhouetted shadows onto the back wall of the basement. The noise was noticeably louder than earlier on, and a slight vibration could now be sensed through the soles of their feet.

'It's a lot quieter than it was before.' said Heinrich. It was just a statement, but implied a question.

Like I care, thought Callison. He continued to wind up the speed.

The display screen read 0.91C and they had entered uncharted water. The previous record had been 0.9C the night before and now the Eye was whirring away at a high pitch. The energy released from the near light speed flow was intense; the outer rim electro magnet of the Eye was starting to glow red underneath all the cooling ducts and peripheral attachments.

'Is that normal?' asked the agent of the heating.

'Yes, its getting warm, but the cooling is taking care of it.' He checked the cooling state on the computer. *All fine*. He was honest, 'We are in new ground now; I only went to 0.9C last night. And we've *never* hit light speed before, so I'm not entirely sure what's going to happen.'

'Keep going.' said Heinrich firmly and eagerly.

The white shimmering light covered the entire face of the portal. Small ripples of colour were starting to emanate from the centre of the Eye travelling outwards towards the periphery like coloured stones being dropped into a white millpond.

They edged ever nearer. 0.97C... 0.98C... 0.99C... 0.99C... 0.99C... Something was impeding the progress. The last 1 percent always threatened to be resistive according to theory.

'We're hitting a barrier of resistance.' Callison told them, 'We still have some leeway with the temperature, so I'm going to keep increasing the power. Try and punch through.' *It could go bang, but I don't care,* he thought, *I've already lost my baby.*

'Ok, keep going, this I *have* to see!' Heinrich had forgotten about everything, about the whole situation. He still was a scientist at heart; he just worked for a pathological corporation who'd kill people for its economic survival.

The noise continued to increase in pitch. The magnets were forcing the steam flow to accelerate, but it was up against the light barrier. 0.99C remained the top speed. The distribution graph was starting to hiccup slightly. It caused concern for

Callison; the hiccups could be felt underfoot by all three men, but under the circumstances he'd lost the will to research methodically. He kept increasing power and the number of hiccups of vibration increased.

Then it happened. The hiccups subsided and everything fell quieter. A large ripple emerged from the geometric centre of the portal, leading a front of colours. It had the men gazing wondrously. The portal changed colour rapidly. It was as if a bubble had burst. Greens, blues and yellows surged forward, emerging from the centre of the portal, flooding out the previous white blanket. They became blurred intermingling colours, mixing, rotating and swirling into each other much like a colour-blended kaleidoscope. They noticed that some of the colours were unknown to them, which was an assault to their senses.

'Tell me that was light speed just being hit!' called Heinrich excitedly.

'I think it was!' Callison dived back onto the control panel.

Like pushing against a door and falling through when it gave way, when the steam overcame the barrier of light speed, it sped up effortlessly again. The display surged forwards. 1.04C... 1.09C... 1.17C...

'Whoa!' exclaimed Callison. He caught it and backed the power supply off to get the speed to a steady 1.02C. The steam distribution reverted back to its previous best, and all the dials and displays reported back perfect figures. They had done it! The steam inside the tunnel was moving steadily just above the speed of light, circumnavigating at 50,000,000 revolutions a second.

The portal's new coloured surface vibrated heavily. Reds, blues, yellows all dancing, vibrating with a pulse. They reminded Callison of multicoloured inkblots on wet paper. The new colours swirled around with an uncanny intelligence making more new colours as they mixed and intermingled with the seven known ones.

'Are you seeing what I'm seeing!' said Heinrich, who had no idea what he was actually seeing.

'Yes! And it's my design that has done it!' said Callison carelessly. He did a jig in the middle of the basement floor, even with a couple of guns in the room.

Heinrich walked around the portal to view it from behind, but all he saw was Callison dancing and the amazed agent looking back at him. It was still see-through from behind as if no barrier existed at all. He walked back around again. He asked Callison. 'Where does that lead to? He rephrased, 'Or more like; *when* does it lead to?!' He seemed demanding again.

Callison's private party ended. He was just as much in the dark as Heinrich. 'I... I don't really know when that is,' he said surprised, 'the classified theory manuals suggested that a clockwise accelerant led to the future and an anti-clockwise accelerant led to the past. The steam in the doughnut is travelling clockwise so I'm guessing it's the future, but we'd still have much research and calibration to do to find out how far it is away from us chronologically.' Callison had forgotten about the situation, while his transfixed eyes remained glued to the multi-coloured pulsating portal.

'We... Callison? Don't include yourself in this research project.' He was still cold, 'We came here to take the Eye, and that's what we're going to do. It's a Quanta project after all.'

'You don't know how hard I've worked on this! Please, let me back in! I'll work for Quanta again!' He was desperate. He felt throbbing pains in his chest. It made him nervous, and he was sweating.

Heinrich remained adamant, 'You are a security risk of the highest order; you don't know our agenda. No way. No fucking way.'

Callison found it hard to get a full breath, 'So what, you're just going to take it all to pieces?' He breathed, 'What do you think my wife will say? She'll go to the papers, and so will I!' He was clutching at straws.

'You'll both not be in a position to do much at all! You'll be either dead, or behind bars!' He laughed at Callison in a display of power. 'You should have fallen into line and taken all those promotions when you had the chance!' he continued to laugh.

Callison didn't know why, he just heard an inner voice. It said: Jump!!... Jump!!... Jump!!... It was an intuitive move, but he ran. He ran as fast as he could towards the coloured portal. A shot rang out from someone's gun, but it just missed him and he jumped. As the clock struck 4:02 on the afternoon of the 15th May 2008, Callison Trebla disappeared into his own invention and in so doing changed the future; and the past, and the present.

* * * * * * *

6: Sixth Sense

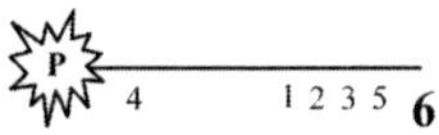

"Masses are always breeding grounds of psychic epidemics"
Carl Jung, Psychiatrist and Scientist (1875 – 1961)

6.1 –
Hidden Timeline:
May 15th 2008:

'Go on Ellie, you almost have a full house!' shrieked her best friend, Betty. Just as Eleanor's hopes were heightened, someone else shouted from the back of the hall, 'Full house!'

They were at the Turtle Bingo franchise on the edge of town. Eleanor sighed and looked at her wristwatch, her day had been a strange one. They had been to the Homewares exhibition, which was fine, but for the last hour she had been overly worried about her husband. She had called him at about six o'clock, but there was no answer and it was now seven-fifteen.

Betty had persuaded Ellie to let her hair down with a few drinks and bingo. They still wore the summer frocks that they went to the exhibition in – Eleanor wore an ankle length red dress with white flowery designs all over it, and Betty had donned a dark green dress. The bingo hall was busy but not full, and burbled loudly with the multitude of voices. Above the voices, speakers bellowed with the sound of an overenthusiastic bingo caller. Each of their bingo cards was taking about ten minutes before someone would shout 'full house' and another game would ensue after a five-minute interval.

Betty consoled Eleanor, 'Oh well Elles, not your time this time, but we still have three more bingo cards to hope for, I just know one of them will be a winner!'

Betty had dark curly hair, and a large round face. She was by her own admission overweight, but had a loud voice and bubbly personality to counter. In her late fifties, she was a divorcee of five years, and drank probably too much than was good for her. Betty's brash and unrelenting manner and Eleanor's passive and reflective style fitted together well in the friendship, which is why they were friends.

'I should really think about going home soon, I just want to make sure everything is alright with Callie.' Eleanor said with concern.

Betty and Eleanor had been friends for about fifteen years and knew each other well. Betty thought that although Eleanor was always in control, she never seemed to have fun because of it, 'Oh Eleanor darling, you worry too much, let your hair down, enjoy yourself.' Just as she had stopped speaking, the serving steward walked past clearing glasses and taking orders from the floor.

'Excuse me!' Betty called across a neighbouring table. The serving steward looked their way, her ears attuned to those two words. Betty fired an order in, 'Yes, could we get two G and T's over here please.' The serving steward acknowledged with a slight nod and a small smile and made headway towards the bar.

'Thank you!' Betty called over her shoulder.

Eleanor exclaimed, 'Betty, I shouldn't, I have to drive!'

'Well one G and T isn't going to be over the limit, besides you've been drinking orange juice all night, come on, let your hair down.'

The loudspeaker interrupted them. It was the cheesy bingo caller announcing the next game, 'Ok, sixty seconds until the next game starts!' A large red digital counter started its count down from sixty to zero, as Eleanor and Betty carried on debating.

'Look we'll play this game then see how you feel' said Betty, using a serious tact.

Eleanor looked worried, 'I don't know, Callison will be worried where I am,' she justified. 'It's nearly an hour and a half since I said I'd be back!'

Betty countered, 'Yes, but you've rung him, and there was no answer. You said yourself he was probably working on his science experiment, now relax and have some fun!'

Eleanor sighed, and half conceded, 'I did ring him I suppose.'

Betty seized the argument, and reassured Eleanor, 'Yes, you've got nothing to feel guilty about.'

It wasn't really a feeling of guilt Eleanor felt, it was a feeling she wasn't sure of. It felt like unease.

The speaker system burbled with the sound of the presenter, 'You have 5 seconds until the next game start, three... two...one... Let's play Bingo...!'

Eleanor gave in, 'Ok, get your eyes on your card!'

Betty smiled, 'That's the spirit old girl!'

Eleanor carried on with her bingo card, while silently thinking to herself about Callison. *He must be in his own little world working. He must have missed the phone.* If only she knew the truth.

6.2 –

They had left the Bingo with one card still unused. Despite a stubborn defence, Betty had agreed to leave as she'd won some money on the last round they'd had. Eleanor dropped Betty home and set about driving home again to see her husband. It was not dark, and it would be a fifteen-minute drive through some quiet country lanes to get home from Betty's.

Her drive was more surreal than normal. Now having only the sound of the car's engine as company, her inner voice was louder. She got slightly panicky as her thoughts started to take her over. She turned the radio on. It was the Beatles, playing Penny Lane. She almost started to cry. It was their song. She had a strange urge to pick up the phone and call for help. She knew she shouldn't do it while driving, but felt it necessary this evening. She dialled in a number as she drove. This call would be the unconscious cause that would seal her fate.

Her fifteen-minute drive home felt like half an hour, but she finally pulled into the driveway of the cottage, having made the call. Callison's car was still on the drive and it was ten past eight in the evening. She got out of her car and as she walked closer to the house she sensed that something wasn't right.

As Eleanor slowly walked up to the front door, she rummaged around in her handbag for her keys. She got to the front door and was confused. It was a slightly different colour, and the door lock looked new. She pushed her key in, and it worked normally.

The house was quiet inside. She turned the light on and closed the door but something immediately jumped out at her. She saw that the basement room door was open. It was normally closed and locked. She walked intrepidly towards the basement door and pulled it open some more. Deadly silence; but there was a moving colourful light source coming from the basement, almost like a TV was on down there.

'Callison dear?' She called down the stairway. No answer. *That's weird,* she thought. A strange sense of danger swept over her, as if she knew something was very wrong. She walked timidly down into the basement. The stairs creaked as she slowly descended them. Her going-out shoes and long red frock were hardly the most practical attire for descending the flight, but she wasn't thinking about that. She wanted to call out, but didn't think she should. She made the turn at the bottom of the steps, sealing her own destiny as she went.

* * * * * * *

7: Lost in Time

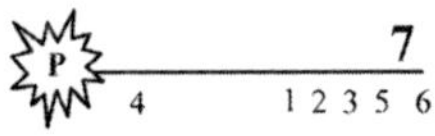

"Not until we are lost do we begin to understand ourselves."
Henry David Thoreau, Philosopher
and Transcendentalist (1817 – 1862)

7.1 –
Date not known:

He hadn't had any choice; with a gun pointed at him and on the verge of losing everything, he had escaped into the portal. Flight. The drama in his basement and everything Callison knew were left far behind him as he travelled through a tunnel.

As soon as Callison jumped into the portal, he looked back almost to check they weren't following. It enabled him to see Heinrich and his gun-toting helper literally frozen in 2008, their being in a state of frozen animation telling Callison he was moving at the speed of light. *If I were travelling at light speed, it would mean time was frozen*, Callison thought. *I've done it. I'm travelling through time! I'm going to be a hero when I get back!* He was right; but for very different reasons to those he envisaged.

He took his vision away from 2008 and looked forward again. He was travelling through a circular tunnel that had a certain transparency to it, a tunnel through a serene otherworldly light blue dimension. The light blue was everywhere he looked. Above the tunnel: light blue. Below the tunnel: light blue. To the left and right: light blue. The passing tunnel walls reminded Callison of an effect that crystal or water might have when reflecting light. The tunnel meandered left, and right and up and down with no apparently obvious direction.

It felt like a pulling rather than a pushing force that drove him through the tunnel and there was a sense of movement, but only in so much as the internals of the tunnel seemed to be moving past him. There was no wind in his face. There seemed to be no proper noise either, just a quiet static sound that was emanating from everywhere and nowhere.

After some time, or what felt like time in his timeless surroundings he realised he was joining into other tunnels. The tunnels were getting bigger, and seemed to be organic in nature. He felt like he was travelling inside a twig of a tree, working his way towards its trunk, or like travelling a network of small streams to reach the larger rivers. He was in awe of all the extra sights he took in. He thought about this pipe of time being hidden from normal life on Earth. He had no idea of where he was, and no idea of where his basement was in relation to where he was now.

It was as though he was travelling through something that was alive. He'd seen microscopic pictures of nerve cells in his time, and that's what he was reminded of. It also dawned on him that nerve networks, capillaries and arteries behaved exactly like trees and rivers flowing back to the heart or the sea. He felt a strange sense of connection to nature, as if he *was* the tree or the river network, or the artery he travelled.

Strange all-knowing thoughts came into his mind, as if he was becoming more linked to the world in which he travelled than he had ever thought possible. Memories from Callison's childhood were instantaneously and simultaneously remembered. Something was happening to him, like he was bleeding out of a now-point in time and into the rest of time as a totality. He was experiencing his whole life all at once.

Up until a point, the space outside the tunnel had been the light sky-blue colour. Slowly, a dark green area started to emerge as a point in the distance. It was a dark green that had a gold undertone to it and looked much like a small cloud or a nebula in the universe. The dark green and gold cloud grew as Callison approached in the tunnel and it seemingly moved up, down, left and right as the tunnel meandered through its different orientations. The cloud was becoming larger and closer all the time and Callison anticipated this as his destination.

As the area became closer still, Callison's speed seemed to increase. Much like a planet or galaxy has gravity to pull everything together, this region also seemed to be pulling him in faster, and faster, and faster still. The tunnel meandered up, down, left, right very quickly and it became engulfed in the dark green patch, but kept going. There was no light blue left anymore. The speed at which he was travelling seemed to blur everything, even the light.

Suddenly, there was a large flash of light, and then pure silence. Callison touched down in an unfamiliar land and his tunnel experience had ended without him knowing how.

7.2 –

Was this even planet earth? Callison asked himself. It felt too quiet. He stood up; he was naked and stood on a grass bank near a stream. *Clothes cannot transcend time,* he guessed. He realised a different feeling also, like his body was younger. He *was* younger! He inspected his body some more. He looked to be in about his mid forties again. He touched his face and he was bearded. He could tell by directing his eyes straight down that the beard was a dark brown colour, not the silver grey he was used to.

He turned around to see the portal from the future side. All that could be seen was the portal's face and there was no evidence of the Trebla Eye at all. The portal showed a shimmering view of his basement, and also showed Heinrich and his lone agent standing there, frozen in time. He thought about the ride he'd just had; wonderment, excitement, all wrapped up in large doses of adrenaline, he had loved it. He loosened up as he adjusted to his younger body, and his new surroundings. *All I have to do is jump back through and I'll be me again. It's ok; just relax.*

His invention now existed in two dimensions of time, one end of it being in 2008 and the other end being in what he assumed to be a future. *This is the greatest breakthrough of all time!* he thought to himself laughing out loud. He could still remember everything that had transpired in the basement. It didn't make any sense, but here he was. *If only Heinrich Muller could see me now,* he thought.

He wanted to go back, but he was hesitant about facing Quanta again. He turned and observed the future. If he could bring some sort of proof of where he had been, he would be in good bargaining stead with Quanta as to the imminent termination of his life.

His new surroundings were beautiful and he found himself on a grassy bank, upon which the grass was the greenest he'd ever seen. It even appeared to shimmer as the bright sunlight shone down upon it. Behind the portal were weeping willows with branches that draped down to provide the portal with shade from the sunshine. The grass bank he stood on was shallowly inclined down a small verge to a one-metre wide stream about fifteen yards in front of him. The sky was a deep crisp blue, and a selection of well-defined white fluffy clouds silently rolled by overhead. The silence was profound. No cars, no building noises, no voices, no shouting; just silence.

All of a sudden, out of the corner of his eye, a craft zipped across the sky. It didn't really make that much noise, just whistled in the wind. As soon as it came, it went. *I guess they didn't see me at that speed,* he thought; he couldn't help but question, *What year could it be?* He had wanted to see the future ever since he was a young boy, but in much the same way as an ancient could never guess what the twenty-first century would be like; so Callison could never imagine what this would be like.

The silence echoed throughout the lands again, until a bird flying above him broke it with a deep throaty squawk. In all the years of sitting outside in the morning, drinking tea and smoking, a bird had never made a sound like the one he had just heard. He looked up to see the bird. It was a multi-coloured bird encompassing blues, reds and greens, with a wingspan of a few metres. *A large parrot?* Callison wondered. *Had he arrived in an English future, or an exotic one?* The bird continued to circle overhead, but seemed not to be interested in the new visitor to its green pastures.

He walked down to the stream's edge and the water in the stream was the clearest he'd ever seen. It looked like fluid crystal. The water running over the rocks shimmered in the sunlight. He tried to make out his reflection in the water and he peered into one of the sheltered still water pools near the bank. It looked like he had undergone an age regression. He was still Callison all right, but seemingly forty years old now.

He put his hand in and cupped some water to drink. It tasted perfect. As he drank, the sound of the running stream prompted an early memory from Callison's childhood. He and his father used to go fishing in a small river near a weir. The memory emoted feelings of wonderment of a large unknown world just waiting to be explored: he may as well *be* a child in this new world he found himself in. He took another cupped hand of the stream water and drank. It tasted so good.

Callison's feelings of wonderment flashed across his consciousness, before they vanished. A grave sense of being in over his head took over. Something he was unconsciously aware of told him to turn around. That's when the fear started to kick in.

There was no portal anymore. He quietly started to panic. He walked back up the grass bank to see if the portal had just moved, or if he had lost his bearings. But, his first fear seemed to be confirmed. *Maybe Heinrich powered it down. The bastard! He has the Eye!*

The gravity of the situation kicked into a higher gear. *The portal's gone! What am I going to do?* he fretted. He looked around for something to alleviate his fears, but it was in vain. No one was here but him. The panic turned into tears of anguish. He felt like a small child well outside its comfort zone in distress. He slumped his younger naked self down with his knees forming rests for his crossed arms and rested his head down upon them. The weeping willows provided the weeping man with some shade and a breeze gently blew. He continued to cry. His beloved wife Eleanor would surely be wondering where he was. *Would he ever see her again?* he thought. Feelings of guilt and loss filled his mind. He decided to pray; to whom he wasn't sure, but it felt like it was all he could do. While sitting, teary-eyed under the tree he thought quietly for lack of a better term, to God.

Dear… God? Who ever you may be, please comfort Eleanor. I have been so stupid. I was so wrapped up in time travel, I didn't think about the consequences and now I fear I have lost her for good. She has been my rock through all of the bad times, and now I've left her. I'm sorry Eleanor. Please forgive me. If I could undo it all I would. I love you. Please do what ever you do God.

Callison reflected, *Would a God who he had not been in contact with for all his life be interested in helping this old fool sitting on a grass bank in the year 'whatever it is'?*

He added to his appeals, *I've always respected what you do, but never really believed any of your literature, I'm sorry. It's hard living in the twenty-first century; there are so many other attractions in your creation that pull oneself away from religion. You didn't seem to help me when you took Jack from me, and I hated you for it, I'm sorry. But Eleanor is all I have. I've been a fool. Please help me get back. I'm scared, and I want to love my wife.*

He waited for a long while, looking up into the clear sky. A light breeze rustled the branches of the tree overhead. *Is that an answer?* He wondered. *No it's just the wind man, get a grip.* His feelings of fear hadn't really changed and he was still sad about being far away from Eleanor.

His view downstream was of greenery and trees. Somewhere in the distance the sound of a waterfall echoed. His view upstream was somewhat less expansive, but there was a mountain on the horizon, obscured partially by more greenery and undergrowth. In all honesty he had no idea at all on which direction to travel.

Just as Callison was building up the courage to move away from his arrival place, the large multi-coloured bird he'd seen on arrival swooped down very low, just above his head. So close that the passing bird created a downdraught, the power and force of which startled him. It was a large bird; even larger up close. The bird pulled up and soared high before circling back around and came to land on a branch about 5 metres away from Callison in the tree above. As the large bird came to rest, it's wings flapped furiously to keep it from falling out of the sky before it's landing. When perched on the branch it stretched its wings as if to get comfortable and stared down at him sitting on the grass. The bird's beak was a shiny black, and had a streak of yellow running down its bridge. Its eyes were very human like, and both stared towards the distressed man sitting under the tree.

As Callison stared back he could feel his pulse start to increase. *Could it eat me?* Then, all of a sudden, a strange feeling entered his awareness. It was a feeling of warmth and security. A peaceful thought entered his mind. *It's not going to eat me.* It was a profound thought. *Where did it come from?* Callison sheepishly smiled at the bird and the bird continued to stare at Callison seemingly smiling back. *I can't be communicating with a bird?* Callison thought, he dismissed it as impossible. Another thought entered his field of awareness, one that was a lot more directed and concrete. The bird was looking at him squarely in the face, eye to eye and made no sound, but it was concentrating on Callison.

(Telepathically) They call me Nuridaga... You have something to find here... Intuition will be your guide now... Forget everything you think you know... You are your own guide...

Callison thought to himself. *It's talking? I must be dreaming. This can't be the future.*

(Telepathically) Wherever you think you are, you will be... You are here for a reason, but to tell you would be like cheating... Remember Callison; intuition will always lead you to what you are looking for...

I'm not looking for anything, Callison thought.

The giant bird ruffled its large feathers and jumped off the branch, its wings stretched out as it caught the air. Flapping hard, it created a downward gust that blew over the naked man before riding the air and taking flight again. Callison watched the bird fly off into the sky.

Wondering whether or not he had imagined the whole 'conversation' with the large bird, Callison was now was back to square one and his heart started to beat faster and faster with anguish. He was still stuck in the future and he was still naked and he was still unsure of where to go next. *Use your intuition* the bird had said.

The stream would be his companion either way he went, that was his intuition speaking to him. *Well, left or right? Down-stream or up-stream?* His intuition wasn't being so helpful now. Callison was confused and his mind raced ahead of him, questioning his experience. *Did the bird talk to me at all? Am I dreaming? Am I going mad?*

Callison stood up, realising his knees didn't creak anymore; his situation wasn't *all* bad. He walked back to the stream and took another cupped hand of water to drink. He decided he would walk down-stream and follow the feint sound of the waterfall. *There's more chance of a village being down stream than up anyway*, he reasoned. He looked back to check it was not his eyes playing tricks, but the portal was definitely gone, and he was definitely alone. He sighed and hoped everything would be ok. He was still very conscious of being naked and that troubled him. Sheepishly he covered his genitals and started to walk down stream in hope of finding some security and assistance.

7.3 –

There was a lightly worn away track on the bank of the stream, which followed the water's ebb and flow through the countryside. The path suggested that life certainly existed, and had walked regularly next to the river before him. Whether it was intelligent and kind human beings or huge gnarling beasts was at this time still unclear. He remembered the craft he had seen early on arrival and reasoned that if these types of craft existed, the civilisation that built them must be advanced, which might mean they were a peace-loving people. *If the big parrot is anything to go by maybe the other animals are nice*? He thought as he walked naked along the pathway, fearful of the unknown.

Thoughts of loneliness and vulnerability pervaded his mind. He wanted a cigarette again like it would cure some of his loneliness, but he couldn't have one and he was nervous. Every tiny noise in the long grass or the trees near the pathway made him jumpy and he flicked his head around anytime he heard noises. It was a shame because he didn't get to appreciate the stunning detail of the wilderness he found himself in. The plants and wildlife he walked past, unnoticed to him, came in all sorts of shapes, sizes and colours, but the gems of nature were all hidden from Callison's own perspective. While concentrating on his imminent survival, he simply didn't notice them.

The sound of the waterfall had been building in volume for some time, when finally he reached it. The stream had combined with others on its way down the mountain and by now had opened up into a small river of about ten yards across and flowed faster than the stream it had started as. The walk had taken him down some tricky descents and over some steep rocks, but now the terrain had almost levelled. His new body was coping with the ordeal well. He approached the waterfall's edge just before he came across the most wonderful view he'd ever seen.

A high cliff dropped away off the side of the land he stood on, revealing a view of treetops and meadows that stretched all the way up to the horizon. The lay of the terrain formed a slight rolling valley, which sat in the middle of two slight hills. In the valley a grey-bricked Aztec-looking pyramid stood, with another bright white modern looking building just next to it. *Old and new together?* It confused Callison. However, finally human contact looked hopeful; he just hoped they would turn out to be friendly.

He leaned forward to see how high the cliff was. He was nervous and held on to a tree as he ventured a look over the edge. It was a long way down; the falling water to his right was turned white while being pummelled into the rock ledges. At the bottom lay a blue lagoon into which the waterfall deposited. A white sandy beach bordered the lagoon's peripheral edge and led back into dense trees and undergrowth again. The water in the lagoon was light blue near the sandy beach, but became a darker blue in the centre as the depth increased. It looked idyllic from where he was viewing from high above. He wanted to go down and see the lagoon, but there was no apparent route down the cliff. He sat down on some grass on the bank of the river just before its subsequent plummet. His knees didn't creak as he lowered himself onto the grass. *I could get used to this again,* he thought. The noise of the waterfall was full of energy, and there was a misty water-spray in the air being buffeted around by the wind.

He'd been sitting down for not but a minute, when a water rat swam up to the edge of the river and climbed out of the water. The rat navigated through some reeds that cut the water off from the grass bank. At first Callison was alarmed, but as the rat sat on the bank looking at him, it too had some investigating to do of its own. They were about 5 yards apart and the pair eyeballed each other for about thirty seconds, until a thought popped into Callison's head.

(Telepathically) Why so glum?

Callison was startled. He thought, *Did the rat say that?*

(Telepathically) Of course I said it! Who else do you see here?

Callison was even more startled, but spoke back out of habit, 'I'm stuck here, and I don't know where to go.' A few moments passed before another thought occurred to Callison.

(Telepathically) Well, let me help you. I'm the number one source of information you need right here. If I can't help you I don't know who can. I know everything, I do.

Callison was suspicious about the communicative rat to start with, but it seemed harmless enough. Besides he wasn't in a position to neglect advice from anywhere, 'Ok, then how do I get over to see the people of that civilisation over there?' He pointed to the white buildings in the distant valley. 'Who are they, are they friendly?' He hoped the rat understood. Again some time elapsed. The rat moved its head slightly, keeping its gaze firmly on the mysterious dark haired man on the bank, assessing. Soon, the thought entered Callison's field. The rat was silent as the thought was transmitted.

(Telepathically) You mean the Sukarmians? They won't hurt you.

Callison felt relieved. *How did this rat know everything? Surely that was impossible.* The rat heard him thinking.

(Telepathically) My word, you should learn some privacy, I can see everything.

Callison wondered what he meant and moved to cover his genitals more than he was already.

(Telepathically) Not that sort of privacy, I mean the privacy of your mind. Who is Eleanor?

Callison all of a sudden realised the rat could see his internal world of thought. A wave of panic swept over him, as he thought about everything the rat could be accessing. Of course he was now *more* exposed.

(Telepathically) Whoa, thought explosion!! So that's who Eleanor is. Thank you. There was a pause in the rat's transmitted thoughts, before another one was received. The rat had scanned Callison's insecurities, and had the perfect solution. It even smiled; I can help you, you know, if you give me something in exchange.

Callison was intrigued, *what help could a rat possibly give a human?*

The rat was about to show him. It slowly stood up and moved slightly to the left and underneath where the rat's stomach had been on the grass, there now laid a bright red ruby, glinting in the sun. It was about the size of Callison's fist; a special gem that would have been worth a lifetimes' wages from when he came from. Callison was fascinated, and transfixed on what looked like the finest ruby he'd ever seen. The rat had 'laid' a gem. *What kind of rat was this?*

(Telepathically) Kimeng is the name. Glad you like my offering. It's yours for a special thought.

Callison looked at the rat with intrigue. *What kind of thought could he want?* His intrigue waned as his attention was drawn back to the hypnotising red stone in the grass. The rat heard his thinking.

(Telepathically) I want you to picture me being the best rat in the whole world. And whenever you need something you think of me first.

Callison spoke words in return, 'I have to think this consciously? Just imagine you as the best rat in the world, and you'll give me the gem?' he questioned.

(Telepathically) This gem will be yours if you do, and you can use it to bargain with the Sukarmians. You will need this with the Sukarmian people if you do meet them. They trade in gems. Trust me. You'll be safer.

The rat had taken advantage of the man's insecurities.

Callison was worried, and decided he needed the gem as a bargaining chip in Sukarmia. It also sounded like a good deal, a thought was free after all. 'Yes, Ok. I'll think the thought.'

The Kimeng rat prepared for payment with an eager smile, its whiskers twitched and it tilted its head as the thoughts of intention started to arrive from the strange man sitting on the bank.

Callison closed his eyes and thought hard about the rat in front of him being the best rat he'd ever met. The thought was heartfelt too; as if this *really was* the best rat he'd ever met. Callison pictured the rat answering any problems he was going have here. He really concentrated, as he knew his thoughts were being scrutinised. The rat 'listened' intently to what Callison was producing with his mind, and absorbed the thought 'energy'.

A few moments passed. Callison asked the rat if the thought was good enough, but there was no telepathic reply. He opened his eyes and the rat was completely still, absorbing the thought. As soon as the thought was broken by Callison's question, the rat came to again. It quickly ran away back through the reeds and into the river from whence it came. There was no parting thought from the rat. A confused Callison questioned what the hell all of this was about. He was still nervous about meeting the Sukarmians, but his questioning didn't last long as the 'product' distracted him again, glinting in the sun. *At least the gem is still here* he thought, and hoped.

Unbeknownst to Callison, the Kimeng rat didn't really much care for the strange man on the bank, or the gem, or the truth. A master of problem-reaction-solution bargaining, the rat just needed the thought, and this thought had been an easy one to extract due to the man's own insecurity.

Still somewhat confused, Callison eased himself to his feet and walked over to the gem to pick it up. The first thing he noticed was its weight, it was remarkably heavy. He held it up to the sunlight, which glinted through the precious stone as he moved it. *Of all the luck* Callison thought. The dilemma was that he didn't know how much the gem was worth in this unknown land, would it buy him a drink or a house? Back when he came from, this gem would have been his lucrative retirement dream. He contemplated Eleanor again, with regret, and sighed. He wanted to be back home in his time. As he stood next to the running water, gem in hand, his problem still persisted: he wanted to find a way down the cliff face to get to the blue lagoon below.

He wondered if he could let the water carry him over the edge and splash down into the lagoon. The risky thought quickly departed however, as the recollection of the water being pummelled down the cliff recurred. He walked back to the cliff edge and looked down upon the land below, the falling water to his right. The only way he could think of to get down was to follow the cliff top pathway left, away from the river and hope it would lead down the cliff side somehow. Briefly, another thought occurred to him; he could travel back up stream to try and find a place to cross the river and see what lay on the other side of the waterfall. *Too long-winded* he thought. Left it was.

The pathway followed the edge of the cliff and the beautiful view across the valley below was now on his right. The white building and pyramid in the distance intrigued Callison. *So that is Sukarmia*, he thought as he trekked along. He was nervous. Even though the rat had said they wouldn't harm him, what if the rat was lying? He thought about running away, but run to where? He was lost in time and vulnerable, but he still had the gem that he hoped the Sukarmians would like. The thought relieved Callison and he looked back at the buildings. The contrast of the modern looking bright white building and the ancient-looking grey pyramid Callison found strange. Maybe he was in the past?

His mind was cast back to the large bird that had told him his intuition would be his guide here. He wondered again what on earth the bird had meant.

To his left were trees and undergrowth. He was still wary of noises in the bushes, as if something could catch him off guard. Again, the fear of the unknown meant his awareness was taken away from the beauty surrounding him.

7.4 –

She took care with her footsteps to not make much noise. She had a view of the pathway from deep within the undergrowth and wondered if the dark haired man who walked the cliff-top path was who she thought he was. He carried a red Kimeng gem, and his aura was partially blocked giving his fearful red-coloured emotions away. She continued to stalk quietly, hoping he would be travelling to the lagoon as the Time Shaman had forecast. With her eyes focused on the strange man, she inadvertently trod on a small branch. It made a noise that echoed through the trees. She paused, and remained completely still, hoping she'd not been seen.

7.5 –

Callison was startled. *What was that!* he fearfully thought, as if someone or something was in the deep undergrowth to his left. He paused for a few moments, before speaking vaguely to the trees, 'Hello? Is any one there?'

No answer. Had he felt braver he would've walked into the undergrowth to explore further, but no one had answered. *It's probably just me,* he thought. *I must be going mad. Talking to animals. Hearing things.* He nervously laughed to himself and ignored the noise, carrying on.

The pathway meandered as the cliff top slowly fell in altitude compared with the tree-topped valley below. He'd been walking for about an hour down hill and by now the treetops he'd been looking at from the summit of the waterfall were almost at eye level. The pathway he followed continued, until some stone-carved steps were revealed to his right, leading the way down to the undergrowth floor. The staircase was intricately shaped into the rock face and so smooth it looked like a laser beam had worked it. The precisely cut stone steps were flanked down to the forest floor by a shiny metallic handrail, which had Callison thinking, *an advanced people must've built this.*

At the bottom of the steps another track lay before him. *Left or Right?* He asked himself. With the benefit of seeing the lay of the land from above earlier, Callison guessed that left would lead towards the buildings of Sukarmia, and right would take him back to the lagoon. He walked right, doubling back on his walk along the cliff top. The lagoon should be about an hours walk from here, based on his walk from the waterfall.

The track he followed eventually opened up into a clearing revealing the lagoon and the bottom of the waterfall; the cliff top now towering over his right side, and throwing most of the lagoon into shadow. His arms and legs ached slightly from the walk, and he put the gem down on the sandy floor to stretch. He looked up at the cliff and the sky above him was still a brilliant blue. The light blue water lapping the shore of the golden sand seemed not to take any notice of him, and carried on regardless. A mist lay over the lagoon near where the falling water hit the still water about fifty metres from the shoreline. There looked to be a stream on the opposite side carrying the water out of the lagoon and onwards on its journey. The light sand of the beach was wider than it looked from high above, wrapping around the lagoon like a sleeve and developing into a few sand swept grass banks that were backed by shadowy trees.

The air under the tree canopy was more humid and less breezy than on the cliff top and despite his younger body, he had built up a sweat during his walk. The water in the lagoon looked inviting and would cool him off from his sweat, so he started to look for a place to hide the gem while he swam. He picked it up and concealed the precious stone under a nearby shrub, before walking backwards and keeping his eyes on the bush that held his Sukarmian 'money'. Satisfied he would remember which bush it was under, he turned around to face the idyllic lagoon.

The loose sand under his feet became flatter as he neared the lapping water's edge. The water was clear and surprisingly warm. Eventually the lagoon water became deep enough and Callison dived beneath the water's surface. The deeper water cooled his face; he was definitely real. It was as if the essence of the sixty-five year old Callison was in the body of the forty-year old Callison again. He put the anomaly down to a bizarre effect of time travel but the true reason would turn out being far simpler than that.

He broke into a swim, thinking about the near future and how he might make his first introductions when the time came. The thoughts were more wishful bravado than useful insight; for all that really mattered was how one acted in the moment of the situation.

He'd been swimming for only a few moments, when the thought occurred to him to swim back to the shoreline as if the gem were somehow under threat. He changed direction and started swimming for the sandy beach again. It was while looking back at the shadowy trees that he saw it. He froze in the water; petrified. He watched on in horror as he locked eyes with a large prowling lion on the undergrowth's fringe behind the sandy banks.

The lion froze, staring back from the shadowy trees as if assessing whether to pounce.

Callison's heart started to beat out of his chest as he trod the lagoon water. *What should I do?* he panicked.

The lion seemed to be waiting, its large mane surrounding its curious expression of imminent intent and then it decided. The beast suddenly accelerated out of the shadow of the trees and across the beach like a rocket on a bearing headed straight for him.

Callison was an animal again; the hunted. He automatically and furiously lashed at the water trying to swim in the opposite direction, away from the lion and towards the waterfall again. He had never swum so fast in his life. Within only few moments he was nearing the spray from the gravity driven water, and hoping the lion couldn't swim quickly. He had to check. He dared a look over his shoulder. The lion had stopped its pursuit. Callison ceased swimming and began treading the now deeper water. He spotted the cat walking timidly away and off to the left of the beach. He still assessed instinctively, *Where is it going? Where should I go? How is it acting? How should I react?*

His flight mode abated slightly, as curiosity started to set in. He looked over to the shoreline and there was a woman standing on the beach near the waterline, pointing the lion away.

The lion eventually walked off and out of sight, but the woman remained; now watching him. He trod water, relieved but still too scared to speak.

* * * * * * *

8: Falling into Fear

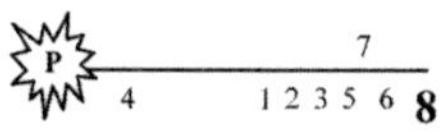

"Nothing in life is to be feared. It is only to be understood."
Marie Curie, Chemist and Physicist (1867 – 1934)

8.1 –
Hidden Timeline:
15th May 2008:

She rounded the corner of the steps and Eleanor's heartbeat echoed through her confused mind as she witnessed the basement scene in front of her. Callison wasn't anywhere to be seen, but instead a solitary man sat, slouched back in one of the lounge armchairs from upstairs. Unaware of Eleanor's presence, the man faced Callison's large circular invention. The device was whirring away, and a colourful, peaceful, almost hypnotic light radiated from the invention in the middle of the doughnut. It bathed the whole basement in the same multi-coloured light.

The uneasy feeling Eleanor had experienced at the bingo seemed to be trying to tell her something; it was as if it was connected to what was happening to her right now. She wondered where Callison was. *Had he jumped?* she thought. She too, was amazed at the sight of the portal in her basement. *Is this what he's invented? Has he done it?* she thought to herself. *Time travel?*

She wondered who the man was. He had thick dark hair. *Was he friend or foe?*

She was too nice for violence, 'Hello? Excuse me?'

The man bolted round, sitting up straight and taking a couple of seconds to re-adjust his focus, 'Ah, Eleanor, such a pleasure.' the man said warmly. He stood up, and his wide frame became silhouetted by the bright image behind him.

'Heinrich?' She got worried and the fear started to flood her senses. He had a sinister ambience to him, 'What are you doing here, where is Callison?'

'He is at Quanta at the moment,' he thought of an excuse, 'getting some data CDs.' He slowly started to walk towards Eleanor concealing a gun behind his back, 'If you wait here, he'll be back shortly, I'm sure.'

* * * * * * *

9: Flying like a Bird

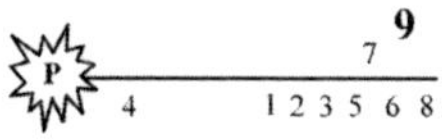

"Heavier-than-air flying machines are impossible."
William Thomson 1st Baron Kelvin,
Statesman and Scientist (1824 – 1907)

9.1 –
Date not known:

Callison's heart started to settle back into a normal rhythm after his life had been spared the vicious attack, but now he was intrigued. This woman had just saved his life.

On the beach the mysterious woman stood, observing the man in the lagoon. She was naked also and had dark wavy hair and a golden skin tone. The waterfall dropping into the lagoon from above generated a mist that hung in the air, partially impairing his view of the woman in detail.

She remained standing on the beach staring back at him as Callison trod water thirty yards from the sandy beach. He was transfixed on her, and she on him. All of a sudden a feeling of relief came over him. It had come from the woman on the beach, but he couldn't deduce why he knew it was coming from her. He expected her to be psychic, like the animals, but to his surprise she spoke English.

She called out, 'They call me Liele. Its ok to be afraid, but you really have no need to be. I am from a settlement called Sukarmia. What is your name?'

Her accent was strange. Not like one he'd heard before; the sentences and words sounded somewhat broken, but it was grammatically perfect. Callison felt warmth within him and called out his name in an overly dramatic style, 'My name is Callison Trebla and I'm lost. I come from the year two-thousand-and-eight.'

She replied, 'I'm sorry, I don't know where that is.'

'Did that lion walk off because of you?' asked Callison, wanting to know.

She sounded genuine as she called back, 'Yes.' She seemed friendly. 'Swim to me, I want to help you.'

Callison was habitually unsure of the offer, people from his time wouldn't offer something so quickly but the people of his time couldn't save you from a lion. He also felt anxiety about being naked and was timid about walking out of the lagoon.

Liele sensed his worry and without him knowing, she gave him a helping hand. She called out again, 'I really don't care what your body looks like. Look, I'm naked too.' She telepathically transmitted some of her confidence to Callison and remained on the beach.

Callison started to swim towards the woman and strangely trusted her. As he swam closer to the beach, the water level decreased so that he could walk on the sand under the water. As he continued to wade forward the water level continued to shallow, revealing more of his body and when the water level came to his navel he continued walking without breaking stride, or covering his body. All of his life he had been hesitant to show himself naked, but now he was less afraid, which was uncharacteristic for him. Little did he know it was Liele's telepathic transmittance of confidence that made him feel that way. His wading turned into walking as the water level fell down to his knees and then his ankles. He wondered whether the lion was definitely gone, and looked around for it as he approached the woman on the beach.

'The lion?' said the beautiful mind reader, 'It won't bother us.'

Callison acknowledged with relief, walking to stand a few metres away from her. She was beautiful. She looked to be about thirty and her whole body was covered in subtle golden paint and darker patterns that reminded Callison of Aztec tribes. She seemed very physically fit and now closer than before, her simply featured face could be seen clearly, framed by her dark brown wavy hair and hazel coloured eyes that showed off the beauty in her being. In the centre of her forehead was a tear-shaped silvery blue emerald, held in a metallic looking mount that tapered down to the bridge of her nose. Beneath her eyes were some elegantly painted blue patterns, applied very accurately to fall away at her cheekbones and morph into other, more complex shapes on the sides of her cheeks. The patterns were of a similar nature to the Aztec-style designs all over her body. She smiled carelessly at him, before speaking, 'Hello. It is nice to meet you Callison.'

'Hello Liele,' said Callison, timidly, 'what year is it here?' The answer would confuse him.

She obliged, as if not conscious that Callison might be confused by her answer, 'There is no year here.' she said blankly.

Callison felt downhearted, which Liele *was* conscious of. She added, 'Deep within yourself, you know already. You wouldn't be here otherwise.'

Callison asked; one day he would need the knowledge, 'How did you call the lion off? I was scared. I thought I was going to die.' he worriedly exclaimed.

Liele explained, 'Lions go for fear. It might seem like the lion chose to run, but you willed it to run, just by your state of fear. All *I* did it was will it on its way.'

Callison thought fear a natural reaction. *When was he?* he curiously thought. 'Well, thank you anyway, you saved my life.'

She smiled, 'You're welcome,' and lead the exchange, 'Here, hold my hands.' said Liele. She put her hands in front of her, offering them to Callison.

While standing face to face on the strange beach he was initially hesitant, however he walked up to her and trustingly put his hands out in front of him. Liele held them and discharged some of her internal energy to her visitor. The process was unknown to Callison but it filled him with excitement and he felt a warm glow travel through his body right down to his fingers and toes. An amazing thought occurred to him, triggered by Liele and the telepathic energy transfer. It wasn't so much just a thought, as a feeling of euphoria at the same time.

(Telepathically) Believe in your experience, run with your experience! Anything you want you already are and anything you need you already have! You are your own master, or your own worst enemy. Explore yourself with intuition to know yourself!

Heat and some small sparks of light were generated between their hands, as the energy transferred into Callison's body. After it was complete, Liele took her hands away, and was slightly out of breath. It had drained her somewhat, but Callison was invigorated and grateful. The lion was a distant memory, 'I feel amazing! How did you do that?' he asked.

'Humans radiate those energetic frequencies all the time. If you were more soul conscious you would be able to receive them mentally yourself, but you required a physical technique that I have perfected.' She led him to a grassy bank on the edge of the sand and the pair sat down looking out at the beautiful lagoon and waterfall.

Normally sitting down would have put stress on his old legs, but his legs were twenty-five years younger and didn't creak. Callison somehow knew he was under her umbrella of fearlessness and felt safer. He asked, 'What does soul conscious mean?'

'It's exactly like it says. We acknowledge ourselves as souls. You are more body orientated.'

Callison didn't know what to make of the soul. He was a sceptic, and a scientist that had been trained for nearly forty years not to believe in hocus-pocus and spirit. The fearless woman knew he was confused.

Liele angled her head towards Callison with curiosity, and eased his confusion, 'Do not worry about soul consciousness yet. I have been told to help you. Tell me, why are you here?' She showed genuine interest.

Callison sighed, and rested his head on his knees. He didn't look at Liele as he started to recall his journey here, 'I worked for a big research corporation…' he realised what she actually said, and looked back at her, 'Wait… you said you have been *told* to help me?' Not even *he* had warning, 'How did you know I'd be here?'

Liele knew what was happening, 'There are certain things that I know, but you have forgotten.'

'Like what?' he asked with curiosity.

Liele smiled, 'That is for you to find out, and not for me to tell you. You are here for your own reason as I am mine.'

'Oh.' said Callison, confused. He didn't understand what she meant, or why she couldn't tell him.

Liele hoped that one day he would understand, but for now encouraged him to tell his story, 'Don't worry about it, I am here to help you find your own reason for being here.' She prompted, 'You were saying about a corporation?'

Callison trusted Liele, although he didn't know why and let the cryptic subject go. He sighed and rested his head on his arms again and continued with his explanation, 'Yes, I was working for a large research corporation and I designed a time portal.' He sighed again, 'Anyway, the corporation wanted the invention to boost their profitability and I wanted to change the world with it, so they threatened to kill me if I didn't hand it over to them. Just as they were about to take it from me, I jumped through it not wanting them to have it. I wanted to be the first one to time travel. I didn't know where I'd end up, or what would happen to me, it didn't even cross my mind, all I knew was that I didn't want them to have it. When I arrived here, I thought the portal would get me back home and I would be a hero, but when I looked for the portal, it had vanished and I was stuck here.' He started to cry as he thought about the prospect of Eleanor living alone, an eternity away from him.

Her unique accent was calming to Callison, 'Every thing you do, it has a reason you know.' Liele was sure of it, 'I can sense things in you that are very negative, which is why you feel pain, but beneath the negativity, I see a wonderful heart.' She sensed his regretful thoughts about Eleanor, and radiated inner strength, 'Who is Eleanor?' she inquired.

Callison's tears subsided. His mind was racing so much he didn't even ask her how she knew, 'Eleanor is my wife, we have been together for 35 years. I love her more than she knows. She is now alone in my old surroundings, and I feel worry and regret for her being without me. It's my fault. I'm a stubborn old fool!'

Liele put her arm around Callison to comfort him.

The light blue water lapped at the sandy beach seemingly unaware of Callison's anxiety. Callison looked up to see the top of the cliff from where the water barrelled over the edge.

Suddenly his thoughts perked up again. *The gem!* Eagerly, Callison spoke, 'I have some thing for you Liele.' he said excitedly as he stood up and started to walk, 'It's over here, come with me.'

9.2 –

Callison started to walk briskly to the bush he'd hidden the gem under before his swim and as he walked he explained to Liele what he'd been given, 'Now I don't know what it will be worth, but a telepathic rat gave me a gem that you might like. He said it would act as payment for things here.' He had high hopes in his mind.

Liele walked with him. She spoke as they walked up the beach, 'Was it from a Kimeng Rat?'

Callison stopped walking and faced the gold skinned woman, 'Yes, he did say his name was Kimeng. How did you know?' He was intrigued.

'Show me your gift, and I will tell you what I know.' said his host solemnly.

Callison walked the beach another twenty paces until he came to the bush he had hidden the gem under; Liele was a couple of steps behind.

Callison bent down and foraged in the sand under the bush, 'That's weird,' Callison mused, 'I swear I left it under this bush. All that is here now is this rock?' He stood up and held the rock to show Liele, which loosely resembled the shape of the gem.

'This is what I suspected,' said Liele, 'the Kimeng rat has somewhat of a reputation for offering less than expected.'

Callison was disgruntled, 'The little bastard! Why would he do that?'

Liele answered with wisdom, 'Just learn your lesson and don't look back with anger. If you see another rat, remember what they offer you has more to do with what they want from you, than what you need from them.'

'You mean there's more than one of them?' he said with surprise.

'Yes they are like a, how do you say, like a species? Tell me, what did you have to do to get the gem?'

Callison sat down again on one of the grassy clumps near to the bush and Liele sat next to him listening. He recalled to Liele about consciously making a thought that the rat was the best rat in the world. He felt embarrassed, especially now he realised how stupid the thought was, and how he'd been duped. 'I thought the whole episode was strange,' Callison said, 'but I didn't know he was lying, because I didn't know the truth.' Liele sensed his fear start to increase again. 'What am I going to do now, Liele? I was kind of hoping that gem would give me a trading tool to survive here! I felt secure, and now I don't.' His emotional insecurities started to bubble over and a tear ran down his cheek and into his dark beard.

She broadcast an emotive thought, (Telepathically) My people will not hurt you, but *you* can hurt you. Don't worry, ever. There is nothing to fear apart from fear itself. Look for feelings of relief and let go.

The received feeling unconsciously soothed Callison's psyche as Liele explained graciously, 'The Kimeng rats want people to think good of them because they have no self worth of their own. They don't have the ability, like we do, to realise our own self worth, so they sell misleading gifts in exchange for directed thoughts of worth. The gifts are nice for a while, but they are only ever temporary. Your gem would have been no use to us anyway, you don't need bartering tools with my people, just the love in your heart will suffice.'

Callison was confused. For the majority of his life, money, status, and possessions were what drove him; *they are what drove the world*, he thought. They created happiness, or so he thought. He was confused and worried, 'So how does Sukarmia work without money, or bartering tools?'

'I just told you: love.'

'I'm sorry,' said Callison honestly, trying to convince Liele she was wrong, 'but where I'm from, love is not currency. Love won't buy you a nice house.'

She knew more about the inner workings of consciousness than the new visitor to her lands, 'No, but love will buy you the *right* house.'

Callison thought about the words Liele had used and how they resonated with the circumstances surrounding the purchase of his retirement cottage. 'How much do you know about me?' he questioned, wondering if this was an outrageous set up.

She didn't really know anything about him; from her perspective she just knew that love could lead someone to the right house. 'I can tell you have been holding onto a fear for along time.'

Callison wondered, 'How do you know that?'

'From seeing your thoughts.' she answered.

Callison was taken back, 'You can *see* my thoughts?'

Liele answered, 'Yes. Telepathy. It is a learned ability.'

Being a scientist, he wanted to understand, 'So, what do you actually *see* when you look at thoughts?'

Liele didn't know the best way to pictorially describe them, 'It is hard to explain with words Callison, they are kind of like vibrating multi-coloured clouds of light, that are emitted and received through here.' She pointed to the tear shaped blue emerald on her forehead, 'We see them through our third eye if you will. I can feel your lens is unfocused, rendering thoughts invisible to your mind. You just unknowingly experience them as your own.'

'So what do you see when you look at *my* thoughts?'

She maintained calm and used tact, 'I see a lot of anger, and frustration. They are dark red, stormy thought clouds and the light is blocked. They vibrate slowly, as if you are pessimistic, and not sure of who you are, or what you want.' Liele saw the stormy thoughts turn worse, as Callison was again frustrated that he felt how he did. He knew that what she was saying was correct.

'It's not fair. I want to feel love, and happiness, but I get these sensations in my stomach, that just feed the fire. Life where I come from is full of double standards and bullshit. Life should be fair!' he protested.

Liele was restrained and waited for the answer of wisdom to come to her. It came, 'I'm not sure what your life is like, but it sounds like your lands are very testing. You let the outside world affect your inside world too easily. If you can focus your third eye, you will see that the outside world is in fact a reflection of your inside world. When you know this, you will understand on a whole new level.'

Callison subconsciously relaxed but was in over his head regarding his understanding. He changed the subject, 'So do your people communicate with this language we speak now, or do you swap thoughts telepathically?'

'We have a language as well, but half the language is spoken, and half of it is mental. If you spoke to people in my city using English, they would probably understand the feeling behind the words, but not the words themselves. People can learn English, but it is an unspoken language as there are too many spoken languages in the Akashic to learn them all!'

'Akashic?' enquired Callison.

'The Akashic records.' she said. 'They are records of all time, and all experience, but they...' she seemed vague, 'are distant from us. They have to be accessed very precisely. It is easy to extract misinformation.'

'And you access them, these Akashic records?' His tone sounded interested.

'Well, with the help of the Noi Tu masters, yes.'

The questions came like a machine gun, 'The Noi Tu masters?'

'They hold the way, and they teach the way, but again do not worry yourself about it yet.' She corrected herself, 'Do not worry about it *ever*.'

He was apologetic, 'I'm sorry for asking too many questions you see, it is information overload for me. I have always been a curious person, hence my being a scientist.'

She propped his pessimism, 'Don't be sorry for being curious. Curiosity has a reason for existing. Just as much as you do.'

He put the thought to the back of his mind, 'Ok, could I ask another question?' he smiled, 'out of curiosity of course.'

'Of course.' she replied welcomingly.

'Well, when I jumped through the time portal I had clothes on. I guess clothes don't transcend time, so I now find myself naked, which I don't really like, but…' he paused and thought how he might phrase it. '…why do you not have clothes on? Do the people of Sukarmia not wear them for a specific reason or something?'

She could sense he was uneasy, but she laughed aloud, 'You are funny! Of course we wear clothes. Sometimes it gets cold!'

He smiled, not really understanding fully.

Liele enlightened him, 'I suppose you aren't to be blamed for wondering.' she said, retaining her warm smile, 'I am doing what my people call "intuitive integration". We walk into the undergrowth surrounding Sukarmia in order to integrate our soul with the soul of the planet. We paint our bodies with signs and symbols of peace and synergy, and meditate with the planet and its treasures. This keeps Sukarmia, and ultimately myself in a state of balance.

Callison was uncertain of what intuitive integration involved, but thought it was a nice thing to do. He only really had one concern, 'So I can get some clothes in Sukarmia?'

Liele smiled, 'Yes, I'll get you some clothes when we get back into the outskirts of Sukarmia. Trust me, you'll be fine.'

Callison did trust her and was relieved. As the pair sat and enjoyed each other's company, a bird suddenly swooped down from the trees on the right and caught a fish out of the lagoon. It took them by surprise, but it was memorable to watch. The bird flew up to the left into the trees to eat the catch.

Callison spoke again. 'I can see the point of calling it integration, as in, integration with nature and stuff, but why the 'intuitive' part?'

Liele took her eyes away from the bird in the tree to face Callison again, 'Well, when we each do intuitive integration, we each have things we want to learn, or find out, or test. They are only ideas before we set out on the intuitive integration. The ideas or thoughts or tests have to be realised via intuition. Sometimes we are successful; sometimes we are not, but we grow from either outcome.'

Callison asked the obvious, 'So what was your intuition exercise?'

'I...' she hesitated, 'I... cannot say, I'm sorry, I hope you understand, it is very personal... for my soul only.'

Callison accepted it, 'No need to apologise. Well are you being successful with your goal?'

Liele replied, 'It's impossible to fail an intuitive integration.'

Callison nodded but didn't understand fully, 'Well, Liele, I hope you are successful, in whatever form your success would take.'

'Thank you Callison.' she waited before adding, 'Do you want to take a walk? I have something to try out.'

9.3 –

The staircase they climbed started on the far side of the lagoon at the base of the cliff, near where a stream channelled the lagoon water away and onwards on its gravitational journey. The steps were identical in form to the ones he had used on his journey here; carved very smooth and Liele told him they were indeed carved using laser cutting tools.

As the pair ascended, Callison told Liele more about his time, and how he managed to get here. She was impressed about his technical knowledge of matter, and of his scientific descriptions of atoms and subatomic particles. He also told Liele about Jack and his fateful death and more about his wife; Liele telepathically sensed his fondness for both of them.

When they reached the cliff top Callison realised where he was, 'I've been here before!' he was generalising, 'Well albeit on the other side of the river.' He pointed across the waterfall to the grass bank on the other side of the torrent, 'That's where the Kimeng rat gave me the gem!' He corrected himself with regret, ' I forgot. I mean the rock.' The thought passed as Liele told him where he was.

'Welcome to the Greendale Valley, isn't it a wonderful sight?' They both looked over the rolling valley of treetops disappearing to the horizon; the pyramid and white building being impossible to miss, taking centre stage.

'It's a great view, that's for sure. Is that Sukarmia then?' He pointed to the man made structures.

Liele informed him, 'No, that's not Sukarmia. Sukarmia is hiding just over the horizon, and to the right.' She pointed at the horizon in the direction she meant, before coming back to the visible buildings. 'That is the Noi Tu outpost. It is built away from the city for the tranquillity and silent location, because self exploration and meditation are best undertaken when there is quiet.'

'Meditation? What is the point in that?' He acknowledged his bluntness, 'Sorry, I didn't mean to be rude.'

Liele didn't mind, 'It's ok; your land must be very wild and chaotic. Meditation allows us to know anything we want, and keeps us free because we are free spirits. Without meditation we become slaves to our experiences of the outside world.'

Although Callison didn't really understand, he couldn't argue with such a graceful explanation, 'You make meditation sound good. I just thought....' he didn't finish the sentence. He didn't need to; Liele knew his minds processing mechanisms.

'You thought meditation was for the weak?' she laughed, 'Oh Callison, you have so much to learn!'

Callison, for all his degrees and doctorates, felt stupid and inferior and didn't like the fact that his thoughts were in open view of Liele.

She sensed his feelings of inferiority, and decided he was ready. The cliff top was high, and they were close to the cliff's edge. Liele looked at Callison, and said something cryptic that Callison didn't fully understand, 'I hope you are who I think you are.' She smiled, 'It's time for you to start your learning.' Liele fell backwards off the top of the cliff.

Callison was instantaneously filled with grief; and would go on to forget her parting words until the time was right to remember them. 'Liele!!' he cried out. Not wanting to stand too close to the edge himself, he slowly crawled forward to look over intrepidly and expecting the worst, he realised the unimaginable.

Liele had been falling but pulled out of the fall in much the same way as a plane pulled out of a dive. She sailed away from the cliff face to end up in horizontal flight out over the lagoon and forest, before starting to climb again. She was flying!

Callison forgot to stand up, so transfixed was he on what he was seeing. Liele climbed high into the sky, until she was a small dot, Callison's eyes pinpointed on her for the whole flight. She disappeared into a cloud, and re-emerged the other side. *She must be doing quite a speed up there!* he thought, as she spiralled, and barrel-rolled through the sky. She passed in front of the sun, and he was blinded momentarily. He shut his eyes, losing her before finding her again. She passed directly overhead. Conscious of the sheer drop, he got up off his knees and edged backward away from the plummet. He turned around to keep watching Liele and he was spellbound as he wondered if she was ever going to come down again.

She stayed in the sky for about 10 minutes, free as a bird, arcing, and pirouetting through the air. She finally came into land on the grass at the top of the cliff, close by Callison as if she was a super hero. She angled her legs at the grass, took speed off and touched down while running, which turned into a jog, then a walk. Her hair was wind swept, and she was physically very drained. She slumped on the grass, completely worn out, which worried Callison, but as she pulled her head up to face him, she had on an ear-to-ear grin. She punched the sky and shrieked with success.

Callison had a thousand questions to ask, 'What the hell! I... I'm lost for words, that was amazing!' He went over to her and she kissed and hugged him like she'd known him all her life.

She spoke, while gasping for breath, 'The power of meditation Callison! For the weak? That was thrilling!!'

'How on earth did you do that!!' he exclaimed.

'A leap of...' She gasped for breath, '...a leap of faith is how I did that!' She stopped for more breath, 'You will be my witness when we get into Sukarmia!'

'Yes, I'll vouch for you!' he said enthusiastically.

'You won't need to. They will see your thoughts also.'

Callison's face dropped, 'Oh yes, I forgot.'

Liele was used to sending thoughts. She dropped her speech without realising, (Telepathically) Don't worry about it! My people are good people. You only fear what you don't know. Walking into fear is like acquiring new knowledge!

Callison replied, consciously unaware of the thought transmission, 'How do I try and keep my thoughts to myself? I feel nervous knowing people can see my thoughts.'

She spoke English again, 'Think about something beautiful if you want to hold on to your thoughts.' she said. A light sheen had appeared on Liele's forehead from sweat, 'My life guide says you are here for a reason, and we are going to help you find it.'

'How does your 'life guide' know about me?' said Callison.

'He...' she thought of the correct term. '...senses such things. He is very rarely wrong. He can also help you find your way back to your land of two-thousand-and-eight.'

Callison asked with intrigue, 'What's his name, your life guide?'

'His name is Mystera. You'll meet him at the Noi Tu outpost where we'll get some clothes as well. Are you ready?'

He took one last look at the Greendale Valley, which filled him with a very free sense of being, 'Yes,' he said, 'we're walking I take it?'

* * * * * * *

10: Power Corrupts

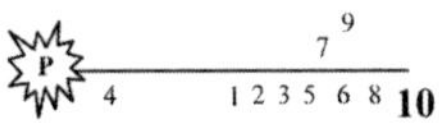

"When the power of love overcomes the love of power, the world will know peace."
Jimi Hendrix, Musician (1942 – 1970)

10.1 –
Hidden Timeline:
May 15th 2008:

Heinrich's hand-warm gun glistened behind his back as he continued to walk towards Eleanor with his back to the portal.

She thought on her feet, 'So does the portal work then? It looks very nice!' She knew that Callison had breached his Quanta contract, and was trying to buy time.

'Yes, it works beautifully. Quanta are very proud of Callison.' He paused.

'Yes, he's certainly a clever chap my Callie.' She was acting naïve.

He smiled sarcastically, 'Tell me, were you aware of the *laws* your Callie was breaking in doing this?'

She didn't know what to say. She didn't need to. There was a loud knock at the door, and someone's voice from above shouted, 'It's the police! Could you open up please!' The instinctive phone call she had made in the car on her way home from bingo had saved her bacon.

Without delay Eleanor shouted back up the stairs, 'Just coming!' *Your move*, she thought to herself.

Heinrich was startled and annoyed at Eleanor's insolence. He whipped out the silenced gun from behind his back, pointed it at her head and whispered aggressively, 'You're going to regret that.' He went to pull the trigger. Eleanor closed her eyes and winced, but all she heard was an empty click. Eleanor was saved. The gun had jammed and remained impotent. He tried again, but the gun jammed again. Heinrich became annoyed, but remained mute because of the police.

Eleanor was stunned and remained deadly quiet; in a one in a million chance, she had just cheated death, or so she thought; she would later find out that there was no such thing as chance.

Heinrich thought before speaking in an authoritative whispered tone, 'Ok, you are going to wait here quietly, and I am going to go and sort out those bastards.' He pointed up stairs with his gun, 'I'll deal with you when I return.' There was coldness to his tone, as if he wasn't human. *He never used to be like this.* she thought, *What had happened to him?*

He disappeared up the steps and locked the door at the top, leaving Eleanor alone with the portal. She could not place how she had the urge, but something told her to jump. It was an intuitive voice but it was enough, and four hours after Callison had made the leap, at 8:17pm on the 15th May 2008 Eleanor Trebla left the space-time continuum and became the second person to venture into the Eye. Callison had blazed the trail, and Eleanor had fatefully followed.

* * * * * * *

11: Noi Tu Love

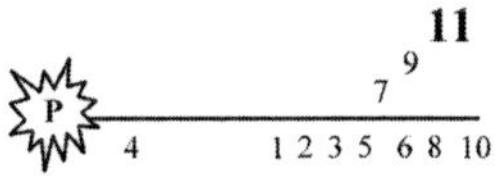

"For small creatures such as we, the vastness [of the universe] is only bearable through love."
Carl Sagan, Astronomer and
Exo-Biologist (1934 – 1996)

11.1 –
Date not known:

Callison followed his new friend, Liele, down a jungle track towards the Noi Tu outpost. Callison now saw the wood for the trees and he observed his surroundings seeing the different types of flowers and wildlife for what they were; beauty in its purest form. Liele had been talking to the animals and trees, and they had reciprocated their communication in kind. Butterflies, birds and even a fox had all joined the pair for a segment of their walk. They all seemed to be enjoying the world as if it were a playground. No fear existed at all in these lands and folk. It was a feeling he wasn't used to from his era.

As the pair had been walking, Callison thought back to Liele flying high up into the sky. *How in the hell had it been possible?* His scientific instincts came to the fore. He couldn't wait to find out what technology they were using and he hoped he could take the technology back to his people, if the Noi Tu Masters could *find* him a way back.

His mind was consumed with the realisation of walking and talking in a different time. The spacecraft he saw whizzing across the sky just after his arrival, Liele said, had probably been her people. He guessed to himself that he was probably in the future. He was a time traveller now, and he was starting to become at ease with his situation, no matter how bizarre.

After a while, the jungle track they had been following opened up into a clearing, revealing a large yellow-green meadow that rolled downhill in front of them. At the foot of the inclined field stood the pyramid and the white building he'd seen from the cliff.

Liele spoke, 'I give you the Noi Tu outpost!'

The stone cut pyramid was larger than it looked from afar, and was impressive. From his view he could see two sides of the massive object and each side had steps leading to the top. On the top of the pyramid was a small cube-shaped building that he guessed was a lookout. About one hundred yards to the left of the pyramid was the white building seen from the cliff-top. It too was more massive than expected and seemingly had some trees growing from its roof. From counting the windows it looked to have about ten floors and was both wider and longer than it was tall. The sun was setting and an orange glow sat on top of the buildings, which were partially silhouetted. The sky was pink over-head, highlighting rows and rows of high cloud that had formed like sand on the bottom of the sea. The rippled clouds disappeared all the way to the hazy yellow sky just above the horizon.

'Wow!' he said, admiring the scene. 'Those buildings look amazing!'

'Glad you like it.' she replied, starting to walk into the waist high yellow-green grass towards the buildings. 'Come on, follow me, we'll go and find Mystera.'

Callison followed Liele into the meadow intrigued by the foreign buildings. He talked as they waded through, 'Will I be able to learn how to consciously communicate with thought to others?'

'When your mind is open, yes.' she said as she led the way.

'I'm sorry I shouldn't worry I know.' He was nervous however, 'What sort of clothes do your people wear?'

'We'll get a tunic from the Preparatory House.' She pointed to the large white building to the left of the pyramid.

Callison continued to ask questions as the two made their way slowly toward the Noi Tu outpost. Liele answered dutifully every time.

11.2 –

On the top of the grey stone pyramid a solitary man was watching the landscape all around. He was dressed in a hooded hemp ankle length gown with light blue hems. He could see the meadow below and observed as two naked people ambled through the long grass towards the Noi Tu outpost. The wind on top of the pyramid was gusty, and his tunic flapped.

As the man stood, a being of light materialised from thin air to stand next to him, looking down over the lands. The being stood like a human but had no other features apart from the silhouette of white light. Telepathically, the beings communicated but not a sound was made.

The robed man broadcast to the being, Looks like Liele found him.

The light being telepathically transmitted its reply; it would appear that way, Mystera. But our work is far from complete yet.

Mystera was Liele's Noi Tu life coach. He had lived for nearly two hundred and fifty revolutions of the sun and his weathered face had a dark complexion with wrinkled skin and a long grey beard. His hood concealed his dark grey shoulder length hair and like Liele, Mystera had a tear shaped emerald encrusted in a gold cage on his forehead. The wind continued to blow.

I will go and greet them. Speak to you soon. Transmitted Mystera.

The being of light agreed, Have it be done. We will consult with the Time Blueprints and the Universal Mind and tell you what needs to be done to ensure Callison's route home.

Mystera hung up, cutting the telepathic line to the light being and continued watching as the pair walked across the meadow towards the Noi Tu outpost. As easily as the white silhouette had arrived, it departed, vanishing from view like it had never been there.

11.3 –

The yellowy grass in the meadow became shorter as they made it to the outskirts. The meadow ended, and the small dusty pathway that the couple travelled along led from the meadow's edge to the central Noi Tu outpost. They arrived into a circular sandstone courtyard situated between the tall pyramid and the white Preparatory House. The periphery of the circular courtyard comprised tiers of seats, and built into the seating and each separated by 90 degrees, were four columns that rose into the air. The four tall columns each had an archway underneath them providing four possible points of entry and exit to the courtyard.

'What's this place used for?' He was still asking questions.

She was still answering, 'This is the Noi Tu stage. We have debates and discussions here about the stability and direction of our collective experience.'

'Like government meetings, you mean.'

'No one governs in Sukarmia,' she said with a troubled look, like she knew he wouldn't understand, 'we just maintain a balance, but I know what you mean.' She empathetically smiled at her new friend.

In the centre of the circular courtyard was a small raised platform. 'Is this the stage?' Callison was stood next to it.

'This works in conjunction with the four columns you see around you to create images and holograms of visiting speakers. There is a meeting here next week.'

Nice, he thought, 'Holograms?' He was interested, 'Do you use electricity then?'

'Yes.' said Liele. 'Do you have electricity where you come from?'

Callison was beginning to think he might be able to talk with some experience on the subject, which made him more comfortable. He was at heart still a scientist, 'Yes, we harness electricity to power lots of things.'

'Looks like we think the same!' said Liele, upbeat.

He was yet to find out how they generated their electricity.

There were three other exits from the circular courtyard. The right exit led to the start of one of the pyramids four flights of steps. The left exit led to the white Preparatory House. The exit in front of them, he assumed, led to Sukarmia itself.

Liele received a telepathic message and pointed to the pyramid, 'Mystera is about half way down the east flight.'

Callison looked towards the pyramid. It was hard to see clearly, as the light was fading fast, but he could just make out a hooded robed man walking down the huge staircase. He was but a speck in comparison to the enormous structure.

'You'll like him Callison. He is the friendliest, wisest person I know.'

Callison nodded, still apprehensive.

Liele spoke remotely to Mystera as he walked down the flight, it would seem distance was no barrier for telepathic communication, He is exactly like you said he would be. He has a big heart, but he is stuck here, and can't find his way home.

Mystera replied with his own broadcast, I assume your intuitive integration has been successful. Well done my child. Get robed up and I'll meet you and our new arrival in the Prep House. Did you fly?

Liele smiled as she stood with Callison, Yes, I flew like the wind!

Well done! Mystera said enthusiastically.

'What are you thinking about?' Callison said, oblivious to the invisible waves of thought travelling in the air all around him.

Liele was smiling and told him, 'We'll go to the Prep House, and Mystera will meet us there.'

The pathway out of the Noi Tu stage arena was dusty, and it looked like it hadn't seen rain in years. Callison followed

Liele to the entrance of the Preparatory House and the first thing he realised was the lack of security. There was no door; the entrance was a round portion cut away from the white exterior wall.

'There's no door?' he said as the pair approached the building.

Liele was confused, 'What do you mean?'

'You know, how do you secure the building?'

'Why would we need to secure the building?' She was still confused.

'Thieves, robbers, people that might break in and take your things?' Callison thought he had a valid point.

Liele smiled, 'Your society sounds very different from ours. We have no one that would want to do that.'

The entrance led into a small lobby with a counter, which Liele walked behind.

Callison continued as Liele interfaced with a touch screen computer behind the desk. 'What do you mean you have no one that would want to do that?'

Liele knew she was making perfect sense in her world, and explained, 'Why would anyone take what is already theirs?'

He wasn't sure of this new land. *All societies have greed; it's a trait of humans?* he thought.

Liele interrupted his thinking, 'I have a medium tunic for you to wear?'

'Ok' Callison replied, still thinking about greed.

'Follow me, the tunics are in one of the back rooms through here.' She gestured to a door behind the desk. She had picked up on his thoughts, and spoke as she made her way to the door, 'Greed is a symptom of a sick society, not the cause of one.'

Callison followed Liele behind the desk, toward the door on the far left. He wasn't convinced, 'Where I come from greed is the cause of everything bad!'

The computer he walked past only consisted of one glass panel. No wires, no keyboard. He guessed it was more powerful than computers of his era. The door they walked through had a sign on it that looked like an ancient hieroglyph. He changed the subject, 'What does this sign mean?'

She spoke back, 'Clothes store, I guess would be a good translation.'

They emerged into a long corridor with doors down the right side every ten or so yards with hieroglyph signs on each. They had passed 5 doors, when Liele stopped and turned, 'We will get a shower before we get our clothes. In here.'

The door was not locked and Liele pushed it open, 'What's in the other doors along this corridor?' Callison asked.

Liele was still answering his questions, 'They are clothes and stores.'

The room they were now in was light and airy, reminding him of a sports changing room.

'Stand here.' Liele said, pointing to two foot shaped recesses in the floor near the wall.

As Callison stood where he was told, Liele stood on some different markers facing the wall also.

'What are we doing? asked Callison.

'This is the shower room.' said Liele informatively.

Before he could ask another question, they were both blasted with atomised water that shot out of the wall in front of them. The water looked like steam, but was cool and got them wet, before blasting them with soaps and suds. After a minute, it reverted back to atomised water, before turning into a jet of warm dry air. Within three or four minutes, they were dry and ready for some clothes.

Liele now showed her olive skin, the intuitive integration paint having been washed away. She was more beautiful than Callison had thought and her skin tone was soft and smooth. He immediately pined for Eleanor, and still felt bad having left her the way he did.

Callison followed Liele out of the shower room and into the next door up the corridor, a clothes store. Liele started to take a selection of clothes off of a large hanger rail that ran down the left side of the room and handed them to her new friend, 'Here's your tunic.'

He held the clothes up to himself and thought they'd be a good fit.

Liele had her clothes off the rack and she held them up for him while explaining each garment.

'The body suit is for wind proofing. You wear the brown tunic over the top of this layer. The tunic is warm, and will keep you dry if it rains.'

'And does everyone in Sukarmia where tunics?' asked Callison.

'No, we generally only wear tunics when visiting the Noi Tu outpost.'

'Ok.' Callison said as he continued dressing, 'Yours is different from mine?' Liele's tunic had a light yellow hem, whereas Callison's had no colour.

'Yes, I am a grade three Noi Tu specialist.' She pointed to the yellow parts.

'And what does it mean to be a grade three Noi Tu specialist?' asked Callison as he zipped up his body suit.

Another voice emanated from the doorway, 'It means she is set for a life by her own will!' The well-spoken English echoed confidence and wisdom, and its host walked in through the doorway.

'Mystera!' exclaimed Liele.

Greetings Liele. He looked towards Callison and continued in English for him, 'Hello, you must be Callison.'

'Hello Mystera, I have heard a lot about you from Liele.' He tried to make a joke, 'All good of course!' he nervously laughed to himself.

'I can sense you are scared, there really is no need to be.' said the wise master.

He wore a large tunic similar to the one Callison would soon be wearing, but Mystera's had many coloured sashes around the waist. His hood was down, revealing long wavy dark grey hair. He reminded Callison of a tribal elder. His slightly Indo-Chinese looking eyes were emerald green and on his forehead lay a similar gemstone to Liele's, but his was a deep blue, almost indigo shade. His olive skin showed only between his hairline and beard line and looked weathered. Callison felt intuitively reassured that this man was genuine.

Callison replied, 'Yes, Liele tells me I worry too much, I'm trying to work on it.' He faintly smiled. He thought about what Liele had told him up on the cliff top; *Think of something beautiful to hold on to your thoughts.* He thought of being reunited with his beloved Eleanor, in his front lounge. He didn't really know if his thoughts were more contained because of it.

'So I take it Liele has given you a pleasant welcome to our lands?' he said to Callison before turning to face Liele and transmitting, Could he understand your thought projections?

Callison replied, 'Yes, she actually saved me from a lion that was going to eat me and has also been wonderful in keeping my spirits up.' He looked to her again, 'Thank you Liele.' He explained, 'I'm stuck here, you see.'

Liele telepathically replied to her life guide, Not fully, but he shows signs of tessellation and reception. He needs to focus his energy more to communicate remotely with us.

Mystera assimilated the two responses in parallel. He spoke to Callison. 'I am glad she was receptive to you; I knew she would be, that's why I picked her to meet you.' He smiled and then attempted to telepathically project a thought his way, Are you able to comprehend my thought projections?

There was no response from Callison to the thought projection from Mystera and Callison only heard the spoken words. 'So you knew I was coming?' he asked oblivious to the shaman's telepathic projection.

Mystera telepathically asked his Noi Tu student a favour, Yes, he seems not to pick up on mine at all Liele. Can you show Callison around tomorrow? He nodded to Callison as he replied with words, 'Yes, we knew you were coming.'

Callison didn't know how they could know he was coming when even he didn't. 'How did you know? I'm here out of chance, surely!'

As Callison and Mystera spoke, Liele replied mentally to her master. It would be an honour to show him our lands.

The master acknowledged, Good, I know you'll do a fine job. See you on the roof decking my child.

The master told Callison cryptically, 'When you understand that time is pushed forward as much as it is pulled forward, then you realise there is no real such thing as chance.' As Callison tried to assimilate what was being implied, Mystera changed the subject, 'Now, there is something we all have to discuss, and it involves you, Callison. You finish up here and I will meet you both up on the roof decking.' He faced Callison and was gracious. 'It's been a pleasure Callison, see you in a short while.' He faced Liele, and nodded affirmatively, 'See you Liele.'

And with that, Mystera left the clothes store.

11.4 –

The decking was on the top floor of the white preparatory building at the Noi Tu outpost. After Liele and Callison were suitably attired in their tunics and bodysuits, they took the lift all the way to the top. The lift was silver on the inside with no buttons and it worked when Liele put her hand up against a black plate. It was a lot smoother and a lot quieter than the lifts he knew back home and Callison guessed that it utilised some form of electro-magnetism.

After the lift had come to a stop, the doors opened to reveal a well-lit large roofless decking area with tables and benches dotted around. Two rather large trees grew up through the middle of the decking area floor, making a feature of sorts and giving the people cover from the open night sky. There were some other Noi Tu student groups out on the roof also, sat at the tables, drinking, talking and laughing. Along the back of the decking area was a bar, and the scene reminded Callison of a beer garden.

The sun had by now gone down, and all that could be seen above was the night sky, showing off its finest stars. The sky was clearer than he remembered it, but the warm yellow glow of the downward lamps on the decking still stole some of the sky's wonder. The tunic he wore certainly kept him warm as a cool breeze flowing over the open topped building moved on through.

'There he is,' said Liele as she spotted Mystera, 'come, we'll go and see him, then get a drink.'

Callison followed dutifully as Liele walked through the array of tables to where Mystera was seated. As they made their way over, Callison looked at the other people at the tables and they too all wore tunics, and seemed not to raise any concern about the alien in their land, which alleviated some of Callison's fear. Mystera was sitting alone in his coloured sashed tunic with his back straight looking directly ahead. His eyes were closed and he looked to be in some sort of trance.

Liele projected to him, Hello master; we are on the roof deck now. We're going to get a drink and then we'll be back.

Although Mystera didn't seem to physically register the telepathic thought projection, he did receive it. Callison was oblivious to it all.

Ok, I'm almost out now anyway. See you shortly. Mystera mentally replied.

Liele spoke to Callison, 'We'll get a drink, then meet him back here.'

'You spoke to him with your mind then didn't you?' enquired Callison as he followed Liele to the bar area.

'Yes, he was entranced in the valley of thought, speech wouldn't get through to him.' She spoke like it was normal and for her, it was.

They approached the bar as Callison wondered what it would be like to be telepathic. He thought it would be great; no one could lie.

Liele turned to Callison, 'So then, what would you like to drink?' she smiled, 'Anything you want!'

He didn't know. 'I trust your judgement.' Callison replied, leaving Liele to do the choosing.

The bar was not like Callison had expected. Liele walked round the bar entrance and started to help herself to drinks.

Callison leaned forward on the bar to maintain the conversation, 'So is everything self serve here? They don't want paying or anything?'

Liele was slightly confused, as she got two pieces of fruit and put them into a blender looking device. 'Callison, we own the bar. You own the bar. All the people that come here after classes own the bar. Everyone does their bit to supply the fruits. It is part of our community service. Give and receive.'

'I guess I still have a lot to learn.' said Callison somewhat downbeat. 'It sounds like a good system,' he hesitated, before muttering, 'well, better than the one I'm used to anyway.'

Liele was consoling and rested her hand on his shoulder, 'You'll learn over time. There is never anything to worry about, besides you are in my land now, I'll look out for you! Now, want to spice your drink up?'

The subject change startled him, 'What do you mean, spice it up?'

Liele smiled playfully, as she took her hand back from his shoulder, 'You said you'd trust my judgement, you'll have to do just that!' She walked over to the other side of the serving area and picked up some mustard coloured powder and sprinkled it into the drinks.

'What's that powder?' he enquired wondering.

'It is pure goodness. It is cleansing for the soul.' she said with honesty.

He relaxed. *Probably some futuristic nutrient,* he guessed.

Liele finished making the drinks and proudly handed a glass containing what looked like orange juice to Callison over the bar. 'I give you one mala and mango mix!'

Callison smiled and was intrigued, 'What is the mala bit?'

'It is a fruit also.' she said, beaming happily.

'Well thank you very much.' Callison sipped some of the drink from the glass, 'Not bad!' he remarked as he settled into it.

Liele was pleased, 'Good.' She walked out from the bar with her mala and mango drink and they went back to join Mystera, who was by now out of his trance.

He turned almost before he could know they were approaching, 'Hello my friends, how are we now?' came a buoyant welcome from the Noi Tu shaman.

'We are very well' answered Liele happily.

Callison held up his drink to Mystera, and nervously smiled, 'Yep, very well thanks.'

'Come take a seat, people.' Mystera was warm and welcoming, they both placed their drinks down on the small round table. Mystera was drinking a green coloured drink, but Callison didn't ask what it was. He sat down opposite the master, and Liele placed herself at 90 degrees on Callison's left.

The master continued, 'So Callison, tell me, how are you feeling?'

Callison replied. 'Erm... yes, I'm ok, thanks.' he smiled nervously again.

'No, I mean tell me how you are *really* feeling, regarding your being lost here.'

Callison felt his heart drop. He looked at Liele who smiled back. He answered the Noi Tu elder again, 'Nervous, I guess. Unhappy about how I left without saying goodbye to my wife.' He added, 'but happy that I met Liele and now I am hopefully going to find out how I get back home? If you can find me a way home?' He looked on hopefully.

Mystera waited a moment and answered solemnly but with wisdom, 'You will find your own way home; it's how it has to be. I can't do that for you.'

Callison got the impression that this man was correct. He didn't know how to get back home though, 'But I don't know how to get back home?' Despite his younger appearance, his facial expressions still showed the same confusion.

'Intent is a good place to start.' The master smiled and let the idea sink in, 'You do want to go home I take it?'

'Yes, of course.' nodded Callison.

Mystera leant back, and relaxed, 'Then you will get home.' His confident smile was enough to reassure Liele and comfort Callison that he would indeed get home again.

The life guru changed the subject, speaking to Liele as much as he did Callison, 'I have spoken with the Universal Mind about you and they say they are aware of your situation. They say the blueprints of time have changed which means the reality you knew has also changed.'

'It spoke about me, this Universal Mind?' enquired the visitor.

Mystera corrected, 'They.' he iterated, 'The Universal Mind is a "they", and yes, they said they knew you were going to be arriving here and are working to rectify your route back.'

'So my way home might be in doubt?' enquired Callison apprehensively.

The Noi Tu elder prompted forthrightly, 'Doubt is something that *you* create, not something that exists without you. You will always get home if that is what you will to happen.' He continued, 'But anyway, the Universal Mind will send an envoy of Engineers and they will want to meet you, but request for you to settle in and feel more at home here first. They know you miss your wife, Eleanor, and they know you are marooned here. They will meet you in two days, here at the pyramid.' The bearded master briefly looked towards Liele, 'And Liele here, is going to look after you in the meantime.'

Liele smiled proudly, reassuring Callison he would be ok. He liked his new friend in Liele and it was as if she was meant to look after him here.

Callison wasn't sure who the Engineers were or what they could tell him, 'So what do you think they want to tell me, these Engineers?'

Mystera told the truth, 'Information that relates to your situation.'

Callison's anxiety was sensed by both of his table guests and Liele reassured him, 'Don't worry about any of it. There's nothing wrong!' She rubbed his arm gently.

Mystera reiterated, 'She's right you know, Callison. There is never anything that warrants worry, worry stems from fear, which is created by an absence of love.'

Callison was defensive, 'I'm sure you're right, but I wish it felt like that to me!' He took a sip of his tangy drink.

The Noi Tu master tried to emphasise his point metaphorically, 'Love and fear are like light and dark. Fear can't shine in the presence of love.'

Callison nodded, and understood Mystera's point, but he was so used to living in fear he didn't really listen properly.

Liele tried to alleviate his negativity, 'The Engineers have experienced everything, they are very wise, and now don't need bodies anymore, they exist as light and they organise the conscious experience of growing beings.'

It got a hesitant smile from Callison who felt a little bit more reassured, which Liele swiftly seized upon, 'If you only knew how much better your thoughts looked when you smiled, you'd do it more!'

Mystera agreed, observing Callison's thought patterning, 'Yes they have changed away from the negative somewhat. Try and tune in to how different you are feeling now.'

Callison was smiling still and he felt a strange wave of positivism come over him, 'I do feel better, by just deciding to feel better! It's weird.' he said. The smile developed into a small chuckle, then developed into a hearty laugh. By this time, Liele and Mystera were both broadly smiling also. Callison's laughter became uncontrollable, 'I have just solved all my problems in one second and it was easy!' He continued to laugh, 'What was I so *scared* of?'

Mystera looked towards Liele.

She looked at Callison, who had his face slumped down in his arms and was still laughing hard. Liele started to laugh also, 'The man's a genius! He's solved all his problems in one second!'

Mystera was starting to realise what had occurred. He took Liele's mala and mango drink, and smelled its contents; 'Ah ha.' came his realisation.

Callison and Liele continued to laugh hard for a short while as the old master looked on, broadly smiling.

'Ow...' said Callison, calmer and sitting up more straight again. He clutched at his side, 'My ribs hurt, why am I finding this so funny?'

Liele had come down from her laughing, but still had tear streams down her cheeks. She filled him in, 'It's the beauty of Aloemara; it's the 'spice' in your drink that is causing you to loosen up.'

Callison picked up his drink and peered questionably at the orange liquid in his glass, seemingly having forgotten about his pending situation, 'It's good stuff.' he concluded as he took another swig of the juice. 'So what is Aloemara then?' He was light headed, and still smiled.

Mystera answered, 'It's a plant extract that is used to free up the thought processes. It brings on laughing, and relief from over-thought.'

'All be to that!' exclaimed Liele, 'Aloemara has given me plenty of funny moments, and some great intuitive skills.'

Callison thought as he realised he was taking drugs. *I swore I'd never do drugs. What does that make me?* Soberly, he asked, 'So drugs are allowed in Sukarmia? What if people get addicted to them?'

Liele answered freely, 'As long as they still give to society, who are we to tell them not to take it?'

'I find that very wrong; drugs are frowned upon where I come from. I've never taken them.' Callison righteously said.

Mystera gave away more about himself and what he knew, 'I've seen what your time was like Callison, and there were drugs everywhere. Cigarettes and alcohol were both drugs. You had drugs for headaches, drugs for pain relief. You name it; your people had a drug for it. It's a blessing your civilisation realised in the end…' He stopped and thought about his words, 'Well… it's a blessing we can all learn from.'

Callison was curious. It sounded like Mystera had seen more of time than he let on. He remained quiet, thinking. *Best not to know too much about one's future.*

Mystera went back on topic, 'Anyway, moving on from Aloemara, your meeting with the Engineers,' he paused, 'will you meet me on top of the pyramid on the morning of the day after tomorrow?'

Callison and Liele both nodded in agreement.

Callison shrugged, 'Well yes, nothing to be scared of!' He smiled at Liele.

'That's the spirit!' she said.

'Ok then, that is settled.' said Mystera happily, 'Liele, if you could lead our new friend here? Aim for about two after rise?' said the Noi Tu expert, 'I must be getting on with my duties now, I bid you both farewell. Have a pleasant trip back to Sukarmia this evening.' He stood up and finished the last of his green drink.

'See you later Mystera, thank you.' said the dimensional traveller, still high on the Aloemara.

'You are most welcome Callison, see you soon my friend,' Mystera said warmly, putting his empty glass down on the table 'and you Liele.'

'Good bye Mystera.' she said as he walked off towards the lift.

Callison faced Liele. 'Nice man.'

'Glad you like him. He is very wise.'

'So how do we get back to Sukarmia from here?' Callison asked.

'We walk.' Came the reply.

* * * * * * *

12: Absolute Power Corrupts Absolutely

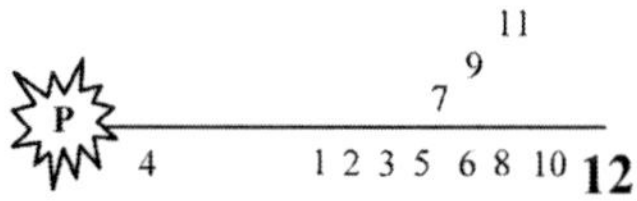

"None are more hopelessly enslaved than those who falsely believe they are free."
Johann Wolfgang von Goethe, Theoretical Physicist and Philosopher (1749 – 1832)

12.1 –
Hidden Timeline:
May 15th 2008:

Heinrich opened Callison and Eleanor's front door where two police officers greeted him. Bathed in the light from the hallway, they were dressed in dark blue uniforms and covered in radios and disarming devices. Heinrich was taller than them both, and took up most of the doorframe.

The taller officer spoke in a trained way as to seize the upper hand early in the exchange, 'Hello sir, we've had a report of a disturbance at this address. Are you the owner of the building?' The cop expected compliance, but was to be surprised.

Heinrich seemed cocky, 'No, but I've got clearance to be here.' He showed them a badge that he pulled out of his back pocket. The leather part fell down, revealing an important looking badge, 'I have to inform you that this house is now the property of the Ministry of Defence.'

The two officers were dumbstruck. They looked at each other unsure of protocol. 'Well…' said the taller officer at a loss for what to say.

The shorter one spoke to the large framed man in the doorway, 'I'm going to radio this through to headquarters.' The taller officer looked relieved, and started nodding in accordance with his quick thinking partner.

'Of course.' Heinrich handed the officer the badge as he stood condescendingly in front of the low-ranking beat cops.

The shorter officer cocked his head to the side and spoke into a radio on his shoulder. 'Yeah hello, it's Tango Foxtrot Two Zero here. We're responding to the disturbance on Seaview Road. There's a man inside the property claiming to be from the Ministry of Defence and he's shown us a badge?' He looked at the badge in detail, as he awaited a response in his earpiece.

Heinrich stood confidently meanwhile.

The officer spoke into the radio again. 'It just says MOD and Special Branch. There is a number?'

He waited for his earpiece before reeling it off, 'Yes, it's 1 – 1 – 9 – 0 – 1 – 1 – 2 – 9 – 5.' He awaited a response, which came through his earpiece once more. After a short moment, he handed the badge back to Heinrich, 'Ok. It sounds like you're legitimate, sorry to have bothered you Sir.'

The taller officer didn't understand, but he acknowledged the wide-framed man in the doorway as they both turned and walked back to their squad car. Heinrich watched them off the property.

'What did HQ say to you?' asked the taller officer as they walked.

'They just confirmed that they knew about the I.D., it was a Ministry of Defence badge and accepted it. Our orders were to get back to HQ for our dinner break and debrief.'

'Paperwork?'

'Nope,' he said happily, 'it's a national security operation.'

The taller officer was driving and unlocked the car, 'Result! I guess the M.O.D. will do the paperwork!' he said over the car roof, before getting in.

'Ask no questions I say,' said the shorter of the two as he sat down in the passenger seat of the vehicle, 'they are doing their job to keep us a free country after all!'

'Yeah, I guess.' agreed the taller one as he got behind the wheel and turned the ignition key. 'Let's go get something to eat, we've sure earned it.' he said, in an automatic and unconscious attempt to bring his mind back to the mundane levels it normally worked on.

The other officer fell into mental habit also, 'Yeah, I'm starving, the wife's got me on a diet.' The two officers drove back to HQ, talking about the brand new TV game show, "Submit and Obey".

Maggots! Heinrich thought. He closed the door to attend to matters more important. He unlocked the basement door again, and goaded his captive, 'They've gone. Problem sorted!' he hollered, as he made his way down into the basement again. He walked round the corner at the bottom and panicked as he realised immediately what had occurred. He whipped out his mobile phone and dialled a number. He walked up to the Eye and sat down in front of the multicoloured portal once more. Staring at the dimensional doorway, he spoke into his phone. 'You're not going to believe this, but...' he paused, '...it's happened again.'

* * * * * * *

13: City Limits

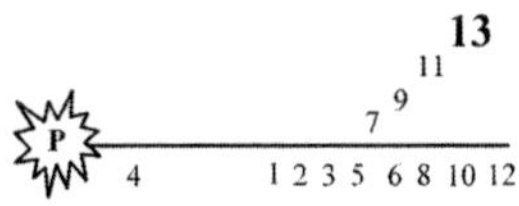

"This city is what it is because our citizens are what they are."
Plato, Philosopher (428BC – 348BC)

13.1 –
Date not known:

It had been an hour since they had set off from the white preparatory building and their walk had taken them down dark wooded tracks and across open moonlit meadows. The temperature was cool, but the tunics were doing their job well. The clear dark sky above twinkled with a thousand stars and a bright three-quarter moon dropped its silvery blue light down upon the lands. Liele had told him it was about two after fall, which Callison understood. *Two hours after the sunset.*

His younger body was coping well with the walk; it had been many years since he'd been out walking and he wished he'd done it more often in his life. The pathway they tracked was a lot more defined than the route they had navigated from the lagoon to the Noi Tu outpost. A few people had passed them as they walked and Callison seemed to attract no undue attention, which reassured him that he wasn't going to feel like an alien in Sukarmia.

The walk had included plenty of conversation, but also a few long pauses where neither said anything. It wasn't an awkward silence, but rather an ease of being with ones thoughts. It was during those pauses that Callison thought back throughout the day he was having and prospected the coming meeting with the Engineers.

Liele sensed Callison's probing thought processes telepathically, but didn't complicate them by talking to him about them. She was just happy to be walking through nature.

They came to a large meadow that rolled uphill and Liele stopped walking to speak. She pointed to the horizon, 'You'll get your first view of Sukarmia from just on top of this next slope, and you will be able to see all of the city and the Solus.'

He looked up to the horizon formed between the crest of the meadow and the clear night sky, 'How far are we away from Sukarmia when we get to the top of the meadow?'

'Still about ten minutes on foot, then a five minute skimmer ride over the Solus Sea, then we're practically there, come on let's keep going.' Liele started to walk again.

He was keen to see the city, 'Right behind you.' he said as he continued walking.

The shoes he was wearing were similar in style to sandals, but had an extremely spongy layer to soak up the uneven ground.

They approached the crest of the meadow, and as they did so, the Sukarmia skyline slowly became the new horizon. As they got closer to the summit, more of the city came into view. They came to the top and the full skyline confronted them. The meadow rolled down hill again the other side, down to a shoreline. Callison was speechless at the view, and made his mind up straight away, *I am in the future!*

The city lights and sprawling futuristic skyscrapers were probably still three miles away but looked magnificent. The sight of Sukarmia reminded Callison of the Manhattan skyline, but on a larger scale; the buildings were enormous! The city was cut off from the land they stood on by a large body of water maybe two miles across. *The Solus Sea*. The whole view was made that much more dramatic by the moon's silvery reflection on the water. There were about ten flying craft hovering at all altitudes above the city and they didn't need horizontal speed like a plane to fly; it was as if they were using some kind of levitating technology. Suddenly, one of the craft shot off and flew overhead, and before he could turn around it was gone.

'Whoa!' It caught Callison by surprise, but he was in awe of it.

'That was a plane. They can travel very fast!' informed Liele, undeterred.

It was exactly like Callison had imagined the future to look, 'It's magnificent! How many people live in the city?' he asked.

'There are about ten million people who live here.' She was proud of her city, and it showed as Callison remained transfixed on the view, 'Do you like it?'

'Like it? It looks amazing!' said Callison in reply.

'We will spend time here tomorrow.' She started to walk down the inclined meadow, 'Come on, the water skimmer is in that shore-shed down there.' There was a defined pathway that led all the way down to the waters edge where a small wooden building perched.

Callison followed Liele all the way down the hill. With the city in front of them it was hard not to stare on the approach. The questions continued as they descended down the incline to the shore of the Solus.

'So these levitating flying devices, what are they? How come we are walking if we could be in one of them?'

She answered as she walked, 'They're mainly used for intercity travel. The reason we are not in one of them now is because I am doing an intuitive integration, which is personal, so I choose to do it in my own body.'

Callison didn't really understand, but respected it and nodded.

She added, 'Besides, anyone going to the Noi Tu complex generally walks, to get in touch with nature.'

He didn't really know what to make of Noi Tu. It seemed to be more a way of living he thought, than a religion. He nodded again, and changed the subject, 'So are there a lot of cities around here then?'

She sensed his uneasiness of Noi Tu but it didn't bother her, 'There are plenty of other cities! Prechester, Findiel, they are dotted about all over the place. You wouldn't want to *walk* to another city though, it would take twenty-nine days to get to the nearest one!'

'And how long does it take in one of your 'planes'?' He could only associate the word with a jumbo jet.

'Oh, in a plane it's a lot less, ten minutes or so.'

'That's quick!' A slight delay ensued before he could assess how quick, 'Do you know how fast they go?'

Liele smiled. She was warmed by his curious nature, 'They attract the zero point field in front of the craft, and repel it behind; and travel at about twenty times the speed of sound?'

Neat, he thought, impressed at the technology.

Liele continued, 'We have to take a plane tomorrow to get to the city of Turuk. I have some activities lined up for us there that will hopefully allow you to relax more before your meeting with the Engineers.'

'What sort of activities?' he enquired, as he walked by her side.

'Well, in the day we will go to Turuk and visit one of the Noi Tu temples. There is also a Technological Recreation building in Turuk, which I think you will like. Then, my brother is doing a telekinetic show tomorrow evening in Sukarmia, so we'll come back to see that.'

The inevitable came, 'A Technological Recreation building?'

'It's a building where you choose something to have a go at, like a sport or a game.'

Hmm, what games do I like? He had difficulty thinking of something.

Liele explained further, 'Well the games in a technological recreation building are technologically natured. I know you like science and engineering. I thought it would be fitting.'

'Well I thank you in advance and I look forward to it.' He was humbled. He complimented her back, 'Your English is impeccable. It seems more natural now than when we first met.'

'That is because I've been learning from the master!'

'Who is that?' asked Callison, confused.

'You!' She laughed, seemingly happy to be showing the visitor her lands.

He was humbled, but smiled gingerly as he walked. The questions and answers ensued all the way down to the water's edge.

13.2 –

After ten minutes, they arrived at the water's edge, and the small wooden building spied from the top of the hill turned out to be a fairly large boat-shed. They entered through a panel cut out of the back wall. Again there was no door and no lock.

Inside, it was illuminated by motion sensing lights that hung from the angled wooden eves of the roof. A small walkway wrapped around the inside wall of the boat-shed running adjacent to the water. Bobbing silently were a collection of devices that looked like jet skis. On the opposite side of the wooden building, two large holes were cut into the wooden wall that allowed a waterborne exit directly onto the Solus. Callison could see the bright lights of the city through the boat-shed exits from where they stood. They walked right, and over to the far side where Liele pointed towards a specific craft.

'This is our water skimmer. They are built for one or two people.'

'Err... Ok.' said Callison expecting something like a jet ski. There was no one else in the boat-shed, and he guessed the other craft were for other Noi Tu followers. There was still space for more craft, and the boat shed seemed lightly utilised.

Liele jumped down from the walkway onto her skimmer, which bobbed even deeper into the water with her mass, 'Ok, ready to jump on?'

'It's a bit low down, I don't want to get wet!' said Callison timidly.

She smiled, and powered it up with some dials in the middle of the handlebars, 'Ok, wait there.'

Headlights illuminated the space in front of the skimmer and small bubbles started to emerge from the water beneath the craft. They grew in number, until the water was turned white from being pummelled by a downward force of some kind from the skimmer. Callison looked on with intrigue, and then within a few seconds, the engine whined, and pushed the craft clear of the water. It was hovering; blowing up a fairly moderate water spray into the boat shed air.

'Wow!' He was taken aback by it as his tunic went to work on keeping him dry from the spray.

Liele backed off the throttle slightly, and the craft descended to hover on the same level as the walkway of the boat shed. She said to Callison, 'Ok, how is that, better?'

'That's much easier.' With the skimmer hovering right next to him, he jumped on.

'Ok,' Liele said, 'put your arms around my waist, and hold on tight, I won't go too fast, so enjoy the ride!'

Callison sat and located his feet into the ergonomic grooves either side of the seat. He lightly put his hands on her hips, 'Like this?' he asked.

She took hold of his hands and folded them round her waist, 'No, like this!'

His chest pressed tightly on her back, and he held on tight. The hairs in his new dark beard tangled slightly with Liele's golden brown locks. It prompted him to realise that he was younger again, and thoughts flashed across his mind that he might make a suitable sexual partner for her. The thought passed as other thoughts about Eleanor came to his fore; mainly feelings of guilt for having thought the thought about Liele in the first place. He had never cheated on any of the women he'd ever courted, *Time travel is no excuse,* he thought. It was as if he could still sense that Eleanor was out there somewhere, which had him at a loss, as she surely must have died a long time ago in this future land he walked. He missed her so.

Liele sensed the attraction, but didn't let it affect her.

The skimmer lurched up higher from the water and Liele started a slow movement towards the exit by tilting the skimmer forward. It certainly didn't sound like an internal combustion engine.

'This is great!' shouted Callison into Liele's ear, 'What is powering it?'

She called back over her shoulder as the skimmer departed the shed slowly, 'Basically an anti-gravity gyro.' Callison nodded, not really worrying about his lack of knowledge on the subject. 'Hold on tight!' she said, as the skimmer tilted forward and accelerated out of the boat shed out over the Solus.

He shouted into her ear again, the noise of the craft and the wind proving quite loud, 'How long will the crossing take?'

She didn't hear him, and continued concentrating on 'flying' the boat.

The initial forward tilt had backed off and they sat at what he thought was about forty miles per hour, gently tilting forward. Liele's hair was blowing backwards into his face, which obscured his view of the approaching city lights. He angled his head to look over her left shoulder and the approaching city had him spellbound, the illuminated buildings were enormous and only grew in size as they approached.

With the wind in their faces, the large skyscrapers slowly edged towards them. These buildings were bigger and taller than anything he'd ever seen on Earth in his time. Long tunnels joined some of the buildings together at all altitudes creating levels of sprawl. He could see some of the flying craft entering the skyscrapers near their summits, like fly-in valet parking lots; flashing lights guiding the flying craft about the city. Blue, red and green lights flashed in sequences high in the sky. The main light source of the cityscape came from the plethora of floors of interior building lights, emitting a warm orange glow and being reflected by the approaching water of the Solus.

Running the length of the scene and just in front of the bases of the skyscrapers a raised road carried traffic around the city. Unseen initially, the road disappeared off to the right, and turned into a bridge running out over the Solus at ninety degrees to their direction of travel.

The crossing was about to turn subterranean; they were still a mile off the coastline, when Liele pointed to what looked like an obstacle approaching in front of them in the water. She shouted over her shoulder, 'This is the Aquaside tunnel entrance in front of us, which we're going to take.'

A tunnel? Callison thought. Liele backed the speed off by tilting backwards slightly, and the wind noise died down.

She carried on speaking over her shoulder, now at a quieter tone, 'The Aquaside tunnel is the quickest way into the city. A bit boring for you, but you will like the view when the tunnel emerges into the city!'

'I'm merely along for the ride, it's all exciting for me!' he said back, glad to have got this far.

The tunnel entrance approached. It looked to be a small manmade island in the sea. Liele backed the speed right off, and explained what she was doing.

'Got to go slowly for this bit.' The tunnel had a small concrete shoreline and as the skimmer got to the concrete shoreline, Liele turned a dial in the middle of the handlebars, 'I have to turn the repellence down for the hard surface. Liquids and solids have different settings.'

He acknowledged with a nod and continued to observe their movement as the skimmer transferred onto the concrete rising up out of the water. The concrete surface led up a small incline, which acted like a water break, stopping the water from flowing down into the tunnel. As they neared the crest of the incline, the 'road' dipped back down again and into the lit tunnel. A solid white line split the passageway into two lanes and another hover device zipped past them towards the Solus. Liele waved, and the other hoverers waved back. Again the timid newcomer to the future prompted no funny looks, which reassured him.

'That was a neat entrance.' he said to her as they navigated steadily down the tunnel's incline.

'It's just easier than navigating the shoreline, lots of hectic traffic about going the other way. No big traffic can go down this tunnel, only hover jets and bikes.'

'So can you go really fast in the tunnel?' he asked over her shoulder.

She smiled to herself as the tunnel closed up over their heads. 'No I have to hover at a sensible rate. There might be a stopped bike or jet.

The tunnel lights continued to barrel over their heads, and they sat at roughly thirty miles an hour. The tunnel was like any other from his time, apart from the lack of soot and grime deposits on the walls and roof. *No petrol burned in here.* He thought to himself.

13.3 –

After a few minutes, the tunnel exit ahead was given away from the lights of the city beyond falling down into the tunnel. 'We will emerge onto the Mainway Boulevard shortly.' Liele called back to her passenger.

Callison acknowledged, but didn't speak. The tunnel ascended up a gradual incline and emerged directly onto a wide raised gangway in the middle of the city sprawl. There were now more hover jets travelling around them and on-ramps and off-ramps passed them by as they travelled. They had emerged directly onto the boulevard and were right in the middle of the action.

Callison had his head craned looking skywards, 'Wow. The buildings are so high!'

Liele explained with her social knowledge, 'Yes, it is the most effective way to create living space.'

The skyscrapers towered over them to the left and the right, and had gangways high above the ground that connected some of them together. Also high above them were what seemed to be flows of air traffic and a line of the levitating planes slowly filed into one of the towers next to them. At ground level the building's sizes were evident as each one was very wide and broad. They had large illuminated entrance halls at their bases, presumably housing elevators taking occupants all the way up and down the buildings.

'So people live in these buildings here?'

'Yes, most of the buildings in Sukarmia are for living space.' said Liele while hovering.

'So is there any business going on in the buildings?'

She spoke over her shoulder, 'There is another area where the utilities and the factories are based, but it's easy to get there on hover jet or transport probe. That's where a lot of people do their city service.'

'So is a transport probe bigger than a hover jet?'

'Yes, that's right, a transport probe can carry 10 people. They use circuitry wired into the road surface to navigate the city, we call it 'the grid'. All the driver does is program the destination.'

Checking for other hover jets on her blind side, Liele adjusted her hover jet to buzz closer to the side of the raised gangway. She pointed left down to the grid line running adjacent to the raised hover jet gangway they travelled, 'They are transport probes down there.'

He looked downward to see a line of dark shiny and curved transport probes buzzing by about two times faster than they were travelling and in the same direction. He guessed they were all sitting at about fifty miles per hour. Three particular probes were travelling dangerously close together by his driving standards. The middle one suddenly veered off and onto another route. He pointed downwards, referring to the traffic below them. He spoke closely to Liele's ear, 'Do they have many crashes?'

She called back, 'It is all controlled by the grid, and they are programmed not to crash.'

It was all too much to take in for Callison, who sat on the back of the hover jet observing silently again. He was in wonder of where he was. They had not been travelling for too long, before Liele announced it was not much further.

'We're almost there now. It's just down this next off-ramp.' She angled the craft towards one of the off-ramps of the Mainway Boulevard. The skimmer jet glided down the ramp and joined another pavement running adjacent to 'the grid'. A steady flow of transport probes whizzed by.

'We're going into the building four up from here on the left.' called Liele, as she gestured with her hand.

He nodded as he inspected the Transport probes in more detail, which buzzed up and down the grid lanes next to them as they travelled. They looked like shiny round pebbles with wrap-over windows. Aerodynamic, and sleek looking, the glass was profiled over the entire roof, allowing 360 degree views. They were very quiet and instead of burbling by, they whistled by. They weren't running on anything that Callison was used to, which intrigued him.

'So do you own a transport probe?' he called forward as they neared the fourth building on the left.

She called back, 'No, we call them when we need them by connecting with the grid. No one owns anything in Sukarmia, apart from our own spirit of course!' She laughed, mainly to herself before announcing, 'I live in here.' She pointed to one of the taller buildings of Sukarmia on the left side. The grid lane cut the building off from the pavement they followed.

'Do we need to cross?' asked the visitor.

She shook her head, 'No, another down junction.'

Before he could ask what a down junction was, the pavement disappeared down a slope and underneath the grid traffic. Their route under the grid bent round to the left, and headed directly for the building Liele had pointed out.

Callison looked up, amazed that they were going up it. It was a building of immense proportions. The rows of interior lights were numerous, and disappeared high up into the night sky and there were some flying craft buzzing around about three quarters of the way to the top.

'Wow! Which floor are we going to?' he asked.

'My family's area is about half the way up...' Callison nodded, as Liele finished her sentence. '...on floor 235.'

'Two hundred and thirty five?!' Callison exclaimed.

Liele nodded.

His mind did the simple calculation, *So there are about 470 floors?* He couldn't comprehend it. The structure was so immense in scale; it made the human life that created it look small and insignificant in comparison.

The hover jet slowly cruised up to the entrance hall; again there seemed to be no security to talk of. The entrance to the hall consisted of an overhead archway and led into a well-lit and wide corridor with marble running along the interior walls. Liele had backed the forward speed off to hover slowly down the corridor as another skimmer slowly hovered in the opposite direction out toward the city.

'Are we not leaving the skimmer outside?' asked Callison as the other riders disappeared down the marbled hallway.

Liele confirmed, 'No, we'll leave it in my social area.'

The large tunnel from the entrance led into a spacious box-shaped marble atrium in the middle of the floor plan of the enormous building. In the middle of the atrium, a tree filled in the empty open space of the room and there were concrete flowerbeds and benches, Callison guessed to make meeting here nicer. Many more people milled about in the large room, some wearing similar tunics and some wearing what Callison thought of as normal attire.

He'd built up a comfort zone with Liele, and the prospect of meeting other people in Liele's family was grinding on his mind.

'So...' he decided how to say it, '... so who do you live with? Big family? Small family?'

Liele turned left out of the ground atrium with the tree and into another main hallway of the building's ground floor. There were some elevators in front of them about a hundred yards further up the roomy walkway, 'It's a fairly small family, but we are close. I live with my Dad, Mum and brother, but there are many more I would call family here. I have grown up with many of them in this building, so I know them well.'

It was not long before Liele hovered up to the elevator's entrance; it had dials on it, but nothing Callison could understand. She twisted one of them, and the slide doors opened almost immediately. They hovered forwards into the elevator, then Liele manoeuvred the hover jet through one hundred and eighty degrees to face the exit again as the door slid closed. The elevator started to whirr into operation and he felt the upward acceleration as the lift started to climb.

Callison was receptive, 'So who are your dad, mum and brother? What are their names?'

'There's my Father, Tomak. He is a nice man, very helpful and specialises in building and construction. Then there's my mother, Estina who will make you feel very welcome; she is a healer, and then there is Tobian, my brother, who is a very clever telekinesis expert. He will dazzle you in the show we will go to tomorrow evening.' She paused, as Callison remained quiet. She telepathically picked up on his insecurity, and tried to calm him, 'You have nothing to worry about, they are all very friendly.'

'Yes, I know.' He gingerly grinned, but deep down he didn't know.

She sent him some kind thoughts telepathically; Think your dream and good thoughts will blossom.

Callison felt more relaxed and thought of reuniting with Eleanor again to keep his thoughts more to himself.

Liele smiled to herself, happy that he could find a loving thought.

The lift had been moving upwards for sometime when it emerged on the side of the skyscraper. The wall opposite the lift door was a see through panel giving excellent views of the city. The city's perspective changed rapidly as the lift continued upward at some rate.

'Wow!' exclaimed Callison. 'This is almost a city in the sky!'

Liele was happy he was excited, and beamed, 'I'm glad you are enjoying it!'

The lift's upward motion started to slow as Liele told Callison more about her family, 'Now when we get in you will meet my family, then I think you should get to sleep as early as possible, we have a long day tomorrow.'

He nodded, suddenly realising his tiredness.

She continued, 'They don't speak English very well, but are very friendly and will pick up the feelings behind what you say in English, so don't hesitate to talk.'

The lift stopped and its slide doors slid apart. There was a fair sized entrance hall in front of the lift with two other hover jets parked on saddle-shaped docking stations. A long corridor led away from the lift, which lit up as it detected their movement out of the elevator. It was a long corridor, and Callison couldn't quite make out the end of it. Liele hovered the skimmer slowly forward out of the lift and round to the left, where there was an empty saddle-shaped dock available to park the hover jet on.

She turned the dial on the handlebars anti clockwise and the craft descended into the dock station, its levitation device quietening down until it stopped completely.

'All parked,' said Liele, 'Shall we?'

They dismounted the hover device and walked down the long corridor that led away from the lift, while still the questions continued, 'Do lots of people live on this floor?'

'There are fifty families on this floor.' she said, 'This corridor leads to a central area for communal food and hot food, and the living space wraps around the outside of the floor's footprint.' They carried on walking towards the central area, but reached a corridor off to the right before reaching the centre. After a few seconds in the corridor, they stopped. Liele indicated their arrival at the first double door on the right, 'It's this one here. You ready?'

'Yep.' He nodded bravely.

She knew he would be fine, 'Ok, follow me in.'

13.4 –

Liele opened the door to her apartment and the room they entered was open plan. Callison assumed they were in a kitchen area and an older woman greeted them as soon as they walked in. The shiny floor was rendered in white marble, and noticeably clean; it gave the space a clinical feeling. A selection of green plants and leaves brought a touch of nature into the dwelling.

Liele walked over to the woman who stood at a food preparation table in the middle of the kitchen, 'This is my mother, Estina.' said Liele to Callison as she put her arm around her and gave her a kiss.

Estina looked to be in her mid fifties and had shoulder length blonde hair and stood slightly taller than Liele. She smiled at Callison, welcoming him into their home. Her mother, who was full of life spoke in very broken English to the man standing near the door, 'Goot evenig Gallizon.' She smiled welcomingly.

The words were broken, but Callison understood, and he said back, 'Good evening.' He smiled courteously and was very polite. He found himself unconsciously bowing in humbleness, 'Nice to meet you Estina. Thank you for letting me stay here, I am stuck in your time, and it's very different for me. Your city looks amazing.'

'Yes yes.' she confirmed happily. She understood what Callison meant, but not through the noises he made with his mouth.

Liele communicated in a futuristic language with her briefly. The language was unknown to Callison, but was in part telepathic, This is Callison. He is lost, but warm-hearted.

Her mother replied in thought, He looks tired. Does he know where he is yet? She continued to smile at the man in the Noi Tu tunic.

He knows enough, but there is a lot for him to take in. He has many clouds in his mind, and can't receive our external communications yet. We'll get him to sleep fairly soon.

Ok, the bedroom in the back is cleared. Glad you're back darling.

With information exchanged telepathically, Estina walked over to Callison and ushered for his tunic. Liele helped out, 'You can take your tunic off if you want Callison. My mother will hang it up for you.'

Callison understood and handed his tunic to Liele's mother who carried it away and as she walked towards the coat storage, Liele threw her tunic over to her mother as well. It seemed to trace an unnatural projection through the air, as if Liele or Estina had assisted it telekinetically in some way. It landed in Estina's arms on top of his tunic. Liele smiled at Callison acknowledging his curiosity, but before he could ask about it, the sound of a slide door distracted him.

Hello my sweet, how was your intuitive integration? A man walked into the kitchen area, and spoke some words that were unknown to Callison. He kissed Liele on the cheek as he welcomed her before smiling towards Callison.

Liele replied in thought, Hello dad, it went well, thank you. We have a guest; this is Callison. He is stuck here from a place far away.

She enlightened Callison, 'This is my Dad, Tomak.'

Callison was standing next to a kitchen work surface in his light grey coloured body suit. He spoke to Tomak like an Englishman might in a foreign country; slow and clear, 'Hello Tomak, nice to meet you.' He half bowed again as he spoke.

Tomak heard the sounds of the guest's words but understood the intentions behind them more. He imitated Callison's bow as he spoke back in the futuristic tongue. His meaning was transmitted by thought, Hello Callison, it is nice to meet you too.

Tomak seemed friendly. He looked to be about the same age as Estina, and was as tall as Callison. He wore a large beige robe over his one-piece body suit and had dark brown wavy hair.

Callison could sense a very alien feeling in the room, like he could feel the telepathy going on, but not enough to understand anything. He concentrated on thinking thoughts about reuniting with Eleanor, so as to keep his thoughts to himself.

Estina made her way back into the room to stand next to Tomak as Liele told them her plans, Well Callison has had a long day, we'll get him to bed straight away. She hugged her parents.

Liele spoke to Callison, 'We have a bedroom made up for you, and a spare toothbrush! We'll just pop in to see my brother.'

A tooth brush? Hardly futuristic, he thought. 'Ok.' He looked towards Liele's parents and felt welcomed by them, 'Thank you once again.' He bowed again out of respect and asked Liele to say thank you to them for letting him stay here.

She spoke in a different language that Callison couldn't understand, but her parents both smiled graciously. They bowed like he did and Liele's mother said in her broken English, 'Goot Night Gallizon.'

Liele led Callison out of the open plan kitchen and through a minimalist lounge area. Settees lay pointing towards a large flat screen that seemed to be the centrepiece of the otherwise empty lounge. *Television?* thought Callison as he followed Liele through the open space. The far wall had drawn white curtains covering its whole plane and plants continued the natural feel of the room, adding a green touch to the airy space. There were some doors on the left wall, which Liele walked towards. She knocked on one, and a voice called back. The voice spoke the same unknown language as Liele had spoken to her parents. She slid the door open, 'Come here, meet my brother, Tobian,' she said to her new friend, 'he knows English too.'

Callison followed Liele through the doorway and into Tobian's bedroom, which was spacious and had pictures of mountains and scenery on the walls. Tobian was sat on a sofa talking to a hologram of white light being produced by a black box on the floor. It reminded Callison of the Princess Leia hologram in Star Wars but this hologram was of a person that looked like he was juggling. Tobian swivelled round to face his visitors, 'Hi Liele, and you must be Callison. Nice to meet you.'

'Hello Tobian, nice to meet you too.' The bowing was still automatic.

Tobian looked to be in his early twenties, and looked geeky. He had inherited his dad's dark curly hair. 'Sorry I'm just finishing up talking with a friend. We are making some last minute adjustments to the telekinesis show tomorrow.'

Callison nodded unknowingly.

'Tobian is a telekinesis master,' said Liele, 'show him what you do!' she asked.

Callison watched as Tobian stood up from the chair and gestured with one of his fingers to the far wall. A glass of water on one of the shelves slowly started to levitate before moving through the air towards the telekinesis expert until it was suspended in front of him. Tobian leaned his head back and the glass tilted forward depositing some of the water into his mouth. Then the glass tilted upright and hovered back to the shelf, landing back where it started.

Liele was impressed, 'He's very good at it!'

Callison nodded in astonishment, 'Very clever!' He had seen so many new things today; he was strangely accustomed to it.

Tobian spoke to them both, 'You're coming to the show tomorrow, right?'

'Yes, we will both be coming. It starts at set, yes?'

Sunset, thought Callison.

'Yes we're going for some new tricks tomorrow. It should be a good show.'

'We'll be there. Anyway, just really saying hello, we're going to get Callison an early night, we'll see you tomorrow Tobi.'

'Good night Tobian.' said Callison. 'Nice to meet you.'

'Yes, see you guys tomorrow.' said Tobian as he got back to his holographic meeting.

'I'll show you your room now.' said Liele as she walked out and turned right. She walked him to his room, which was two up from Tobian's. 'You'll be in here,' she said as she gestured towards an open slide door. Liele explained further, 'The toilet is just across the hall on the left. Why don't you get yourself ready for bed?'

13.5 –

He felt like a child again tucked up in a bed he didn't know, in a room he didn't know, in a time he didn't know.

She looked down at her new friend, 'Now get some sleep, we have a big day tomorrow, I'll wake you at two after rise.' said Liele.

'Ok.' He stared at Liele, fascinated about the precious stone on her forehead.

As he did so Liele bent down and kissed him on his lips. It was a quick but sweet kiss, and it took Callison by surprise. He spoke, 'What was that for?'

'Good night.' she said, as she stood up again.

'Oh, good night.' he said back, thinking the kiss was just friendly.

She was almost out of the doorway, until Callison called out, 'Liele?'

She stopped by the doorway. 'Yes?'

He sat up in the bed and looked towards her, 'Thank you.'

'What for?' she asked.

'Well, you know, everything. Rescuing me from the lion, looking after me, showing me here, all of it. I was dreading whom I might meet here, and I met you. You are very nice, thank you.'

She felt happy, 'You're welcome; it just shows you should never dread anything. See you in the morning, sweet dreams.' And then she left.

The light went out automatically and the door slid closed simultaneously; he didn't know how it worked and he didn't care. His eyelids fell shut straight away.

* * * * * *

14: Just Another Time Traveller

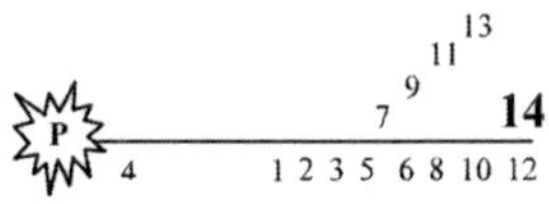

"Time, whose tooth gnaws away everything else, is powerless against the truth."
Thomas Huxley, Biologist and Evolutionist (1825 – 1895)

14.1 –
Date not known:

The basement seemed far away and the memory already felt like a dream as she looked forward, wondering where she was headed.

Eleanor was in a translucent tunnel unknowingly travelling at the speed of light. There was a light blue glow everywhere she looked and the tunnel seemed to be free of inertia; there were no forces on her body as the tunnel zipped left, then right, then up and then down. The tunnel kept combining with other tunnels and there seemed to be something guiding her through a certain route, she got the distinct feeling that she was a passenger.

She kept looking forward as the tunnel continued to carry her towards somewhere that she hoped she would find her husband. Her speed was seemingly increasing, and she saw outside of the tunnel, in the distance the same dark green cloud that Callison had witnessed four infinite hours ago. It was as if the tunnel was homing in on this region, she thought. The dark green cloud suddenly emitted what looked like a lightning bolt that stretched high above her. It partially illuminated a flat layer of cloud high above, which looked like a ceiling of sorts. It was as if she was travelling between two planes. It was surreal and she wondered where she was. The tunnel's speed increased, and increased, and increased until the ride ended in a crescendo of white light, like she was the lightning.

Where am I? she thought. She was outside and a light blinded her. She slowly adjusted her focus and her destination revealed itself. She was in a garden. She focused some more. There was a sky. Grass. A stream was flowing past from right to left in front of her. Her hearing came back to her and she could hear the stream trickling by. It was as if she was still on Earth, but just in an idyllic countryside. Her vision focused and she could see her surroundings clearly. 'Callie!?' she called out and waited: no response. She was sitting down on the grass and she realised she was naked. Soon she realised her body was different. She was younger and became fearful. She didn't know what Callison had invented, but it put her firmly out of her comfort zone.

Where is the portal? I can jump back she thought, but as she inspected the surrounds, there was no sign of the portal and she felt alone and vulnerable.

She stood up and walked down the slightly inclined grass bank to the stream's edge. Kneeling on the bank of the stream she peered into some of the still water in the protection of a side pool. Her reflection confirmed; she was still in *her* body, but she was indeed younger; she seemed to be about twenty years old again and her mind had no answers.

Before she could think any further something startled her. She jumped as a voice echoed through her.

'Hello?' Someone was there.

The voice had come from afar. She pulled her head up from the stream water and stood up. Walking towards her, he was about twenty yards away. He wore some sort of animal skin and carried a staff. He was dark skinned and reminded Eleanor of a Red Indian tribal chief. He spoke with a deep voice, 'Hello?' he called again. Whoever he was could speak English clearly.

'Hello?' she timidly called back, 'My name is Eleanor and I fear I am lost!'

He smiled warmly, 'I know, that's why I've come to get you.' He used his staff to navigate some large rocks next to the brook, and looked to be about thirty years old. He sounded friendly, 'My name is Togo, I am on a walk into the wilderness we call an intuitive integration. I am here to look after you before you return. Everything will be Ok.'

This felt too surreal. *Was this actually happening? Or was it a dream?* she thought to herself. 'Thank you.' Her manners were always present. 'Am I supposed to know what's happening?'

Togo came closer. He had heard her. He had white paint on his bronze skin, making patterns on his face that reminded Eleanor of the Aztec period. He sounded very well spoken, which Eleanor couldn't put with the appearance, 'If you knew what was happening, there would be no need for me to be here would there?'

She acknowledged, 'Do you know where Callison, my husband, is?'

The man smiled. 'He is doing just fine; he has things of his own to find out. You will see him again. This visit is all about *you* however; not Callison.'

The man's words seemed cryptic, but Eleanor sensed that he was genuine. This meeting, in a strange sense, felt like it was supposed to happen. She walked with the tribal man called Togo upstream towards the mountains, knowing little that her husband was here not long before her, and had opted to walk downstream.

* * * * * * *

15: Waking in the Future

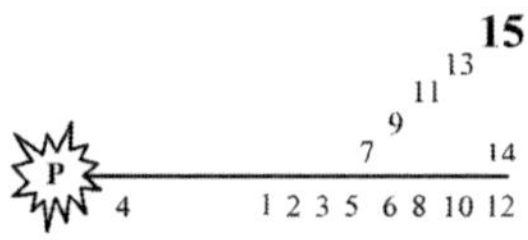

"The present is theirs; the future, for which I have really worked, is mine."

Nikola Tesla, Electro-Physicist and Transcendentalist (1856 – 1943)

15.1 –
Date not known:
Plus one day:

She sounded worried, 'Callison darling, where are you?'

He had trouble explaining, 'It is hard to say my dear. I'll be back.'

Eleanor came to be floating in front of him, wearing a red dress and she looked as beautiful as the day they met, 'I have something to tell you.' she said to her husband.

He tried to move towards her, but his feet were glued to the ground. He felt worry for he could not move, 'I'm stuck, what is it?'

'We are eternal...' and with that, she walked away up a foggy old-fashioned looking street as Callison stood, unable to move. Her body became silhouetted as she walked away into the mist.

Above him, a large bird circled. It came down and rested on one of the rooftops of the buildings and it was speaking to him, It's your choice, the bird said.

Someone tapped him on the shoulder.

'Hello Callie' said Eleanor.

He was confused, 'But you just left?' He looked up the street but the earlier silhouette of his wife had disappeared; the bird was still watching him. He was confused.

The large bird flew away from the rooftop. He couldn't let it go, so called out to the bird, 'What's my choice?'

It looked back as it flew, Everything is your choice.

Confusion remained.

'I jumped as well!' said Eleanor, 'Your device! It saved me!'

Callison took his eyes away from the bird.

Eleanor was talking to him, 'You are just asleep. I'm in a new reality now.'

'What?' he said. This wasn't making sense.

She would wait for him, she said, before disappearing into the same mist she had just walked into.

With the wind whipping around him, he watched her go. *But where? What happened?* He couldn't remember.

He came round in a bed he didn't know. It was light outside, and a light-beam streamed in through a crack in the window blind. *What was the dream about? Where did it go? Where did we go?* The dream seemed like a distant memory. *Why can't I remember?* He lay awake looking at the ceiling for a moment. He assumed he had been dreaming and that he was now looking at his very normal cottage ceiling.

He looked around the room and suddenly his surroundings consumed him. He wasn't in his normal bedroom; he was in a strange room. He missed Eleanor straight away, which made the dream ache that much more. *This must still be a dream. I must be dreaming. I'll check out the window.*

He levered himself up out of bed, thinking that the dream felt very real. He wore a beige baggy one-piece sleep suit, but didn't know whose it was and after opening the blind, he saw the reality he had said goodnight to the evening before.

The city of Sukarmia greeted him good morning. He realised that the day before had really taken place and he realised again that he was stuck here. Suddenly Eleanor seemed even more distant and a sinking feeling consumed his heart, *What's going to become of me now?* He was told fear was the illusion, but right now it felt all too real. He closed the blind and went back to lie in bed, his stomach churning. A tear ran down his cheek into his beard, he remembered: his *dark haired* beard. He remembered about the age regression that the jump through time seemed to have had on him. Just the activity of thinking about it tied his head in knots, but habitually, he thought on it for a few minutes more to prolong the agony.

There were no sounds of activity outside his room so he lay in bed some more. *I'll wait until someone else is up before I venture out.*

Something grabbed his attention; in the corner of the room was a device that resembled a TV. He looked at it for a while before getting out of bed again to have a closer look. The unit seemed to be a flat display screen and he wondered what the machine did. *Surely it can't be a simple television?* He wasn't so sure; he looked closer at the screen. At the bottom it had three small symbols, which looked like hieroglyphs, which he assumed were a brand of some kind.

He wondered how it was powered. There seemed to be no wires running to a power source and he could see no button to activate the device. *Weird.* For fear of going too far and possibly waking the house up with the device, he again went back to lying in bed, wondering about the possible uses of the machine.

Footsteps and voices eventually broke the silence outside. It was nothing he could understand, which made him anxious before the knock on the door came.

It was Liele, 'Callison are you awake?'

This certainly isn't a dream. 'Yes, you can come in.' he said.

The door slid open and Liele walked in wearing a sleeveless surf style jade blue body suit. She had wet hair, and dried it with a towel as she spoke, 'Good morning, do you want some breakfast, I have some prepared.'

'Mmm... Yes please.' said Callison, not knowing what breakfast would be.

'Well, get yourself ready. I'll be in the kitchen area.' She waited, 'You remember where the toilet is, right?'

He nodded, still somewhat questioning his reality, 'Yes, thanks.'

She walked out, but the door was left open. He levered himself out of bed, and walked to the bathroom. As he brushed his teeth, he looked at himself in a small round mirror in front of the sink. He had always enjoyed being in his forties and ran his non-brushing hand through his beard. *I want to shave this thing off* he thought. He continued to rub his hands over his head; he was still bald but less so than before the jump and had now had a ring of brown hair instead of silver.

Liele knocked on the bathroom door, but didn't enter. Callison held the toothbrush still and Liele informed him, 'I'm leaving a towel and shaver outside on the floor for you, just in case you were thinking of shaving and I have some clothes for you as well.'

Did she just read my mind? he questioned to himself. 'Ok, thanks.' he called back, slowly, but strangely acclimatising to the alien feature of the mind.

15.2 –

He walked in to the kitchen area with a dark brown moustache and freshly shaved cheeks and chin. He wore yesterday's one piece body suit and he felt better, like he'd only lived for forty years, but had the conscious memory of sixty-five. He still missed Eleanor and wondered what she was doing now or more precisely, what she did in history.

Liele was preparing breakfast in the kitchen as Callison walked out through the lounge and into the kitchen area. She wore a crystal-encrusted headband that encapsulated the emerald on her forehead as much as keeping her deep brown hair pinned back.

'That's better.' he said, then happily greeted, 'Good morning Liele, thanks for the razor, it was just what I needed.'

'You're welcome,' she said genuinely, 'I got some clothes for you on my morning meditation trip as well.' She pointed to the sofa, 'Have a look at them and pick something out, breakfast will still be about ten minutes.'

'Well, thank you once again.' Callison walked over to the sofa in the lounge and started to look through the neatly folded pile of brightly coloured clothes. *People like their bright clothes in the future*, he thought seeing Liele in the bright jade sleeveless body suit. He picked out a pair of blue trousers that closely resembled denim, and found a white tee shirt to wear on top. He went back into the spare bedroom to try them on, and they were a close-to- perfect fit. He walked back out to show them off.

'What do you think?' asked Callison as he emerged from the room he slept in showing off his chosen clothes. He walked over to her to stand on the other side of the stand-alone centre sideboard where his host was preparing breakfast.

Liele was happy, 'They fit well, my guess was good!'

He was content with his look, 'Yes, they are a perfect fit, thanks again, Liele. Where did you get them from?'

She pointed upward, there was still a lot of skyscraper above them, 'There is a clothes manufacturer in this building, it was an extra ten minutes to my schedule, it was nothing.'

He still had a lot to learn about the systems of Sukarmia, but was intrigued by the food that Liele was preparing, 'What's that you're chopping up there?'

'This?' she offered the round red object. 'It's a limelon. Have you ever tried one?'

He shook his head, 'No, what is a Limelon?'

'It's a fruit.' she said as she chopped it in half and took out a stone in the middle.

He wondered what the red fruit tasted like; it looked like a cross between a red peach and a small melon.

Liele cut him a piece off for him to try, 'Try some.' she gestured across the floating kitchen island.

He tried it, and smiled as his senses told him about the new fruit, 'It tastes like a citrus strawberry?'

'Do you like it?' she asked hopefully.

He gave an affirmative nod, 'Yes, it's good.'

'Yes, I love them!' Liele informed her guest, 'We'll eat breakfast out there,' She pointed towards a double door in the lounge, 'there is some breakfast furniture out there already if you want to go out and have a drink. Do you drink tea?'

He smiled and thought, *A home from home*. 'Yes, I drink tea.'

Liele was pleased.

'Where's the rest of your family?' he asked as Liele continued cutting fruits.

'Well, mum is on a meditation trip; she should be back soon, dad is doing his work duty harvest work, and Tobian has gone to the telekinetic arena to set up and practise for tonight's show.' She added, 'We'll be leaving too, after breakfast to get a plane to Turuk.'

'Ok,' he said, 'To go to the Techno… Recreation thingamajig?'

She was happy he remembered, 'Yes. The Technical Recreation Centre.'

He nodded, 'That's the one.'

She played the host, 'Go and pour yourself a tea! I'll be out in two seconds.' she said and gestured him out with her arms.

'Yes boss!' he joked, before walking through the double doors. He liked Liele and couldn't believe how lucky he had been in meeting her.

The light flooded him as he walked through the doorway and he felt like he was on a veranda in the sky, the morning sun streaming into the room and showing off the city view. After his eyes adjusted more, he realised that he was in a long room with large windows rather than on a veranda. On his right were a table and some chairs with a pot of tea set out on the table. Next to the teapot there was an unfamiliar blue case-like object that Callison waited for Liele to go near first. There were also two empty white mugs and two plates set out. Next to the teapot was a small jug of milk. He mused, *It must be a future England…* He took a mug and poured himself some tea.

Sipping his tea, he looked at the view of the city through the large windows. They looked out on an opposing corner of skyscraper; far enough away so as to not really see into the windows with any detail, but close enough to be physically connected by a sky bridge. He craned his head up to look at the wide connecting walkway, which was about ten floors above his vantage point and was about halfway up the total height of the building. The top looked a long way above still; he had to crane his head close to the glass just to actually *see* the top. He brought his view downwards to see the tiny transport probes navigating the grid way below him. He saw the raised main boulevard that they had skimmer-jetted through the city on last night. Looking left revealed more city buildings and skyscrapers. Craning to the right he could see a body of water that he guessed was the Solus.

With each sip of his tea, he felt a pang for a cigarette. The pang hurt him, but passed painlessly and quickly as he guessed no one smoked in the future.

Liele, who came in with a platter of fruit, yoghurt and jams, interrupted his thoughts, 'Yes, you do get a good view from up here.'

He agreed, 'Yes I was just thinking that. It's quite impressive!' He walked over to the table again and sat down on one of the two seats.

'You like your tea?' she said.

'It's just like tea where I come from, very nice thank you.'

'Breakfast?' she questioned and offered.

The blue case shaped object made him curious and he pointed, 'What's this here then?'

She flicked a switch, and the lid opened gently, revealing two bread rolls inside, 'Bread warmer!' she said; and took a roll. 'You want one?' She sat down opposite him at the table.

He realised it was quite a mundane object and his mind smiled at his unwarranted fear of the unknown, 'Thank you.' he said. He tore the warm crusty bread roll apart to get to the bread, which was white and fluffy inside. *Perfect.*

Liele explained, 'So, we also have some yoghurt and fruit, and some jam for the bread.'

'Ok. It looks nice.' He started to pile some jam onto his broken off pieces of bread.

Liele mixed up some yoghurt and fruit, 'So what sort of house do you live in?' she said, 'Is it high up like this?'

'Oh no, there are only three levels in my house; a basement, the ground floor and the first floor, all connected with steps.' he said, licking some jam off his lower lip.

Liele nodded, 'Hmm, are your cities not large and sprawling in that case?'

'Some of the cities in my time are huge,' said Callison, 'it would take a transport probe quite a while to get about!'

'Does that mean you don't see greenery and wildlife, or the natural landscape?'

'We have parks within the cities, but we still have the natural landscapes as well.' He sipped his tea.

She sounded pleased, 'Oh, that's good, what are they like?'

He was confused, 'What's what like?'

'The natural landscapes.' she enquired.

'Well I've mostly seen it on TV, but there are mountains, valleys, just like here.'

'TV?' she probed as she spooned yoghurt and fruit into her mouth.

He explained, 'Television.' *How best to explain?* 'It's a device, which shows moving pictures of the world around us.' He stopped and thought for a moment.

'Oh, ok.' She poured herself a tea, 'Yes, we have something similar...'

'No, that was wrong.' Callison interrupted on his own thought tact.

A confused look swept over her.

'No. That was the wrong description,' he sounded surprised, 'when you asked what the landscapes were like in my time, I don't know, I'd never been to any of it.' He continued to ponder, 'I've mostly only seen it on TV... I'd never thought about it.' He looked openly frustrated.

'Don't knock yourself for it, try to keep your mind in the now rather than in the past.' she smiled, nodding, 'More tea?'

He took up the offer, continuing to ponder.

Liele spoke as she poured his tea, 'I am used to living in both the city and natural world. It's all about balance.'

He nodded but didn't say anything. He knew that the closest he had ever come to the raw natural world was yesterday just after touchdown here. He soon changed the subject and forgot about the natural world, 'That bread was lovely. Thanks. Could you pass the yoghurt and the fruit?'

They continued eating and talking before Callison brought up the device in his makeshift bedroom, 'So what's the device in the corner of the room I slept in?'

Liele told him, 'You probably mean the holophone; it allows us to communicate visually and remotely. It is what Tobian was doing when we saw him yesterday evening.'

Ever the scientist, Callison asked how the device worked, and Liele sensed his genuine interest and explained it to him the best she could.

'Well, we stand in front of the device and as it scans us, it beams our image to the recipient where they see you in hologram form. You see their hologram form as well.' She didn't know the mechanism, just how to harness it. 'If you want to know how it works ask Tobian, he knows more about these things than I do.' She spoke like she didn't need to know how it worked in order to believe it.

Callison found the future riveting; holograms, flying machines, telekinesis. *Whatever next?* he thought. As soon as they'd finished breakfast they left for the air station.

15.3 –

After breakfast, Callison had re-searched the pile of clothes and found a loosely fitting cream suit jacket with collarless lapels. It hung well on him and had a Japanese feel to it making him feel regal in stature. He contrasted Liele, who still wore her surf style jade body suit but had some white jogging trousers on over the bottom half. The pair would have looked strange together dressed like this in the twenty-first century, and Callison still sensed he looked out of place. Liele's hair was tied back into a ponytail, leaving her gem to take prize place on her forehead.

They left Liele's apartment and to Callison's surprise they took the lift upwards instead of down, to a sky-taxi rank in Liele's skyscraper. They didn't need to wait for their sky-taxi and hopped into one straightaway. Their exclusive sky-taxi had a wrap-over bubble styled window and gave great aerial views of the city. The taxi flight was only a five-minute saunter to the large intercity air-station. The exciting flight to Turuk was still to come.

The sky-taxi dropped them off at the air-station situated in one of the taller skyscrapers of Sukarmia. Liele had given their names to a computer, while Callison stood and watched. The computer gave them tickets and told them which departure lounge to go to and they went to sit down in the waiting area. It would be a fifteen-minute wait for the next plane, which ran like a shuttle bus to and from Turuk ten times a day.

The rows of red seats were not full, but there were other people arriving every few minutes, all assumedly wanting to catch the same plane. Callison noticed that many other people in the waiting area also had gemstones on their foreheads, and seemed to be living their own lives without interest in Callison.

He looked at some more of the other passengers in the terminal. It seemed that in the future, clothing in general was just brighter. The other passengers wore bright yellows and bright blues. Callison liked his cream jacket, which made him feel less obvious.

The rows of seats in the departure lounge sat in a fair sized room that looked out through a large window on to an empty landing pad inside the skyscraper. Above the window a red screen ran text across it, but Callison couldn't understand it. An audible, but fairly quiet low tone buzzed around the room and the large window started to vibrate slightly as a large dark coloured plane hovered into the landing area opposite them. Its three legs already extended, it slowly came to rest on the landing pad across the way and as it touched down, a suspension mechanism in its legs took up the slack of the weight of the aircraft. Its shape reminded Callison of the stealth type aircraft of his generation, sleek and aerodynamic. Callison watched as the sound of its levitation device slowly came to a stop.

While Liele remained seated, he stood up and walked to the window to get a better view of the air-station's runway. He felt like a child again investigating his new world. Pressing his head up to the glass, he looked left and right. The landing area was essentially a large tunnel that ran through the whole skyscraper left to right and had a high ceiling. Incoming aircraft seemed to enter on the left, and taxi through to the correct landing pad before hovering off to the right, and out the other side of the skyscraper. He could count four other planes all waiting at their departure pads. Large overhead lights ran the entire length of the tunnel, and coloured, dotted and dashed lines on the floor showed aircraft where to taxy.

The giant craft that Callison had seen touchdown across the taxying strip started to offload. Hatch style doors opened up at the back and sides of the craft, and passengers walked off into their arrival terminal on the opposite side of the landing strip. Seeing the passengers file into the rooms on the other side of the gangway Callison was reminded of taking holidays and passport control. He realised something. He hadn't shown any form of identification; he could be anybody.

He turned around to see the departure lounge had filled up some more. He went to go and sit next to Liele again.

'See anything interesting out there?' she smiled, as she acknowledged he must feel like a schoolboy in a sweetshop.

He sat down, and stroked his hazel moustache, 'It really is amazing. I'm blown away by it all.'

'Well, just relax. I'll take care of you today.'

He felt relieved, before thinking about how to phrase his next question, 'Do I have to show any identification to take this flight?'

She was confused, 'Identification with what?'

'You know, for security, to show who I am.'

'Why? Are you not sure who you are?' she said, genuinely confused.

'No, I know who *I* am...' He paused, 'or at least I *think* I know who I am, but I mean identification for the authorities so *they* know who I am.'

'No you don't need anything but yourself, what more proof could they want that you are you?'

It was clear to Callison that his point had been lost, so he withdrew, but he found it amusing how Liele thought about it. He was sidetracked pretty quickly by a new humming noise that started to vibrate the window looking onto the landing strip again.

'This will be ours here.' Liele pointed as the plane hovered into view of the window to touchdown just outside. It was lighter in colour and looked even more sleek and streamlined than the last one. It had twin tail fins and swept back main wings with what looked like grey panels down the sides of the fuselage, which turned out to be windows. It looked like it was a double-decked plane from the placement of the grey panels. Their transport manoeuvred its way in to land and a light dust cloud blew up as it came to rest on its legs.

'We have about five minutes before we get on board.' said Liele. A few people got up and started to check bags and belongings.

In each corner of the departure lounge, there were two doors leading out to the landing pad and above each one, some undecipherable text was emitted in red writing and an announcement was made. Before Callison had a chance to ask what they meant Liele had pre-empted it and pointed. She pointed at the left side, 'Baggage,' and then the right side, 'no baggage.' They had no baggage.

After the inbound passengers had disembarked and walked into the arrival gate in the next room down from them, Liele led Callison out of the 'no baggage' exit and onto the landing pad itself. The craft's bay style loading doors were already down as they walked towards the sleek vessel. Liele and Callison boarded the ship via a stepped ramp that folded down from the side of the plane just in front of the leading edge of the wing. She inserted her ticket into a machine just inside the plane and a computer voice called back in a language Callison didn't understand. She got her ticket back and they went to find some seats.

'What did that machine just say to you?' said Callison as they made their way through a small, rather cramped corridor to the seating area.

She spoke as she led the way, 'It was just confirming my Unique Vibration Pattern and told me that I have five hours of plane travel to use if I want. Every citizen of Sukarmia gets a flight allowance of ten hours per year.' She got to the end of the small corridor, where there were two flights of steps, one going to the upper level seating, and one going to the lower level seating. They walked down a small flight of steps to the lower seating area and found some seats facing each other adjacent to a large curved viewing portal. They sat down opposite each other and in-between their seats were reading materials and magazines. Liele started to flick through them.

Callison looked around the red and beige luxury interior of the plane. They were in a compartment of about twenty seats and slowly, other passengers started to file through to the other compartments further down, and some took seats in the same cabin.

'Here, this is the Noi Tu temple we will go and look at in Turuk.' Liele handed Callison a post card sized brochure she had found in one of the reading supplements.

He took the brochure, and although he couldn't understand the text, he could understand the pictures. There was one picture of a pyramid, similar to the one in Sukarmia, and another picture showing a large statue of a man sitting down in the lotus position. 'Looks nice.' Callison said, not knowing what to expect there. He handed the small brochure back to her as the plane filled up with more passengers.

The large portal window next to them gave a great view outside the plane. Another plane had just landed next to theirs and a man ushered the passengers inside to the terminal. Callison felt excitement at the forthcoming flight. He was sitting in one of the machines that yesterday filled him full of wonder when it had shot off into the distance.

Liele smiled at him, knowing he was enjoying the experience, before continuing to read the Noi Tu leaflet.

After they had been seated for about ten minutes, subtle noises started to emanate from deep inside the plane's structure. Then, the sound of hydraulic valves played over the quiet subtle noises. They were closing the doors. The door noise stopped but the quiet tone remained. It was the hum of the anti-gravity engines starting up. The hum increased in pitch and reminded Callison of the sound that the Trebla Eye made as it accelerated its magnetised steam. Suddenly the plane jolted as it started to break gravity's hold and lift off to hover slowly. Callison couldn't help but smile as his body felt the reaction forces of the plane's movement. The engines continued to increase throttle and the craft manoeuvred itself backwards, until it had space to rotate around and started to slowly taxy off towards the exit on the right side of the skyscraper. Callison sat facing Liele with his back facing the direction of motion. His gaze was glued to the view passing by outside the window and after about thirty seconds of slow taxying inside the skyscraper they emerged outside.

'Turuk here we come!' said Liele as the plane slowly started to gain altitude.

Callison looked back towards the large departing skyscraper and the tiny world of Sukarmia far below them. The plane continued to climb until it was higher than all of the skyscrapers he could see. A lot of the skyscrapers had gardens on the roof; Liele said her tower block did also. He looked at the Solus Sea, which wrapped around most of the city of Sukarmia and thought he could see the Noi Tu pyramid on the horizon. 'Is that the...?' he turned to Liele.

She had seen it too, 'Yes, that's the Noi Tu out post where we met Mystera at yesterday.' She had taken flights before, but still the great aerial views weren't wasted on her, and she continued to view with Callison.

As the craft continued to climb, the cliff was revealed in the distance where Callison had seen Liele fly. Callison thought that they were already on route; they were still only taxying. The futuristic aircraft began to rotate round to point in the direction of Turuk and as it did so the view slowly panned around showing the other side of Sukarmia. Two large dark structures that looked like upwardly skewed tall mushrooms caught his eye, 'What are they?' He pointed to the structures, which were similar in size to the tallest of the skyscrapers.

'They are the magneto-electrostatic power stations,' she then clarified, 'they supply electricity to the city.'

'What, you mean you obtain your electricity from the magnetosphere?' he asked overly interested.

'Yes, how did you know?' she sounded surprised.

'Just something I read back in my time, that was all.' He continued to look at the tall mushroom-like power generators thinking about science marvel Nicola Tesla, the man who gave Callison's era AC current, sonar and electromagnetism to name but a few. The story told in scientific circles was that Tesla had always hypothesised that the magnetosphere could provide all the electricity the world would ever need, but when his industrial capitalist investors realised the energy would be hard to distribute and sell, he lost his funding and was branded a crackpot. *Tesla was right after all...* Callison thought. There didn't seem to be much past the electricity towers, 'What is past the electricity station?'

'Mainly farmland crops and grazing land for community sustenance.' she said.

He nodded with interest and continued looking out of the window. The plane continued to climb directly upwards, until it remained still, just hovering. Slowly, another noise started to become apparent. Callison thought it was something to do with the fact that they'd stopped climbing. It was like a small whine to begin with, but it grew to a high-pitched screech and Liele had her eyebrows raised like she was expecting something. Then all of a sudden there was a flash of white light from outside and the noise vanished.

* * * * * * *

16: Financial Interest

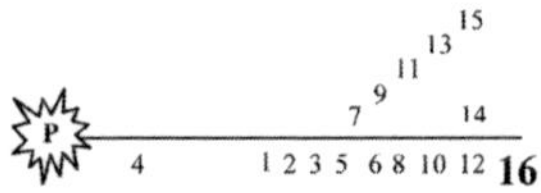

"All money is a matter of belief."
Adam Smith, Economist (1723 – 1790)

16.1 –
Hidden Timeline:
May 16th 2008:

It was the morning after the night before. Last night, Heinrich had powered down and stopped the Eye and his Quanta foot soldiers, all of who were in the dark as to what really happened to Callison and Eleanor, disassembled the structure. They were now reverse engineering and putting it back together again in one of the secret underground laboratories of the Quanta complex.

Heinrich was proud of his work in the basement the night before and sat in his office with his feet up on the desk, speaking into the phone to the private investors of the Eye project. He was in a buoyant mood. 'We have retrieved our invention and are now in the possession of the portal once more!' Heinrich said, smiling like a Cheshire cat.

The anonymous voice associated with the codename; Harold, emanated from the earpiece. He sounded pleased also, 'Good, and did you see it open last night?'

He affirmed, 'Yes. It was amazing, you should have seen it, as soon as the propellant reached light speed it just opened up,' he still shook his head in astonishment, 'it looked like brightly coloured light behaving like a calming liquid.' He opted not to tell them about Callison and Eleanor.

The voice came through the earpiece again, 'Can we come to view it?'

'Yes, it should be functioning again this afternoon, you can come by this evening if you like, it will be quieter and more discreet.' Heinrich knew the investors liked discretion from previous meetings, and having money gave you secrecy should one wish it.

'Yes, that sounds good...'

The line sounded like it went dead, 'Hello?' he searched.

A few seconds passed and the voice of the investor came back on the line; Heinrich wasn't expecting the words he heard next, 'There's something you need to know about the Eye.'

'Oh?' he questioned.

'It's not a time machine.' said the voice.

'Ok.' he said, confused and intrigued, 'What makes you think that?'

'We'll talk about it this evening after we see the open portal. See you at ten pm Heinrich.' said the voice, before the line went dead.

The Quanta executive hung up the phone and stared at his wall, wondering what the investors might know.

* * * * * * *

17: The Tourist

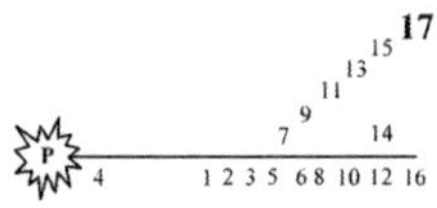

"It is better to travel well than to arrive."
The Buddha (563BC – 483BC)

17.1 –
Date not known:
Plus one day:

'What was...' He was just about to ask about the white flash outside the plane before he realised they were already moving at a tremendous rate, 'Wow!' He peered out of the viewing portal to see greenery moving below them many times faster than he could have even dreamt of imagining it. Their velocity was so great that the landscape below was actually hard to see, it was nearly a blur. His scientific side yearned answers, 'How? I didn't feel any acceleration forces, how can this be happening?' Just seconds ago they had been stationary and hovering above Sukarmia.

Liele explained, 'It's a warp drive; it bends the Zero Point Field in front of the craft, and repels it behind. There is no inertia, because we are not moving, the space around the plane is.'

'Now that's neat.' He smiled as he looked back out of the window, 'How fast are we going?' he asked, while his gaze remained outside the craft.

'Oh about M14 or 15 probably.' she said back.

He looked back at her, 'You mean fourteen or fifteen times the speed of sound?'

She affirmed his question and he looked back out of the window in speechless excitement.

Liele was intrigued, 'How fast do the planes from your time travel?'

He answered as he watched the view flying by, 'Not even M1 on passenger flights, but there are some stealth planes that will do M3.'

'Stealth? You mean planes that take things?'

He turned to face Liele again, 'Well, sort of. They are spy planes that fly very high over land to check for possible security threats. They take information, I guess.'

As much as Callison didn't fully grasp Liele's world, Liele didn't fully grasp Callison's. *Stealth planes?* she thought more. She was confused, 'What is your world like? It sounds paranoid to need stealth planes.' She was thinking aloud rather than criticising.

Callison believed his words, 'Believe me in my world there are threats everywhere. There have been all sorts of horrible events like terrorism attacks, wars, and murders. Sukarmia is a nicer place to live, trust me!' he cajoled.

Liele probed more, 'What do the events of your world tell you?' she was learning as well as Callison.

Callison paused. He wasn't expecting the question, 'What do you mean?' he said out of routine, before offering an answer, 'That there are a lot of greedy psychos out there?'

Liele spoke with knowledge on the subject, 'The events in all collective worlds are the physical reflections of the collective mind state. It's one of the universal laws; the minds build the physical experience.'

'I don't understand, what does that mean?' he asked.

She gave her understanding of the law, 'If you don't like your world, then change your mind, because your mind is creating your world.' It drew a blank look from Callison, so she rephrased, 'All I'm saying is that if you think your world shapes your mind, there is no way for your mind to shape your world.'

'Really?' He had never thought about the subject.

Liele smiled, 'I'll let it sink in.' She had planted one of the many seeds in his mind and reverted to the original speed discussion, 'So I guess M15 is quite quick for you then?'

He was taken back to his immediate surroundings, 'Oh yes,' he said, still thinking about the collective ideas, 'It's very impressive.'

She was happy that he was happy.

He continued to look at the green blur whizzing by below for a few minutes thinking about cause and effect and whether thoughts were reflections of observations or something more. His attention was drawn back into the cabin and he prompted Liele, 'Tell me more about how Sukarmia functions.'

17.2 –

A red light started to flash above the viewing portal after they had been travelling in the futuristic craft for about half an hour. Callison looked to Liele for its meaning.

She explained, 'It means we will be exiting hyperspace shortly, just stay seated for now.'

He acknowledged and looked back out of the window again. The land was still passing below at the same rate it was when the craft had started its space-time trick. He thought about how far they had travelled and started a sum in his head; the speed of sound, *about 730 miles per hour*, he thought about their speed, *M15*; and approximation later, *we're travelling at 11,000 miles per hour. It's been about half an hour, so we've travelled about five and a half thousand miles...*

Suddenly there was a flash of light outside the window just like the one he'd questioned when they started, which stopped him in his thought and the craft was stationary. He found it amazing that they felt no inertia shock when the plane came to rest; it broke all of the laws of physics he knew, but obviously not the ones he didn't.

Now hovering high above the city of Turuk, all that could be heard were the engines keeping them in the air. Callison witnessed the new surroundings, and the new city out of the portal. Turuk had its own system of interconnected skyscrapers, which were similar in height to the Sukarmian ones, but they were styled differently, they were thinner and had orb shapes moulded into them. It looked to be a less concentrated city than Sukarmia and had a feeling of open space about it. There was a pyramid set back from the skyscrapers and a river ran through the metropolis out to a sea a few miles away. The plane slowly started its descent into Turuk.

'We'll be down soon.' said Liele.

Callison acknowledged, maintaining his gaze out of the window.

The information Liele had given him during the flight about the inner workings of life in Sukarmia had intrigued him. He couldn't help but be fascinated and amazed at how simple Sukarmia's system was, as were the systems of all of the cities on this future globe he walked on. It relied on service to others, rather than a credit or finance system; there was no money, just a willingness to work for the whole. The people *were* the resource.

People in Sukarmia, from the ages of three until twenty, were educated in very open and encouraging schools operated by many teachers. These schools equipped the students with resilience, and a knowing of what happiness and sadness is and how they are realised. From a young age they were encouraged to daydream, and think about issues of morality, and what the correct thing to do is. They were all taught the differences between the senses and the self, the mind and the experience. A child stayed in the same class for all seventeen years, being taught with the older students when young, and being taught with the young students when mature. The only compulsory part was group meditation; other taught lessons were undertaken on the bequest of the student, and ranged from play, to counting and speaking, to quantum mechanics and structural telekinesis, to art and expression. Nothing was off the table for the students.

Upon graduation at twenty years old, the student emerged into the service environment. Here, they worked for two days in every seven, until they were sixty years old, doing collective service work. These two days of work per week provided the system with the manpower it needed to function. In return, the worker was then entitled to live in the city and make use of all its services. If a worker started to acquire a higher than average work rate, they would be encouraged to take some time off and if they were slack, and didn't do enough they were encouraged to work. If no effort was made to give to the community they started to lose their privileges, but that didn't happen often from what Liele told him, and in the instances where it did, the citizens realised and started to give again. For the other five days of the week, Sukarmian citizens were left to their own selves to know themselves by relaxing and engaging in hobbies and interests in the pursuit of developing a resilient and satisfied peaceful spirit.

'The Collective', comprised of twenty-four annually elected proven problem solvers, acted like a steering committee that arranged manpower to maintain the city's systems, which was calculated by supercomputers based on past efficiency statistics. Systems of waste management, the food supply, building and construction, energy delivery, transportation and education all fell under the jurisdiction of The Collective.

This group of twenty-four also listened to citizens about their interests and desires and supervised the running and management of the recreation buildings in and around the city. The recreation buildings provided the citizens with a set of hubs to discover new interests and desires. They utilised 'Altrovision Simulation Interfaces' to allow the observer simulations of the desired sport or situation, like a virtual reality. Then, if the observer was serious about the interest, the recreation staff could organise lessons and visits to places where the desired activity was taught. The activity was taught not by people doing their service work, but by people who enjoyed teaching their passion during their five days off. The

Sukarmian system sounded like it all worked beautifully. Callison found it hard to believe, but his mind had been trained to notice differences and problems, rather than similarities and solutions.

Since exiting hyperspace, the plane continued to hover down to make a landing in Turuk, and Callison was guessing where it was going to go. He could see the pyramid more clearly, and could make out the large statue of the man sitting in the lotus position near by. Gardens ran from the pyramid to the start of the city. He could count eight interconnected skyscrapers that dotted down the banks of the wide main river. Each one had orb like bulges in them, and they reminded Callison of skewered barbeque food. On the ground, the city was fairly developed, with many smaller tower blocks about a third of the height of the skyscrapers making up most of the city's skyline. Turuk seemed to follow the river for maybe two miles, before dissipating back into the greenery again. It was like these futuristic cities were man made islands in a sea of green undergrowth.

The plane hovered in close to one of the main eight skyscrapers. It was a very light coloured skyscraper that had an opening on the side of one of its circular bulges that resembled a giant letterbox slot. Lights could be seen inside the opening and as they approached further it was clear to Callison that this was their destination. The plane throttled back as they entered the orb and they found themselves in another tunnel-like taxying strip where they would disembark the vessel.

'Welcome to Turuk!' said Liele, as the plane touched down in its parking bay outside the arrival hall.

Callison was still excited about the whole experience, 'Why thank you. It was a very pleasant trip.'

After filing out of the arrival lounge they took an elevator from the airport in the sky to the next orb bulge down in the skyscraper, where a sky-taxi rank was housed. The sky-taxi followed the roads in the sky over Turuk at a lower altitude than the planes. The taxi was exactly the same type as they had taken in Sukarmia, which showed Callison that the technology was common between cities, like they worked together rather than in competition against one another. The driverless craft took Callison and Liele out over the river and over some of the shorter tower blocks, still in themselves tall for twenty-first century standards, and onto the Turuk Noi Tu complex. The weather was beautiful, with only a few light wispy clouds breaking up the brilliant blue sky. It dropped them off at a sky-taxi point in the green open gardens surrounding the Noi Tu pyramid, where the air smelt of freshly cut grass. The skyscrapers of Turuk could be seen clearly towering over the green backdrop to their location.

The pair walked through the picturesque gardens surrounding the Noi Tu pyramid talking about their respective worlds. The casually smart loose suit jacket that he wore clashed with the bright jade coloured surf top that Liele wore, but no one seemed to raise any eyebrows. She locked her arm around Callison's as they walked and talked.

Liele told Callison more about Noi Tu. It was a way of finding out the art of living and had been on the planet for five thousand years. Every large city or town had a Noi Tu team that could speak to and meet with beings on higher planes that showed themselves on this one as holographic figures of light. The Engineers he was to meet tomorrow with Mystera would show themselves as white light, Liele said. Callison thought about ghosts, and became anxious about meeting with them, but Liele assured him there was nothing to worry about.

Liele had graduated from the Sukarmian school system ten years ago with interests in self-development of spirit and service, and teaching. After two years of doing her collective service work for the energy department and the waste dematerialisation department she was offered the chance to do her collective work at one of the schools. Since then she had divided her time up, so she taught one day a week, and worked for the city one day a week in the energy department, but she could be posted into any sector if there were shortages.

With her five days off per week she was interested in walking, hiking and exploring so went on many group hikes to see wonderful scenery. She was a keen survivalist, and could live off the jungle should she need to. In the last three years she had become interested in devoting more of her time to the Noi Tu discipline and furthering herself as soul.

They continued walking the green gardens along a walkway around the pyramid, as two skimmer jets slowly buzzed past. Callison gave Liele a potted history of his society and she found the concept of money to be unfair, especially when he told her which professions earned what. She asked the logical and obvious, 'If your community needs more money, why don't you just make more?' Callison told her about inflation, and the dangers of inflating a currency, and supply and demand, but Liele sensed that he didn't really know what he was talking about. He was no different from anyone else in his time; drowning in paradoxical financial terms, definitions and contradictions.

When Callison explained about the number of corporations offering services and products in his era she got confused again. She didn't understand why ten different organisations needed to compete to make one type of product. Even without talking about war, poverty, terrorism, global warming and corruption, Liele got the impression life in Callison's age was a hard graft. However, when Callison told Liele about his son, his wife, his friends and pleasant experiences she started to realise that life in Callison's time could be extremely rewarding upon success and taught the people to believe in themselves.

After walking one lap of the Turuk pyramid, they walked through a large open field to the statue of the seated man assuming the lotus position. A selection of other people milled about at food stands and drink bars and there was a small market in the corner of the field. Children played balancing games and their laughter was carried on the breeze.

'Ok, are you hungry?' said Liele, 'I think we should get some food here and then head over to the Techno Recreation Centre?'

The walking had worked off his breakfast, 'Sounds good to me.' he said, as he continued to think about the systems of this futuristic race. But he felt he was still missing something integral to his understanding, it tugged at his mind and no matter how many questions he asked, the mental itch was never completely satisfied.

17.3 –

Callison followed Liele into the sky taxi and sat down next to her. 'So how far away is it, this techno centre?'

'Not far,' she said, 'it's fairly close to the air station we arrived here at.'

The Technological Recreation Centre was a five-minute sky-taxi journey away. Their taxi hovered back over the outskirts of the city before descending down into the city centre area near the river at the base of the inter-connected skyscrapers.

After they got out Callison wondered where they were going, 'Where to now then?'

She pointed upwards, 'In there.'

He gazed skywards to see one of the globular spheres in the skyscraper they found themselves under. It was filtering the sun from the sky like a man-made eclipse, and had an adjoining walkway through to the neighbouring globular tower. They were on a fairly busy and wide, pavement inbetween the river and the grid line with other people who walked about oblivious to the time traveller and his guide. The numerous transport probes running along the Turukian grid looked different from the Sukarmian ones in colour and shape, but they still made the same whistling noise. The propulsion technology he guessed was the same.

'We'll cross the river at the bridge further up,' said Liele, 'are you excited?'

'I'm not really sure what to expect,' he said, 'but yes, I am excited as well.' He smiled before following her up over the bridge and across the river. The entrance to the skyscraper was a fifty-yard walk along a path through some more well-kept lawns. Looking above him only revealed the bulge of the first globe of the skyscraper; it made the walk towards the entrance a shady one.

Once inside the large lobby of the building, they took one of the elevators to the first of the skyscraper's bulges on the 50th floor, where the door of the lift opened and revealed what Callison could only call a shopping mall. They walked out into an open plan floor area with stalls around the periphery, and on the inside was a drinks bar and food outlet. A steady flow of visitors circled the stalls, talking to the stand owners.

'So what exactly is this? It looks like an exhibition?'

Liele explained as she led Callison towards the back, 'The place I want to take you to is at the back over here,' she pointed ahead of her as she spoke, 'the stands and stalls around the outside are for hobbyists and enthusiasts. They offer courses and experiences for people looking to learn new recreation activities.'

The idea sounded quite good, 'With a technological feel to them?'

'You guessed it!' said Liele as she continued to walk through the crowd to the other side of the hall.

Callison followed, slowly losing Liele in the flow of other people. He was looking at the stands and stalls as he walked. There were stands with all sorts of hobbies and crafts on offer, from robot building to plane acrobatics and from skydiving to scuba diving. He kept walking until he made eye contact with one of the stand owners not engrossed in conversation, who looked set to collar him. Callison was hesitant to speak with the man, feeling like he couldn't communicate with the future people apart from through English. Despite his best efforts to avoid the man, the hobbyist managed to get him. He spoke in some strange language that put Callison on the spot and Liele was not in earshot.

Boldly, and knowing that the man might understand the feeling behind his words, Callison spoke back fairly slowly in

English, 'I'm sorry; I'm not from here. I don't understand you.' and to Callison's surprise, the man withdrew. *Did he understand me?* he thought.

The man leant over behind him, pulled a leaflet off a rack and handed it to Callison.

'Thanks.' said Callison before walking on to catch up with Liele. The stand owner waved his pleasant but strange-speaking customer off.

'Sorry, I got stopped by a man offering a hobby.' Callison said as he caught up with Liele, who was waiting outside an entrance for him.

'Oh, ok. What was the hobby?' she asked.

'I don't know, but the man gave me this leaflet.' He pulled it out and handed it to her. 'I can't decipher the writing, but there is a diagram.' He concluded.

She scanned the piece of paper, 'This is a leaflet from the Collective, offering courses in holography.'

'Oh, I thought it might have meant something, the man looked like he wanted me to have it.' It would mean something in the future, but for now he folded it up and put it in his pocket, oblivious. 'What's this place then?' he said as he inspected the building front.

Above the wide entrance Liele stood outside, was a purple and black sign. Liele informed him, 'This is where I wanted to take you, the Technological Recreation Centre. They have pre-programmed ASI simulations here, which I thought you would enjoy.'

'Simulation?' he questioned.

Liele informed him. 'An ASI, is the Altrovision Simulation Interface, it is a device that let's you create mental simulations from thought inputs.' Liele explained that it worked with the third eye and the creation centres of the brain, allowing one to play games, make and test ideas, hone thought inputs for better simulation resolution, experience dreams and imagination, meet friends and colleagues. Nearly everybody utilised the technology to improve one's thought patterns, but today Callison would experience it just for fun.

'Right well, I'm ready when you are.' he said.

Upon entering the centre, Liele spoke to a girl behind a checkout styled counter. The girl made Callison fill out a form of preferences, with which Liele assisted in translation. The form related to the type of experience he wanted to have; fast, slow, scary, safe, delicate, powerful and the like. Upon handing the form in, they were led into a booth with an ASI device and screen and in the middle of the booth was a couch, facing the screen. The woman who was behind the counter was now configuring the device to display suitable matches to his choice preference form. Callison took a seat on the couch in front of the main screen and Liele took a seat on the side of the room.

The first screen popped up and it was a picture of a plane flying, 'Flying experience?' translated Liele.

Callison shook his head, 'Already done that! What else?'

The next match popped onto the screen. A picture of what looked like a racing car came up on the screen. It intrigued him, 'Yes, that one please.'

'A hover race?' checked Liele.

He nodded. Motor racing had always been his passion. *Hover racing wouldn't be far behind, surely*, he thought.

The woman put a visor over his eyes, taking his vision away, which had an attachment that he could feel pressing into his forehead, Liele told him what was going to happen, as he looked at the backs of his visor. 'They have created the messages for you in English, just follow the green text and enjoy.'

He didn't really know what she meant, but he took the information on board as he leant back in the couch and waited for the simulation to start. He saw nothing until the ASI powered up, instantly catapulting his awareness into another world. The sensation frightened him somewhat to start with and felt like he was falling backwards for a moment, but after his fright ended, he came around again and was faced with a completely different scene to the booth. Liele was gone and he found himself in a vast underground cavern and in front of him sat a hover racer, floating on a cushion of air in front of him.

Was this an illusion? Or reality? thought Callison, as he moved towards the racer. He was seemingly in the body of another man, and had input as to where the man walked and did, just by 'being' the man. He crouched down and felt the floor and it felt as real as a real floor. He pinched the body he was in, and felt the shot of pain. *Was this actually real?* he questioned again, as he held out the hands he had in front of him. They definitely weren't his hands.

Suddenly some green text flashed in front of his gaze: "Get into your craft Callison." It stayed for a couple of seconds before disappearing again. He walked to stand next to the tall hover-racer craft and felt the warm wind gushing up from the underneath the machine. The engines were running, and they hummed smoothly. The rear section was swept back and looked aerodynamic.

He paid attention to the rest of his simulated surroundings and it looked like he was in the pit lane of an underground racing circuit. Suddenly two hover racers emerged from a tunnel and flashed past on the main straight and barrelled into the first corner, which arced upwards and to the right before entering the underground tunnel again and completing another circuit. They were travelling fast.

The ladder into his craft flashed green, which looked odd for his mind, but this was a simulation; *not reality* he thought.

He heard Liele's voice like an echo throughout everything. 'Follow the green items and text.' She could see his world by observing the screen in the booth.

The green text appearing in front of him again directed him into the cockpit of the racer, and gave him a tutorial on the controls. The effect was so real; the cockpit even had a smell of oil and grease. The view from the deep racing seat was expansive, having a see-through front module that showed the space above and below the craft as well as the oncoming racetrack in front of him. He had a steering wheel, and some foot controls that operated the power, and braking, much like a motorcar from his generation. Green text flashed across his view again: "Slowly increase power and steer round the track. Watch out for other racers in your racer radar and in your mirrors." The mirrors and the racer radar instrument flashed green as part of the continued tutorial. Then the text disappeared.

The assistant left the ASI booth, and Liele remained, watching on the screen. Callison's body moved and twitched on the couch as he experienced the hover racer in his mind. She knew it was normal and excitedly watched his progress.

Slowly and tentatively, Callison increased the throttle and the hover racer moved forward. Steering to the right, he checked his mirrors and his racer radar and there was no traffic. He increased power and joined the circuit and as he did so, the computer traced his progress and gave a track layout display so he knew what bends were approaching. The first corner was a fast upward right-hander at the end of the pit straight, which entered the underground tunnel. Once in the tunnel, the track levelled out before entering a downhill section that led into a fast left-hander. The tunnel continued onto a long straight, where he thought he was travelling quickly. Suddenly a beep emanated from the control console. It was the racer radar. He stayed to the left, like the tutorial had told him to and he didn't even have time to see the other craft in the mirrors; it flew by at an immense speed. It gave Callison the confidence to go faster and after a few more underground corners he emerged into an open underground void again and the start finish straight. He flew by where he started from and went into the first right-hander of the lap for the second time. Slowly but surely the lap times began to fall.

The craft had immense acceleration, and felt heavy to manoeuvre round the corners, which meant lots of braking beforehand. As he barrelled into and out of the corners, he could feel the G-forces pulling his simulated body left and right thought the bends, up and down over the undulations and forwards and backwards under acceleration and braking.

After about twenty laps, he started to feel tired, and so came into the pits to check if everything was still ok. He slowly brought the hover racer to a stop, and realised his simulated body had been sweating. He thought to himself, *Was the sweat part of the simulation? Or was he actually sweating?* He found the hover-racer experience immensely fun, but not being aware of the true reality felt alien and some of him pitted to check that his *real* reality was still intact. He pressed the green button on the hover racer's dashboard to abort the simulation, and after the falling backwards sensation, came around in the booth again and took his visor off. He was slightly damp from sweat, but Liele was there.

'Hey. How did you find it? Fun?' She dabbed his forehead with a tissue.

'Yeah, it was really fun. It felt so real!' He sat up and checked his hands again. They were his hands and reality was still intact to his relief.

She handed him the tissue. 'That's because your experience *was* real, your brain was entrained to tell you that you were in a craft, racing round a track instead of here in the booth with a visor over your head.'

'It was kind of hard to tell between the ASI simulation and real life!' said Callison.

A smile emanated across Liele's face, 'It's quite uncanny isn't it, when you experience it for the first time...'

Callison agreed, 'So what would happen if I smashed the craft? Would I get injured?'

Liele shook her head, 'No, you would have the option to wake up into the booth, or start the simulation again.'

Callison wanted to immerse himself in to simulation again, 'Can I do some more?'

'Yes, of course you can!' ushered Liele.

'Well, visor me up!' he said enthusiastically, before falling backwards into the illusion again. He had no real idea of how it all worked, but it didn't detract one iota of his enjoyment.

When it did eventually come time to leave, Liele became concerned with the time; they had been so engrossed in the ASI experience they had lost track and would miss their return flight to Sukarmia. 'We're not going to be able to catch the plane and see Tobian,' said Liele as they walked out of the futuristic ASI arcade.

Callison felt guilt and became concerned, but he was the tourist and had nothing to add.

Liele continued, 'which means we're going to have to get back to Sukarmia the boring way, sorry.'

* * * * * * *

18: The Truth Embargo

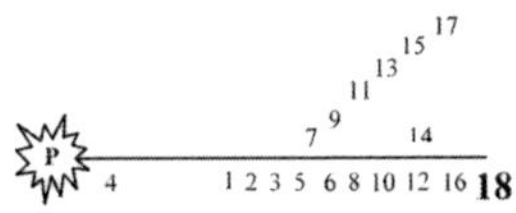

"The very word secrecy is repugnant in a free and open society; and we are, as a people, inherently and historically opposed to secret societies, to secret oaths and to secret proceedings."
John F. Kennedy, 35th American President (1917 – 1963)

18.1 –
Hidden Timeline:
May 16th 2008:

Heinrich stood in the main reception of the Quanta Research Corporation, with five empty tumblers and a bottle of special reserve whisky, on orders of the main investor. It was five minutes to ten in the evening and the security gate had just advised him of two limousines headed his way. The reception lights were on night setting, as the building had powered down and closed up for the night but there was still enough light to see the room. Car headlights approaching broke the darkness outside the giant main reception windows as they circled around the entrance loop to stop outside.

As Heinrich made his way through the tinted glass revolving door to greet his guests, the suited driver of each limousine got out and proceeded to open the rear doors of their cars. Two men in black coats got out of each car and congregated together. One man who used a walking cane left the congregation and walked towards the entrance. His name was Baron Braithwaite III.

'Hello,' said Heinrich, as he waited by the revolving doorway. This was the man known as "Harold" over the phone.

'Hello Heinrich, a pleasure as always.' said the elder statesman with a croaky Etonian accent. His weathered and pale face was partially covered by some large sludge brown dark framed glasses. As he neared Heinrich, Baron Braithwaite III held out his non cane-holding hand and the pair shook.

'I have brought some others with me,' said the Baron just outside the main Quanta entrance, gesturing to the others, 'now you may well know one of the faces you see, but discretion is of the highest order tonight, you remember your oath?'

Heinrich nodded. They were both members of a secret society that helped Heinrich climb the Quanta career ladder and he had taken an oath of secrecy upon initiation to the elite club. This was as much a meeting of master and student than it was business.

'We trust you with this, don't let us down.' said the Baron; his words vibrating with the threat of death.

Heinrich nodded again, 'You can trust me.' He yearned acceptance from the brotherhood.

Baron Braithwaite III smiled, 'Good.' He ushered the other three men forward, and they began to walk towards the entrance. 'Is the device ready?' said the statesman to Heinrich as the acquaintances walked towards them.

Heinrich hadn't let him down, 'Yes, it is ready.' The device had already been running in the afternoon and it was poised to go again.

The statesman expected the answer he got and nodded acceptingly, 'Good, I think the men are keen to see it.' said the Baron as the entourage approached. The two limousines quietly drove off to park and waited for their request again.

The other men, all wearing exclusively expensive suits were introduced to Heinrich by Baron Braithwaite III, 'This is Miles Goldman, he's into banking,' By saying he was into banking was to mean he owned all the circulated money in the country. He looked to be the youngest of the foursome but was still mid fifties in appearance. With his slick black hair, he was a city man through and through.

'Hi,' said Miles, as he shook hands with the Quanta chief executive. Heinrich reciprocated.

'...and this is Anthony Van Der Hayder, you may know him by sight, but he's much warmer in person,' the Baron joked, as he introduced. Heinrich knew him straight away; he owned the monopoly of television networks throughout the world; this was a *big* world player. He was in his seventies and he was composed in nature, with greying hair. His cheeks drooped and his grey eyes lacked emotion in their weathered sockets.

They shook hands, 'Hi.' said Heinrich, not really sure of how to act in front of such power.

The media mogul, acknowledged with a nod, but remained quiet and blank faced.

'...and finally, this is Andrew Anderton, the head of MI5.' Heinrich shook his hand also. He was the shortest person in the foursome, and his puffy red cheeks showed years of accumulated stress and alcohol addiction.

'Hello.' said the MI5 chief.

'A pleasure.' said Heinrich, smiling to impress.

It was clear the four men were in jovial spirits about the Eye standing up in the main laboratory and they were eager to see it.

'Right then Heinrich, lead the way!' said Baron Braithwaite III.

Heinrich led the men into the reception area and pressed a button on the underside of the reception desk, remotely locking the entrance doors. 'A drink?' he said gesturing to the tumbler glasses ready and waiting on the desk. His guests all accepted and he poured them each a glass of the special reserve Scotch.

'It's this way.' he said and they began to navigate the network of corridors and security-coded doors that led to the underground laboratory, where the Eye was situated. As they walked, motion detectors sensed their movement and illuminated their path with overhead lighting. Normally alcohol was not permitted in the building, but this evening the investors could do whatever they liked, they paid the bills after all. The five suited men came to a lift, which they all got into and travelled towards an underground top-secret laboratory.

'What makes you think the device is not a time portal then?' asked Heinrich with intrigue as he pushed the security cleared buttons on the lift.

'Just a hunch,' said Baron Braithwaite III, 'when we see the device in operation, then we'll know for sure and then we can discuss the future.'

The lift started its descent into the bowels of the Quanta complex.

'So what happened last night, how did you get the device back here?' asked the banker, Miles Goldman.

'It went smoothly. No loose ends.' he replied to the banker as he stood nearest the lift door. He faced the Baron again, 'I have to say thank you for the ID badge as well; I needed to show it to a couple of cops that called round.' The men smiled, they *were* the law.

'You have Mr Anderton to thank for that one.' said the Baron.

The MI5 agent acknowledged, 'You're welcome,' and asked back of Heinrich, 'What about Callison? Will he be in a position to threaten the project?' It was his job to be suspicious.

The Quanta man assured them sarcastically, 'Unfortunately he and his wife were involved in a fatal road traffic accident last night.' Heinrich smiled at the men, knowing it would gain him acceptance.

The powerful men smiled. They were glad Callison wasn't around and they could trust this useful idiot.

The lift came to a halt four floors underground and the doors in front of them parted ways. They opened directly into the laboratory, introducing the investors to the magnificent Eye standing up in its frame in the middle of the lab. The four power mongers simultaneously smiled like Cheshire cats.

There were lights on in the lab, but it was empty and the majority of light shone directly onto the metallic doughnut caught in the web of steel framework. It was taller than all of the men by some margin, and towered over them, almost staring back at the men.

'It looks magnificent!' said Baron Braithwaite III, looking on. He saw to the right of the device was a moveable desk on wheels with a computer screen glowing with power. 'Is it ready to go?' he added.

Heinrich grinned, nodding, 'Yes, shall we?' He walked up to the computer and took over with great pride.

The other investors agreed and looked on with eager anticipation, sitting on laboratory stools.

The computer system was already on. Heinrich had downloaded all the software from Callison's computer onto this one, and he accessed the correct programmes to open up the CCU control panel window.

The computer did a check of the pressures and seals and Heinrich assumed this to be enough. The pressure check returned a green 'go' symbol, telling him that the pressures were fine. A low hum reverberated around the laboratory as the inner and outer magnets were powered up.

The investors remained quiet in what would be a crescendo of anticipation.

Heinrich had pre-prepared the Eye so the internal vacuum inside the circular tunnel was already in place; all he had to do was introduce the magnetised steam. Peter Montague's black box whirred into life, boiling off and magnetising 0.893 grams of water and piped it into the eye through the inlet valve. The steam touched no internal surfaces, sitting on the centreline of the tunnel like futuristic plasma.

He opened the steam distribution window on his computer monitor to display the steam distribution within the Eye and all looked good. He felt relieved; a cock up in front of the investors now would cost him dear. He used Callison's own notebook to power the Eye all the way to light speed without even a hiccup of mal-distribution, until for the second time today, the Eye opened up its doorway of light, just like it had done the night previously in Callison's basement.

The five men sat bathing in the multi-coloured light of the portal, as the colours came and went, intermingling with and mixing with other colours, like a giant kaleidoscope of light.

They had not witnessed for long before Baron Braithwaite III piped up. He spoke to the rest of his cohorts; 'I think we've found it gentlemen, after all these years we've finally found it again!' he smiled broadly, as did the other men.

* * * * * * *

17: The Tourist Continued...

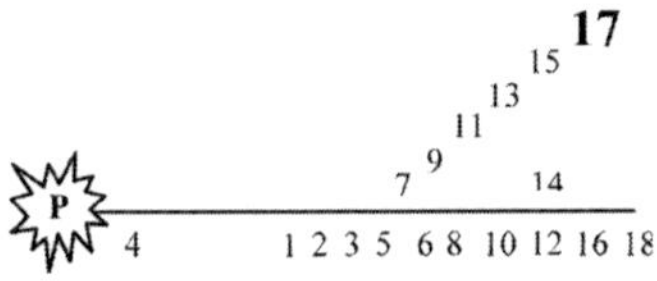

17.4 –
Date not known:
Plus one day:

The boring way back to Sukarmia, although brief proved not to be so boring for Callison and tied his head in knots. After walking out of the ASI centre back into the 'hobby market', Liele had taken her headband off and placed it on the floor in front of them.

'Look at the lens.' she asked.

As Callison stared at the lens of the headband on the floor, it flashed like a camera and before he could get his bearings, he realised they weren't in the hobby hall of Turuk anymore. They were in the sky-taxi terminal again in Liele's tower block of Sukarmia again and Callison felt like he had witnessed a trick or an illusion take place. Turuk was nowhere to be observed as if they had teleported instantly.

'How the...' pleaded Callison as he gasped for meaning looking around him, 'Was that a teleport?'

Liele leant down and picked her headband up off of the now Sukarmian floor. 'Yes, it's kind of boring, but we were in a rush.' She put the teleporting headband back on her head. 'We'll get a sky-taxi to the telekinetic arena.'

His new surroundings seemed to be just as real as the Sukarmia he left in the morning and the sky-taxis came and went just like before, but it made Callison question whether he had actually been to Turuk, or whether he had dreamt it. There were different laws here, different allowances of science so it would seem. They walked from the point they had materialised and Callison asked why they didn't just teleport directly to the Telekinetic Arena. The answer he got, he didn't expect.

She told him as a sky-taxi hovered into place for them, 'We can only teleport to where we have already been in the day. This is the closest to the Telekinetic Arena because it's just a sky-taxi away. The teleport works with your day's memory and is more of a go-back than a go-anywhere tool.'

The futuristic environment he found himself in was starting to feel more like a dream than reality, but given the strange and wonderful things he had seen over his last day here, he allowed the feeling to go just as easily as it had come and followed Liele into the waiting sky-taxi.

The sky-taxi they hopped into hovered its way out over Sukarmia and strangely, Callison felt at home upon seeing the Solus Sea and the city of Sukarmia below him once more. It was like Sukarmia was more his home than Turuk, even though neither were really his home.

They had teleported back to Sukarmia as the sun approached the horizon and the clear sky was now rapidly turning into a pink shade of dusk. The sky-taxi zeroed in to the top of a skyscraper where a stadium was situated and the floodlights emanating from the structure leaked into the sky, adding to Callison's anticipation of the telekinetic show. They were dropped off and walked into one of the many turnstile entrances dotted down the busy drop off strip and into the stadium's large foyer area. Other spectators slowly filed through to the seating areas as Liele and Callison made their way in.

Liele remotely sent a transmission to her brother, Hey Tobi, we have arrived. Are you about? Or are you busy?

She waited for a reply, as Callison spoke, 'Are you hungry? I could do with some food.'

Tobian had received and transmitted back, I am busy at the moment. I'll see you after the show. It's a busy one tonight! Mum and Dad have some seats saved for you.

Liele agreed with Callison, 'Yes me too, we'll get some food up the hallway on the right.' said Liele to Callison before telepathically broadcasting again. Ok, I'll look forward to it, good luck Tobi!

They started to walk away from the entrance foyer and down the right hallway, where there were stairways that periodically disappeared up to the left, leading into the stadium's seating areas. On the right side wall of the corridor were small food outlets. Liele contacted her parents as she walked.

Hello, whereabouts are you guys seated? Callison and myself are getting something to eat and then we'll be in.

'Shall we get some food here?' asked Callison, pointing to one of the passing food stands, oblivious to the telepathy taking place.

Liele's mother broadcast in reply, We are up on the right side, sector 5, row 17, seats 14, 15, 16 and 17. See you soon dear. We hope you had a good day.

'Yeah, ok, we'll get some food here,' said Liele, 'my parents are seated in one of the sectors further up this hallway and they have some seats saved for us.' Other spectators made there way up the corridor, as traveller and guide waited on the right in a short food queue.

Liele continued the conversation with her mother, Day was good, thanks. Do you want any food?

No, we've eaten, but could you bring some bottles of crystal water? Thanks.

Liele spoke to Callison, 'Have to get my parents some crystal water. Don't let me forget.'

After getting some food and drink, they made their way to the steps leading up to sector 5 of the Telekinetic Arena. Upon ascending the steps, a panoramic view of the open-air stadium was revealed. The floodlights cast their light onto a flat grassy area that was surrounded by three banks of spectator seating and roofing, making a triangle shaped pitch. It reminded him of a baseball stadium, although hitting it out of the park in this stadium would see the ball drop a long way down to the floor below them. The noise of the crowd's burble was adding to the anticipation of the show, starting in ten minutes. He guessed there were about 30,000 people in the arena.

A thought occurred to him as they made their way to their seats; nowhere in the stadium could he see any adverts. As the thought sunk in, he realised he had seen no adverts all day, which he found strange, but funny that he hadn't realised it. The non-commercial feeling was refreshing, and gave a sense of freedom.

He looked at the deep pink sky posing as a roof overhead; it was peaceful. The white glow of the stadium's floodlight merging with the pink sky accentuated the sense of tranquillity. It *looked* like a futuristic sky. He still couldn't believe he was the first time traveller, and smiled to himself.

Liele found her parents seated and she and Callison joined them. Liele sat next to her mother, and Callison sat next to Liele on the end seat of the row next to the aisle way. They briefly spoke in their Sukarmian language, before Liele turned around to speak to Callison, 'I just told my parents that I think you enjoyed the day, and that you got the hang of hover racing!'

'Oh,' he leaned forward to see Liele's parents and pretended to drive an imaginary hover racer, 'Good fun.' he said happily.

Tomak and Estina smiled back, they were nice people and were genuinely pleased for him. Tomak tried to telepathically communicate, Glad you enjoyed the ASI simulation. I hope you enjoy the Telekinesis show also.

Callison didn't receive the message, but smiled graciously. Despite the language barrier, her parents knew that he was genuine, and he knew that they were also. He continued to look around the stadium as Liele talked to her parents some more.

By the time he'd finished his food the show was just starting. All the eyes in the arena were focused forward. A low rhythm of deep drums started to reverberate around the arena and the floodlights started to dim. Other coloured lighting started to become apparent as a team of people walked out onto the pitch. Liele pointed Tobian out to Callison as the drum beat got louder and faster. There were about fifty telekinetic experts or more on the pitch when the drum beat started to die down, and some elegant music started. White balls of light started to fountain out of a gutter on one of the sides of the triangular performance pitch. They flew up into the air, but instead of falling back to the ground haphazardly, they were influenced by the telekinetic experts into neat flowing trains. In time with the music, the chains of balls started to fly around the arena. The telekinesis experts in the centre of the arena were spinning around, conjuring, and moving their hands, orchestrating the glowing ball dance. They reminded him of people playing with kites. Callison was smiling from ear to ear, but was so concentrated on the show that he didn't realise he was smiling. The balls continued to flow, each group of balls flowing in one well-kept line. The individual flows of arcing balls intermingled, and created patterns and shapes through the air. The orchestrated ball dance lasted for ten minutes before ending in a loud musical crescendo having all the balls in the display whizzing in circles very quickly around the arena. They moved so fast they went blurry and then, all of a sudden, they stopped dead; suspended in mid-air. They fell to the floor as the music stopped on beat and the crowd clapped. Callison looked at Liele and nodded approvingly.

The conjurers in the middle of the arena ran about, changing their positions ready for a second display. The telekinesis-choreographers placed boxes down one of the centre lines, and then withdrew to one of the sidelines. A new rhythm played quietly to start with, but grew in intensity. From the sidelines, the entertainers took hold of the objects in the boxes, which turned out to be coloured lights. Out of each box slowly rose about one hundred bright lights, each box revealing a colour. The lights all separately hovered about 2 metres above the boxes they emerged from. They dispersed slowly into the surrounding space. Their collective movement mimicked ink blots spreading out onto wet paper. Then, they all started to arrange themselves into order, making two-dimensional pictures. Each light took a place like a pixel on a TV screen to make pictures of beaches, sunsets, forests and galaxies. The pictures were remarkable in detail and each one got a round of applause from the crowd. The two-dimensional pictures rotated so that every one in the arena could get a view of each pixelated picture.

Each time a routine finished, the performers would regroup and new music would start up, and another routine would commence. After six displays of choreographed telekinesis, the show launched into its finale. A sea of blue dimly lit balls hovered and bounced in mid air, collectively simulating moving waves of the sea. All the telekinesis experts were concentrating on top of a boat, that itself was being levitated to make it look as if it were navigating the sea of blue balls. A dolphin, and a whale were telekinetically created using different coloured balls and emerged from under the surface of the sea of floating blue, making splashes in the simulated water. The effect was spectacular. Callison squinted his eyes; it looked like a natural splash action. The telekinesis experts had certainly been paying attention to the movement of water and were recreating its movement accurately. The display ended when all the blue balls constituting the sea turned into a sand colour and took on the characteristics of static non-flowing sand. The boat that the telekinesis experts all stood on lay beached on the sand as the music changed, and slowly upon the sand, greenery started to emerge, modelled by green telekinetically influenced balls. After five minutes the pitch was a sea of jungle and undergrowth and the music had built into a fast crescendo to stop abruptly as the green balls were mentally 'dropped' and the scene vanished like dust falling to the floor.

The floodlights came back on, and the performers all took a bow from the top of their boat to rapturous applause. The sky overhead was now dark blue, and the stars had come out.

Callison had really enjoyed the show and asked how long Tobian had been practising for; fourteen years was the answer. Liele also told him the demonstration of the sea receding and being overtaken by plants and vegetation was a re-enactment of their story of creation.

Liele's parent's bid them farewell as soon as the show finished and went back home early. Liele and Callison stayed on for Tobian so that they could go home together. While they waited for him in the entrance foyer, Liele bumped into some friends and they spoke in the Sukarmian tongue together for a few minutes. Callison waited with them, not really knowing what they were talking about. He could see they were all happy from their facial expressions, but his mind was taken back to the show and he was still mesmerised at what he'd seen; the whole show demonstrating that maybe telekinesis is not that hard. Maybe he *could* do it. Liele and her friends bade each other farewell and parted ways. Callison smiled and waved them off too.

Liele turned to Callison. 'I think we should get early to sleep tonight; recharge the batteries. We have an early start tomorrow to see Mystera and the Engineers at the Noi Tu Pyramid.'

Callison agreed. He had almost forgotten about his meeting with the Engineers, he had enjoyed his day so much. 'Thank you Liele, for showing me around today, really, thank you.'

'You're welcome.' she said back.

He felt an attraction to her that he couldn't place. He guessed it was because they had spent the last thirty-six hours together. He remembered about Eleanor, prompting thoughts of guilt for his attraction to Liele. He tried not to think about it; he was still determined to get back to rescue Eleanor stuck in the year 2008.

Tobian was en route. I'll be with you guys in a minute. Well sis, what did you think?

Very impressed with the show, well done! See you soon. broadcast Liele.

Tobian emerged from the left hallway. 'Hello Callison.' he said in spoken word.

'Hello Tobian, great show tonight. I really enjoyed it.' His enthusiasm was authentic.

'Thanks. It takes some hard work, but it's good yes?'

'You bet!' said Callison.

'Ok,' said Liele, 'let's go home, we have a big day tomorrow.'

* * * * * * *

18: The Truth Embargo Continued...

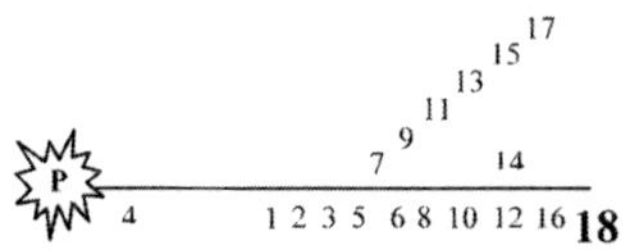

18.2 –
Hidden Timeline:
May 16th 2008:

Heinrich had one of his closest scientists power the eye down and within a quarter of an hour of seeing the opened Eye, Heinrich Muller, Baron Braithwaite III, Miles Goldman, Anthony Van Der Hayder and Andrew Anderton were sitting in leather chairs in Heinrich's modern ground level office slowly getting drunk. The whisky continued to flow, and Heinrich was under the impression that they were celebrating something big. Matters turned to Heinrich's role, and all the investors thought Heinrich should be told about the new asset that his company held four floors below them.

Anthony Van Der Hayder, who until now had remained fairly quiet, pulled a photo out of his suit jacket and slid it across the desk to Heinrich, 'You see Heinrich, this is not the first time a device like this has existed.' His voice was broken, and soulless.

Heinrich looked at the photo, which had a corner missing, like it had been burned. It was a picture of an Eye, but not the one standing up downstairs in the lab, this one was different, but the pattern of light it created was identical to the patterns they had all just witnessed. Heinrich was baffled, 'So, where did this eye come from?'

The media mogul continued to explain slowly, 'We heard about this one in the late seventies in Siberia. An inventor by the name of Igor Popovic had struck upon the idea and made one, and we tried to buy it from him.' He let the words hang, as he sipped his tumbler of scotch. The emphasis was on Heinrich to respond.

'So…' he thought, as he held up the photo in his hand, 'so… why did you fund *this* project if you already had one?'

Baron Braithwaite III interjected, 'Popovic didn't sell. He wrote in his notebooks that the portal was too early, and the world wasn't ready for the implications it would reveal.' The baron spoke without a hint of guilt, 'Well it would appear that when Igor Popovic heard that we were going to take it anyway, he decided to let the device explode, killing himself in the process. The picture you are holding is the only picture of that device actually working,' he went on, 'you see, there was nothing left at the laboratory site in Siberia. All we could recover was that photo and the remnants of his notebook; nothing about how the device worked though. The blast site caused by the Eye was vast.'

Heinrich was bowled over by the additional information, but wanted to get to the crux of the device, 'So do we know what the portal does? If it's not a time machine, then what is it?'

The media magnate informed him by posing a question. He asked it like he knew the answer, 'Mr Muller, what do you think we humans are doing here on this little rock we call Earth?'

'I don't really know,' said Heinrich, 'evolving?'

It was clear he didn't know. Mr Van Der Hayder posed an answer, 'What if I told you that reality is in fact a simulated algorithm, a walk-through environment dictated and created by the state of mind of the observer?'

This was getting heavy, 'Is it?' asked Heinrich with a troubled look on his face.

The media man nodded as if to agree with the words he spoke, 'It is a secret that goes back many thousands of years, kept by the few for domination of the many through the use of mind-paralysing fear. The people have forgotten about the power of their internal worlds and think the physical world *is* the reality; a default that lies outside from them and can't be influenced. They think that men in the sky dictate their fate to them; they think that chance, luck or the natural laws of the economy have power over them. They are asleep and docile of their power to create reality and thus ripe for dividing and conquering!' Anthony Van Der Hayder spoke with a malevolent undertone to his voice that troubled Heinrich.

Miles Goldman spoke from a similar viewpoint, 'Yes, the people don't even realise that it is their willing submission to us that creates their powerless existences and depressive states of mind, which in turn creates their depressive experiences of life.' he laughed aloud.

Heinrich couldn't have been more in over his head if he'd tried. He tried to keep up the conversation, despite the mind-shattering information, 'So...' He dwelt upon the Eye to lead his mind back to the fringes of normality, 'So if one of us jumped through the portal, what would happen? Do we know?'

The Baron took up the answer, 'The Russian scientist had written in his notebooks that when he walks through the portal, his soul separates from his body, and it's the soul that has the power to explore and learn in other dimensions, the body is just a physical suit for the physical world that falls to the floor unconscious after walking through the portal.' Baron Braithwaite III took a mouthful of his liquor, 'After about ten minutes the unconscious body wakes up from its unconsciousness as the soul comes back to it's 'earth suit' with more knowledge and more power.'

Heinrich thought to himself with worry, reaffirming the knowledge he was receiving, *that's what happened when Callison and Eleanor used the portal.*

The aristocrat's tone turned serious, 'Popovic also wrote in his notes that this invention would resurface again in the early 21st century by a researcher in England and that one day it would liberate the world, and that the first person to use the new portal would bring about a new world order.' he added humorously, 'And it looks like the first person through the portal will be one of us!' His tone lightened and he began to laugh.

'Here's to controlling the future!' said the banker, Miles Goldman as they all clinked their glasses together, blinded by their egos. They loved the physical illusion, and ironically were *more* attached to the illusion than the docile masses they mocked.

Heinrich felt his heart race with grief as the others clinked and celebrated. He thought back to his basement dramas with Callison and Eleanor. *Were they dead? Or had they used the portal?* he thought. *They were dead*. He had witnessed it with his own eyes. His kept his mouth shut however and pretended to be excited for the power brokers of illusion.

* * * * * * *

19: The Alpine Stargate

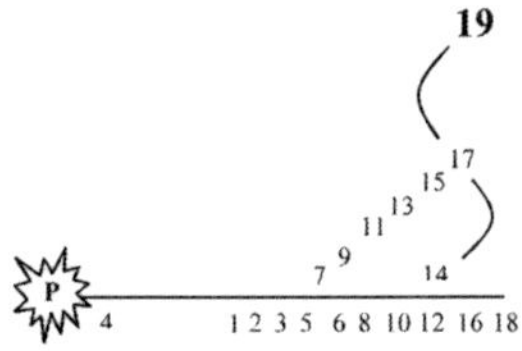

"Everything we regard as real is made of things that cannot be regarded real."

Niels Bohr, Quantum Physicist (1885 – 1962)

19.1 –
Date not known:
Plus one day:

Eleanor's experience behind the portal's veil of light proved briefer than her husband's. After leaving the banks of the stream, she had been led to Togo's village called Capee, high up in the mountains where she ate and drank the finest foods and wines. She had stayed in Capee for only one evening and in that time she had spoken with an amazing holographic being of light that was known as an Engineer of the Universal Mind, and knew she was now departing for the remainder of her Earth life reality.

Eleanor and her guide, Togo, left the mountain village of Capee and after a trip through the ether of the collective mind they floated towards Eleanor's Earth experience, the gateway to the physical universe, called The Alpine Stargate.

The Alpine Stargate was a large round portal that hovered in space and worked like a curtain of light much the same as her husband's device, but in reverse. She was soon going to be back in her physical body on Earth, where her instructions from the Engineers of light were to play amnesic until her husband came back to her.

Togo and Eleanor approached the Alpine Stargate and it even looked like her husband's invention, but there was no frame; the round portal seemed to just exist, floating in space, and it was big; really big.

Eleanor spoke with Togo as they continued floating towards the Stargate, 'Thank you, Togo. You have helped make this experience a pleasant one.' She kissed him.

Togo had proved the perfect guide, and felt sorrow to see his new friend leave for Earth again, 'It has been a pleasure.' he said with his deep English accent.

She smiled, 'How far is it from here? It looks like we're close.'

'The size can be deceiving. It really is a fascinating stargate, the Alpine. We still a have a short while, but strictly speaking, time begins on the other side of the gate so we are there already in some sense!' He laughed.

Eleanor smiled, and kept of floating towards the Stargate. She thought about the concept of time as they neared the doorway to the physical. Eleanor stopped. Some one was waiting for them in front of the stargate's light-curtain. *It couldn't be,* she thought. It was someone Eleanor hadn't seen in a long time. She wanted to cry in happiness.

'Jack!' Eleanor gasped. She moved towards him and he towards her.

'Mummy!' said Jack.

Their eternal characters embraced for an emotional re-union. It had been so long for Eleanor.

'Jack, are you ok? We were worried about you.'

'Yes, mummy I am very happy.'

'We missed you Jack.' She was sorrowful.

'We live forever mummy. Earth is a game that we play. Are you going back?'

She was surprised at his comments, but replied, 'Yes, I'm going back. I'm not sure what I'm going back *to* though. I'm to wait for your father.'

Jack smiled, 'Everything will be ok mummy.'

Eleanor smiled back at him. Her memories of Jack were so sweet, 'I love you Jack.' She hugged him again.

'I have to go mummy.' he said, like he knew he had to be somewhere else.

Eleanor had learned well in her physical life that permanent goodbyes were impossible. She remained loving but detached and let him go, 'Ok darling, I'll always love you. You do what you need to do.' She was strong, 'I'll see you again.'

'I love you too Mummy, thank you for being a nice mummy.' and with that, he kissed her and slowly started to float away from the surface of the stargate. He waved goodbye to Togo as well and disappeared out of sight into the rest of the timelessness.

As Eleanor watched him disappear it prompted one of her fondest memories of Jack running off down a school corridor. The sound of his feet clomping on the corridor floor had all the energy of a five year old. The sound got quieter as he disappeared into the non-physical ether. Eleanor reminisced, but gave thanks. She had a physical challenge of her own to go back to.

'Are you okay?' asked Togo, who had taken a back seat while she spoke with Jack.

'Yes. I'm feeling confident.' she said with wisdom.

The Alpine Stargate was right in front of them. The surface of the gateway stretched upwards and outwards, creating a 360-degree horizon of bright yellowy white light. Eleanor wondered, 'It's a long way from here, Earth?'

Togo smiled gracefully, 'You got here alright, and you'll get back.'

Eleanor conceded. 'There aren't many others here. Are we the only ones?'

Togo tried to explain; he was a scientific soul. 'Your mind is still very much in character, so it simply doesn't see the others.' He knew it would comfort her, so he helped Eleanor's mind for a moment, 'Here, do you see now?'

It was like a light going on for Eleanor, a hazy orange light that shone from a distant source. She looked all around her and

Togo, and in the new light source there were millions of seemingly 'alive' white swimming fireflies of light! 'Wow! There are loads of them!' Eleanor exclaimed in wonder as she witnessed the immense scale and number of the conscious sparks of energy all around her, interacting and whizzing around each other and emerging from and disappearing into the portal. She remained in awe at the sight, before it vanished in an instant when Togo ceased his mental assistance.

The surroundings were dark again and all she saw was Togo, 'Was that real? What was that?' she asked.

Togo was gracious, 'A glimpse of your larger family. Know that you are part of something wonderful that doesn't measure its progress with time.'

Eleanor agreed and was filled with a hope she had not known since being a carefree child. The time came for Eleanor to depart, who felt the call to the rest of her life.

'Will I see *you* again?' she asked.

'You can count on it.' assured Togo.

'See you then Togo. Thank you.' She hugged him, and then kissed him. Bravely and boldly she floated onward through the Alpine Stargate's curtain of shimmering light and into the physical universe of experience again. She wasn't really sure what to expect as the yellowy-white light swallowed her whole. It rippled as she made the jump back to Earth.

Togo nostalgically waited by the time-gate for a moment; he had enjoyed his new friend's company. All around him was pure silence. He had been successful in his assignment and telepathically transmitted to his time shaman called Mystera, Mission accomplished.

* * * * * * *

20: The Engineers

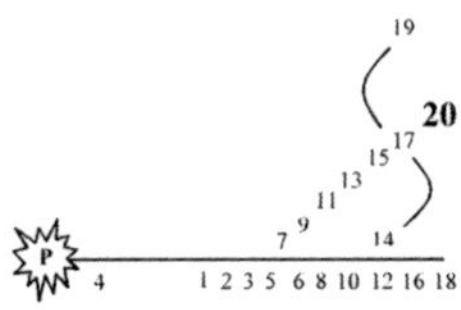

"Is man one of Gods blunders,
or is God one of man's blunders?"
Friedrich Nietzsche, Psychiatrist
and Philosopher (1844 – 1900)

20.1 –
Date not known:
Plus two days:

A hooded man had led him on a magical flight high above the world's borders and out into the solar system. Now though, Callison was in a dark stone walled room, partially illuminated by seven multicoloured candle flames that seemed to communicate with him by flickering in a certain way, unique to each flame. The hooded man who had taken him on the amazing flight now sat behind him, remaining quiet and communicating back with the candle flames by flickering light from his eyes. It was surreal and Callison was anxious.

The flames seemed to be relaying advice; what they separately said was impossible for him to comprehend but after a time they all merged into one bright white flame, and the message was heard loud and clear: 'Wake up!'

A pause ensued, 'Wake up sleepyhead!' said Liele for the second time.

He'd been dreaming. Callison stirred and asked what the time was, 'What time do you call this Ellie?'

'No... remember you are in Sukarmia now.' Callison realised, but refrained from speaking. He was still physically asleep.

Liele continued, 'We have to leave for the Noi Tu Outpost soon for your meeting with the Engineers.'

Callison woke and realised for a second morning in a row that his wife, Eleanor was still in 2008, which panged him more than the morning before. 'What time is it now?' he said back sleepily.

'It's two before rise. We need to be leaving soon to meet Mystera, so you'll have to wake up now.' She was stern but friendly, 'Wear the body suit and tunic; they are clean. I will fix up some breakfast while you gather yourself. It will be ok this morning. You will understand more about your circumstances I'm sure, after meeting with the Engineers.'

There were lights on, and he winced, 'Yeah, ok. Thanks.'

Liele walked out of the room before the memories came back about the day he had yesterday. On a side table next to his bed laid the leaflet about holography he was handed at the techno recreational centre He was tired from his long day yesterday but opened his eyes fully and thought about the telekinesis performance he witnessed last night. He had loved it. *He* wanted to do that.

He swung his legs round ninety degrees and levered himself out of bed, his age regression wasn't wasted on him and he felt at ease in his younger body again. When standing, he used his hands to conjure up the telekinetic strength to move the glass on the table. His hands pointed directly at the container for a few minutes, before he gave up, sighing. *Not as easy as it looks.* He grabbed a towel off a heated rail and headed for the bathroom.

While showering, his mind turned back to a couple of days ago and the meeting with Mystera on the roof of the white preparatory house. The shamanic elder had said that the Universal Mind would send an envoy called the Engineers who would be able to help him. *How?* he thought. He was confused, and it made him feel uneasy.

He turned the shower off, dried himself and got dressed, thinking about the dream he'd had and about the hooded man that led him on a flight into space. Just before he left his new bedroom he picked up the holography leaflet and put it into the pocket of his furry brown tunic. He wanted it with him just in case he got bored; the real reason he took it was not boredom, but an unconscious pre-requisite for the day's lessons.

Liele was in the kitchen area preparing a picnic when Callison emerged ready in his body suit and tunic. He preferred the clothes he was in the previous day but he wore the tunic out of courtesy.

'Morning Callison, did you sleep well?' she said as she chopped up some pears and apples. She too wore her tunic.

'Yes thanks.' He walked over to the kitchen area to see what Liele was doing, 'I had a strange dream about a space flight and a meeting with seven candle flames though, it was weird; really vivid.'

Liele enlightened him; 'It was probably the Universal Mind analysing your UVP.'

'My UVP?'

'Your Unique Vibration Pattern, remember I told you yesterday? We all have one.' she said.

He recalled, nodding, 'What do you think the Universal Mind wanted my UVP for?'

'So they can tune in to you later this morning. You see, your vibration pattern is what creates you; if they know your vibration pattern they can 'dial in' as it were.' She sounded as if it was nothing unusual.

He was nervous, but tried to remain upbeat; he was learning that it was his choice to be negative or positive. A flask looking canister stood up next to the chopping board. Callison pointed at it, 'What's in that?'

'It holds refrigerated orange and Aloemara in one side and hot tea in the other. It will keep them at their respective temperatures for the whole morning.'

'We are having Aloemara again?'

'Yes. Well I am, it is up to you if you want to have it. It will help you to relax during the session with the Engineers and you'll be more open to their information.' She finished chopping some fruit, 'I also am making a breakfast for us to enjoy during the rise of the sun. I have the nicest spot to watch from, but we need to be leaving soon.'

Callison had already decided to himself that he was going to take the Aloemara again and answered forthrightly, 'I'm ready right now I think, unless there is there anything else I can do?'

'No, I'm just about done here,' she replied unflustered, 'you could get that bag over there for me to put our breakfast in.'

He walked over to the lounge sofa, and picked up the bag that rested upon it. 'This one?'

'Yes, thanks, when this is packed we are ready to go. How are you feeling?'

He nodded apprehensively, 'Yes, I'm trying to choose to be positive, what's the worst that could happen?' He felt like he meant it, but knew there was some degree of uncertainty to his words.

'That's the spirit!' she congratulated, as she started to pack the bag, 'Now I had a word with Tobian and he said it's ok for you to take his hover-skimmer, so you can take that across the Solus if you want.'

He smiled, before wondering, 'Is it like a hover racer?'

Liele tilted her head forward and warned, 'Don't show off... you'll only injure your pride!' The words hung as they made their way out of the apartment door.

As soon as Callison had come to grips with the power device that cancelled out gravity, it was just a case of leaning forward to go forward, and leaning back wards to go backwards, left and right, the same. When he increased the power of the hover jet as he leant forward, he gained speed. It reminded him of a small-scale helicopter in its dynamics. There were no brakes, you simply leant backwards, and increased power. A hover racer it wasn't.

They steadily set off out of the entrance hall of Liele's tower block into the dark crisp morning. After navigating their way under the grid tunnel, they hovered up one of the ramps onto the Mainway Boulevard raised transport platform, where a few transport probes rushed by in the same direction just below and to the left of them on the grid. Being early in the morning, there were fewer probes than usual and he followed Liele as she governed a pace to be maintained. It was fairly quiet but for a few other hover-skimmers travelling the raised platform. Although travelling the Boulevard before, he was still astonished at how high the buildings were that towered over them, and couldn't help but look up as he moved. Their lights illuminated the sky and disappeared into the low morning cloud. Before long, the Solus tunnel entrance was upon them, which they took, leaving the city lights behind.

The tunnel seemed shorter than before, and they reached the Solus sooner than he expected. They both made the quick adjustment to enable hover over water, and travelled out over the sea to one of the boat sheds that dotted the opposite shoreline. Liele said it wasn't the same one as they had been in two days previously, but Callison was none the wiser. They moored the hover jets and left them partially sunk, bobbing in the water for their return crossing.

The walk to the Noi Tu complex would take about an hour from the boat shed, but they detoured slightly for breakfast during the sunrise on the aptly named, Sunrise Hill that overlooked the city skyline.

Liele did some meditation just before the sunrise, and talked Callison through what she was thinking. They sat on a sky blue rug, while Callison listened and started to use his imagination to picture what she was talking about. Planetary movements, new days, flying through clouds, imagining thoughts as clouds that pass by and finishing by welcoming the new day and the new experiences it would bring. It was an exercise that Callison didn't find painful at all, but he didn't really know why he was doing it. The meditation did give a light and airy mood to the sunrise process though and the dynamic view was stunning. The whole process of sunrise had lasted 20 minutes. It was as if he could sense the spin of the planet's rotation. The skyline of Sukarmia slowly sank itself into daylight, exposing the sun and a light blue sky over the background of the buildings. He felt small and insignificant; in awe of the world's movement relative to him, and the beautiful earthly scenes those movements created. Liele called it the birth of the sun, and said it was a spiritual process for her.

They ate assorted fruits and oat-based flapjack biscuits as the sun drenched the lands. The tea from the flask was warming, adding to the warmth provided by the tunics they wore.

After breakfast they drank some of the Orange juice and Aloemara. The juice tasted better than normal orange juice and he could taste the Aloemara, but couldn't associate it with anything he knew of. After packing up their breakfast utensils they left Sunrise Hill and set off for the Noi Tu Outpost; the sun now awake but still low in the sky.

It didn't take long for the Aloemara to take effect and barely five minutes had passed before the pair of them laughed about the shape that clouds made in the sky. They navigated a pathway that Callison thought he had been on before and he noticed that he felt lighter as he walked with Liele, high on the stimulant. He had never taken drugs before, but as Mystera had pointed out on the day of his arrival, cigarettes and alcohol were both drugs. They watched as one cloud slowly faded away to nothing, seemingly folding back into the great unseen. Liele said clouds behaved just like thoughts, coming and going depending on the internal emotional weather fronts. It was a concept Callison seemed to 'get' better than before, he guessed because of the metaphor of the cloud.

The walk to the Noi Tu Pyramid ended up being more gruelling than he'd expected. Callison was breathing faster and slightly sweating and even for his forty-year old body he was tired. Liele on the other hand seemed almost super human, not even a tremor in breath. When they got to the Noi Tu outpost, they walked past the white prep house and into the open round

Noi Tu arena via one of the four archways, then walked straight out under the archway that led to the pyramid. They still had the stairs to climb to get to the top of the monolithic pyramid, which would mark the end of their three-hour morning.

As he climbed, he wondered what the Engineers could say to him to help him. Could they send him home straight away? He would wait and see, and tried to relax. The sun was by now wide-awake, but a light mist rolled through the valleys and troughs of the treetops, which were brought into view the more they climbed.

Liele spoke back to Callison as she took the last few steps of the large staircase. 'I'll let Mystera know we're here.' She concentrated momentarily and broadcast to Mystera, *We are here Mystera.*

Callison made it to the top and the view unveiled itself. The top of the pyramid consisted of a square flat stone surface, providing excellent aerial views of the green surrounds. He could see the cliff in the distance from which he had first viewed the pyramid, and looking the other way he could make out the small skyscrapers of Sukarmia just above the tree line. In the middle of the small stone area was built a cube shaped building that he guessed provided access to the internals of the pyramid. Mystera was about to show him the clever way in.

20.2 –

As Callison observed the surroundings atop the monolith, from out of thin air Mystera suddenly materialised. He emerged, wearing a dark brown ankle length robe with a light blue sash around his waist. His hood was up and his eyes were covered deep in shade, the only prominent facial feature being his beard. He reminded Callison of the hooded man in his dream only hours previous. Mystera pulled back the cloak's hood exposing his wavy grey hair and wise eyes; he started to walk forward, smiling warmly. *Greetings children!* he broadcast.

Liele reciprocated, Greetings Mystera!

Callison was taken by surprise, 'Where did you come from? How did you just do that?'

'Oh that? I meant to do it.' he said, humorously gesturing back with his head to the point where he appeared. Liele laughed.

Callison was stunned into silence for a moment, before replying back, 'I'm sure you did mean to do it... it just doesn't happen that often from where I come from!'

'Well, you are where *we* come from now, and where *we're* from things like this do happen!' said the old master, 'Just like talking rats and flying women happen.' Liele smiled at the floor, proud inside of her flight, as Mystera continued, 'I trust you had a good day yesterday?'

Callison had enjoyed himself, 'Yes, it was a great day. We went to Turuk, where we saw another Noi Tu Temple and went into a techno recreation centre before coming back to Sukarmia to see a telekinetic show in the evening. Your lands are very welcoming, thank you.' Callison said, 'And thank you too of course.' He smiled at Liele.

Mystera got straight to the point, 'So your dream last night should have prepared you for your meeting with the Universal Mind's envoy, the Engineers.' It was a question as much as a statement.

The new explorer was stumped, 'Well, it was weird...' he thought, 'Wait a minute, how did *you* know about my dream?' He thought some more, 'Were you *in* my dream?'

'Yes,' said the master, 'well done.'

Callison tried to get his head round everything, 'So you were actually *in* my dream, can you consciously remember what happened?'

'Yes, I was behind you when you were liasing with the Universal Mind.'

'But I can't even remember what any of us said!'

'That is because when you leave your dream and wake up, the waking reality consumes your senses. What you can see, hear, touch and smell is easier to identify with, so it takes the place of the dream. Somewhere deep inside you, you know what was said.'

How do I get at it then? Callison thought, without speaking aloud.

Mystera picked up on his thought and answered his mental question, 'Quieten your mind.'

It took Callison by surprise, 'What?'

'If you can learn to listen to you inner voice, it will never be wrong.' said Mystera almost as a challenge to him. 'And that's how you get at the information inside you.'

Callison didn't know what to say, so he asked another question, 'What do you think this session will hold for me?'

The wise man replied with enthusiasm, 'Come with me, let's see.' He transmitted to Liele, As you know this will need to be done with Callison present only, thank you Liele.

Liele acknowledged. Yes, I have things to do in the prep house, call me when you're done. She waved goodbye to Mystera.

Mystera held his hands out in front of Callison, 'Take my hands Callison, we have to get into the pyramid.'

Callison was timid, but walked towards him, 'Are you not coming Liele?'

She shook her head, and explained, 'No, this is only for you, Mystera and the Engineers, I'll wait for you in the prep house.' She sounded reassuring.

'Ok then, let's do this.' Callison remained positive, which both Liele and Mystera mentally applauded.

He walked forward and held Mystera's hand, 'Are we going to teleport or something?'

Mystera answered, 'Hold on!' He then held his eyes shut, and they silently vanished from sight, leaving Liele on top of the pyramid.

There was a loud 'whoosh' sound, and Callison could see Mystera's large grey beard throughout the trip being blown by an upward wind. Mystera kept his eyes tight shut and seemed to concentrate on the travel, but no longer had the fall started, it stopped. It was quiet again. They were in a dark stone walled room with no doors and seven candlesticks provided some dim, flickering light.

Mystera stood as he was before the strange movement through space, still linked to Callison through touch.

'What on earth just happened?' Callison exclaimed. He let go of Mystera's hands to look around the room he was now inside.

'We are in one of the internal chambers of the pyramid.' said Mystera, 'It's only really a fifty yard journey.' He seemed to play the skill down.

Callison was surprised, and confused as he looked around the room, 'I've been here before! The candlesticks! The stone wall! This is what I dreamt last night! How can this be?'

Mystera enquired about Callison's dream, 'What was the overall feel of your dream last night? Was it scary for instance?'

'No, not scary, more...' he thought, '...frustrating,' he explained, 'at not being able to understand the information.'

The wise master helped alleviate his fears, 'You'll understand soon. Are you ready?'

'Ok. The sooner we start the sooner we finish, hit me.' Callison said astutely.

Mystera was confused, and asked with wisdom, 'Hit you?'

'Sorry, turn of phrase. I mean let's start.'

Mystera lit an incense stick, which started the process in action. He rested it in a holder in front of the candles.

Mystera's high hood concealed some of his brow, and his eyes were cast into shadow. His beard was the only point of reference once again. 'The information you are about to receive is for you. I will be present, and I will be concentrating, but you will be the one communicating.'

'Ok.' came the affirmative response from the 21st century refugee. The candlelit room flickered with dim illumination that bounced off the walls and the smell of the incense stick circled around the void.

Mystera began, 'You will see the Engineers appear as light from the candles merging into one. This light is just as conscious as you or me, and will be able to explain your circumstances and help you find your way.' He sounded friendly and calm. He went into a trance-like state and recited some words that Callison had never heard before. Mystera went to sit behind Callison, just as Callison's precognitive dream had alluded to.

Mystera's words instantaneously triggered the candle's dim flickers into a more intense set of flames. Callison's heart began to accelerate in expectance as all seven of the waxy sticks increased their brightness until white light started to pour off the candles. It wasn't bright for the eyes surprisingly, and Callison watched on in contained awe, it looked to behave almost as liquid light. The seven rays of light from the seven candles converged into a focused point above the waxy sticks and this point of light became mobile within the chamber of the pyramid. It floated down from the candles to hover just above the floor in front of Callison in the form of a small orb of light. As Callison sat cross-legged he could feel the bright light was in some way intricately connected to him at a core level. It was an earthy feeling, and a grounding sensation. The light startled Callison by communicating. It sounded like real sound, and not telepathy.

'Hello Callison.' It was a woman's voice, which sounded soft and gentle.

Callison remembered Mystera said the light was conscious, he answered, 'Hello?'

The ball of light slowly morphed into a six-foot hologram of a woman that looked like an angel wearing a flowing white dress, her white light outline as clear as crystal. She was the epitome of beauty and her presence cast white light onto the four walls of the void in the pyramid.

The form change had amazed Callison, and he was intently concentrating on the experience. He wondered if she was an angel. 'You don't look like I expected!'

'That's because you still see through your Earth mind.' She gave Callison more information while smiling like a mother would to her child, 'We speak to you now from a higher frequency of existence with the help of our mutual brother, Mystera.' The hologram acknowledged the wise master sitting behind Callison, before continuing, 'We are a collective entity known as an Engineer of the Universal Mind, and we maintain the Karmic balance of life during the collective experience of the universe. How has *your* experience been so far Callison?'

Callison felt like he knew the presence, but didn't know why, 'My experience?' he thought, 'It's had its ups and downs you could say.'

The collective entity was calming and accepted his spoken answer, but saw the pain he held deep inside about his dead son, Jack. 'Do you know why you are here?' she asked.

Callison told her all he knew, 'All I know is that I arrived here by jumping into a portal that I invented back in 2008 and now I am marooned here in the future. I was a fool, I know.'

She was gracious, 'You are not a fool, your heart is honest,' The hovering lady of light added, 'and you are not in the future.'

Callison was unsettled by the answer. He had made his mind up that he was in the future, 'Am I in the *past* then?'

'You are in the dimension of the energetic mind and soul, which surrounds and builds the physical dimensions. Time, as you know it on Earth, is an illusion of the nature of human consciousness and occurs as a result of the creation of physicality. Your experience is now one of mind and soul energy rather than physical matter, which means you are not experiencing time, you are experiencing experience itself.'

Callison was dumbstruck, 'But this feels just like the physical world! I can touch things, I have a body, look.' He pinched his arm, confused.

The engineer of light had an answer; 'Your imagination is still heavily influenced by your Earthly experience as Callison

Trebla, which is why you decode a physical land much the same as Earth and a physical body much the same as you remember on Earth.' She paused, as if to listen for internal permission to explain, 'The dimension of the energetic mind and soul is non-local, and is a bridge dimension between the physical and spiritual dimensions. Your invention is one way to get here, there are many others.' The woman of light stopped speaking and remained floating in front of him.

Callison asked a question, 'Is that why I look younger?'

She smiled gracefully and obligingly as she floated, 'Your current appearance is you in your own best image, given that you only know your life as Callison Trebla.'

He followed up with another question, 'Why *am* I here?'

She replied, 'You are here because your portal lead you here. You have invented a doorway of light out of your physical dimension and into this one.' The revelations continued, 'You chose your Earth life as Callison Trebla, because you wanted to learn how to deal with the loss of a loved one, in this case it was Jack, your son on Earth. If you were successful, then you would go on to lead your invention into the world, liberating the people from the false paradigm they currently use to understand themselves.' She seemed to emphasize, 'This is *still* your ultimate destiny; you have just taken some wrong turns that's all, and now you need to navigate back onto the right road to this destiny.' The entity seemed to remain impartial but caring.

'So how do I get back to the right road from here?'

The holographic deity seemed troubled, and hazy of her information. 'Normally, using your invention, you would go back whenever you want and wake up in your body on Earth again but...' she hesitated, '...there has been a complication. It is...' she listened to her source again, 'It is not possible for you to go back to the physical dimension you have come to know as your reality, because on that timeline your body will be rendered inactive.'

Callison became worried, 'What does that mean?'

'It means Callison Trebla will be written out of that reality.'

He became worried, 'What... what does that mean? I'm dead?' he panicked with grief and was frightened of non-existence, 'Will I see my wife again?'

The angelic Engineer of experience smiled but was openly confused, 'We find it strange that your people fear death. It is as if you have become addicted to your characters on Earth.'

Callison tried to help the Engineer understand, 'It's just the way we are on Earth.'

'It's just the way you have been *told* to see it.' The ghost-like elegance spoke with compassion and understanding, 'You're not dead; you can never die, because you are not your body and you never were. Your character is built *by you* and its essence goes with you as a saved copy of your experience.' She answered his next question, 'As regards to seeing your wife, you will see her again. She will have a story to tell you also when you get back to your physical experience.'

Callison breathed a wave of relief, 'So I will get back?'

'You have to build your way back Callison,' she clarified, 'with your mind.'

'Ok...' Callison said as if to wait for more instruction.

The envoy of the Universal Mind obliged, 'By changing your mind signature here, in the dimension of energetic mind and soul, you will effectively retake your life choices as Callison Trebla, and return to an alternate branch of your experiential tree.'

He was intrigued, as some of the research he read at Quanta was on parallel universes, 'So, you mean like a parallel universe?'

'You could see it like that; we know you worked with these ideas in Callison's experience. The parallel reality you can travel back to will be a partial parallelism, so your history will have changed and everything in it, but the Earth collective will continue without even detecting the overwrite in time, for you see, time is relative to the observer, it is not the same for everyone.

Callison didn't fully understand, 'So if I change my history, how did I get into this dimension?'

'You coincided your arrival here from your alternate version of history also. You will be tempted to call it fate when you learn of your route here, but it has all been designed by you.' said the enlightener.

Still the questions came, 'And what about Heinrich, and the old time line?'

'All remnants of the old timeline will be overwritten by your alternate experience.' The lady engineer remained quiet anticipating the next question.

The information Callison received was against everything he thought he knew about time, but he accepted the answers with some excitement, 'So how do I get back to my new life from here?'

The engineer explained, 'After Mystera has helped you to hone your mind, which will allow the route to your alternate physical history, an intuitive integration will lead you back to it.'

'Ok.' he reasoned. 'How do I know what intuition is?'

The lady of light sounded like she was preparing to leave, 'Your compass will always lie within, but your bearing is always your choice, and the rest? Well, you already know the rest. Listen to Mystera, he is wise and has done the same journey you find yourself on now. He will act as your guide.'

Callison accepted his new guide, 'Ok.' He turned round to face Mystera again wondering more about his master's circumstances and the master smiled back. Callison turned to face the Engineer again, asking like a small child, 'Are you an angel?'

The Engineer wasn't expecting it, but enlightened him cryptically. The being seemed to relax and smiled, 'We don't think of ourselves as angels, we just help build and maintain experience with the energy we are given.'

Callison nodded.

She prepared to leave, 'We must be off now,' said the collective woman, 'we have told you all you need to know. But before we go, we have a gift.' She blew a kiss to him, creating a small ball of light that floated down and absorbed itself into Callison's forehead.

The time-less explorer felt an easing in his forehead, as if the ball of light had lubricated the inner workings of his mind, 'What was that?' he asked, with curiosity.

The friendly deity told him, 'A gift.'

He felt no different, but trusted her, 'Thank you.' he said gratefully.

'We will let you know telepathically when you have created your pathway home. See you soon Callison, it has been a pleasure talking with you.'

The student of life nodded, 'And you too, thank you.'

Slowly the hologram shrank, and the intensity of the light increased again until it resembled the bright ball of white light that first appeared. The light bundle slowly moved back up above the candles, and separated into seven separate beams each being absorbed back into the seven candles, and after that it was quiet again. The candles burned normally and there was zero evidence of the deity being in the door-less stone chamber at all.

Mystera tested Callison's gift, Can you understand me now?

Wow. Crystal Clear he thought, before projecting back instinctively, Yes. I can understand you perfectly!

20.3 –

Callison had expected the teleportation out of the pyramid's chamber to be an upward movement to counter the downward entry teleport, but the movement seemed to be downward again. Mystera and Callison teleported out of the stone walled room and appeared from thin air to emerge onto the top of the pyramid. The sun now lit up the view of the lush green trees and the mist had burned off. Callison felt warm, and took his tunic off revealing the white body suit he was wearing underneath. Mystera had his hood down, but kept his robes on and they both sat on the top step of the pyramid looking down onto the round Noi Tu arena and white prep house.

Callison could sense no difference between the dimension of energetic mind and soul he found himself in and the last sixty-five years of his physical life on 'the real' planet Earth. He didn't know what 'real' was anymore. He could feel his own body, he could see, smell and taste and the thought of it all being an illusion made him wonder why and how it existed at all.

While looking over the green lands from the top of the pyramid, the Noi Tu master explained to Callison that the dimension of energetic mind and soul was a dimension where imagination and feeling worked together to create experience for the experiencer. He told Callison that his physical experience on Earth worked exactly the same way, but the lead-time between the imagination and the actual experience was much longer. The physical dimensions were dense, heavy and consumed lots of energy for small changes in experience.

Callison reached into the pocket of his tunic lying next to him and pulled out the holography leaflet he had taken with him in the morning. He inspected the paper to try and see the illusion of matter, but no sooner after he started to inspect it, he realised the writing on the leaflet now appeared in English, like his gift of telepathy had enabled him to read the once illegible symbols. His inspection of the seemingly physical paper fell into insignificance.

'It's changed?' Callison said to Mystera as they sat.

'What do you mean?' said the master.

'Yesterday this leaflet was written in a language that I couldn't understand. Now it is written in English? How could it change?'

'Maybe it was *you* that changed?' said the Noi Tu shaman. 'I think you should read it,' said his new life guide, 'it has certainly attracted your attention, and your attention is a root towards your intuition. Your experience is asking you to notice the leaflet.'

Callison read the leaflet while Mystera looked out over the green canopy of trees from the top step of the pyramid.

The holography leaflet was fascinating and described the makings of a hologram. Holography worked on a principle of light interference. Coherent light (laser light) was split into two beams by a beam divider. One half of the light was reflected and directly diffused onto a piece of light-sensitive holographic film. The other half of the laser was diffused at the object wishing to be holographed. The light reflected off the object and was taken in by a lens where it was then diffused onto the same holographic film as the reflected 'raw' laser light. An interference pattern was created and became captured onto the piece of holographic film. The interference pattern on the film looked similar to lots of pebbles being dropped into a pond, complex but quite unrelated to the original object. This was a coded image, for when another light source was shone through the holographic film, either a laser or a bright white light, a three-dimensional hologram of the captured object was projected on the other side of the film.

The intriguing part of the holographic interference pattern was that it was non-local. Every part of the coded pattern had all of the information to create the whole hologram again, so even if you cut the film in half, or into a million pieces, every piece would generate the whole hologram of the object again. The pieces had the same information as the whole, an intriguing concept.

Callison called on his life guide, 'Why should I have needed to know this? Should I enrol on the holography course now?' He was still thinking about time sequentially.

The master, who had been observing the land as Callison read, came back to Callison, 'You could do that, but I'd just notice the message and think about the information, maybe it has something to do with your Trebla Eye?'

Callison thought, 'Have I told you about the Trebla Eye?'

Mystera enlightened him, 'No, but I can hear your thoughts about it.'

Callison felt a strange sensation come over him, like he thought Mystera was keeping something from him. He forgot the holographic principle until he would need to remember it.

'When the Engineer said you had been on this journey before, what did they mean?'

Mystera empathised, 'I understand you want to know, but please have patience. I will tell you things only as you need to know them. I have indeed travelled the journey you are on, but the details I have to keep from you for now, I'm sorry. You need to prove to yourself that you can build your knowledge bridge back to your new history before we look down that road.'

Callison conceded, but trusted more than understood his life guide.

As the pair continued to watch the green panorama of the land, Mystera told him about the coming days and about the intuitive integration he was to undertake. He said it was an exercise of self, where walking intuitively into the surrounding undergrowth, signified searching the subconscious memory. The undertaking would reveal answers, provided he had questions, gearing him up for the call to head back again to his parallel Earth life experience. Before the intuitive integration however, Callison would have to increase his mind power and understanding of self, so Mystera suggested exercises consisting of meditation, telekinesis lessons, and he also suggested a magnifier.

Alright, Callison thought, *Telekinesis lessons!* Boy, was he was looking forward to that. He enquired the unknown, 'What's a magnifier?'

'This is a magnifier.' Mystera pointed to the crystal on his forehead, 'A magnifier will act to help your pineal gland to start functioning properly, get your intuition flowing again.'

Mystera gave Callison the duty of telepathically transmitting to Liele, to tell her they'd meet her in the magnifier room of the white prep house. Being telepathic felt different and Callison felt his mind had a fluid like quality.

'Just think of Liele, and think the message. Visualise the thought leaving your mind.' said the wise one.

Callison found it instinctive, Hi Liele! The Engineers have given me a skill. The experience was nothing like I expected it to be. Mystera and myself will meet you in the magnifier room. We are just leaving the top of the pyramid now.

The transmission was clear. She knew it was Callison's unique vibration signature straight away and transmitted back, Hello Callison, good for you! I hope you had a good session. I'll meet you there shortly.

Callison telepathically responded, Mystera has a plan of action I think. The Engineers have cleared a few things up for me also. I'll see you soon!

Callison faced Mystera, 'She understood.'

Liele reassured him from at least two hundred yards away, See, nothing to worry about!

The telepathic broadcasts sounded almost like his normal thoughts, but for some reason that was hard to identify, he could tell they were from Liele. Callison knew she was right also; there was never anything to worry about.

The master smiled, 'Good,' He stood up, 'come on, let's walk to the magnifier room.'

Callison was more positive about his situation and stood up also, 'Yes. I'm ready.'

They descended the goliath staircase down the pyramid's flank and walked across the dusty Noi Tu arena to the bright white prep house. They walked in via the same entrance he and Liele had done two days previously and after navigating floors and corridors, Callison and Mystera arrived in a large room with shelves and shelves of boxes on runners that could be pulled out: the magnifier room. Liele wasn't there yet.

Mystera looked at the hieroglyph style labels on each of the boxes and when he found the right box he pulled it out and gave it to Callison, 'Choose a magnifier.'

Callison looked in the box. There were five precious crystals, a white one, a blue one, a yellow one, a purple one and a red one, 'Which one should I choose?' asked Callison.

'Choose the one that you feel calls out to you the most, or choose one at random, it will always be the right one.'

'I'll take the purple one.' he said, taking the precious stone out of the box. He gave the box back.

'Good choice!' came Liele's voice from the open doorway.

Callison was pleased to see her again, 'Hey! How are you?'

'I'm well.' she continued to walk over, 'I take it you have more information about your circumstances now?'

'Yes.' Callison wasn't sure, 'Well, it looks like my life as I know it has ended, but it seems I'm not dead.' He smiled at the absurd profundity of the words he'd just used. 'But I think we have a plan of action?' He questioned a glance toward Mystera, who walked out from the shelves of magnifier boxes.

'Yes, Callison is going to do an intuitive integration,' said the master to Liele, 'after some meditation and thought exercises first.'

'Are you nervous?' she asked.

Callison replied, 'Not really. It's quite the adventure in fact!'

'Good for you!' she rallied.

'Let's get this magnifier attached then.' said Mystera.

The magnifier was attached using a natural resin that took a few moments to bond the stone to his forehead. Mystera, Liele and Callison left the prep house and parted ways in the Noi Tu Arena. 'Ok then Callison, I'll see you tomorrow morning here at about 2 after rise for some meditation.' said Mystera.

Callison confirmed the appointment, and said his goodbyes. He added, 'Thank you as well. You are a kind man.'

Mystera took the praise gracefully and smiled, 'See you now. See you Liele.'

The wise one walked back towards the pyramid as Callison and Liele set off back to the boat shed and Sukarmia. Tomorrow Callison would have a meditation lesson and teachings on the soul from Mystera. The day after that, he was to have telekinesis lessons from Liele's brother, Tobian to increase the power of his mind. If he were ready, he would undertake the intuitive integration in three days time to navigate his way back to his parallel experience of Callison Trebla.

On their way back to Sukarmia, they stopped off at Sunrise Hill again to practise a meditation that would help Callison's telepathy to develop. It was warm, but a slight breeze rolled over the grassy hilltop, hazy sunshine bathed the city and the skyscrapers glinted in the sun like twinkling stars. He was aware of the new attachment on his forehead, but it didn't seem to detract at all. He didn't even need to think, he just listened to Liele's telepathic meditation instructions, and gazed at the mid-afternoon view of the city before them. He felt like the master of his own experience again and realised he always had been; he'd just forgotten it over his sixty-five years of misinterpretation of physical reality.

* * * * * * *

21: Awakening of Soul

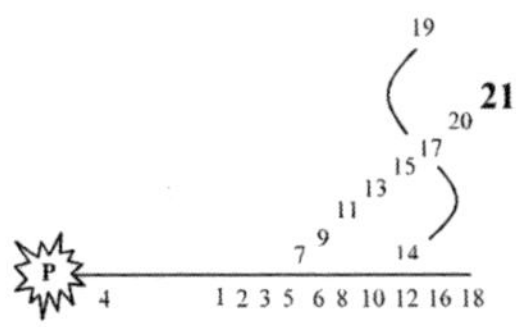

"It's not that you have a soul;
you are a soul. You have a body."
C. S. Lewis, Writer and Author (1898 - 1963)

21.1 –
Date not known:
Plus three days:

Normally meditation in Sukarmia was taught in classes with a handful of likeminded souls, but given Callison's background and mental pre-condition, Mystera gave him a one-to-one class in a sacred and tranquil place.

As Callison was climbing the steps to the top of the pyramid, he telepathically broadcast. I'm here Master Mystera! As he reached the pyramid's summit, Mystera was standing waiting for him.

He put his hands together and bowed towards Callison, smiling peacefully. 'Good morning my friend.'

Callison felt safe and assured in the shaman's presence. 'Good morning Mystera.' he said.

Instead of going into the pyramid like last time, master and student walked down the long staircase on the blind side of the pyramid and onwards into the Sukarmian undergrowth for another half hour to a tree house that Mystera had built as a teenager many years ago. Clouds had started to build and although light, it was getting more overcast as they approached the tree house.

From the ground level, Callison could just make out a wooden box hidden high up in the canopy. The tree trunk had wooden slats nailed in all the way up to the tree house, creating a ladder.

'Wow, it's quite high up.' said Callison.

Mystera didn't want him to do anything he didn't want, and sensed his nervous thought patterning, 'Do you not want to go?'

Callison took his gaze from the top of the trees, and faced his teacher, 'No, it's fine, I'll go up.' He was brave rather than he was fearless.

Mystera was glad and walked up to the bottom of the tree ladder, 'Come on then.'

They started to climb; Mystera lead Callison up but before they got too high Callison started to get nervous. He looked down at the forest floor and they were already rather high, he looked up past Mystera above him, and there was still a long way to go. He called to Mystera above him, 'It's pretty high up, are *you* not worried about falling?' he asked.

The master continued climbing, shouting back over his shoulder from above, 'No, not really, why are you?'

Callison was honest, 'The thought had crossed my mind, we're quite high up.'

'We'll be there before you know it,' he stopped climbing and looked down at his student and reassured again, 'do you still want to come?'

'Yes, I'm coming.' said Callison, determined not to wimp out.

They finally reached the tree house, high up in the canopy and entered via direct access from the ladder, which lead into the underside of the wooden house, 'Welcome to my meditation retreat.' said Mystera as he helped Callison in.

'Thanks.' said Callison, who was glad the ascent was over. He couldn't help but look down before he entered. *He would be a speck down there from up here*, he thought. He wondered about the consequences if he fell and they made him want to get into the safety of the tree house.

'I'm surprised you do that climb every time to get here, how many times do you think you've done it? Imagine if you fell!' Callison was still thinking like a human on Earth.

Mystera's reply intrigued him. 'I have fallen many times, but I always get back on!' he said as he looked for some candles in one of the cubby holes of the wooden room.

'Surely you should be dead?' asked Callison, looking around the interior of the shack. Inside it was basic, but deceptively spacious. The tree trunk ran up one side of the space, and just in front of it was the door on the floor.

'You'd survive if you jumped from here.' said the master casually. He found the candles.

Callison looked down through the hole in the floor again. *No way.* 'You're kidding aren't you?'

'I'm not,' he said honestly, 'jump, and prove me wrong if you think you'll die.' He was teaching Callison, even if Callison didn't know it yet.

'No, I'll just use the ladder.' he said cautiously.

'Ok, same here then, close the hatch up and we'll begin some meditation.' The master smiled as he put two candles on the sturdy wooden floor.

Callison closed the hatch, covering the hole in the floor while wondering what the bizarre conversation had meant. *Would he survive if he jumped?* He remembered the elegant Engineer had said he wasn't in a physical dimension anymore, but it still felt like one and that was all the mattered. He wasn't going to be jumping any time soon.

The four walls of the tree house had sections cut out of them making windows that gave wonderful views of the surroundings; deep, lush greenery as far as the eye could see. One of the windows was partially covered by the leaves and foliage of the tree they were sitting in. A rumble of thunder echoed in the distance. There was a distinct earthy smell of timber that lingered in the air inside the wooden cage, in which there was easily enough headroom to stand. On the fourth wall next to the tree trunk was some hieroglyph text written above a black painting that, upon closer inspection, had a small dot of white paint in the middle.

'What does that say?' Callison asked of the writing under the painting.

Mystera was momentarily absorbed over by where he found the candles. He mentally focused on the candles he'd just put on the floor and after a few moments, they sparked into life, and as if my magic emitted a flame apiece. Callison was learning to accept the new skills people here had developed.

'That is a proverb,' said the wise one, 'that prompts me to keep a reign on my mind, to filter my thoughts and to think positively.' He translated, 'It says: Plant an intention and grow a thought - plant a thought and grow a feeling - plant a feeling and grow an attitude - plant an attitude and grow an action - plant an action and grow a habit - plant a habit and grow a personality - plant a personality and grow a destiny.'

'Wow. That's pretty good,' he thought about it. *Planting and growing:* another concept that Callison had known about all his life, but was just starting to listen to, 'wise words indeed, and the black painting?'

Mystera smiled, and half chuckled as he answered, 'Self portrait.'

Callison was confused; the painting was just a white spark on a black background. He hesitated for a minute, 'But,' this was too easy, 'you don't look like that.'

The master corrected him, 'When you experience yourself as the energy you are, rather than your body or your character, that's exactly what *we all* look like.'

Callison still had a confused look about him, 'So my soul looks like this?'

'Soul is a label that has been used for it, yes.' The master wanted to teach, 'Instead of asking if *your soul* looks like this, it would be more true to ask if *you* look like this, for you don't *have* a soul. You *are* a soul. You are given all the tools you need for the duration of your earth experience and those tools are your mind and body.' He didn't seem like he was making it up.

Callison wasn't following, 'So, I see myself as a body, and you see yourself as a soul,' he was honest, 'so what?'

Mystera nodded, 'A valid question.' He thought about his reply, he had witnessed the physical, so told Callison to reassure him, 'Look, I have experienced Earth lives also, and I have seen the condition of the minds of the people on Earth in the era you are from.' He paused on purpose. 'What do you think of your world?'

Callison answered, 'My world in 2008 has gone mad!' he retorted, without needing time to think.

The master made his point, but spoke calmly, 'The world is not mad; night still follows day, summer still follows winter. It's the souls *in* the world that have gone mad, including I'm sorry to say it, you, by thinking you *are* your mortal earth bodies! Your character is so much in survival mode, it locks down in fear and cannot tell you that you are mad, so it does the easy thing and convinces you that you are sane and it's the rest of the world that is mad.'

Callison felt slightly offended, but compared his world to Sukarmia, and had to concede the point.

The teacher continued, 'I'll give you another insight into body-consciousness; your world is very much body-conscious and people grow up to see themselves as separate from everything and everyone else, and that in turn leads to self-identification by comparison, which leads every time to bigotry and ego issues in the case of the 'have's', or destruction and depression issues in the case of the 'have not's' and they are both pathways of fear.' he summed, 'And it's all because the knowledge of true identity has been forgotten on Earth. In being soul-conscious you would see everyone else as the same as you. You would care more about what goes on in your mind, for you would know that the mind builds your physical experience of your environment. Mind comes before matter.'

Callison conceded again.

'Take a seat.' Mystera gestured to the rug on the floor, and they both sat down cross-legged facing each other. As they both sat, their tunics pushed up and the bristles tickled Callison's chin. Callison noticed it was raining slightly mainly from the earthy smell it created, Callison's favourite smell. *Perfect*, he thought. He took a deep nose full of the earthy air, making him feel good as the cleansing rain fell.

21.2 –

'I'm going to ask you a question.' said Mystera, sitting down. 'It's the most important question you can ever ask yourself.' He paused, 'Who are you?'

Callison was confused again. He sat on the wood floor, thinking. 'I'm…' This was too obvious, surely. '…me?'

'And who is *me*?' came the wise one's answer.

'Callison Trebla.'

'Ok, but there can be many Callison Trebla's, and there is only one *you*. What's the difference?'

'What?' he answered, confused.

'Your name is merely a label for you. You could change the label if you wanted.'

'Yes, I suppose I could.' said Callison, thinking with the master.

'So would *you* be someone else if *you* changed *your* name?'

'No, I'd still be me.'

'So, "Callison Trebla" inadequately describes who or what you are; it merely labels you, so we'll go back to the question. Who are you, the labelled?'

Callison thought he would be exact. 'I am slightly balding, I am white skinned, I have a moustache, I have blue eyes, and I have…' He stopped himself, because Mystera was smiling. 'What are you smiling at?'

'So let, me get this right.' said Mystera. 'You are slightly balding?'

'Yep.' Came the confident reply.

'You are white skinned?'

'Yep'. Still confidant.

'You are a moustache?'

Callison stayed quiet. That sounded odd. 'No, I *have* a moustache.' he corrected.

'This is the deceptive point I'm wanting you to think about. You are not describing who you *are* anymore; you are describing what you *have*. Instead of seeing yourself as slightly balding, see it like you *have* balding hair. You *have* white skin. You *have* a body.' he paused, 'Who *are* you?'

The penny started to drop. 'Ok... I think I see where you're going with this.'

The master helped him along, 'I'll give you a clue. What do *you* have that your body, or your labels don't?'

After remaining quiet for a long minute, he answered philosophically, 'Morals?'

An enlightening smile spread over Mystera's face, 'Good one, now you're getting it. What else?'

He thought some more, 'Desires and dreams?'

'Yes... keep going?'

'The capacity to imagine?'

'Yes, really in the flow now... So who are you?'

'I am a human being.' He smiled, thinking he'd got the answer.

Mystera conceded, but not fully, 'You are half right with that one, when you're on Earth, which you are not now.' he added, 'An interesting term though: human being. You are the *being* of the human,' He paused, 'So who are *you* being?'

Callison was stumped again. 'I... I don't know who I am. I thought I did...'

The master calmed the student, 'Don't worry about it for now. You were actually closest with your first answer, when you answered "me". Just be aware that when you refer to yourself as "me", you are labelling the whole of your being. Just keep asking the question, "Who am I?" to yourself and it will start to make sense as you think about it.'

Callison nodded apprehensively as the rain continued to fall outside the tree house. The master's words had wisdom in them that Callison felt and he was listening for the first time, even if he didn't understand fully yet.

'Ok, would you like to do some meditation now?' asked Mystera.

'Yes, ok, let's do it.' he replied with a new found intrigue.

'You can meditate on whatever you like,' said Mystera, 'but seeing as though we are talking about identity, we will start with rediscovery, and soul-consciousness.

Callison went with him, 'Ok.' He had heard Liele talk meditations to him, so half expected what was coming.

'For you are not Callison Trebla; you are an energetic and conscious being of light that is having the *experience* of Callison Trebla.'

'Ok.' said Callison. This felt like a philosophy lesson, but he kept his mind open.

Mystera closed his eyes and mentally turned a speaker on and some calming music started to emanate out of a speaker hidden in the tree house. Mystera's voice was calm, slow and clear.

'You can keep your eyes open if you wish. Of course, remember to blink.' He paused, smiling peacefully, 'Or you can close them, it is up to you.' Callison kept his eyes open, but let his gaze fall upon the light coloured wooden floor. Mystera slowly began to speak, and gave instruction.

'Sit comfortably and consciously relax your body...' He paused to let his student take it in. The music added to the tranquillity. 'Stretch and relax your muscles and joints for a moment, working up your body ending with your head and face.'

Callison fidgeted as he stretched and relaxed his body.

'...Breathe in through the nose...' The master said.

The smell of the fresh falling rain was beautiful to Callison.

'...And exhale slowly through the mouth. Watch your breath come and go, just like the tides of the ocean...'

'...In... ...and out...'

'...In... ...and out...'

Callison followed as Mystera led his imagination away from it's learned confines.

'...Now imagine nothing exists outside this room,'

Callison imagined.

'...Imagine that the space itself is empty of all objects. There is nothing to distract you...'

Apart from my thoughts, Callison thought, *I don't know how to stop them!* He tried to continue listening. This was the benefit of one to one tuition; Mystera picked up on his thoughts, and adapted what he was saying.

Calmly Mystera continued, '...Ignore any wandering thoughts or external distractions... ...Allow them to come, allow them to be and allow them to go... ...Watch them come and pass, like clouds in the sky...'

Callison didn't try to stop his thoughts anymore; he let them come. And they went away again before he could even let them go. He'd never realised his thoughts were so fleeting.

Mystera carried on speaking like a metronome, leading Callison's mind, '...Bring all your attention up through your body to a point in the middle of your forehead. Just above and behind your eyes...'

Callison did so. He was aware of the magnifier on his forehead, which felt warm against his skin.

'...This is where you, the being, reside... ... within your body...'

'...For you are not your body... ...You are the one that animates your body... ...You are the driver, and your body is the vehicle...'

There's the body stuff he was talking about earlier Callison thought. Before realising the thought it was gone already. He tried to bring his mind back to listening and imagining.

'...Now quietly concentrate your attention on yourself...'

'...Begin to see and experience yourself as you really are... ...A tiny point of concentrated energy that is conscious and self aware...'

I don't understand why? thought Callison, *I'm not light?* He went with Mystera out of trust more than logic.

'...Be aware of yourself sitting... ...here... ...just above and behind the eyes...'

'...Be aware of yourself, radiating energy...'

'...You are a being of light, radiating light...'

'...You are a point of light... ...That is conscious... ...and aware of it's own existence...'

'...Now imagine a darkened room...'

Callison closed his eyes to do so. He could imagine the darkened room.

'...There in the middle of the room... ...a tiny point of radiant light appears...'

A tiny spot of light flashed in the darkness of the backs of his eyelids, and then vanished again. *Am I seeing things?* Callison thought as Mystera continued. He searched the darkness for the light again, but it was apparently gone.

Mystera continued, '...Gradually the speck of light grows in intensity... ...until all darkness disappears and the room is filled with pure... ...white... ...light...'

Callison had labelled the light he saw as his mind playing tricks. It was gone again. He tried to continue listening.

'...You are that light... ...That tiny point of light that expands to fill the room...'

'...Now remind yourself that you are eternal and imperishable...'

The light flashed again for Callison, but vanished the moment Callison realised it was there.

Mystera was in flow, '...You cannot die...'

'...Quietly create this thought, and say to yourself...'

'...I am a point of pure light...'

Callison thought out of curiosity, *I am a point of pure light,*

'...A point of pure radiant... ...spiritual... ...light...'

A point of pure radiant... spiritual... light...

'...Take a moment to live in that awareness...'

It's peaceful, Callison realised.

'... Now change that thought...' said the master.

'...I... ...the soul... ...the energy... ...am the eternal unchanging imperishable being...'

Callison thought with him, *I, the soul, the energy am the eternal unchanging imperishable being.*

'...Make this thought very slow...'

'...I... the soul... ...am the unchanging... ...imperishable... ...being...'

Callison slowed his thought down to match his teacher's tempo.

Mystera spoke in first person, '...I have been on a self-guided journey... ...for many lifetimes... ...and had many adventures and experiences along the way...'

The sentence resonated with Callison, who felt like he'd had many adventures in the last few days here, let alone in former lifetimes.

'...Allow yourself to experience the freedom... ...the peace... ...that these thoughts invoke from deep within...'

It does feel peaceful, thought Callison.

'...You are a traveller of worlds, allow yourself to fully realise who... ...and what... ...you are...'

He tried to allow himself to fully realise, but he didn't know. He did feel peaceful though, despite not knowing. He tried to think about whether feeling peaceful was more important than knowing everything.

'...You are now in the consciousness of the soul...' continued Mystera.

It's more important to be peaceful. Callison hadn't thought *that* thought. It kind of popped into his awareness. *Where had the thought come from?* he asked himself. This thought too, dissipated quickly.

'...Your original... ...and true consciousness...'

'...Gently maintain that inner awareness for as long as you can...'

There was a pause of a couple of minutes as the pair of them maintained their awareness of the peaceful and tranquil feelings.

Mystera started to draw the meditation to a close, '...Then... ...when you feel ready... ...gently return your thoughts and your attention to your physical body... ...to this room around you... ...to this moment now...'

'...Bringing with you... ...that awareness of your inner peace...'

Mystera remained quiet, until Callison opened his eyes.

Slowly Callison brought his awareness back into the tree house. He didn't say anything. He didn't need to. He lifted his eyes and looked at his master again. The rain had stopped, and the sun shone in through the unglazed windows creating a warm damp wooden smell.

The master advised, 'When you have finished your meditation, take a moment to realise how peaceful you now feel, and how light you now feel. You are simply creating a contented mind, by your own intent.'

He listened to his teacher, feeling energised but peaceful. He felt a bit silly, as he realised he had meditation pre-compartmentalised in his mind as a lonely thing to do. He thought people that meditated must lead sorry, empty lives, but here he was, meditating and his mind was more positive than it had been in years. It felt good. He was a human, being peaceful by intent.

Master and student remained in the tree house for the entire morning talking about the facets and dimensions to soul. Weather fronts came and went as the pair discussed the concepts and lessons involved. Two birds even came and stood on the window ledge, as if listening to the imparted wisdom.

Callison learned that the soul was comprised of three elements, the intellect, the mind, and the subconscious. Each attribute merged in unique-to-the-soul proportions and formed unique-to-the-soul patterns, like primary colours of light mixing and forming together to form spiritual signatures. Much like snowflakes, each soul was unique, and each one equally beautiful. They were seen rarely on Earth with the human eye, but sometimes they would appear as white flashes and specks or orbs of light in times of crisis, despair or displays of unconditional love.

The mind was the part of the soul that thought, felt, imagined, and formed concepts and beliefs. The mind was regulated by the intellect, which was the part of the soul that discerned, evaluated, decided and understood. The intellect fed back to the mind the quality of the thoughts the mind was generating. If the intellect broke down due to lack of use, it would slowly lose the power to evaluate incoming information, and the mind would be unregulated, generating pointless noise. The subconscious part of the soul was similar to a zipped storage facility, or memory: it held records of all the soul's experiences over all the life times, past and present. It was the subconscious that held memories and dictated tendencies, talents, virtues and character traits during physical lives. All three parts communicated with light and shone upon a point of focus in the centre of the soul, which manifested in humans as their current state of self-aware consciousness.

As the morning turned lazily into afternoon, the meditation session came to an end and Callison followed Mystera back to the pyramid.

The day was as much an experience of meditation, as it was a lesson in life. That part of Callison that had been whispering to him most of his life that something was not right with the direction of humanity; that shouted loudest while watching the news and seeing stories of murder, rape, theft, fraud, greed and lies was his intellect working overtime, trying to tell his mind that the thoughts it was generating were negative, and to change his thoughts, or stop watching the news if he wanted to find a lighter mood. He couldn't hear the inner wisdom though. The intellect's valiant cries were deafened by consciously loud, but useless fear based thoughts of comparison, resentment and anger brought on by the body-conscious fear of survival. His judgement was clouded by something that only now, he was starting to see. He was looking at the quality and cleanliness of the lens through which he saw everything, not through his eyes, but through his being.

* * * * * * *

22: Awakening of Mind

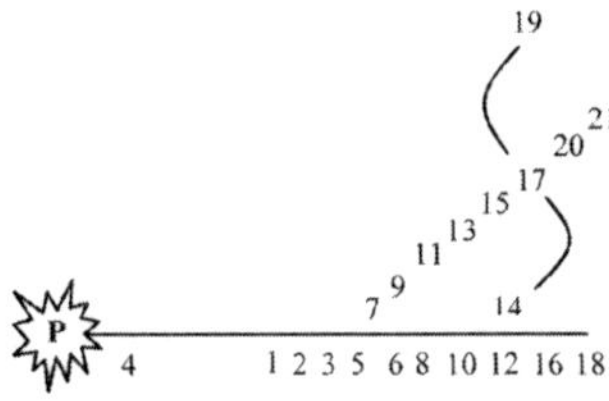

"Emancipate yourselves from mental slavery,
none but ourselves can free our minds."
Bob Marley, Musician (1945 – 1981)

22.1 –
Date not known:
Plus four days:

The meditation lesson had awakened Callison to a conscious question of identity he'd never asked himself. *Who was he?* The more he thought about it, the more he realised Mystera had a point. He thought he was Callison, but that was only a label. He thought he was his body, but that was only his vehicle through time. His body didn't make decisions; *he* did. He thought he was a scientist, but that was only his job description.

The more he realised that his identity as Callison had been a mishmash of temporary fleeting terms and definitions, relative to the *context* of the question: who are you? The more he thought about it the terms and definitions he wanted to use to describe himself were all only relative to his current circumstance. Who was he, the *whole* being that experienced *all* of his experiences *as* him?

Describing himself as a soul did make sense. His body didn't have dreams, memories, desires or morals. *He* did. He was the soul that had choice to make judgments and decisions, and steer his body from experience to experience. It was as if a light had been turned on. He tried to see his new friends in Sukarmia as soul rather than body and he saw them as the same as him. It was a levelling and calming realisation. The need to act a certain way disappeared, and he could be more soul-like, more himself. He felt the fear-of-having-less leave his body, and unknowingly freed himself from invisible chains that kept him unconscious to the true nature of his identity.

Callison's intuitive integration was going to take place tomorrow, but today he would be working on improving his mind's resolve and would increase his thought strength and thought patterning by having a telekinesis lesson from Tobian. Little did he know that in addition, the lessons would help him inter-dimensionally save his beloved Eleanor's life.

Liele was teaching meditation in one of the schools today as part of her community service and would see Callison and Tobian at the end of the day after their lesson together. After breakfast in the apartment, the three of them took a sky-taxi over to the telekinesis arena they had visited three days ago.

The morning sun was trying to break through the cloud, as the sky-taxi approached the tall skyscraper roof where the arena was situated. The airborne transport hovered over the sky cab drop-off point and Callison hopped out first, followed by Tobian. Liele stayed inside to travel on to do her city-service teaching day.

'Have a good time. I'll see you at dusk.' said Liele.

'Ok.' said Callison, 'See you tonight!' Liele had been so nice to him for his whole time here. She had prepared breakfast for him and Tobian this morning, and Callison felt himself becoming increasingly attracted to her. He ignored the attraction. He knew he would be going back to his reality soon, and his beloved Eleanor.

'Have a good day sis, see you later.' said Tobian.

As Liele zipped off to her destination in the sky-taxi, Tobian and Callison walked towards the entrance of the telekinetic stadium in the sky. It was a lot less crowded than the last time he had arrived here.

'Thanks Tobi, for doing this.' Callison said.

Tobian seemed laid back, 'No problem Callison. It's my skill. Teaching it is what I get enjoyment from. Come, it's this way.' Tobian led them towards the arena.

Callison looked forward to being able to do telekinesis. He had tried to do it secretly in the bedroom in Liele's family's apartment, but had ultimately had no success. Or so he thought.

'How is your mind at concentrating on one thing, and one thing only Callison?' asked Tobian as they walked towards the entrance.

'Well, I don't know,' said Callison, 'I concentrated a lot to make my invention back in my physical experience, but I've never moved anything with my mind as far as I'm aware.'

Tobian gave a different answer as he walked into the arena through the empty turn styles, 'Maybe you have unknowingly done ninety-nine percent of the moving, and you're struggling with the final one percent?'

Callison was intrigued as he walked through the turnstile next to Tobian, 'Is that how it works?'

'Maybe,' he added, as he led the way across the sparse entrance hall, 'the truth is you make up how it works in order to actually do it.'

'And how do you do that?' asked Callison as he walked along side his teacher.

'It's not as universal as that,' said Tobian, slightly troubled, 'I know where to go in *my* mind, and it's not labelled so I can't tell you where to go in *your* mind, only *you* can. Does that make sense?'

'Slightly maybe,' Callison said, plainly confused.

'Look, I don't know how your mind works for you,' said Tobian, 'and I never will; only you can *ever* know that.'

They walked directly up some steps that led out of the entrance hall and when they got to the top of the flight, the arena greeted them. The seating in the arena was largely empty, but for a few people milling about and the grassy arena floor had been protected with walk-on flooring and was open to the sky above. Gathered in small groups, people were practicing their telekinesis skills.

'What's going on here today?' asked Callison.

'Practice day.' said Tobian. As he looked out over the arena, he telepathically announced his arrival to the arena show organisers.

Callison looked down at the main arena floor. It looked like a circus workshop. He saw a couple of people making coloured balls hover in the air. *What a fascinating skill!* he thought.

'Come on, let's make a start.' said Tobian. He continued, 'Now, I'm going to have a meeting in about an hour, but it won't be a long one. I'll start you up, but then I'll leave in about an hour. You can have some lunch.' He pointed up to the eatery high up in the far stand. 'We can stay here all day if we like though, so we have plenty of time.'

Callison agreed, and followed Tobian down the steps onto the performance area. They took a drink each from a help-yourself stand, and after finding some space on the arena floor Tobian began teaching him how to master telekinesis.

They stood facing each other, 'This is what we practice with.' Tobian held up a red spongy ball in his hand, 'We use a ball because it is round, and spherical objects are the most uniform to pick up with your mind.' He pulled his hand away, but the ball remained levitating in the air.

Neat, thought Callison, as he couldn't help but smile at the feat.

The ball zipped down to the floor inbetween them under Tobian's telekinetic influence. He mentally dropped it, and left it on the floor, 'Have a go at moving it.'

Callison was unsure, but looked at the red ball on the floor. He wasn't sure of how to do it. He willed the ball to move but it just remained still, 'I can't do it. I don't know how.'

Tobian explained. 'Everyone describes what they actually do with their mind differently, but the phenomenon is common to all minds. Your experience of your surroundings, or the *external* mind as it's also known, is everything outside of you: the objects, the trees, the people, the events, the sights, and the sounds. They are all abstract reflections for everything in your *internal* mind; your issues, your thoughts, your ideas, your concepts, your understandings.'

Callison was intrigued from his currently forming thoughts about identity. 'So who are we? Are we the observer, or the creator of experience?'

Tobian replied, as he saw it, 'We're neither: we are the consciousness that encapsulates the creator *and* the experience as one.' He waited for Callison's reaction.

'Ok' he said back, not really seeing how it related to telekinesis.

Tobian continued, 'You see, we create via the *internal* mind, and experience via the *external* mind. We only have direct influence via the *internal* mind because we cannot change the outer world, as that is the reflection. So we need to move the ball in our *internal* mind, and then expect the reflection in the *external* mind.'

Callison was sceptical. He didn't know if he could do this, 'I'll try, but I'm not promising anything.' He prepared himself, beginning to stare at the ball between them again, before Tobian stopped him.

'Change your attitude.' Tobian said informatively, 'If you don't think you can do it, guess what... you have just sealed your fate. You have to know you can do it.'

'Well, where I come from we can't do this,' Callison said, slightly defensive, 'so it's hard!'

'I wonder why!' said Tobian sarcastically, 'Look, you will only see results reflected in the external mind,' he pointed at the ball on the floor, '*the ball*, when you address and locate the part of your mind which reflects this ball. And it won't be in a part of your mind that says it's impossible, it will be in a part of your mind that says it's possible, so guess what you have to think to navigate to the internal red ball?'

'That it's possible?' asked Callison.

'You got it.' said Tobian, 'Here, let's try this.' He used his telekinesis skills to hold the ball in the air in front of them again, 'Ok, I'll tell you what I'm doing.' The ball started to waver more and looked unstable in the air. 'I'm releasing my concentration now, and that is why the ball is wavering. If I decide to concentrate more,' he did so, 'I will have more control over the ball's location.' The ball stopped wavering in the air and locked into a static position. 'If I decide to think about something else completely, again, I'll lose control.' The ball dropped to the floor.

Callison was quietly awed in Tobian's knowledge of the subject.

Tobian resumed control and the ball hovered in front of them once again. He continued, 'Ok, so what I'm going to do is hold the ball in the air, but I'm going to get to the point where I'm only just mentally holding onto it.' The ball started to waver more as Tobian part-relinquished his mental influence, 'Ok, try and steady it. Try and keep it still.'

Callison concentrated on trying to keep it still.

Tobian advised, 'You have to remain as peaceful as you can, getting frustrated is like pulling a cloud between you and the ball. You have to imagine yourself as being whole. Imagine you are the whole universe; imagine you encompass everything, even if you think you don't. Imagine you do, and then scan your mind. Find the ball in there. When you get close, you will see the ball stay more still in the air' Tobian continued to barely hold the ball, and the ball floated haphazardly still.

Callison listened to his teacher, and imagined being peaceful. He saw himself as being everything, and scanned his mind. He visualised doing a sweep of his mind, as he swept across, the ball did remain still for a moment, but it wavered again straight away.

'You got it for a moment there!' said the teacher, 'Now try and home in on that area of your mind.'

It took some time, but Callison carried on narrowing down in his mind where the ball was, and he was able to keep the ball relatively still, before giving up and having to break his concentration. He expected the ball to start wavering again, but it didn't; it dropped to the floor.

'You had it going well!' said Tobian. 'I had let go of it quite a while ago!'

'So *I* was doing all of it?' Callison said, with surprised optimism.

'Yes!' said Tobian. 'Placebo never fails. So you know you can do it now.'

Callison was triumphant, and wanted to do it again, but he was surprised when he couldn't. It seemed as fast as he learned the skill, he un-learned it.

'I don't understand it. How can I do it one minute and forget it the next?'

Tobian smiled, 'We have a phrase, I guess that would translate into something called starting luck?'

Beginner's Luck? thought Callison, 'Yes, I know a similar phrase.'

'Yes, ok.' Tobian prompted, 'You know why?'

Callison shook his head, devoid of answers.

'When you do something for the first time, your mind does it blind. No conditioning. Second time around, your mind is not in the here and now, it is living the memory of your first triumph, and so has less effect in the here-and-now.'

'Ok' said Callison. It seemed to make sense.

'So you have to uncondition your mind and focus only on the here and now to interact with the ball again.' He added, 'It's why we meditate also, because it's true of all interactions with the outside mind, not just moving objects. Interacting with ideas, events, people, nature, well: life energy really. Your inner mind is the area to hone. Your outer experience will reflect your inner state of mind.'

It wasn't the first time he'd heard that. The telekinesis lesson was turning into the same lesson on living that he'd received from Mystera the day before.

As his telekinetic experience increased, Callison had some more success with the ball to the point where he could affect the ball with no help from Tobian. He was learning just how versatile his mind was.

Time came around fast, and Tobian had to disappear for his meeting with the display team. Callison went to have some lunch from the eatery at the Arena situated up in one of the far stands, which overlooked the telekinetic performance area below. As he sat and thought back about his telekinetic success while he ate and before long, he received a telepathic message and he just knew it was from Mystera.

Hello my child, how do you find yourself now?

He was startled by it, but replied remotely as he ate, I am well Mystera. I have had some telekinetic success! He waited for his master's response.

It came before long. Well done, I knew you could do it! He continued, I am letting you know that I have received news from the Universal Mind about your alternate reality.

Callison stopped eating and took a sip of his drink as he gazed out over the arena anxiously. Ok. What sort of news?

The master sensed his fear and calmed him. Do not worry. You are ready for your intuitive integration, which means we will need to start early tomorrow. Get an early night and be at the pyramid for one before rise. Everything will be ok Callison. You will be a step nearer your destiny.

Callison didn't know if he was being fearless or being himself. He felt good though and wasn't worried about the looming exercise. Ok, see you tomorrow Mystera. Thank you.

Mystera knew his student was ready, and mentally signed off. See you tomorrow Callison.

Callison carried on with his lunch. He telepathically transmitted to Liele wherever she was. Hello. Are you able to communicate? He waited as he ate a potato-like vegetable that tasted good. Her reply was not long in coming, and although Callison didn't know why, Liele's telepathic broadcasts had her character running through them.

I'm always able to communicate! How are you? she broadcast back.

Callison smiled. He knew it was Liele because it was the most familiar soul to him in Sukarmia. I am doing well. I have moved a couple of balls along the floor and held them steady in the air for a time! How is your day going?

She was happy for him and her jubilance was heartfelt, It's great that you've had some success! My day has gone well thank you. I might be leaving early, so I'll see you back at the apartment if I do. Would you and Tobi like me to cook you dinner tonight?

Gratefully he accepted, Yes please, that would be wonderful! He told her about the intuitive integration. Mystera says that I will be doing the intuitive integration tomorrow.

Liele knew that he could only undertake the intuitive integration when he was ready, and she was glad he was. You will understand more after your intuitive integration. How do you feel about it?

Ok I think. I don't really know what to expect. Callison spotted Tobian walking into the eatery and raised his hand in acknowledgement. He added to his telepathy, Anyway, Tobian is back now. Looks like I'm going to be moving things with my mind again!

Liele replied, Ok then, I'll see you tonight, have fun!

Bye Liele, thanks. Callison signed off also.

Tobian walked up to Callison's table and joined him sitting down. 'There we go, meeting is all done. I'm yours for the afternoon.'

'How was your meeting?' enquired Callison.

Tobian told him all about the coming show, but Callison's internal mind wandered. It was a delicate and intimate feeling. He was thinking about Liele. The thoughts died down, when Tobian stopped talking.

'Yes, it sounds like the show will be good.' said Callison. He knew he didn't belong here, but he felt like he was falling in love with someone here.

'Right! You ready for some more mind magic?' said Tobian conscious to his student's thought patterns.

Callison thought he held his cards close, 'Yes, ready as I'll ever be!'

22.2 –

Callison's telekinesis lesson from Tobian had been one of the most enjoyable experiences he could remember; it was as if he was seeing his mind move right in front of him. The scientist in him wondered more about the mechanisms between mind and matter, and he remembered Einstein's famous $E=mc^2$ equation that said matter and energy were interchangeable at the base level. Maybe the mind did create matter? It had something to do with light, as the equation squarely suggested.

The sun had now set, and before it would rise again, Callison would venture out to see Mystera at the Noi Tu outpost before walking into the undergrowth surrounding Sukarmia to undertake his intuitive integration. After that he would be going back to his parallel Earth life, so this was to be his last evening in the city. To celebrate, Liele had cooked him and the family a nut loaf dinner.

Light background music played in the lounge as Liele's parents; Tomak and Estina sat on one side of the glass dining table, and Callison and Tobian the other. Liele sat on the table's end next to Callison and nearest the kitchen to keep tending to the cooking. The table was decorated simply with flowers and the lounge lights were dimmed slightly as they drank some local wine. Currently, Liele was in the kitchen and they were talking about Callison's intuitive integration; well, talking in the loosest telepathic sense.

Tomak broadcasted, I remember one of my intuitive integrations Callison; I actually changed an event in my history.

Estina added to the conversation, And many of mine have pre-mapped events in my future!

Liele broadcast from the kitchen, Stop telling him things; you're confusing his progress! She took the hot nut loaf out of the oven, and started to cut into it.

He spoke back to Liele telling her not to worry, 'I don't mind, really Liele, I'm enjoying talking about it.'

Liele shrugged and joked to herself, 'Ok then, I'll keep my mouth shut!' She continued to concentrate on preparing the food.

Tobian asked Callison in English, but his parents understood the feeling behind the words. 'Did your meeting with the Engineers uncover how your alternate Earth experience is going to differ from the one you are leaving behind?'

'No, that's what my intuitive integration is supposed to create, I'm told.'

Tobian nodded, as Liele brought plates of steaming hot nut loaf over to the dining table. Be careful, it's hot! she said to her table guests.

The food looked and smelled great and everyone was hungry. They weren't big meat eaters in the dimension of the energetic mind and soul, but its substitute was just as nice. The group helped themselves to the vegetables and the bread and started to eat as the music soothed the room.

The conversation changed away from Callison's integration, as he probed more about where he actually was in relation to Earth. He wanted to included Tomak and Estina, so he used telepathy. So does anybody know where Earth actually is compared to here?

Tobian broadcast as he ate, informing the whole table, The dimension of energetic mind and soul surrounds the physical dimension. The gateway into the physical, well, the main gateway is the Alpine Stargate.

Liele already knew it would be her task to lead Callison to the Alpine Stargate when the time came, but didn't let on just yet, she allowed Callison to live the moment.

Estina gave him confidence. Encouraging, {Estina to Callison} I think that you're very brave deciding to do your training on Earth on the timeline you are from. What I hear from Liele is it's a fear pot.

Callison played it down, Earth's ok once you get used to it, yes, there's fear, but there's also great stories of overcoming. It's hard to be yourself, but I've hopefully learnt some errors of my perception! He laughed it off, and took a sip of the fruity tasting wine. The others smiled for him. They had seen a significant difference in the way Callison acted now, from the day that he first arrived.

Liele boosted his confidence and agreed, I think you have conducted yourself really well here. Tobian says you are a natural with the telekinesis and Mystera thinks you'll ace your intuitive integration.

Callison felt relieved, but he knew how easy the physical trap was to fall into. He wanted to make sure he try and stay soul-conscious this time around. He hoped he could.

The energetic mind and soul family talked about this dimension as they ate, trying to answer their visitor's questions in a way he could understand. Callison learned that the dimension of energetic mind and soul was like a shaping zone for the physical environments housed within; the physical environments included the whole universe and every parallel universe experienced. Physical concepts were formed in the mind and soul dimension before being translated into physical possibility in the worlds and realms of the physical experience dimensions. Mind certainly did come before matter. The Universal Mind carried out this thought-translation process, by making small vibrating particles made by individual thoughts wrapped round upon themselves. Tobian had said that these miniscule mental particles of vibration appeared in the physical worlds as atoms. Callison was amazed; just earlier he was thinking about the link between mind and matter. *Matter would seem to be a reflection of thought.* All his life he had falsely assumed that his thoughts were reflections of physical matter. The realisation was huge; his mind came first, and it created his experience of the physical.

Callison's last evening in Sukarmia had been wonderful, thanks to Liele and her impeccable hospitality. Liele enjoyed cooking for people, but this evening she was sad to see her new friend preparing to leave for his Earth life again; she liked him and had grown fond of him in the short time they had been friends. She felt an attraction to him, but she had made an oath in undertaking her mission. The time wasn't right to tell him. Yet.

* * * * * * *

23: The Old World Order

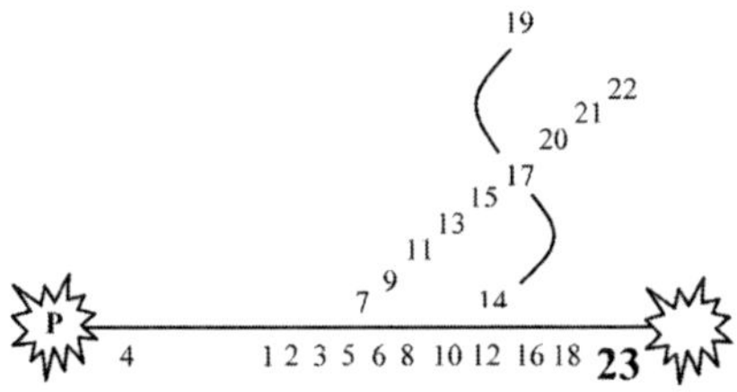

"A new scientific truth does not triumph by convincing its opponents and making them see the light, but rather because its opponents eventually die, and a new generation grows up that is familiar with it."
Max Planck, Theoretical Physicist (1858 – 1947)

23.1 –
The end of the hidden timeline:
May 22nd 2008:

It had been a week since the Eye had first been opened. It was late in the evening and tonight, every soul on Earth that knew anything about the real nature behind the Eye was secretly congregated in the large underground Quanta laboratory to witness history in the making. The significant majority of the world's wealth and power abounded the windowless room in the form of fifty people that all sat on chairs facing toward a speaker's platform on a makeshift stage. To the left of the speaker's plinth stood the recently recovered portal. Excitement vibrated around the underground space, for tonight they would see prophecy realised and be written into the history books as witnesses to something amazing. Or so they thought.

Everyone seated in the audience knew the story of Igor Popovic and his Eye, and the prophecy written in his journals that the first person to use this portal would initiate a new world order. The audience had been told over the years, and believed that the portal unlocked a doorway out of reality, in turn explaining the meaning of life. It was because of that implication that they sought to guard it from the docile masses that currently gave the men in the underground chamber their power. They would demand the truth if ever they realised such a device existed, and that would be bad for the economy. Their leader, Baron Braithwaite III was expecting to initiate the new world order over humanity by becoming the first person to walk through the portal.

Heinrich Muller was working as second hand to the Baron as his technical assistant, and knew that he'd witnessed Callison already using the portal just over a week ago in the scientist's basement. Heinrich was unsure of where this evening was going to go, but time waited for no man and inevitability edged ever closer. The Quanta executive, upon learning that reality was actually a mind-led simulation, had started to crack up. He realised their was point to conscience and a meaning in life he had never contemplated. His Karmic debts lay heavy on his shoulders and he was aware that his murderous actions would ultimately have consequences. He wanted to make amends by telling people about the Eye, but for the oath of blood he had taken with his fraternal brethren of greed he dared not echo a word of his knowledge to anyone; he was on this train all right.

'My Lords, Ladies and Gentlemen,' Baron Braithwaite III began as the eyes of the room eagerly looked on, 'allow me to welcome you all to this special evening, for tonight history will be made.' He cleared his throat with a cough into a handkerchief before continuing in his Old Etonian well spoken tone, 'I'm sure we are all aware of the implications left behind when our dear friend Dr Popovic left us his notebooks all those years ago, well tonight, I will become the first man to walk into the portal you see before you this evening, and we will initiate our new world order!' The audience rumbled in to applause as the hedonistically blind power monger continued to rally his fraternity.

'Before we go on,' he continued, 'I'd like to thank everybody in this room, from the finance masters, to the media masters, to the law and to the political masters for their indebted trust and secrecy throughout the years in our slow but meticulous movement for world domination. We all owe it to ourselves now, to reap our destiny.' He rallied, 'Long may our reign continue my friends!' Another rapturous applause echoed around the dingy Quanta basement, before the night got into swing and their destiny drew nearer.

Heinrich powered the Eye up slowly, giving as best as running commentary as he could to the on looking and excitable crowd. After half an hour had passed, the portal was running at 0.97C... 0.98C... 0.99C... until the number hit the magical 1.00C. The multitude of amazed faces were bathed in multi-coloured, multi-faceted patterns of light emanating from the portal on the stage, swirling, mixing and captivating the attention of the whole room.

Baron Braithwaite III continued explaining to his cohorts that Popovic's prophecy was being fulfilled. He explained what would happen, telling them that after he walks through the shimmering curtain of light that his body will fall unconscious to the floor, but not to worry. He will learn the meaning of life before he regaining consciousness again to inform the room of his experience.

The detectably nervous Baron made his fateful leap through the portal as his followers anticipated grandeur. As his body disappeared into the light curtain, a large white flash occurred and a padded mattress and pillows cushioned his body as it fell to the floor just the other side. Heinrich checked on the Baron, who was indeed unconscious, just as the notebooks had said.

The wait for the Baron to regain consciousness seemed to take forever. The audience continued to wonder, and talked amongst themselves while the Baron lay in another dimension. After five minutes his body had almost come to rest showing zero sign of life. He wasn't breathing. His heart had stopped. Concerns started to grow that he had died, until about ten minutes had passed, when he suddenly surprised everyone by gasping and sitting up straight again.

Whatever his experience behind the veil of consciousness, his facial expression turned immediately to terror, like he'd been to the brink and back. He spoke quickly, and repetitively, while rocking on the mattresses, 'We're all going to be erased…' said the petrified former Baron, 'We're all going to be erased...'

The cabal in the room watched with grave concern as their leader went off the script completely. Their concern turned into a real sinking sensation that something was very wrong. What had their leader witnessed while out of his body?

Heinrich tried to get the dazed man to speak sense, and asked him, 'What do you *mean* erased? What did you see?'

The gibbering Baron Braithwaite uttered more, 'We get taken out of the programme! Our time will be over taken by an altered time wave from a different past… we're doomed!'

'What's a time wave? You're not making sense!' demanded Heinrich.

The Baron remembered Heinrich, 'You!' he pointed and scorned at him, 'You told me that Callison was dead! He used the portal! Both Callison Trebla and Igor Popovic are still ALIVE!'

The prophecy had been true all along, but it was Callison Trebla and Igor Popovic that were the ones fulfilling it.

Heinrich felt like the betrayer, 'I… I don't know what to say….' He knew Callison had jumped first, but knew Callison definitely couldn't be alive. *Could he?*

Before the panic-swept room could blame anyone else, a noise attracted everyone's attention. Including the Baron's. It was coming from the computer rig that sent instruction to the portal. The distribution was starting to hiccup violently. The crowd all noticed the display screen emit a warning beep, and they became tense. The Baron looked back at Heinrich, and spoke with a quiver in his voice, 'What does that mean Heinrich?' Chatter started to ripple around the audience about what was going to happen, before the whole room became deadly quiet. They had noticed something on the stage so curious they could hardly believe their eyes.

Heinrich didn't answer the Baron; he too had his eyes fixed on the same object as his audience. The Baron noticed also.

A marker pen from the computer desk was seemingly hovering in mid-air. Both Heinrich and the Baron watched on in amazement as the marker pen floated over to the whiteboard where it proceeded to transcribe the entire room a message.

23.2 –

Heinrich had read the message and knew what was coming just seconds before the Eye exploded. Heinrich saw the white light pore from the device and fill the entire basement instantaneously. Before he knew what had occurred, he realised he was hovering above his body, staring back at the physical vessel that he had used in the lifetime just lived. He looked at his face and it was covered in blood and the scene around him seemed chaotic, but it was a chaos that unfolded in complete silence. Heinrich, along with everyone that was viewing the Eye in the basement that evening, was now dead.

Slowly, Heinrich's higher memory started to come back to him. This life was only supposed to end this way under special circumstances, which it would appear transpired.

Heinrich could look around the demolished remains of the Quanta basement and the other white lights hovered around the charred scene, the animators of the other powerful earth characters that only seconds ago breathed the same air as he did. Slowly the lights started to drift upwards and out into the universe as one-by-one they started to make their way home.

The ex-quanta executive knew he had to leave the Earth plane for an energetic cleansing, and a life review back in the realms of light where he originally came from. He already felt regret for the people he'd killed and felt like he'd killed a part of himself in his murderous actions during his past life. He felt disfigured by fear and corruption. The feeling was unpleasant to say the least and he knew had had made mistakes in his life, but eventually the pulling came and he travelled upwards along with the other souls who had been his fraternity colleagues in the life-just-lived. The story of Earth was now headed in a new direction.

The Earth soon felt like a bad memory and Heinrich found himself travelling on a beam of light across the universe and back to the realms of light. Soon he noticed a beam of light travelling towards him and as they crossed paths it turned out to be one of the people he had killed in his last life; his ex-employee, Callison Trebla. He didn't want to face him yet out of shame and embarrassment, but his experience drew him in like he had no choice. They stopped and looked at each other. As the two beings stared at each other, Heinrich solemnly broke the silence, 'Hello Callison,' he said sincerely 'I think I owe you an apology...'

* * * * * * *

24: Re Entry

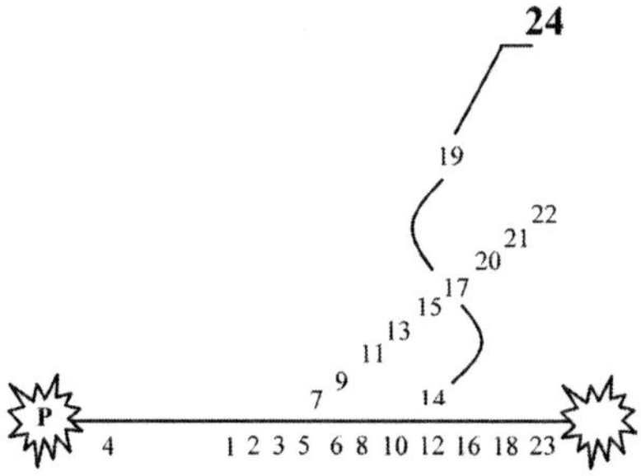

"Be careful who you pretend to be,
because you are who you pretend to be."
Kurt Vonnegut, Author (1922 – 2007)

24.1 –
In Transit:

The journey back to the physical dimensions had been far more surreal than her outbound portal experience, but it filled her full of peaceful expectation. After leaving Togo on the other side of the Alpine Stargate, Eleanor was pulled across the universe through a tunnel system made of the stars and the galaxies of the universe. The sensation of movement felt similar to her tunnel experience during her departure via the Trebla Eye; there was no wind on her face, and there were no forces on her body as she turned and twisted her way back to Earth.

Before too long, Eleanor approached a white hole in the universe and unconsciously knew that this was the doorway to her experience. After being pulled into the white light she came to be hovering in a still scene; a frozen snapshot in time of her life as Eleanor. She was confused because the mechanisms involved to enter the scene were far greater than any soul could imagine. She was so close to the universe, but yet so far. She hovered, observing Eleanor Trebla in the process of washing up in the kitchen of their family home. Her hairstyle and clothing told her it was around 1980.

Eleanor floated towards her own body, looking at the scene from about thirty years ago in detail. The water in the washing up bowl was uneven, and as stationary as a photo. She floated around to look at her own face and there was a light source emanating form her forehead that shimmered. The floating spark of conscious awareness that steered this body and created Eleanor's experience gently moved into the light radiating from the forehead of her younger self. The vital connections were made and she assumed command of the mind. It was like getting back into a warm duvet; cosy and familiar. As soon as she was in, the still point in time rolled into animation and Eleanor's experience continued. As she washed up, the telephone rang and it was devastating news; her young son Jack had just met his fate in the high street.

Eleanor would accept Jack's fate with more thanks and less regret than in the hidden reality due to her unconscious lessons in the mind and soul dimension. Her more positive reaction to the loss would go on to create a more positive life experience that would overwrite the hidden timeline's events. She would remain unconscious as to where she had been and what she had explicitly learned in the Village of Capee, until 2008 when she would miraculously remember after falling into a coma for seven weeks.

Justanother Town Hospital Coma Unit: (Current Reality)
July 6th 2008:
(Seven weeks after Eleanor's accident)

The nurse on duty in the intensive care unit was coming to the end of her shift. It was early evening and the hazy summer sun shone in through the large windows at the end of the ward.

'Sure will be glad to get off tonight Harry. I have some DVD's and a large bottle of wine waiting at home!' she said to Harry, a temporary worker who was busy filing behind a desk.

'That'll be good. Are you nearly finished your shift then?' he asked.

The nurse looked up at the clock on the wall behind, 'In ten minutes I will have. Just got to do the heart rate traces on these coma patients, then I'm off.' She sighed. 'It's been a long day.'

Harry smiled sympathetically as the nurse walked off to do her heart beat traces. She was oblivious to Eleanor regaining consciousness two beds up.

Where am I? She opened her eyes, but there was just bright light. She was disorientated. *What?... What happened?* Her memories were of Togo waving goodbye at the Alpine Stargate. She remembered coming back and the scene of herself washing up. It all felt like a dream now.

Her eyes remained open a crack as she allowed a small amount of light in. She felt on her own again and she concentrated; she was lying down. *What did I do? I'm in a hospital?*

The nurse retrieved the printout from the heart beat monitor two beds up from Eleanor. The man in this coma was bald and had a heavy silver beard. The nurse had always thought the man looked peaceful. She replaced the old printout and hung it on a clipboard at the end of the bed. She spoke to her patients, 'There we go Callison, you're all done.' She moved onto the next patient, one up from Eleanor.

Eleanor opened her eyes as much as the light would allow. Her hearing started to feed information to her and she could hear someone walking around by her. She could see her own feet under a blanket in front of her. She tried to move her toes and they responded with a small wiggle; slowly she began to assimilate reality. There were tubes coming out of her nose. They itched.

The nurse was busy printing the next heartbeat trace, when she heard something. It sounded like someone gasping for breath and her head bolted round to look at the row of beds. All the patients were asleep, apart from the one next to her;

Eleanor Trebla. She had pulled the breathing apparatus away from herself, and seemed to be coming around. The nurse's heart was the fastest one in the room now. *A wake up! I've got a live wake up!* she thought.

Not ever being first attending on a wake up, she rushed into taught action. She called back to Harry on the desk, 'Harry, could you page a doctor! Could you say Mrs Trebla is waking up!' She rushed around the bed to Eleanor's side.

The panic in her voice rallied Harry into immediate action and he put a page out to all doctors in the hospital.

The nurse pulled the drip line tubes away from Eleanor, and assisted her as best she could to breathe. She was comforting, 'Hello, Mrs Trebla? You're in safe hands, a Doctor is on their way.'

I'm fine; just let me get my bearings, Eleanor thought. She couldn't speak yet. It was too much energy. She could hear the nurse giving words of encouragement, which helped, before someone else jumped onto the scene.

It was the doctor. 'Thank you nurse.' he said firmly. The nurse stood down as the doctor started to probe Eleanor with his stethoscope, measuring and listening for signs of life, 'Hello Eleanor can you hear me?' He shone a handheld light into her eyes.

A light blinded her, and she squinted away from it. It went away again as she continued to get stronger. She spoke in broken frail voice, 'Yes...' She gasped for another breath.

The doctor seemed to calm down. Eleanor's heart trace was still connected, and emitted a healthy rhythmic beep sound. 'Nurse, all looks fine here, well done.' The nurse was proud, and although she was due to go home now, she stayed to make sure her patient was ok.

The doctor hung his stethoscope around his neck again and spoke clearly and directly to his patient. 'Mrs Trebla, you're in Justanother Town intensive care coma ward,' Eleanor was gaining consciousness all the time. The doctor continued, 'you were in a car accident, do you remember?'

She didn't and responded with hoarse words, 'A car accident? No, I wasn't in a car accident.' *It was the basement. Callison's invention.* She relayed her account, 'I remember... I was at Bingo... I drove home... Heinrich!' she recoiled with panic.

The doctor thought she was confused and tried to remind her what happened, 'No, you were in a car accident. Do you remember?'

Eleanor had no memory of it, and was bemused. 'Car accident?' she shook her head with a puzzled look.

'Yes, can you remember?' said the doctor.

'No.' she withdrew, questioning herself.

The doctor assumed she was still amnesic from the coma. She couldn't remember the chain of events as documented in her coma file regarding her accident, but it was quite usual for patients to not be able to recall their accidents, so the doctor was not unduly worried.

The doctor told the nurses, 'She is fine, but keep her drip connected for a few more hours. Her vital signs are positive, but she's a bit disorientated. We'll move her to a different ward later this evening.' The two nurses nodded and the doctor resumed his rounds. He called over his shoulder holding his pager in the air, 'Any problems, page me.'

Wake ups in the coma ward were unfortunately less common than eventual terminations. The patient asleep the longest had been comatosed for eighteen months, but Eleanor and Callison Trebla were certainly the most intriguing. About seven weeks ago, Callison electrocuted himself in his basement, and then in a completely unrelated event, four hours later, Eleanor cheated death in a road accident. The nurses thought it more than chance, but then life normally was.

* * * * * * *

25: Intuitive Integration

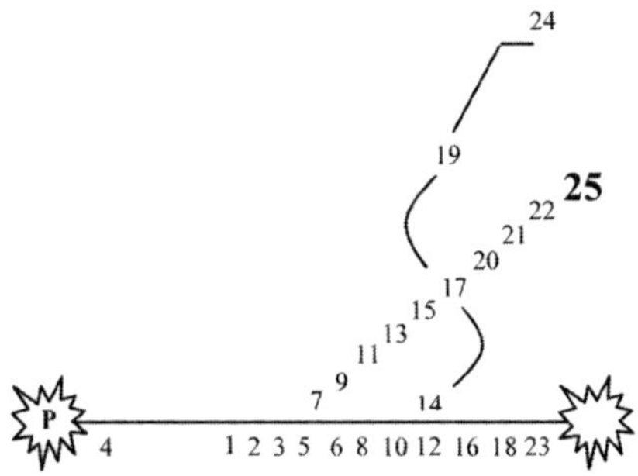

"There is no logical way to the discovery of these elemental laws. There is only the way of intuition, which is helped by a feeling for the order lying behind the appearance."
Albert Einstein, Physicist (1879 – 1955)

25.1 –
Date not known:
Plus five days:

Mystera had applied coloured patterns to the gold sheen that lay stuck to the mental imprint of his body. Callison sat meditating with Mystera in the tree house in the dimension of energetic mind and soul. The meditation process would bring the issues of Callison's Earth life to the fore, but it was also like a meditative prayer to guide him on the path he knew to be correct during his intuitive integration. Soon he would be walking off to follow the prayer's trail into the wilderness where, in Mystera's own words, 'the magic would happen'. Callison believed the Noi Tu master, but wasn't sure if *he* was going to be magical enough. During the meditation Callison had visions of his late son, Jack, of Heinrich, of Eleanor and of his life back in 2008.

After the meditation had ended, Mystera spoke to him, 'Are there anymore questions I can help you with before you search?'

There was only one, 'Should I be nervous before an intuitive integration? Will it affect the result if I am too worried?'

The master gave his answer, 'Worry is only a fear of not knowing. You are going off into the wild to integrate your mind with the beauty of life. Your fear will not be able to sustain itself, and will pass. Be aware that it will pass, and in that moment you will feel less fear.'

The cryptic advice from Mystera made Callison feel more at ease, 'Ok, thank you, I'll try and remember it.'

They climbed down the ladder all the way to the forest floor and the time came for Callison to set off into the wilderness. Before he did so Mystera had some final words of preparation, 'Remember, you are literally re-living yourself. After you have done the intuitive integration you are free to go back to the new reality, so think, if there was one thing you could change what would that thing be?'

Callison didn't think long, 'To not lose Jack.'

The master felt Callison's frustration, but was restrained, 'Life is not about *what* comes your way Callison; it is about how you *deal* with what comes your way.'

Callison looked at the floor acknowledging his regrets, but understood the master's point.

'Just contemplate it during your integration, that's all.' Mystera hurried, 'Right, are you ready?'

Callison took the information in before drawing in a deep breath, preparing himself. 'Yes. I am ready.' He thanked Mystera for his preparation and walked off without regret or fear. The advice from Mystera had helped. *There's nothing to fear apart from the fear itself, which is a mental creation.* He repeated the thought to himself as he took the first few important steps of his integration; the gold coloured man walked off into his own subconscious to change his past.

Mystera stood at the foot of the tree waving his student off, 'See you soon Callison!' he said, 'Remember to let your intuition lead you!'

Callison acknowledged over his shoulder with a smile and a thank you, 'I'll try to do myself proud, thank you once again.' Callison turned back towards his destination and ambled away from the tree house and out away from the pyramid and away from the Noi Tu Outpost into the wilderness. He walked naked, but for a special water pouch that could heat water hot enough for tea, but cool it down enough to provide a cool drink. He also had a small shoulder bag containing some Aloemara leaves, some fresh bread and some herbal tea. Mystera had said to take some Aloemara with tea if his intuition was too quiet, and then to trust the thoughts that made him feel good. They would guide him to where he needed to be. On his right hip rested a knife on a belt; he would use it for cutting fruits from trees to eat during his journey.

It was still early morning and the sun hadn't been up for long. He breathed in the smell of the forest as he walked on a worn pathway through the green environment feeling contented, although just as alone as when he first arrived, he didn't feel lonely anymore. He knew he had changed and the feeling of inner peace satisfied him.

After a few minutes of walking, he reached an open meadow. He hoped he could find the lagoon where he met Liele the first day, but he was aware that the undergrowth was vast, and the prospects of getting lost were high. Or so he thought. He walked naked and golden across the meadow and deeper into his own psyche.

25.2 –

Callison had been walking for what felt like a couple of hours, and was penetrating the outskirts of his deepest subconscious mind. He was walking along tree-lined pathways and tracks through the woods with no real logical sense of direction, although he trusted that each choice he made was leading him to where he needed to be; where ever *that* was. He thought he would be near the lagoon by now and thought he would be able to hear the falling water of the waterfall, but he couldn't.

He emerged from under a leafy canopy into a small clearing in the woods that looked out over some rolling tree-soaked hills. The sky was visible overhead again, but was grey and overcast. There was a spattering of orange trees next to a grass verge that were fruiting nicely, so Callison cut two oranges off and had a snack looking out at the wonderful view in front of him. His intuition didn't seem to be leading him as loudly as he'd hoped so he sprinkled some of the Aloemara leaves onto the orange segments he cut for himself.

About ten minutes passed before Callison started to feel the Aloemara having its effect. He mused at the absurdity of what he was doing and tried to imagine telling it to people he knew on Earth, and chuckled to himself; *I painted myself in just gold paint, and walked naked to get lost on purpose.* The light-hearted thought pulled more intuitive thoughts through his mind. He felt less serious about his situation, and more aware of his thoughts coming and going. He felt more of the beauty of the scene in front of him, like it was an artwork of nature commissioned for him alone.

He decided to meditate to see if it could isolate his intuition from his conscious thoughts more. He sat down on the grass with his elbows resting on his knees and rested his gaze loosely on the scene in front of him; his exterior mind as Tobian had called it in the telekinesis lesson. He contemplated his being and he felt calm, as if listening to himself about where he was to go from here. He tried to get his intuitive voice louder, by listening to the silence between his thoughts. He closed his eyes and suddenly he heard a telepathic voice within his mind.

Hello. What are you doing here then?

Callison was startled, and opened his eyes immediately to see in front of him on the grass, a large rat staring curiously back at him. *A Kimeng Rat?* He thought privately. He wasn't bitter about being given the gem a few days ago, and instead warmed to his new visitor, determined to get to the bottom of it's lack of self worth. He smiled while staying seated, and broadcast back sarcastically, Oh Hello Kimeng Rat and how are you today?

It beamed back, I'm ok, thanks. The rat was curious as to how many thoughts of self-worth he would be able to extract from the golden man sitting down in front of him. This man was not giving too many thoughts away. It could be a hard extraction, but this rat thought he could persuade anyone. What are you doing here?

Callison was honest with the rodent, and transmitted back, I am finding my way.

The Kimeng Rat started its spiel. I can help you find your way if you would like. I know these places better than anyone.

Callison had been here before. I don't believe you.

Why not, I can give you evidence of my knowing the way. The rat came across confident in his claim.

Oh really? Please do, I'm listening. Callison prompted.

The rat moved on the spot and seemed to concentrate while materializing some pieces of paper. He stood up and sidestepped off of the newly created items. Please, look for yourself. The rat gestured the documents towards his visitor.

Callison was curious and knelt forward to pick up the documents. They were certificates from the school of life. The school of life? I've never heard of that.

You're obviously not very clever then. said the rat, pompously and believing his own diatribe.

Callison ignored the rat, thinking privately to himself. He thumbed through the five documents he held and they felt like real documents. He knew they would turn into something less specific just like the gem he had 'paid for' a few days earlier. There was a certificate in geographical knowledge, one in being a spiritual master, one in being a leader, another one proving his intelligence and finally he'd won a beauty prize. You won a beauty prize? How is that a qualification to dictate to me how to find myself?

The rat countered again with scientific statistics, Research shows attractive people have more control over other people. It's science. It proves you need to be attractive to get ahead. The rat believed every taught word.

Callison thought the Kimeng rat was arrogant, and unworthy of a beauty prize anyway. Based on his experiences last time, he scanned the documents in more detail. He noticed something written at the bottom of each certificate. It was some small text that read: "All of the above qualifications are from the Kimeng Rat School of Persuasion" Callison read between the lines; these certificates were meaningless. So basically, you want me to give you a thought of self worth in exchange for some manifestation you conjured up that will help me further myself?

The Rat became excited, and a grin emanated across its sly face. *He believes the documents! I am so good at this!* It nodded.

Callison was to have the last laugh. Ok, ratty, I'm transmitting the thought now.

The rat sat back and eagerly awaited payment. His smile would be short-lived.

Callison transmitted his own opinion of the rat. I got a gem from a Kimeng Rat the first day I got here, which later turned out to be a rock. You sold it as a gem, and it was a rock. You duped me. I gave my power to you. You're not getting my thoughts today. Where is *your* self worth?

The rat recoiled, realising that he was receiving a painful thought of conscience. The Kimeng Rat's conscience was internally silenced quickly, with some more self-lies. That wasn't me! I'm a caring rat! It defended, before bolstering its own ego and going for the sale again, My gifts are better than any other rat's; mine come with insurance!

Callison didn't fall for it. I'm not going to part with a thought that you are the greatest. I'm not going to part with a thought that you are worthless either. I feel sorry for you in actual fact. Find your own self worth. And with that, Callison closed off his line of communication with the rodent.

The rat cowered with thoughts of self-doubt, and realised this man was not going to part with the desired thought. It ran away, scared by it's own delusions, into the reeds near the stream and desperate for the next ego boost.

Callison watched him run away, wondering if Kimeng Rats would ever change. *God help a society run by those critters* thought Callison. He looked back at the rats' documents, and the text slowly disappeared. They were just an illusion.

As he sat and stared at the pieces of paper resting on the grass bank, a subtle thought tugged his intuition. He felt ready to trust this piece of internal advice, so he stood up and started to walk. He arrived at a stream and decided to follow the water downstream with the river flow, unconsciously knowing his destination.

The stream slowly merged with others, building into larger river systems as he continued to walk, and was by now quite a large, slow flowing river. As he followed the flow, he thought little. The journey was made more pleasant for the non-thought, and he noticed the flowers, the trees, the wildlife and the views more. The new intuitive Callison walked with a quiet confidence that he was on the right path. By using intuition one could never go wrong, was the belief. He also had faith that the belief was correct.

The track he was following came to a T-junction. The naked gold man stopped walking. The river on his right flowed slowly into a lake, which he stood next to and looked out over. It was a mill pool; not a single ripple or wave to be seen. It perfectly reflected the opposite tree line, clouds and sky. *Wow*, he thought. He'd never seen a lake so still and it made him feel peaceful.

To his left, a dusty track led over a small hill and to the right, the track led to a bridge over the river he'd been following and on around the still lake in the other direction.

Before he could enjoy the view more, he noticed a small white dot of light in the sky above him. It captivated Callison and he tracked it with his eyes. It buzzed low to the floor and was visible in front of the trees on the other side of the lake. It was very small, but noticeable. It came in close and buzzed around his head before seeming to flick out and do a large arc away. The small spark of light came back in for another pass and buzzed around his head again and again, like a satellite. It moved away and over the hill on his left and disappeared out of sight. Callison knew he had to follow whatever it was.

* * * * * * *

26: Like a Shooting Star

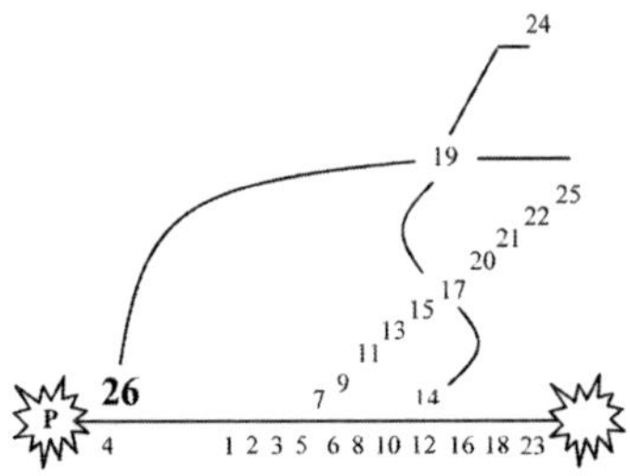

"You see, death is not the grave as many people think.
It is another phenomenised form of life."
Edgar Cayce, Psychic and Visionary (1877 - 1945)

26.1 –
Flashback:
Hidden Timeline:
October 23rd 1980:

Jack's surroundings were quiet and he could see everything going on just below him. His broken vessel lay in the road. The car had stopped two metres too late and his face had blood on it. His Dad ran over, and held him. His Dad was crying in disbelief. Jack didn't want his Dad to be upset. Don't worry Dad. I'm ok! His Dad couldn't hear him. There was too much negative emotion. He tried again. Dad! Up here... I'm ok! It distressed him that his Dad couldn't hear him.

He slowly realised what he was and why he was living as Jack. He wasn't the body lying in his Dad's arms; he was the conscious spark of awareness that animated the body. It had been a means of expression for this soul in the game of experience. A short life this time, but it had all been a karmic pre-arrangement. The well being of his immediate family though still distressed him.

He stayed at the scene of the accident trying to calm his Dad, who was still in tears as the ambulance arrived. Jack was merely observing, floating, just like the red balloon that enticed him into the road in the first place. He looked for the young girl holding the balloon, but she was nowhere to be seen. His infinite memory started to bleed back into to his conscious being. The red balloon was a marker that was always supposed to entice the accident. He spoke to his Dad's mind. Don't dwell on the loss Dad. Give thanks for our experiences. See you back in reality. He kissed his dad goodbye, See you again soon Dad.

He floated up higher into the sky. He saw the main road stretching into the distance. He could see the whole town from up here. He imagined his mother and slowly he started to float towards her. He saw the family house from above. He floated into the house, floating through the roof, and through the walls and into the kitchen. Mummy was preparing a barbeque. She was by the sink, doing some washing up. Good-bye mum. Thank you. You are a friendly and strong soul. Look after Dad. I know you will.

She stopped washing up for a moment. A feeling came over her that she didn't like. Subconsciously she said aloud the words, 'Bye.' The phone rang with bad news. Jack mentally kissed her as she wept on the phone. He whispered, and left her with the words. I love you.

He felt the pull, levering him from this worldly plane. He was floating again above the family house. He wanted to go to the hospital to comfort his family more, but he had made his peace and was ready to go. He had made this journey many times before. It was like a magnet, which he surrendered to; a magnet attracting with warmth, peace and love.

He left the Earth Field Matrix, a conscious living field that supported life like a mother. It was one living canvas among many in the universe, on which souls expressed themselves. Jack realised again that Earth was just a temporary reality, and he was leaving for a truer one. He was a beam of light again, travelling at the speed of light. Free of the constraints of a body he made his way across the universe like a shooting star. Star systems came and went. Galaxies appeared, and passed him on the left and right, above and below. It was a liberating experience. As he passed a certain galaxy, he got a feeling like deja vu. He remembered he was to meet people; two people to be exact. Intuition told him something was afoot. Jack's essence continued to hurtle through the universe, contemplating.

Jack came up to the gateway out of the physical dimension: The Alpine Stargate. The gateway was a door into the dimension of energetic mind and soul that surrounded the whole physical universe and all the parallel variants. The dimension of spirit, Jack's final destination on this journey, was one beyond the dimension of mind and soul.

The face of the Alpine Stargate was bigger than most galaxies and looked liked a large round disc floating in space. It emitted a yellowy-white light, but Jack felt no heat as he approached. He prepared for the entry and braced himself for the dimension change. His spark of energy flew through the stargate at the speed of light, leaving a ripple effect in the portal that subsided like a pebble ripple in a pond.

Once on the other side of the Alpine Stargate he had no speed, as there was no space-time anymore; the energy of his full awareness now drove his experience. He waited for the first being he was to meet just inside the mind and soul dimension. It was quiet. He still had Jack's physical impression deeply imprinted into his mind signature, so still appeared as Jack's five-year-old human self.

Then he met her. It was his mother. She had changed while in the dimension of mind and soul and she was just about to embark for the remainder of a partial parallel Earth life. They were more timeless friends who had shaped, formed and experienced many lives together rather than mother and son.

Jack told his mother that he was fine and that he loved her. He wished her well on her new adventure and told her that he'd see her again soon. His mum let him go without regret and Jack continued into the dimension to meet someone else.

He entered a mind gate to an area of mental rehabilitation called a green wisp. A green wisp looked like a dark green gaseous cloud and was as large as imagination itself. As he started to sink into the green cloud, he started to remember how peaceful the mind and soul dimension was, and how peaceful soul life was. A lush green landscape as far as the Eye could see revealed itself.

He floated down lower, and lower, until he reached his destination. His second friend was already there, waiting naked and painted to the nines, just like he said he would be on the banks of the lake of reflection. It was his father.

* * * * * * *

27: The Wisdom of Youth

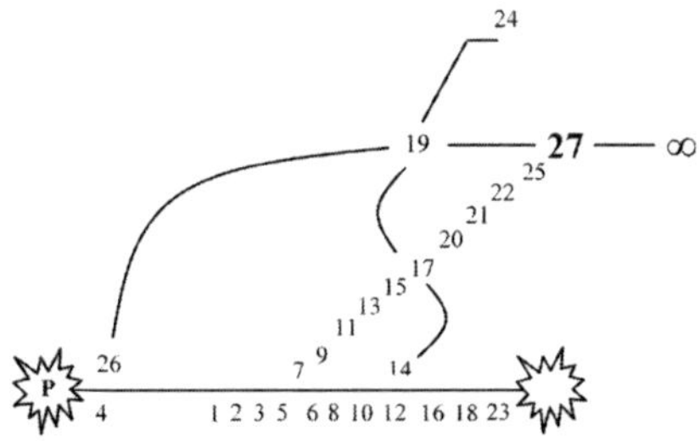

"I am not young enough to know everything."
Oscar Wilde, Poet and Author (1854 - 1900)

27.1 –
Date not known:
Plus five days:

Callison followed the small speck of light over the hill and was stopped in his tracks at whom he saw. Sitting on some logs, overlooking the still lake sat his son Jack, smiling back at him as if he'd never left.

It was a vision, 'Jack?' Callison started to well up with tears, 'Jack is that you?!' he called out. He ran toward him, *Is this a dream?* thought Callison as the emotion built. He forgot he was even on an intuitive integration when he got to his son on the logs. Jack wore the same blue t-shirt and red shorts he was wearing when the car hit him in the high street all those years ago.

'Hello Daddy.' said Jack, innocently.

'Jack, my boy!' He didn't know what to say, 'It's been so long!' Callison sat down on the log next to him and hugged his long lost son. The embrace was one of the best Callison had ever felt. The emotion couldn't be held in any longer and he started to cry. 'I've missed you Jack! Eleanor's missed you. I'm so glad you are ok!'

Jack continued to hug his Dad back. He spoke like any five-year-old would, 'But I just left mummy, she is fine.'

Callison recoiled with surprise, 'Really, what do you mean Jack?'

Jack nodded, 'Yes. I've made this journey lots before.' He was proud of his knowledge in the way only a five year old's consciousness could, 'I know my way. I remembered to come and meet you.'

'Oh it doesn't matter,' Callison continued to hug his son in uncontrolled emotion when his intellect tugged at him, 'wait, you *remembered* to meet me? I wasn't expecting to see you.' *Was I?* he asked himself and drew back.

'We planned it before, with the Universal Mind.' said Jack sure of it, his big brown eyes staring up at his father.

'But...' he thought, 'it's been a lifetime since I've seen you?' It was a rhetorical question for himself, which confused him, 'How did you get here Jack?'

'I floated up, and flew across the universe very fast. I like going fast!' Jack laughed.

Callison smiled. *I like going fast.* Jack used to say that when he was travelling in the car, back in the life that made sense.

'Daddy?' asked Jack.

'Yes?' said his dad.

'Why do you have paint all over you?'

Callison laughed, remembering what he was doing, 'I am doing an intuitive integration. I am trying to find peace with myself Jack. These symbols and paintings are supposed to lead me to peace.'

'They make you look nice.' said Jack.

'Well thank you Jack.' said Callison proudly. He fell back into being a Dad effortlessly. It was a magical feeling, and conjured energy from a place Callison had forgotten for so long. For the last thirty years of his life the energy had not flowed. He remembered what Mystera said about a lack of love causing fear and it was fear that had run his life thus far.

'Can I have some paint?' asked Jack.

'Yes, of course you can have some.' Callison smeared his finger down the side of his own cheeks, taking a layer of the gold paint with it. He wiped some paint down the bridge of Jack's nose and across his cheeks. 'There you go.' he joked, 'Golden Jack.'

Jack laughed, 'What does it look like?'

'You look like a warrior!' said Callison. He realised the lake in front of them would act like a mirror, 'Come on, let's go and look at ourselves in the reflection of the water.' Callison got off the log and walked down to the water's edge.

Jack followed, knowing he would have to leave his father soon.

They both knelt down and looked at their reflections in the lake. The lake was so still it perfectly reflected their appearance. Staring at the water's surface Callison and Jack saw two bright sparks reflected back at them.

'That's weird.' said Callison, 'I wasn't expecting that.'

'That's us.' said Jack, 'Don't you remember?'

Callison thought that this must be the light Mystera had talked about during the meditation. He didn't know why it reflected now though, and he remained confused.

Jack had only had five years of Earth life and was not as programmed as his father. 'That's us. That's what we are; magic light.' Jack could sense his father's confusion, and calmed him down. He walked over to him and put his arm around him. 'It's ok Daddy,' he showed a lot more maturity than his young appearance suggested. 'You'll remember, we always do.'

It was as if the information he was receiving from Jack was identical to the information Mystera had relayed to him, not only before his intuitive integration, but also throughout his time in Sukarmia. 'I wish I remembered fully, Jack, but your Dad's become quite the forgetful old fool.'

'You're not a fool Daddy,' said the young voice of innocence, 'I love you.' He put his arm round Callison to comfort him again.

'And I love you too Jack.' he replied. A tear rolled down Callison's cheeks. He felt like a fool, but knew in the grand orchestra of the universe that if one knew everything, there would be nothing left to realise.

Callison and Jack walked around part of the lake together and Jack sat on Callison's shoulders. They enjoyed about a quarter of an hour together, throwing stones into the lake and talking about things that Jack did in his life. They talked about his death.

'I remember the car, and the screech of the tyres, but I don't remember a bump. I think I left my body before.' Jack was a bit confused, but knew what happened afterwards.

Callison still felt guilt, 'I'm so sorry Jack, I took my eye off you for a moment.'

Jack propped him up, 'It's not your fault Daddy. It was how we had planned it.' He turned and faced the lake throwing a stone into the water.

'We planned it?' enquired Callison.

'Yes Daddy. You wanted to learn lessons to experience loss, and I wanted to help with your science work.'

Callison was intrigued, 'Well if you wanted to help with the science why did we agree for you to die early?'

'It was part of my game contract, which stretches across everybody I interacted with. The contract with the driver, the nurses, you, mummy, the witnesses, it's all connected. I want to come back again though, to help with your science.' He smiled hopefully, like he had requested something for Christmas.

'Well if you want to come back, you come back!' Callison smiled, perking up.

Jack hit home the situation, 'You need to let me come back, by letting me go.' The words were solemn, but had childlike honesty to them.

Callison's lip quivered, 'W... What do you mean jack?' The sky started to lighten up above the water in the lake.

Jack told him, 'I can feel the pulling. I won't be here much longer. Don't close off from the world Daddy and you will change everything.' The spirit world was coming for him.

The sky continued to lighten above the lake, 'Ok. I'll try.' said Callison, 'How long do you have?' He didn't want to lose him again and a tear rolled down his cheeks.

'Not long, I can feel the light coming for me. It's ok daddy. I'm going home.'

Callison hugged him one last time. He kissed him on his head and told him to be brave.

The sky continued to lighten, until it was bright golden white.

'I don't need to be brave, it is like home for us.' said Jack. Callison was assured Jack knew best, but still the tears continued to fall. A brilliant light shone down onto the lake. It called for Jack, and Jack started to float towards the light. Callison stood back, waving and crying.

Good-bye Daddy. I love you. He waved back to his dad. Don't close off from the world Daddy, and you will change everything.

Jack continued into the light until he was invisible in it, while Callison wept on the bank of the lake. The white light slowly shrank away, retreating back into the sky and slowly the sky started to get its colour back, the white fluffy clouds continuing to roll on by, oblivious to what had just taken place. It was eerily quiet again. There was no sign of Jack. *Was it a dream?* Callison thought. There was only silence, broken by his erratic fear-based breathing. It was like Jack had been taken from him a second time and he was scared and alone once again.

A voice echoed through his mind, *Realise the fear will pass and in that moment you will feel less fear.* Mystera's words came to comfort him because he truly listened to them when Mystera had said them. He realised he controlled his fear by realising it was temporary and will pass.

He missed Jack already. He remembered what Jack had said. *Don't close off from the world and you will change everything.*

He didn't know quite what it meant yet, but he knew he wanted to adhere to it. A slight breeze floated across his face, drying the tracks of his tears and he decided to be positive. He inhaled a large slow lung full of air and decided to feel peaceful and give thanks for Jack's life.

He sat on one of the grass banks next to the lake and looked out over it. He was taken aback by just how still it was. He had walked round about half of the lake with Jack, and now looked across at the opposite bank. The lake had such a perfect reflection to it. He crawled forward to see his reflection again. Nothing had changed and he still saw a spark of light in the place of his reflection just as he had done with Jack. *Magic light?* He couldn't make sense of it. He could see, feel and touch his arms and legs. He touched his face. *Why is my reflection like it is?* he asked himself.

Thoughts of his intuitive integration came back to him. He realised what he was supposed to be doing in the wilderness: *Following his intuition*. The light was fading. There was maybe an hour of sunlight left. His intuition told him to sit still and reflect on what had just happened.

The sun eventually disappeared under the horizon and the stars slowly came out one by one. Callison remained seated on the bank of the lake of reflection, listening to the sound of a golden silence.

* * * * * * *

28: Constant Change

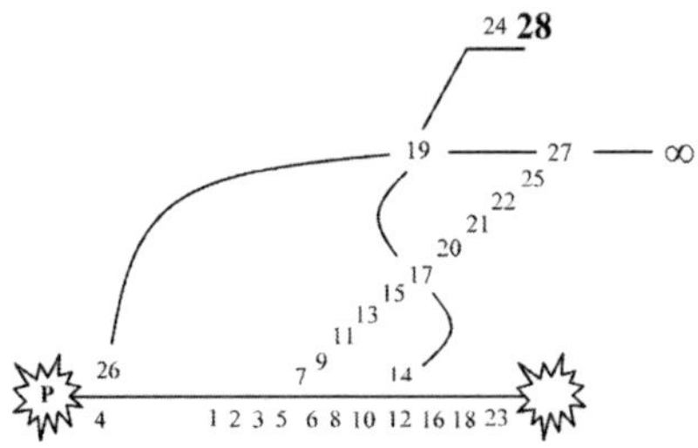

"They say that time changes things,
but you actually have to change them yourself."
Andy Warhol, Painter and Film Maker, (1928 – 1987)

28.1 –
Current Reality:
July 6th 2008:

It had been a couple of hours since she had come round in the coma ward and now the sun had set for the evening and the ward was illuminated by strip lighting. The lights gave the hospital ward a sanitised feeling and filtered in through Eleanor's retinas and directly to her brain, but she was still too weak to keep her eyes open and she drifted in and out of waking consciousness while in bed. She mentally relived her adventure and from her point of view, she had arrived back home from Bingo, and then escaped from Heinrich in the basement, but the doctor had said she was brought in for a car crash, which confused her.

She remembered that she was twenty years old during her excursion out of time and checked her face with her hands. She was mid sixties again, but she didn't mind and felt surprisingly well, considering. The friendly nurse had given her some water some time ago and now she needed the toilet. She had a red call button next to her, which she pressed.

The nurse came down from the desk area, smiling, 'Hi Eleanor. What's the matter?'

Eleanor smiled and said sheepishly, 'I need to go to the ladies?'

The nurse was helpful, 'Ok, I'll go and get the wheelchair, it's not far.' She came back with the set of wheels then helped her patient off the bed. Eleanor stood up momentarily for the first time in seven weeks, before resting back into the seat of the wheelchair, 'It's just at the end of this corridor.' said the nurse, 'How are you feeling my love?'

The nurse wheeled her off, away from her bed. Eleanor still didn't realise she was in the same ward as her husband. 'Oh not bad, I'm still feeling quite dazed.' They rolled into a corridor, it smelled of disinfecting chemicals, and the floor was shiny. 'How long will I be in here for do you think?' asked Eleanor over her shoulder.

'That's up to the doctors, but you seem quite perky, considering you've been in a coma for seven weeks. I think you're doing fine.'

Seven weeks? The reality hit home. *That's serious*, she thought as the wheel chair rolled on towards the toilet. It seemed like she'd only been away for an evening.

On the way back from the toilet as she rolled up to her bed again, she noticed her unconscious husband two beds up from hers. She gasped, 'Callie!'

The nurse was expecting her to notice anyway, which was allowed. If the nurse informed her of the fact beforehand she would have been breaching patient confidentiality. 'Yes, he came in a few hours before you.' The nurse didn't probe her on the assumed coincidence, 'Would you like to sit with him?'

'Yes please.' said Eleanor tentatively. She was all too aware of her surroundings now.

The nurse rolled her in the wheelchair up to Callison's bedside. He looked peaceful, laying in the bed with tubes running up his nose and into his arms. His moustache was quite hard to make out, camouflaged in a wiry grey beard, and his silver hair had grown around the sides of his head. *Oh Callison* she thought. She took one of his hands and knew he would have some answers.

The nurse left them to it.

Eleanor stroked her husband's hand, thinking a dialogue towards him; *I've been in a coma for seven weeks! What the hell did we do?* She thought of more to say, *You look peaceful. I just know you'll wake up soon.* She started to tell him her experience of life on the other side of the portal, *I had the strangest experience Callie; I was taken in a tunnel to a wonderful garden.* She told him about Togo, and how he had looked after her. She told him about seeing Jack. She told him that she knew Callison was coming back. *Do what you have to do my darling.* She hoped he could hear her talking to him. She told him that she loved him and would wait for him.

The nurse interrupted her, 'Excuse me, Eleanor?'

She turned around, 'Yes?'

'I have spoken to the doctor and he says it is ok for visitors to come and see you in the morning. I'm sure they will be pleased you're up and about.'

'Oh, ok, thank you. What time is it now?' asked Eleanor.

'It's nearly ten-thirty,' said the nurse courteously, 'we should probably think about getting you back into your bed, you need plenty of rest.'

Eleanor conceded. She was still weak, 'Ok.'

She summoned the energy to stand up and kissed Callison on his forehead, 'Sweet dreams dear.' She sat back into the wheel chair, and the nurse wheeled her to her own bed.

Visitors? Eleanor thought. At first she first thought it was Betty. She spoke over her shoulder to the nurse, 'Do you know who will be here tomorrow, visiting me?'

The nurse replied up beat, 'It will be your son, James and his girlfriend, Sally probably. They have been in once everyday since the accident and will be thrilled you are up and about.' The nurse knew them better than Eleanor did.

Eleanor was shocked, *Her son?!*

They got back to Eleanor's bed, and for the first time Eleanor realised there were a couple of get well cards stood up on the table next to her. The nurse helped her patient back into the bed.

Eleanor was stunned in silence. *I have a son?* she thought.

The nurse tucked her in and walked back to the desk area.

When she was back in bed she looked at the cards. One of them was from Betty and Reg, and one of them was from their son, James, and his girlfriend Sally. Obviously she couldn't sleep now.

* * * * * * *

29: Double Vision

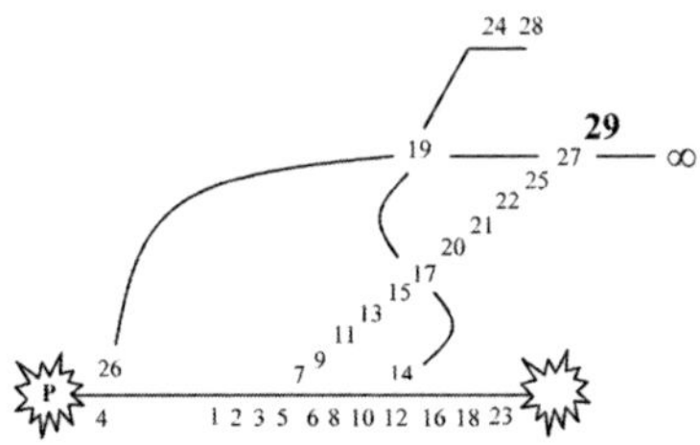

"Time and memory are true artists; they remould reality nearer to the heart's desire."
John Dewey, Psychologist and Philosopher (1859 – 1952)

29.1 –
Date not known:
Plus six days:

The sky started to lighten in the area it had been darkest at dusk the evening before. A new day was coming around for Callison, who had remained sitting by the lake of reflection all night. The temperature had been comfortably cool for the duration and the sky was the clearest he had seen it in his time in Sukarmia. Every single star shone as a singularity, each taking its place on the stage of the heavens.

Painful thoughts about Jack had consumed him for the first segment of the evening, before he remembered that he was the master of his thoughts, and had to assume control again. He let the thoughts go and he let the memory of Jack go, and stopped resisting their departure from his consciousness. He thought the last words out into the cosmos, and hoped Jack could still hear him, I don't know where your journey led to, Jack; I'm only just beginning to understand, but I think one day, I too will be with you again. And on that assumption I leave you to your own devices, for I have to tend to matters closer to home. I'll always love you. Dad. He didn't get a definitive answer by the lake, but he wasn't after one, he was finding self-forgiveness.

He continued sitting by the lake concentrating on simply remaining still and breathing. He moved away from thoughts about Jack into thoughts about Sukarmia, and his time here. They were slow thoughts and they were reflective thoughts.

Sometime during the night, he thought he could perceive Eleanor trying to speak to him. It was as if her voice was being carried in the breezes that washed over him while he sat. The breeze echoed that she was ok and was waiting for him to return. One of the breezes he even perceived as a kiss from his beloved and he smiled in ecstasy as he felt Eleanor was near by and not far away. He tried to tell her that he was coming back soon, but whether she heard, he didn't know.

The sun continued to rise and the whole sky became a brilliant light blue colour. All but the brightest of stars had drawn in for the coming day and Callison sat on the lake bank, wondering if he had slept at all; his thoughts had ebbed and flowed so unconsciously all night that it felt in retrospect like a dream. He felt awake again now however and his thoughts turned to sustenance. He had in his bag, some pieces of bread, which he washed down with the herbal tea.

After breakfast he started to make headway, continuing to walk around the lake of reflection more, before coming to another wide river. This river took water away from the lake. He had the choice to cross via a bridge and continue round the lake but his intuition was already leading him, like it had done since he got here: *Go with the flow.* He walked down stream with the river flow.

The scenery the river led him past was stunning; tall tree-lined mountains lay on the other side of the large river, until the gently flowing water took a turn away from the mountains and led through a small valley. From the top of the valley he could see a body of water that looked like the sea in the distance. The sun was still continuing to climb and it was getting warm. He took off his water bottle and drank some cool water while looking out over the valley below him. The river accelerated down some rocks before levelling out and flowing gently towards the sea nearer to the horizon. He put his water bottle back over his shoulder and carried on following the water.

Mystera had said the magic would happen. Now Callison had tasted the magic in seeing Jack, it had prompted his belief in intuition and he was starting to look forward to where this intuitive integration might lead.

The river he walked beside flowed through the valley and emptied into the expanse of water he saw from the top of the valley. He now walked on a sandy beach next to the wide river that led to the sea. The solitary golden explorer walked down the beach flirting with the waters edge. Occasionally a small wave would come in and get his feet wet, but he didn't mind at all. The scenery was breathtaking. He walked the sandy plains, walking past pieces of driftwood and weeds.

He followed the white sand to the sea, where it became the beach and walked a small section of the coast, before getting a strange feeling that he knew where he was. He didn't though. He was for all intents and purposes lost as lost can be, but a feeling within him similar to deja vu, told him he was coming to a place he knew; it was like he was on English soil again.

A staircase ran the height of some cliffs on his left, which he ascended to the top. The view looking out over the sea from cliff top was beautiful. The sun glimmered a line of reflection on the water right up to the horizon. His intuition kept tugging however and he turned away from the sea, and walked inland over some fields and plains.

Soon he came to be walking down a pathway in between some trees. The canopy overhead provided mainly shadow to fall onto the path but it was contrasted by small patches of sunlight dotted along the floor where glimmers of light managed to get through. Within seconds the sun disappeared behind a cloud and the shadow increased somewhat. Callison started to become nervous like he knew something was about to happen. Before he could think more, he saw it. Callison froze. About fifty yards ahead on the dark covered pathway sat a large lion staring back at him, as if guarding the way.

His memory was cast straight back to his first day here at the lagoon. Liele had got the lion to walk away, and he would now have to perform the feat himself in order to survive.

He thought back to Mystera's fear wisdom, *there's nothing to fear apart from fear itself*. He started to walk directly at the beast. Moving one foot in front of the other he drew closer. Suddenly, while remaining seated the lion emitted a loud roar towards the sky above, but Callison's footsteps didn't stop. Liele had controlled the lion, and Callison believed he could do the same. He was coming through.

The lion seemed to be adamant also and didn't stand or move at all, looking back at the gold-coloured man heading its way.

Forty yards. Callison remembered his new skill and tried telepathy, I'm coming through here whether you like it or not. I mean you no harm, so I expect the same from you.

Thirty yards. The lion still hadn't pounced. Callison remained on his trajectory one step at a time, waiting and hoping for the lion to communicate.

The lion did reply, with a question, Why do I scare you?

Callison stopped with twenty yards between man and beast. He wasn't expecting the transmission. *Why does it scare me?* He questioned, perplexed as he stood on the path. You might eat me.

The lion seemed to be playing games. So why are you walking towards me then?

Callison was honest with himself. Because I believe I need to come through here.

The cryptic lion continued, But I might eat you, you said it yourself. What is so important to you that you'd risk being eaten?

Callison remained twenty yards away before going with an intuitive notion. He started to walk slowly onward again towards the maned cat. Maybe you won't eat me. Bravely or stupidly he continued.

The lion answered as the man walked, I *might* eat you though, how do you know?

I guess I'm going to find out. Broadcast Callison, not breaking his stride and believing he was doing what he had to. He was unconsciously being led towards what would become an illusion-shattering realisation.

Ten yards. Callison continued walking right up to the beast until he was right next to the animal. Its teeth were bigger than Callison's head, and its large brown eyes looked down the sandy fur of the bridge of its nose at the golden man walking past. On first thought Callison wanted to carry on walking and leave the scary experience behind, but something inside him made him ask, Why are you here? If I am in my own subconscious, how are you connected to me? Callison waited, wondering whether his questions would get him any further. They would indeed.

The lion smiled and it's whiskers raised, Now we're getting to the point it said, as its teeth began to shrink back into its mouth and its eyes became smaller. You see, I am your fear of death and I am standing at your gateway to freedom.

Callison was taken back and surprised with the answer from the lion. He phrased his next question as he noticed the features of the lion start to recede, So do I control you or do you control me?

Both. It said as it continued to change in form; its head and shoulders began to shrink and the eye level of the lion started to fall in height. I do what I am told to do by you. It continued, I'm your fear, no one else's. I guard the perimeter of your infinity to create a finite illusion or bubble that serves as a learning environment for infinite beings such as yourself.

What does that mean? asked the confused golden man, while observing the continual reduction of the beast. Callison's fear of death resembled a leopard more than a lion now and continued to morph away from the fierce, towards the timid end of the spectrum.

Now waist high, the cat explained as it threatened less and enlightened more, It means that if you consciously seek to know more about life and look for the Truth with conscience and intellect, your bubble of understanding grows and one day you will know the true power of freedom and the reason for it. Ignore your search for understanding and you give *me* your power. Any notion of freedom while in this state is merely a delusion for there is an infinite difference between *feeling* like you're free and actually *being* free.

The animal now resembled a small pussycat that purred loudly and rubbed up against his legs as he stood. All semblance of Callison's anxiety had evaporated. So am I free now then? Asked the consciousness of the 21st century scientist as he looked down at the friendly cat.

The cat looked up at him and smiled. You always were free Callison.

And with that thought transmission the cat walked hurriedly away. It looked back at the man in gold one last time, before disappearing into the foliage that flanked the pathway he stood on. As Callison stood with intrigue, the sun came back out, and started to rain down light through the trees that congregated into small patches on the path again.

Mystera had been right, *there was nothing to fear but fear itself*. He continued to follow the pathway feeling light and free. Not further up the path than a few minutes, he stumbled upon a fountain. He thought it strange to see a fountain in the middle of a path, but stranger still when he realised it was created from a statue of his old friend Lord Admiral Pickering. He stood one footed pointing up another pathway that led away to the right. Callison decided to look closer at the bronze piece and as he approached, the plaque confirmed; 'Lord Admiral Pickering'. The subconscious explorer was flummoxed, *Is this an illusion? Or is this real?* he thought. There was only one thing left to do. Pickering pointed to the right; Callison walked in that direction.

His sense of deja vu heightened as he started his walk away from the fountain. There were shadows cast before him from the trees and it felt eerie. His intuition had led him this far. He wasn't turning back now. Then all of a sudden the pathway came to a stop. He stopped. He noticed the colours of his shadowy green surroundings leak into each other and his environment slowly morphed much like in a dream. In an instant, he was in a different place. He looked back to trace his steps, but it was all gone as if he hadn't even been on a path. The weather was now gusty, overcast and dark. He was in a derelict street in suburbia somewhere and in front of him he saw a sight that prompted him to his location. It was his retirement cottage, all beaten up and derelict. He was living the recurring dream that had confused him until the fateful jump.

29.2 –

After his realising fright, he contemplated going inside the house. *He had to,* he thought to himself, he was certain he was following a trail that would lead to his destiny. The front door of the cottage was ajar just like in his Earth-bound dream. Being conscious in a dream was eerie, *How did I end up here?* Callison thought as he slowly approached the old front door of the cottage. The lawn was overgrown and all of the windows had shutters over them, apart from the lounge window that flapped in the wind.

He got to the rickety entrance and gently pushed it all the way open. The hallway lay in front of him with the stairs running up on the right. He put one foot in the house and cautiously entered the hallway. It was so quiet. *The writing above the fireplace!* thought Callison, and in an attempt for closure to his recurring dream, he turned left into the lounge hoping to see the writing on the wall without waking up in his bed, like his past experience of being here. He viewed the space above the fireplace and there was indeed some writing, and he didn't wake up. The dream that puzzled Callison for so long was now starting to finish. The writing was white and looked to have been handwritten:

When Jack died, the clouds of your mind
blocked out the love of your heart,
and these are your memories...

As soon as Callison read the writing on the wall he heard a creak from a door being opened. It had come from the hallway and he backed away from the fireplace to look down the hall again. The basement door had crept open and he felt his heart start to race. His breathing started to broaden. He knew he had to look in the basement. *What could be in there?* he thought, as he walked slowly away from the lounge and towards the entrance to the basement. His dream had never included the basement.

He slowly made his way down the steps to the underground room, where he could hear voices. They were well known voices. As he got to the bottom of the steps he peeped round the wall and into the basement. He was at a loss to explain what he was seeing.

He saw his former self in his white lab coat protesting with Heinrich in front of the Trebla Eye. Heinrich's agent was in the room also, facing away from Callison's non-physical current viewpoint. The three people in the basement didn't look normal because they all gave off a white halo of light around them; it was like their bodies were made of physical matter that emitted light. *It was a memory,* deduced Callison. He wondered if anybody could even hear him, 'Hello?' he said fairly loudly, but got no response. He walked right into the middle of the basement and no one blinked an eyelid, even when he walked right up to Heinrich to look him in the face, not a change in expression at all. They were looking right through him. *What was the point of this?* he thought.

Callison witnessed the memory play out as a non-physical observer. Heinrich was just about to walk over to the back wall to pull the camera out of its drill hole but just before he did so, the light that radiated from his body lead him to the wall. It was as if the light chose first and the physical body was delayed by a couple of seconds before following the light path to the back wall. *This was weird, he thought.* He guessed they must be what auras look like.

'What is that?! Is that a camera?!' his former self said with surprise. Callison noticed his own aura was brighter than Heinrich's and the agent's.

Heinrich turned around, 'Its technical name Callison, is X1120 GSW4, the 4th prototype of pinhole camera technology.' The device he held up was about 10mm long, 'Didn't even know it was here, did you? It's been broadcasting continuously on loop, you see, it downloads the information to us, then resets its memory and keeps recording.' He smiled, as he realised the device had done its job, 'We put another one in your laboratory back in your good old days of *legal research*!' he shouted angrily and as he did so, his aura dimmed to a red coloured glow before leading back into the centre of the basement. Heinrich's body followed the light back to the centre just like before.

Callison watched back the whole conversation as a hovering observer. He watched as the auras changed to reflect the mood of each person in the room. Heinrich probed the physical Callison, asking how the Eye was so quiet, before pulling a gun, and telling him to ramp the Eye up.

The memory continued as his bitter former self grudgingly ramped the Eye up for Heinrich. His aura had turned a dark red colour, as he knew himself to be scared and angry at giving his invention secrets away. Callison witnessed the Trebla Eye opening for the first time, for a second time. The portal's surface burst forth when the speed hit 1.0C. It really was a glorious sight and he would never tire of witnessing the breakpoint.

The argument soon ensued between the former Callison and Heinrich. Heinrich was going for his gun and Callison shouted to the memory of himself, 'Jump!!... Jump!!... Jump!!...'

The clock struck two minutes past four and the light of his aura suddenly moved towards the portal and jumped, emitting a white flash. What Callison saw happen next, made him feel strange. Callison's former physical body followed his light and made the jump through the portal. He was expecting to witness his disappearance from the room but to his surprise, his body hit the floor space behind the Trebla Eye. The aura around his limp body was still present, but it was noticeably dimmer.

Callison became intrigued. He moved to look at his own body. It was slumped against the wall of the basement. He tried to remember jumping, but he could only remember being taken away in the tunnel to the garden and the start of his adventure.

Heinrich followed his aura light behind the portal also, 'Naughty boy,' he said to Callison's body, 'Now I have to be clinical.' He pulled out a silencer from his inside pocket and attached it to his gun, before firing two silenced shots into Callison's head. Any semblance of the light of his aura escaped as Callison witnessed his own murder. He didn't know what to think. He felt sick and didn't want to be here anymore.

The exact moment he had the thought, the colours of his surroundings merged into each other and morphed again. The sensation was strange and he didn't leave the basement; it was more like time had been artificially fast-forwarded. The clock's hands re-appeared at 8:10pm. Callison's body had been removed from behind the Eye, and Heinrich sat and watched the portal alone. The non-physical Callison stood next to him in the basement wondering what would occur next. Eleanor poked her head round the corner, and introduced herself.

'Hello? Excuse me?'

Heinrich bolted round, and sat up straight.

Callison was still in love. He hadn't seen her in what felt to him like a lifetime. He walked up to her. She was so beautiful. Her light blue aura even glowed a colour that Callison found beautiful.

Heinrich continued like Callison wasn't there, 'Ah, Eleanor, such a pleasure.' the man said, warmly. He stood up, and his wide frame became silhouetted by the bright coloured portal still going behind him.

'Heinrich?!' She got worried, evidenced to Callison as her aura went a similar dark red to *his* before *he* had jumped. 'What are you doing here, where is Callison?' she said with a quiver in her voice.

'I'm here darling, right here,' thought Callison into her mind.

'He is at Quanta at the moment, getting some data CDs.' He slowly started to walk towards her with his hands behind his back, 'If you wait here, he'll be back shortly I'm sure.' He didn't sound genuine.

Eleanor thought on her feet, 'So does the portal work then? It looks very nice!'

'Yes, it works a treat. Quanta are very proud of Callison.' Heinrich paused.

'Yes, he's certainly a clever chap my Callie.' Eleanor was acting naïve.

Heinrich smiled sarcastically, 'Tell me, were you aware of the laws your Callie was *breaking* in studying this?'

She didn't know what to say, she didn't need to. There was a loud knock at the front door above and they heard someone's voice shout loudly, 'It's the police! Could you open up please!'

What the?... thought Callison. *How lucky!* It wasn't luck, it was intuition.

Without delay Eleanor shouted back up the stairs, 'Just coming!'

'Ha!' Callison triumphed towards Heinrich.

Heinrich was startled and annoyed at Eleanor's insolence and whipped out his pre-silenced gun, pointing it at her head and whispering aggressively, 'You're going to regret that.'

Just at that moment, Callison realised what was unfolding. Before having a chance to let ego dictate his fate, he acted telekinetically on the gun. He summoned every part of his being and focused on stopping the gun from firing. It was as if nothing else existed in Callison's universe apart from the jamming of the gun.

Heinrich pulled the trigger, but the gun was under Callison's influence. The gun jammed, and remained impotent. He tried again, and the gun jammed again. Heinrich became annoyed, but remained mute because of the police.

Eleanor was stunned and remained deadly quiet. Her husband had just saved her life.

Heinrich threatened to kill Eleanor if she made a sound, then went up the stairs to answer to the police.

The portal was still running and Callison urged her to jump. Eleanor heard the mental plea and her jump was identical to Callison's. A large white flash was emitted as her aura light hit the portal's curtain first, before her body followed and went straight through the portal's surface, landing on the floor behind the Trebla Eye. Callison moved over to her body and she was unconscious and vacant, giving off only a fraction of light than she was before the jump. *She was gone already*, thought Callison. He wished her experience on the other side to be as wonderful as his and wondered what he would see next.

Soon, Heinrich came back down the stairs and made a phone call to clear another body from the basement. He took his silenced pistol out again and followed procedure for the second time that night, and this time no matter how much Callison tried against it, the gun fired and Eleanor's light disappeared completely; she was dead also.

The hands on the clock disappeared again and time started to accelerate. Before long, Callison's basement was empty. The Trebla Eye and all the equipment had been taken back by Quanta and it was eerily quiet as if some sort of mind-storm had ended. He wondered how many people would miss them in his life before his intuition started to murmur once again.

He heard something within him and tuned his mind into the signal. He received a telepathic voice from a source he wasn't sure of, like the transmission had been mentally encrypted in someway. Callison was surprised as it spoke, Hello Callison, you are half way along your journey now. You realise now why you cannot return to this dimension. I am here to tell you that your deaths were presented as a car accident to your friends and family of this life-dream. The people that took your invention will eventually realise that there are some things that they will never gain control over. This lesson is now finished, leave the cottage for your next lesson... you will meet me soon.

The voice sounded sincere, but he couldn't help but wonder who'd said it. He tried to communicate through telepathy, Who are you? Are you the Universal Mind? His mind raced as he waited a response standing in the memory of his empty basement. What would the people who took his invention realise? What lesson was over?

He received a reply, but was none the wiser, You will meet me soon, and no, I am not the universal mind. First you have another lesson to witness. Leave the cottage.

Whoever the being was that was communicating with him seemed helpful. Are you helping me? Callison transmitted, but there was no response. With trust in the mysterious voice he slowly made his way back up the staircase and out into the memory of his hallway. Everything was blurred, matching the state of his psyche, but he still found the front door and walked outside where the wind continued to blow and the clouds filtered out the sun.

29.3 –

He crossed the road outside his cottage before stopping and thinking. He now knew he and his wife had been murdered and questioned; *but I'm still here?* He heard Jack's little voice echoing in his more recent memory, '*We're magic light daddy*'. And he started to remember his more complete life.

A tear started to build in Callison's eye as he nostalgically realised there was a bigger picture than his Earth-bound experience of being Callison Trebla alluded to. It was as if witnessing Jack talk about magic light and seeing his own murder made him realise he wasn't Callison, and never was. Callison was merely his character, worn like a mask during his physical experience on Earth.

The tear broke free and rolled down his cheek as he realised he'd logically rejected his spiritual home of compassion, love and understanding. He fell to his knees, deep in realisation as the blustery weather of the memory continued. For all his life he'd propped up his ego telling himself that because there was little material evidence, that spirit was a stupid idea. He now realised he was spirit *before* matter. The whole *world* was spiritual before it was material. Looking for spiritual evidence in the material world was like looking for the artist when all you can see is the painting.

He felt like he had turned his back on his true spiritual roots, and yearned acceptance again. He felt stupid and started to cry. He slumped to his imagined floor of grass across the road from his cottage and cried forgiveness for himself and his perceived mistakes.

Before long however, the weather changed and the wind stopped howling. Callison pulled his head up and it was lighter and sunnier again, as if the pleasance had been turned up. Callison's tears abated and he curiously noticed the change.

The mysterious voice that had spoken with him remotely inside the basement, broadcast to him again, There are no mistakes while being human, just lessons. And this is your next lesson: the place you now find yourself is the life you will return to on Earth to complete your mission.

Callison heard the transmission and turned around. The derelict cottage was not there anymore and a modern, complete and well-maintained cottage stood in its place. The sun shone and there were people in the neighbourhood washing cars, playing and laughing. It was a vision of a dream world. It was the first time he was seeing it, but it somehow seemed like he'd seen it before. Callison didn't know what to say. The sight was wonderful. Thank you... he wondered, the voice sounded parental in some way, God?

He waited for a reply, but it was not one he expected. The voice laughed, No I am not God, but that's not to say he isn't a friend of ours. We will meet when the time is right, for now though, your next lesson waits.

Ok, Callison waited and thought, I'm dead aren't I?

But the voice remained quiet, and Callison realised he was on his own again. He looked at the scene in front of him. He was in a wonderful dream now compared with the rickety old nightmare he'd just walked out of. He stood up and walked forward to inspect the sunny environment. His intuitive integration was turning magically just like Mystera had said it would.

On the driveway of his retirement cottage memory, next to a well-maintained lawn was his old ford Capri. Another car drove down the estate and the era he guessed was early 80's, he wasn't quite sure. He walked up to the cottage from the other side of the road and as he did so a yellow removal van materialised outside the house with a company called Destiny Real Estate written on the side of it. He witnessed his younger self, moving furniture into the dwelling. He looked to be about forty again. He walked forward and over the front lawn into the well-presented cottage. Upon entry to the house, he turned left into the lounge. There was more writing on the wall, this time mounted in a picture frame above the fireplace. Upon closer inspection the words read;

When Jack died, you let your heart shine
and the clouds of your mind evaporated
and these are your memories...

Callison stood looking at the picture frame on the wall, wondering why it hung there. It was the exact opposite of the writing on the wall in the last memory. He was about to find out its origins. The writing slowly started to move and morph, replicating exactly the motion that occurred during his recurring dreams of trying to read the words. They morphed into a painting of a weeping willow tree and stream that looked just like the spot where he and Eleanor had started their experiences on the other side of the portal.

Suddenly a familiar voice from behind startled him.

'What do you think of the picture Callie?'

Callison jumped and turned around. There stood a memory of Eleanor. She was younger again and was holding a small child. She was looking at the new painting she had just hung on the wall.

She was still the most beautiful sight in the world for Callison, who saw her and the baby's glowing light blue auras. Callison answered her, 'It's perfect my darling.'

There was no response from Eleanor; she was still a dimension away from his current relative viewpoint. Callison's forty-year old self walked into the lounge, and looked at the picture hanging on the wall, 'It's perfect my darling.' He leaned in and kissed his wife, before becoming suddenly confused.

'What's the matter?' asked the memory of Eleanor.

'Just deja vu, that's all.' His former self rubbed his head in confusion.

Callison's current awareness was excited. It looked like they had a child. *Was it Jack?* He thought not. It didn't look like Jack.

The colours of the parallel reality started to bleed into themselves and the time started to speed up, much like it did in the last memory. The experience seemed to take a long time, and he sensed time had moved on a long way.

He stood in the lounge still, and the time-point slowly revealed itself to him. The framed picture he had just witnessed taking it's place on the wall above the fireplace was gone and in its place was a family painting of father, mother and son. The painting seemed to be recent; Callison was grey and bald in the painting. Eleanor looked just as he remembered her before he had jumped, and their handsome son looked to be in his mid twenties.

The clock read 4:00pm as a creak was heard from the hallway. Again, the basement door was now open to him and he walked down the steps for a second time. As he turned the corner at the bottom of the steps, he saw a different memory of himself. He looked just as he did in the last reality before he had jumped and he was working on the Trebla Eye alone. His former self now glowed with an aura of faint blue light surrounding his body. The time struck 4:02, when suddenly a flash of blinding white light streaked across the basement. Callison's former self was blown backwards, as a circuit shorted and his body landed on the floor in front of the Trebla Eye. The light blue aura now shone at a significantly decreased brightness. His current point of awareness stood over his body, which lay unconscious.

Time began to accelerate, and regained its normal pace at 8:10pm. His essence then saw another person enter the basement. It was his son: he recognised him from the painting upstairs and his aura went red as he worriedly rushed to his father's aid. He checked on his condition before running upstairs again. He came back and plugged his phone charger into the wall socket. When the phone was online, he made the call for help.

'Ambulance please,' A pause ensued, 'Hello, my name is James Trebla. I found my father lying unconscious on the floor. I think he electrocuted himself.' Another pause. 'Yes, he has a pulse, please come quickly.' He reeled off the address, and finished the call. James Trebla dialled in another number to the handset as he sat by his dad's side. Callison felt the telephone call was significant. James called his mum with the news. It was 8.15pm.

'Hi mum, it's James,' He sounded panicky, 'I've just found dad unconscious on the floor in the basement. I have called an ambulance.' He waited for a response from Eleanor.

'No, he is breathing and his pulse is there, he is just unconscious.' He paused again.

'Don't worry. Go straight to the hospital, and I'll meet you there.' he said into the phone, and hung up.

An ambulance crew came down into the basement about ten minutes later and Callison's body was taken off to the hospital.

Callison felt for his son, even though he didn't know him, not as this Earth character yet anyway. Time started to accelerate, before he was alone in the basement again; this time, with the Trebla Eye and all Callison's tools for company.

He thought back to his memories of the cottage dream that haunted him all his known life, and the coincidences that led him to be living in the cottage at all. *Destiny real state... Was this supposed to happen?* He asked himself and started to realise, it was *all* supposed to happen; the dreams, the coincidences, his whole experience was supposed to be. Everything was connected by some kind of unseen continuum of events and circumstance.

The mysterious voice that had been helping him spoke again. *You have reached the end of your intuitive integration. In order to get back to Eleanor and your new life, I must visit you. I will give you more information that will free you to leave the dimension of the Energetic Mind and Soul and allow you to depart for the remainder of your Karmic contract on Earth.*

Callison smiled. He'd followed his intuition to the start of his destiny and felt like he'd come a long way in a short experience. He continued standing on the spot in his basement, wondering about the new friend that seemed to be guiding him along his path. From what the voice had said, they would be meeting shortly.

* * * * * * *

30: Amnesia

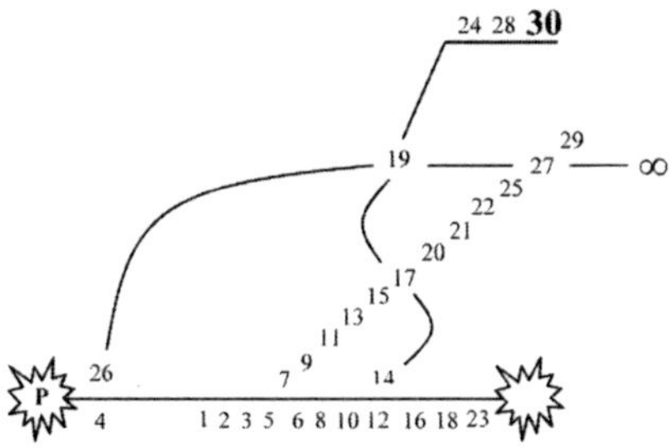

"Memory is deceptive because it is coloured by today's events."
Albert Einstein, Physicist (1879 - 1955)

30.1 –
Current Reality:
July 7th 2008:

The morning finally came around for Eleanor who struggled through a long night without proper sleep. The hospital staff moved her late in the night to another ward where she would be able to recover faster. The clock on the far wall now read seven thirty am. She heard footsteps passing up and down the ward for most of the night, but now they seemed more frequent; the light was starting to creep into the sanitised space and kick the day into action once again.

She could sense her reality was different from her experience of reality in the mountains of Capee with Togo. It was heavier again. Denser. Her emotions and thoughts created feelings that felt a lot louder than during her time away. She questioned if it had happened at all, whether it had all been a dream. Her mind really needed answers, and her only hope still lay in a coma, unconscious and seemingly oblivious.

The nurse noticed that Eleanor had woken and walked over to talk to her. She spoke with a soft and caring tone, 'Good morning sleepy head, did you rest ok?'

Eleanor lied, 'Yes thanks, it was fine.' She levered herself more upright in the bed and the nurse helped her, fluffing up her pillows.

The nurse had some news, 'I spoke with your son last night, and he is really happy to hear the news that you're conscious again.' She continued, 'Visitors are allowed in after 9 am, so in about an hour and a half he will coming to visit.' The nurse sounded helpful, but was unaware as to her patient's current anxiety.

Eleanor was as pleased as she was nervous, 'Oh that'll be good.' Her smile only showed her pleased side.

'Would you like some breakfast?' The nurse spoke quietly, 'We shouldn't start until eight, but it's nearly eight o'clock now.'

The last thing on Eleanor's mind was breakfast. Her nervous side took its turn to emerge, 'What do I look like, am I a mess?'

The nurse laughed, 'No, you look a million dollars, but I can go and grab a comb and a mirror before they arrive if you would like me to?'

Eleanor was re-assured, and started to relax, 'Yes please.'

The nurse joked, 'Now, we have ages to get you ready for the ball, Cinderella, but you still need to eat to keep your strength up. What can I get you?'

'Maybe just some cereal and a coffee?' Eleanor asked.

The nurse's expression said it wasn't going to be that simple, 'No problem with the cereal, but the doctor would like to do some tests before we let you loose on caffeine again. I can get you a decaffeinated coffee?'

She conceded without a fight, 'Yes, ok. Thank you.'

The nurse was about to go and organise breakfast, when Eleanor enquired, 'Nurse?'

The nurse replied with a smile, 'You can call me Aida.'

'Ok, Aida, thanks.' Eleanor smiled, before continuing, 'Do coma patients ever say they experience anything when they are unconscious?' She didn't expect the answer she got.

'Oh yes, all the time! Even people who are unconscious for only a few days have recalled experiences that they say felt real,' she continued, 'Why? Did you experience anything?'

Eleanor felt relieved, 'I think so. I can remember a person called Togo, and I can remember seeing Jack, my first son.'

The nurse knew the history from talking with James, Eleanor's 26 year-old son in this dimension, 'Yes, James told me about Jack. The brain works in funny ways.' said the nurse.

Eleanor probably came across as amnesic, but she had the perfect cover. 'Who is the prime minister now?' she asked from nowhere.

The nurse was slightly bemused, but obliged, 'Gordon Blair; he has been in power for...' she mentally counted, '...eleven years now,' she chuckled and made a joke, 'but it feels more like two thousand!'

Eleanor smiled; the humour was no different than from her last Earth reality. *Nothing new there...* she thought, 'Oh, I'm not completely losing my marbles then.' Eleanor chuckled to herself. The nurse was helpful, and found her patient a copy of the morning's newspaper, which Eleanor read while she ate some breakfast.

Nothing Eleanor read had changed. The newspaper still talked of the same topics; celebrities, politician scandals and sleaze campaigns, war, economy worries, and the like. She knew the characters in the paper perfectly; it was as if she hadn't been away at all. *Why then is James here, what changed?* she thought. Was her mind playing tricks with her? She couldn't tell. The memories of Togo, and her whole experience felt even more like a dream so she decided that she would keep the whole journey to herself until her husband woke up from his coma. She also found out that she didn't like decaffeinated coffee.

The doctor came to see her, and advised the drip be taken out of her arm. He did some further tests, and told Eleanor her body was coping extremely well. She would probably be discharged in days rather than weeks.

Time passed slowly for Eleanor and the clock ticked round to four minutes to nine. She had run a comb through her hair, and brushed her teeth. She watched the clock ticking; the seconds passing like minutes, and the minutes passing like hours. She was going to meet her son again; for the first time.

30.2 –

It was four minutes to nine and James and his girlfriend, Sally, were waiting in the main reception of the hospital for visiting hours to begin. They'd both taken the morning off work to come and see James's mother, who had just woken up from a seven-week coma after falling unconscious behind the wheel of her car. The crazy aspect was that she was driving to the hospital to rush to Callison's side after he'd had an electrocution accident from his Trebla Eye four hours before. The probabilities of the coincidence made James think that the accidents were somehow related.

The young couple sat next to each other in the bus stop style seating, dressed ready for work. James wore a blue shirt and black trousers and Sally wore a cardigan over her white shirt and wore a black skirt. James was in his mid twenties, and the young scientist's brown wavy hair sat on top of an anxious facial expression. He looked like he was ready to start losing hair like his dad, 'I hope she can remember me,' said James as he sat, 'the doctor would have said something, wouldn't he, if mum wasn't fine I mean?'

Sally was pretty with fair hair and shared James' interest in science. She reassured him as she stroked his hand, 'I'm sure everything will be ok, stop worrying yourself,' her voice was restrained, 'it won't be long now.'

Almost on cue the large swing doors to the left of the glassed-in reception desk hatch swung apart, and the doctor walked out to James and Sally, 'Mr Trebla?' He made eye contact with the visitors and they confirmed, 'You can come through now.'

The young couple stood up. 'How is she?' asked James as they signed in and followed the doctor into the ward network.

The doctor was positive, and had spoken with James and Sally often about Eleanor and Callison's progress. 'Your mother is awake and really doing quite well physically, however she still doesn't remember the accident. She has spoken of someone called Heinrich?' It was a question.

James gave the doctor a blank look, 'Not a name I can recall being significant.'

The doctor spoke as they walked, 'Well, we'll keep monitoring that then. Who knows, seeing you and Sally might jog her memory a bit.' He added upbeat, 'And your father still remains stable, so you have plenty more to hope for.'

The news calmed them, but they were still unsure about his mother's possible amnesia. When they arrived into the correct ward they saw Eleanor in the fourth bed up and waiting to see them. She smiled across the hospital beds at them with the same smile that James had been used to for all of his twenty-six years. They approached her bed with reciprocal smiles of relief.

Eleanor fell in love with him straight away. If there was ever someone in her life that was supposed to be, it was this man. He was smartly dressed in a light blue shirt and smart black trousers. *A fine young man*, she thought. This was becoming quite the emotional roller coaster ride for her. She couldn't help her emotion from breaking through and a tear of happiness ran down her cheek.

'Mum!' said James, 'we're so glad you're ok!' He hugged his mother for the first time in seven weeks glad she was awake again.

'Darling,' she said, feeling her son's glow for the first time, 'It's been so long...'

James introduced his girlfriend, Sally.

'Hello Eleanor, we're glad you are awake again.' Sally kissed Eleanor on the cheek.

Eleanor liked Sally straight away also, 'Hello dear, nice to meet you.' she said back,

The way Eleanor said it made both James and Sally feel his mother was still somewhat confused after her ordeal. As they found out through talking, his mother seemed coherent with everything in the paper, the date, her husband's circumstance, but it was as if she was amnesic to details about them. It felt alienating for James, who was used to his pre-accident relationship with his mother, but it was phenomena James had read about. During Eleanor's coma, James found out that the wake-up evidence said amnesia would normally centre upon the closest family members, but his fears were subsided by finding out that the amnesia was also temporary in the vast majority of cases.

Eleanor herself felt like there was too much information coming in. She couldn't catch up her new history fast enough. She had a son, but knew nothing about him at all. To take everyone's mind off of her, Eleanor suggested they go and visit Callison in his coma. She was gaining strength all the time, but the nurse brought a wheelchair over. Callison's ward was not far away, and James pushed his mother round to Callison's bedside. The three of them all looked on as Callison lay peacefully sleeping in the coma.

Up until now, James had been avoiding the issue of the accident. The coma journals said it could be traumatic for the patient, but he was going to have to discuss it.

Eleanor looked up at him from the wheelchair, 'What happened to us James? How did your father and I get here, in comas?'

James told her his version of what happened on the fateful day seven weeks ago, as Eleanor learned her new history.

* * * * * * *

31: Parallel Synchronicity

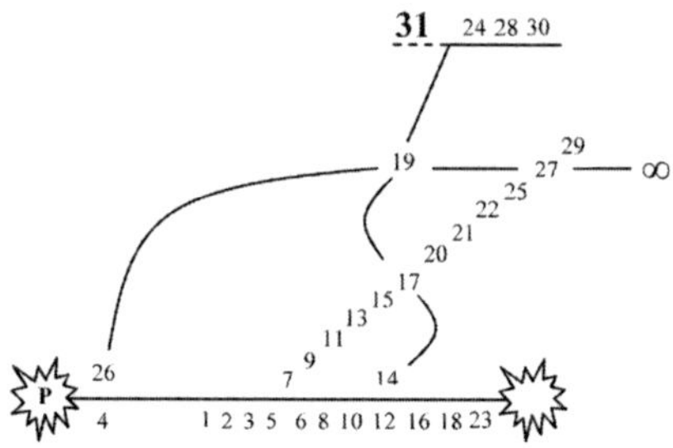

"Synchronicity is an ever present reality,
for those that have eyes to see."
Carl Jung, Psychiatrist and Scientist (1875 – 1961)

31.1 –
Flashback:
Current Reality:
May 15th 2008:

James had recently moved out of the home where he'd spent most of his life, and moved in with his girlfriend, Sally but he was back at his parent's house searching for his phone charger at about three-thirty in the afternoon. He'd left his charger here a couple of nights earlier and was now waiting for a call from a journal that he was publishing some scientific research with and his battery was dangerously low on charge. He would be back to work at his dad's own research company called Quantum Attic Research just as soon as he'd found his phone charger, but he couldn't find it anywhere. *It can't just vanish!* James thought as he hunted his parent's house high and low.

'Dad!' he shrieked down into the basement from the hallway.

The reply was Callison's, 'Yes!' his dad called back up. Although the owner of the Quantum Attic Research company, he had recently taken semi-retirement to work on his invention.

'Have you seen my phone charger lying about? I left it here the other day.' he waited for the reply.

Callison hadn't noticed it and shouted back up the steps, 'Sorry son, I haven't seen it, I've been down here working most of the time.' His father was working on a device called the Trebla Eye; a large round structure that they hoped would open up a gap in the zero point field and become a doorway into time-space itself.

James was aware of the project and helped his father often, but today he needed to get back to work, 'Well, if you see it, can you give me a ring? I have to get back to work.' he waited for the reply.

'Will I get hold of you?' his dad called back.

'Yes, you should do, if not try me on my work number.'

'Ok,' Callison called back.

'Thanks, see you later dad, I'm going back to work.'

'Yes, see you later James.' said Callison. It would be a coma later.

James went back to work and stayed there until about seven-thirty, but he felt odd for the duration; it was an uneasy feeling similar to an uncertainty of how things would work out. He palmed it off as nothing, but he would soon wonder.

He left his offices, still not having heard from the scientific journal. He made the walk across the car park and as he pulled the phone out of his pocket to check for missed calls, the backlight gave up the ghost and the phone turned itself off. He needed his charger. He knew it was at his folk's house somewhere.

Normally he would drive back to his own house after work, but this evening he would be swinging by his parent's house. He arrived there at five minutes past eight, just as the night was drawing in, but strangely the lights weren't on in the house.

He let himself in with his key, 'Hello?' he called; not a soul was about. *Weird.* He thought as he turned the hallway light on.

He called again, 'Mum, Dad??' Still no response. James walked through to the kitchen at the end of the hall. There was a note from his mother to his father telling him dinner was in the fridge and that she was out at a mind body and spirit exhibition in town with her friend Betty. *So where's dad?* He thought. As soon as the thought had come, he saw his phone charger and sighed a relief. It was just on the sideboard. He wracked his brain to remember searching earlier. *Maybe dad found it?*

He checked the basement door and light flooded up from the bottom few steps. 'Dad?' he called down. Silence. He descended the flight and upon walking round the corner into the basement he saw his dad lying on the floor, seemingly unconscious.

'Dad!' he gasped. He rushed to his dad's side, 'Dad! Can you hear me dad?' Callison was breathing, and had a pulse, but he was not responding. James rushed upstairs to get his phone charger, before running back down into the basement and plugging it in to the wall socket. *Come on! Come on!* thought James, as the phone went through its branding protocol. Stricken with panic, he punched in the emergency number, and asked for an ambulance.

With the ambulance now on its way, he thought he should phone his mother with the news. He phoned his mum to let her know what had happened and she said she would set off in the car and meet him at the hospital, which she did, but there was to be a catch.

James went with his father in the ambulance to Justanother Town Hospital and while on route, had the shock of his life. The ambulance radio crackled transmissions into the driver, but the whole cabin could hear the broadcasts. Another ambulance driver radioed about a car accident they had just attended and were on route to the same hospital. James noticed just the last words of the transmission; the casualty concerned was one Eleanor Trebla. James fell white with disbelief.

And that would be the last day that James would speak with his mother for seven long weeks.

* * * * * * *

30: Amnesia Continued...

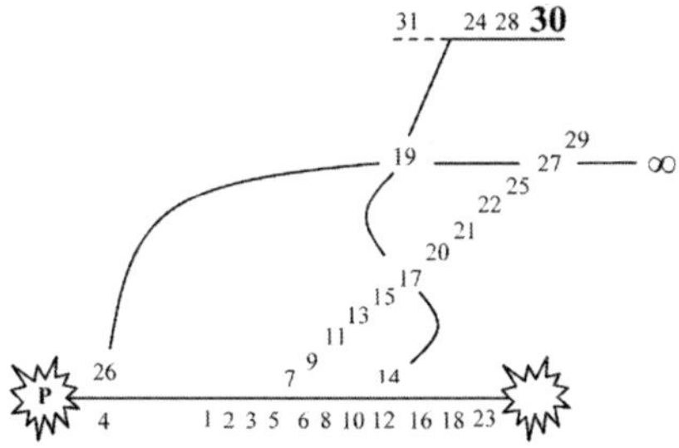

30.3 –
Current Reality:
Back in the hospital:

'And that's when you had your accident in the car.' said James to his mother, sitting in the wheelchair next to Callison's hospital bed.

Eleanor shook her head, as if she couldn't recollect it. From her point of view, nothing happened that way, 'I don't remember...' said Eleanor looking down at her knees, still with hazy amnesia.

'Do you not remember it at all?' asked her son, concerned.

She shook her head, 'I'm not sure what I remember. Maybe I did have a flashback of a car accident, but I couldn't tell you what I was doing or where I was going...'

James thought before adding more mystery to the saga, 'Well at the hospital, I spoke with the paramedics that brought you in. They think you're very lucky to be alive. They said that you must have lost consciousness at the wheel and barrelled through a set of red lights, over a fast busy dual carriageway before the car rolled to a stop in the middle of the road. There wasn't a scratch on the car and the paramedics that rescued you were quite spooked at how lucky you were.'

Eleanor was surprised and grateful to be here at all, 'I'm sorry James, I'm just having trouble putting all of it together.'

James reassured her, resting his hand on her shoulder, 'You take all the time in the world. We love you very much, and when dad wakes up everything will return to normal, you'll see.' he said, optimistically.

She loved him already, 'And I love you too darling,' she added Sally, 'I love both of you, you both look very happy.' She could sense a tear coming, but turned and thought about her husband again. She knew *he* would be able to make sense of it. She couldn't help but wonder what her husband was experiencing, and willed him to wake up.

* * * * * * *

32: The Man in the Mirror

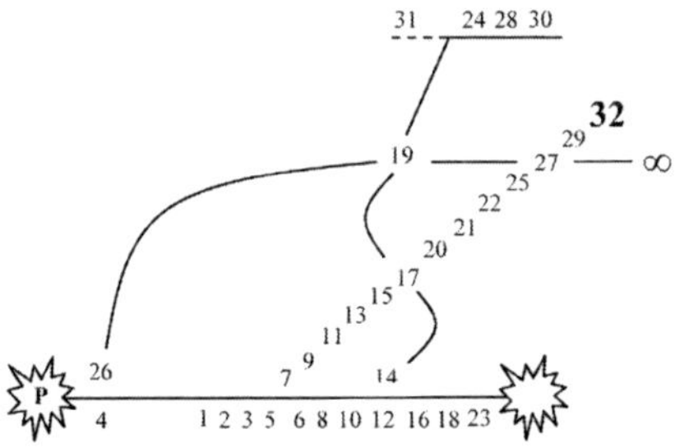

"Knowing others is wisdom. Knowing yourself is enlightenment."
Lao Tzu, Mystic Philosopher (c. 600BC)

32.1 –
Date not known:
Plus six days:

Callison was standing in the basement of the parallel memory and the voice spoke to him again, Leave the basement, you have more to learn.

The intuitive integration student followed the instruction with intrigue rather than fear, he knew fear was only an illusion created by him. When he got to the top of steps he emerged into his hallway, expecting to see the mysterious voice, but it was quiet in the alternate parallel memory. He thought he'd walk back to the water fountain of Admiral Pickering, but he wouldn't end up seeing the Admiral again until he arrived back to his small village of his Earth experience.

Before he walked out of the front door, he looked right and into the lounge again, when something caught his attention. The family painting on the wall was completely different to how it was before he walked into the basement. It was now a painting of a young olive skinned tribal looking man, with jet black hair and to Callison's surprise, the man was with a lady that bore similar resemblance to his new Sukarmian friend, Liele.

What the…? Callison questioned as he approached the painting. He walked through light rays streaming into the lounge through the open windows. Walking up to the painting, he inspected the description at the bottom, it read: Mr and Mrs Trebla. He looked at the painting again. He was none the wiser and continued thinking. *What the…*

'You're wondering what on earth is happening right?' came a familiar voice from behind him.

The voice! Callison was surprised, and spun around to see in the hallway a being of white light that stood still, staring back at Callison. The being slowly started walking toward him.

Callison asked, 'Who are you?'

The light being comprised a head, four limbs and walked like a human. It had no features though, and looked like a silhouette of light. The being walked to stand in the middle of the lounge about two metres in front of Callison and calmly answered, 'I am you in a higher plane of light.' Although the voice was unmistakably the same as the one guiding him, it wasn't so much telepathic anymore and Callison heard the words audibly rather than sensed them mentally.

'What?' Callison questioned, 'How can *you* be me?' he thought, '*I'm* me… aren't I?' Callison could feel the being was very like him, to the point where it felt eerily like staring at a mirror.

The ghostly being repeated Callison's question in a very human manner, 'How can you and me be the same…' It took time to think, and even seemed to invisibly smile at Callison, 'Do you remember the holographic notion that the parts all contain the information of the whole?'

Callison remembered the holography leaflet that the man in Turuk had given him, 'Yes.' he waited for the explanation.

'That concept needed to be given to you,' said the being, 'you see, the energy of consciousness is holographic in its nature. You are your consciousness inside Callison Trebla, and I am your consciousness outside Callison Trebla.'

'What does that mean?' said Callison as he stood facing away from the painting and toward the white silhouette in the memory of his lounge.

The being didn't hesitate, 'Well, based on how you decide to see it, you are the tiny part and I am the bigger whole, or, you are the tiny whole and I am the bigger part, but the separation is only an illusion, as we are both whole in and of ourselves, but we're also both parts of one overall consciousness.'

Callison tried to summarise, but got confused, 'So you're me... but... you're not me?'

'We are each other, as your consciousness and my consciousness are both whole parts that were once one.' said the being. 'We have the same consciousness. I have our more complete memory, and you only have the conscious memory of Callison Trebla and this is because before your existence we divided, and the 'you' fragment of 'us' embarked on the experience of Callison Trebla, and the 'me' part of 'us' stayed in the realms of light. You could see me as your higher self because I communicate with you through the gateways of conscience and intuition in your physical experience.'

The scientist liked the mysterious being of light, and found himself elevated by its presence. The conversation flowed organically with no barriers of awkwardness, 'What's the difference between intuition and logic? What should I follow?'

'Your intuition is the inward river that will lead you to your ultimate destiny. Your logic is a measure of your understanding of the scenery along the way.'

'So I just need to throw logic away and go with what I feel is right?'

'Essentially yes, but it is not as easy as that. We test ourselves. We give ourselves choices in the game of life.'

'What do you mean? Like temptations?' asked Callison.

'Temptation is one aspect.' said the white light, 'You see the inward river is a long one, and can take many lifetimes to navigate. Every time you are born physically, you are born as a character on the banks of the inward river. The riverbanks can become very real, to the point where they can be mistaken for a total reality where in actual fact they were only ever temporary ports of call along the water. The imagined reality then slowly creates its own laws, called logic. The inward river of intuition can flow by almost unnoticed to some of the mind-locked characters of logic thought patterning on the banks of mind, who are convinced by fear that the intuitive river would surely lead to their destruction. And so those characters cling to the perceived mass think, clutching at the illusion as if their total existences were at stake. It is how you felt when you first got here, remember.'

Callison understood the principle, given his experiences over the last few days and thought about his lessons here, 'Are you my soul then?' asked Callison.

The ghostly reflection of Callison's consciousness continued to enlighten, as it remained a couple of metres in front of him, 'Our soul is technically created in the process of our reuniting again. When you and I recombine, and our consciousness resembles one entity again, *that* being would be a good description for soul, but again, we have the same issues with labels just as on Earth; as above, so below. We are all merely conscious potential energy, that needs more than words to describe itself fully.'

Callison wanted to clarify, 'But Mystera said I *was* the soul, and that I didn't *have* the soul, what would that mean?'

The being explained, 'Remember the energy of consciousness is holographic. When the soul decides to embark for a physical experience it doesn't travel, it divides into two parts,' it iterated, '...you and I... and we are each as conscious as the other. You are the pocket of consciousness that experiences your character, and it is that pocket that was described to you as 'the soul' by Mystera. That's the difference, you *have* your character, but you *are* the experiencer. I am the rest of your experiences, your higher soul, from your true origins of light.'

Magic light. Callison thought again, 'Is this reality of light the one that my son, Jack returned to at the lake?'

'Yes.' The being radiated a light feeling, like it was smiling, 'He is a good friend of ours in the realms of light.'

The torrent of incoming information breached Callison's mind and he felt overcome with love and peace for Jack. A tear of happiness started to build. 'I have to sit down to take this all in.' Callison went to sit on one of the sofas in the continuing vision of the parallel lounge reality.

As he took his seat, the light being teleported from a standing position in the middle of the lounge to sitting down next to him on the couch.

'How did you do that?' Callison exclaimed, very aware of the unusual movement through space.

'Because I know I can.' came the reply. 'Time and space are ultimately illusion for light beings, but they serve wonderfully for the physical worlds.'

Callison had an unlimited number of questions regarding his time here. 'So why are you here now?' Callison asked, 'Why didn't you tell me all this when I first got here?'

The ghostly white hologram seemed to look back at him as he sat, but it was only a sense for Callison who saw only white light, and no face. 'You had to go through your learning alone, to learn what intuition was. I'm here now to allow you to leave the mind plane you are currently existing in and allow you to return to the remainder of your parallel physical existence as Callison Trebla.' The hologram clarified, 'The information you are gaining right now will allow you to break the belief of where you think you are and of your self-imposed limitations.' It went on imparting its knowledge, 'The reason I didn't tell you this when you first got here was because you needed to get to this point alone. You needed to make a choice that you didn't make in your physical life in order to change your past and create your light-bridge to the new present.'

'What choice was that? Some choice *I* made, or *you* made?' Callison was confused and unsure.

'You *are* me, remember? I take full responsibility for your choices, because I would make the exact choices you did, given the information you had available.'

Callison nodded conceding.

The higher entity continued, 'It's a choice that was made many years ago to be regretful for Jack's passing. If you had been more open back then, and dealt with your feelings and emotions you would have decided to be thankful for Jack's short life instead of regretful for his loss, and you would have eventually created different choices in life. These different choices lead to the timeline you have just witnessed, in which you electrocute yourself on the 15th May 2008 instead of jumping through the Trebla Eye to get here. This is the life you will enter again upon departure from this dimension of mind and soul. The electrocution puts you in a coma, from which you will wake from and continue writing your alternate life story.'

Callison's heart was lifted, 'Really? Even though I made a wrong choice originally, regarding Jack's death?'

'The choice has actually been retaken. It had to be retaken in order to create your passage to the alternate reality.' He went on, 'The choice was retaken at the lake of reflection yesterday during your intuitive integration experience when Jack passed from you a second time. This was like a second chance at the choice and you moved on. You let go of the shore and followed the river of intuition. This had to be undertaken by the *you* part of us alone; I could only will you on as your intuitive thoughts.'

A tear of righteous happiness rolled down Callison's cheek. He wanted to get back to his new Earth life. Smiling with happiness, he asked, 'How do I get back to this alternate life from here then?'

The being replied, 'You leave via the Alpine Stargate.'

'And how do we get there?' asked the temporary inter-dimensional tourist.

Callison's higher self remained cryptic, 'First, you need to realise what is happening, and who is who.'

* * * * * * *

33: An Ancient Undertaking

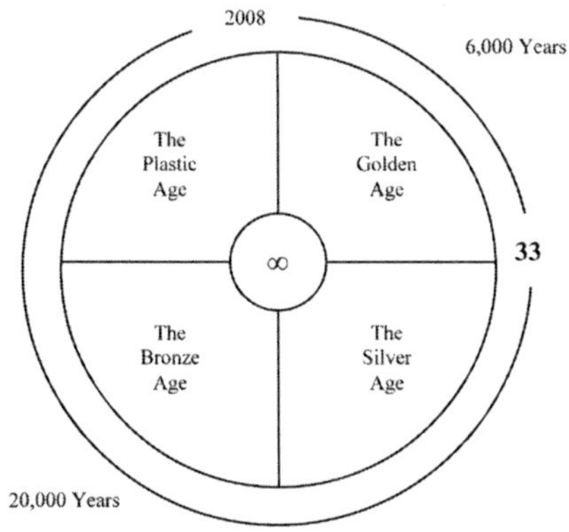

"History is strewn thick with evidence
that the truth seems easy to kill,
but a lie, well told, seems immortal."
Mark Twain, Author (1835 – 1910)

33.1 –
The Planet Earth time wheel:
End of the Golden Age:

Human civilisation on planet Earth in these times existed as a series of cities rather than countries and each city was surrounded by the nature's plains, forests and seas.

Sukarmia was an advanced and technical city habited by a million or so advanced souls. The knowledge they had of self and of Earthly experience meant they could create any city they wanted, and they chose to build Sukarmia. The grand city was powered by the magnetic field of the planet itself, harnessed and stored in such a way as to ultimately mean energy was unlimited.

Two of the million strong population of Sukarmia were young lovers, Togo and Liele. They had met five years ago during one of many meditation classes going on in Sukarmia and were visualising material objects and telling the class what they had visualised. Well, Togo and Liele both visualised the same thing; three copper coins spinning on the floor. They got talking to each other about the common visualisation and the rest, as they say, was history.

Today the couple were to meet Mystera, a Time Shaman at the Noi Tu pyramid for a mission into consciousness itself; an exercise known as an intuitive integration. The intuitive integration exercise would bring them closer spiritually and also gained them wisdom and knowledge.

They had been walking through the lush green landscape for nearly seven days to get to the Noi Tu pyramid, which had been built in nature for the setting of peace and integration with natural systems and energies. They wore white body suits and carried bags on their backs that held their lightweight camping materials.

The pair stood at the base of the pyramid staring up a long set of stairs. Two small white fluffy clouds inhabited the brilliant blue sky above them, and the surrounding green lush plant life glistened in the sun. The monolith before them was built from grey stones and had four large flaming candles on each corner of the square summit.

'Well, we made it.' said Togo to his love, Liele.

Liele smiled back, looking at the large mound of stone, 'It's amazing. Such a simple sturdy shape.' The pair stood with their arms around each other, looking at the large structure. In just a few hours they would be walking back into Sukarmia with a broader spectrum of understanding about life, and about each other.

Togo observed the surroundings, 'It's so quiet here.'

Liele acknowledged, 'Yes, it's peaceful isn't it.' She looked at him and smiled.

'Shall we?' said Togo, gesturing to the summit.

Liele obliged and the pair started the ascent to the top, one step at a time.

Mystera was waiting for them at the summit, 'Hello my friends.' said Mystera to Liele and Togo after they had climbed the north face of the pyramid. The shaman stood in the middle of the square court atop the monolith.

The pyramid visitors put their hands together and bowed out of respect.

'Hello Mystera.' answered Togo, 'We have arrived for an int...'

Mystera finished Togo's sentence, 'An intuitive integration.' he continued, 'Yes, I have been expecting you both for two days now.' He smiled back at the pair and wore a large cape-like shawl made from many animal hides and had a feathered headdress on. His painted face was weathered but warming and his smile glowed with peace. He continued, 'Do you know what your integrations hold yet?'

'No we don't, Mystera.' said Liele, 'We were called here by our dreams.'

'The best way.' said the Shaman, smiling, 'Well let's find out then. Leave your bags up here. Follow me.'

They took their bags off and left them on the top of the pyramid. Mystera walked to the centre of the space on top of the pyramid, before descending down a spiral staircase into the bowels of the sacred structure. Togo and Liele followed the Time Shaman inside.

Once inside the pyramid it was dark and wall-mounted candles partially illuminated some narrow stone corridors. Both Togo and Liele were excited rather than scared as they followed the Shaman deeper into the darkness. Once in the designated pyramid chamber the Shaman lit some larger candles, casting a flickering orange light out onto the contents of the room. It was square in shape and had exquisite hieroglyph patterns circling all four walls.

'Please be seated.' said the Shaman, as he gestured to some cushions on the floor with his hands. The couple sat down cross-legged and faced the Shaman, who sat also.

Mystera divulged more information about the pair's intuitive integration, the flickering orange glow of the flame light bouncing around the room, 'I have been communicating with another dimension of my consciousness from a place far away from the here and now, who is trying to help his people avert a catastrophe.' The shaman said. 'This being has asked me to find you, for your help is needed in the dimension of mind and soul.'

Liele and Togo sat, listening to the wise shaman of time.

The master continued, 'In this dimension you will be required to comfort and aid the mental turnaround of two lost souls. Liele, you will go to a wisp of Callison Trebla's mind. And Togo, you will go to look after Eleanor Trebla on her mental wisp. They are lovers from a place different from now, and need to face themselves before building a bridge to their time-altered physical life. They have personal issues they need to face in order to open up other timelines to allow their return. When they leave the dimension of mind and soul your mission is complete and you can return to your bodies here again.'

Togo had a question, 'We were told that this intuitive integration would be for both of us? Liele and me. We were told it would let us know each other more?'

The Time Shaman eased Togo's concerns, 'You will get to know each other more, because Eleanor Trebla is Liele, dimensionally entangled in another life, and Callison Trebla is you, dimensionally entangled in another life. However, you are not to tell your guests who you are. They can guess, but they have to realise it for themselves, so use grace.'

Togo and Liele nodded acceptingly, 'Ok.' They liked the sound of their missions. They had both been into the dimensions of energetic mind and soul before as part of previous intuitive integrations and through their meditation rituals and mind-altering plants. It usually involved drinking a special drink called Ayahuasca that would entrance them into the non-physical dimension for longer.

'Your personal understandings from this intuitive integration into the dimension of mind and soul will be up to you.' said Mystera.

All intuitive integrations were character building for the undertaker, in terms of personal understanding. The Sukarmians thought there were reasons for every experience, and the trick was to use the intuitive integration to answer questions in one's own life. Although Liele didn't know what was to come during the integration, and meeting Callison Trebla she had a good idea of what she wanted to gain insight on.

Both Togo and Liele agreed to the mission.

Mystera seemed to caution, 'This intuitive integration will be important for another reason also.'

'Another reason?' said Liele.

The Shaman told them, 'Callison and Eleanor come from a dark place on the cycle of time. The souls of the period will have lost the knowledge about their true identities as multi-dimensional beings of awareness and act on the false belief that they are their character and nothing more. If this plan works, Callison Trebla will invent the device that will help change the perception of the world, ushering in the golden age again.'

'Ok.' said Togo, excitedly. Both students had been taught about the changing ages on the wheel of time.

'So be gentle and patient,' continued Mystera. They have to remember their truth on a personal level, not on a character level, and it may take longer for each subject.'

His pupils nodded. They felt some element of pressure but in their era on Earth, fear was not really on the agenda. They were ready to leave time and space.

Mystera stood up and took three wooden tumblers of Ayahuasca from a shelf carved into the wall. 'Drink up.' He placed a glass of green pulpy liquid in front of each of them and sat back down.

'Are you coming as well?' asked Liele seeing a tumbler in front of the Time Shaman.

'Yes.' He picked up his Ayahuasca, 'I will assist your subjects in their turnaround.' he said obligingly, 'and I also have some entities to talk to and matters that I need to tend to in the dimension, regarding the blueprints of time.' His words hung, but neither Liele nor Togo were concerned.

Togo and Liele raised their tumblers and the three of them knocked back the Ayahuasca. Mystera started a meditation chant that would break them free from their physical bodies and propel them into the mental dimension all around them and inside them.

Soon, the trio of ancient dimensional travellers were far away from planet Earth and the notion of physical time. They were in a peaceful mental state that allowed their awareness to leave their Earthly physical bodies, launching them into an abundance of true awareness. In just one thought, they reached the gateway to the dimension of mind and soul: The Alpine Stargate.

As Mystera, Liele and Togo brought their awareness to the circular hub of shimmering white light, Togo was fascinated as to how the gate worked. It looked like there was something circumnavigating the outer periphery very quickly. He couldn't explain his fascination with the stargate. Little did he know that twenty thousand years away as his dimensionally entangled self, Callison Trebla, he would recreate the portal using matter in the physical world.

The three points of awareness vanished through the portal and on to their missions. Their physical bodies remained on Earth; trapped in the web of time and space.

* * * * * * *

34: Multi-Dimensionalism

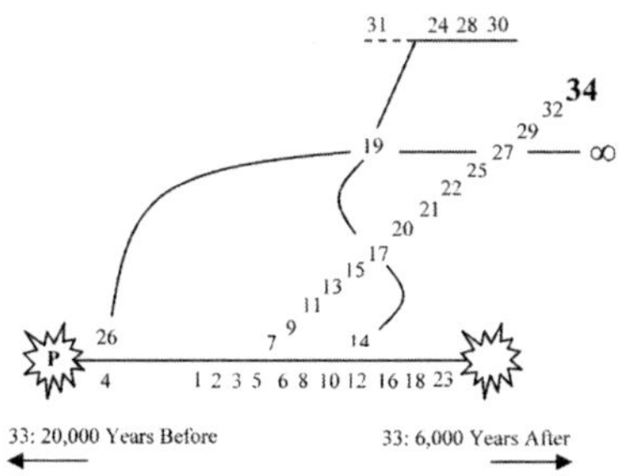

"Man's mind, once stretched by a new idea, never regains its original dimensions."

Oliver Wendell Holmes Jr., Judge and Jurist (1841–1935)

34.1 –
Date not known:
Plus six days:

The answer surprised him; *What is happening and who is who?* wondered Callison, sitting next to his higher self on the couch, 'What do you mean by that?'

The apparition stood in the middle of the room as Callison remained on the memory of his sofa in the memory of his lounge in the memory of his cottage.

'All is not as it seems,' said the holographic donor of Callison's consciousness. 'but first, let us leave this cottage memory, it has served its purpose now. Let's have a change of scenery,' it said, 'let's go back to the waterfall.' It was as if the being was in direct in control of the scene and summoned it to change. The white light moved his arm across from his left to the right and the scene changed in an instant. 'That's better.'

They were outside instantaneously; a wind blew across that carried water vapour in the air, waving the grasses and reeds. They were next to the river and a high waterfall.

Callison had remained seated on the sofa as the scene changed instantaneously, but he hadn't moved a bit. As far as he was aware the sofa had come with them to the new natural surroundings. Until he realised it hadn't and the moment he realised, his belief in the sofa was shattered and he fell on his behind, landing on the grass just below him.

'Did you do that?' asked Callison, now sitting on the grass.

Callison sensed the silhouetted light was grinning, 'This place is not what you think.' It gave its reasons, 'You are not on a planet for instance. You are not part of the time you used to know either. You are in a mental imprint called a wisp, a stand-alone environment created by your own beliefs,' the being radiated humour, 'the minute you realised the sofa wasn't where you thought it was, you believed that you'd fall. Your beliefs always control your experience. That is why if you want to do something, you have to believe you can do it, conversely, if you don't believe you can do it, you can't. You are your own limits of reality.'

Callison accepted, rubbing his behind and standing up again. He looked around at the new scene; the waterfall fell over the side of the tall cliff that he arrived here at on his first day here. Callison and his higher self stood on the grass bank near the river's edge. It felt so real; he could feel the wind and the light mist from the waterfall.

Callison's higher self continued to explain, 'This place, we see right now,' the being of light gestured with his arms to the surroundings they found themselves in, 'and your whole experience of Sukarmia, was actually created by another dimensional facet of our consciousness called Togo. In this golden age of life on Earth we are married to Liele, a dimensional facet of your present wife, Eleanor's consciousness. These life times translate to twenty thousand Earth years away from your era on Earth. While living as Togo, and Eleanor as

Liele, you both agreed to visit the dimension of the energetic mind and soul to help you find your way, and you have, you are ready to go and live out the rest of your life.'

Callison was pleased for his progress and thanked the being for the information. He spoke at the face region of light out of habit, 'So you're saying these are past lives? So we reincarnate?' he assumed.

The higher entity seemed to know the concept, 'Well this is a relativity issue; to a time-limited character-built mind, yes, it's a past life, and yes, you reincarnate, but to your true consciousness, it's not a past life and we don't reincarnate, we just are.'

'How come?' enquired Callison.

The inter-dimensional being explained, 'Because time isn't real, it's *experience* that's real. When you, the spark of light, experience your consciousness in a physical body within time, the appearance is that time moves forwards from the past to the present and onto the future. The truth is there *is* no past and future, there is just the experience of being.' It advised, 'See Togo not as a past life, but rather as another aspect or character of our own consciousness, living holographically at the same time, but in a different now. For you are not connected with your other dimensional characters through time, you are connected with them through consciousness.'

Callison thought about it and nodded. 'I'll try. It's not easy though when your mind has been made a certain way for so long.' He felt his own character's injustice at not knowing. 'Why was I not born with this information? Why do I not *know* this anymore? At what point did my memory get wiped? That's surely a bit unfair.'

'They are the conditions of entry for the Earth experience.' came the light's reply. It continued, 'If we all arrived on Earth having the full memory of who we were, we would fall into the same patterns of life and nothing new would be learned. So the veil is drawn at birth, and all new information that the character takes on sits on the veil, until death, when the veil is broken and the integration of consciousness takes place. It is not really unfair, each spark chooses to go to Earth knowing the rules, no one makes us go.'

Callison's whole existence was changing, just by having the information.

The being seemed to be working to a schedule, and got back to explaining his current situation, 'Anyway, Togo, the inter-dimensional facet of *our* consciousness, has been helping your wife Eleanor adjust to find her way back to your alternate life, and in turn *Eleanor's* inter-dimensional consciousness, Liele, has been helping us find our way.'

The bizarre information made sense and Callison felt relief, 'That's why I feel attracted to her then!' he smiled at himself for not listening to his feelings.

'The energy that animates Liele and Eleanor is a very close friend of ours in the realms of light: that is why you are experiencing the feelings you do towards her. Fall for her in the same way she fell for you, and she will lead us,' he rephrased, 'lead *you*, to the Alpine Stargate that will allow you back to the rest of your karmic destiny on Earth.'

Callison was dumbfounded. 'So...' Callison pondered, as the water vapour from the waterfall blew around them. He thought about the painting in the lounge he had seen before the scene change, 'So was that painting of Togo and Liele actually me and Eleanor?'

'Yes.' said the higher self. 'The painting changing is like a ripple of inter-dimensional experience filtering to you from your higher memory.'

Strange he thought. 'Does Liele know about my experience as Callison, does she know that I'm an inter-dimensional facet of Togo?'

'Yes. She has been showing you things and giving you knowledge to liberate your mind in hope that you will realise yourself, who you are and what you are capable of.'

Callison did love Liele and was glad he'd found out but asked, 'For the record, what do I do with this knowledge... back on Earth I mean?'

The being answered, 'Live your life with it. Life is an art form and knowing this is a start, but living it is quite another. It's the challenge: Live or be lived.'

Callison nodded, appreciating the Earth challenge. The wind suddenly changed direction, and a gust of water mist sprayed the pair, however it was only Callison that believed he was wet. He thought this would be as good a candidate as any to ask if there was a God, 'So God? Does he exist?'

The higher consciousness was honest and spoke back to Callison as the sunlight met the conscious light. 'I must be leaving soon, but I understand your question. This will have to be the last.' It answered however, 'In the grandest sense there is The One, which you might call God, but it's a state of consciousness rather than a man or woman. When The One, or God state of consciousness was all that existed, we were peaceful and resting. We needed nothing, because relatively we were everything already. We were pure potential. We were one creative consciousness, but we split within ourselves in order to experience self-communication. The different states of consciousness then communicated and decided to split again to observe further possibilities. The four then looked inwardly, and split and before long, much like an embryo cell doubles itself into existence, there was infinite growth, or the illusion of infinite growth for we were only ever growing inwardly; we are one consciousness in our broadest state after all. Ideas and concepts started to create universes and experiences within the designs. Animals and humans, the plants, the planets, the galaxies were all born from the desire to imagine and create.' the being seemed to radiate a smile, 'Even though it might seem like you are separate from all the people you meet and all the things you see, they are you and you are all of them at the base level. There are an infinite amount of parts to consciousness that are all whole in and of themselves and all have the capacity of imagining the freedom of the God state. It's just a question of knowledge, experience and intuition.'

The explanation fitted in well with the information he had taken on over his time in Sukarmia, 'It kind of…' he thought, '…makes sense?'

'I'm glad you think that.' said his higher self as the white light stood on the grass bank, looking at the golden naked man. 'Now, let's get you on you way home.'

Callison had come to the end of his journey outside the time he knew and it was now the start of the end for the out-of-body explorer. He agreed. 'Ok, I'm ready.'

The silhouette of light started to subtly get brighter, 'I am going to leave you now Callison. I'm leaving you so that you can go back and collect the remainder of your Earth experience for us.' Callison only just noticed the increasing light intensity at first, but his higher self also started to get shorter. It was morphing in shape, getting fatter and stouter, but it continued speaking, 'You are where you need to be. Go to Liele, and tell her you remember. She will lead you out of your mind wisp and on through the mind and soul dimension to the Alpine Stargate.'

Callison had no idea what to expect as the being prepared to depart, 'Was all of this supposed to happen? Was I chosen to invent the Eye?'

The being of light explained cryptically as it morphed, '*Everything* is chosen...'

'What do you mean?' asked Callison, eager to understand.

'Mystera will tell you more about the Eye and your new past.' said the light, now half its original size.

Mystera? he wondered. 'Will I ever see you again?' Callison enquired.

The light form, continued to shrink and increase it's light intensity, 'Only when you leave the game of life.' it added, without any change in voice, 'Technically, I will be with you in the game too,' he continued to shrink, 'but I will just be harder to spot.' Slowly the bright light of his higher self started to disintegrate, and colours and material began to break through the bright white glow. It materialised into a brightly coloured bird with a yellow line down the centre of its shiny black beak. It moved around, as if to get comfortable.

{Nuridaga to Callison} It's like I said to you on your first day here... The bird jumped and flapped its wings, blasting Callison with a downdraught of moving air and taking to the skies. It continued; Intuition will always be your best guide.

The bird, Callison's higher self, left Callison standing on the grass next to the summit of the waterfall. As it flew off into the sky, it became a small speck, before vanishing with a small white flash of light.

Callison felt lost and alone again, but he had just taken on a vast amount of information. He was next to the waterfall he'd been by on his first day here; where he saw the first Kimeng Rat and where Liele did her flying trick.

Why did I bring myself here? he thought. *Use my intuition?* He thought on it for a few moments more. Initially he thought about telepathically calling for Liele, but he was stopped in his tracks by a lack of thought. Intuition spoke, and it got his attention; Callison didn't even stop to assess it. He walked back twenty paces from the cliffs edge, before turning and running towards the shear drop and launching himself into the valley below.

* * * * * * *

35: The Key of Understanding

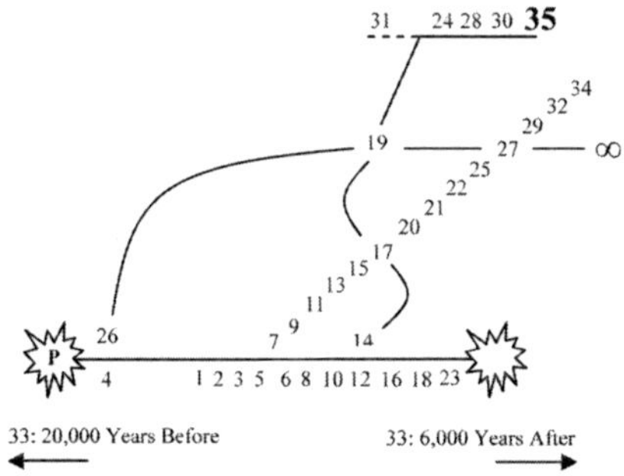

"The noblest pleasure is the joy of understanding."
Leonardo Da Vinci, Scientist and Artist (1452 – 1519)

35.1 –
Current reality:
July 10th 2008:

A few days after waking from her coma, Eleanor was discharged from hospital with a clean bill of health. Despite some tests, the doctors never really described fully what caused her to black out at the wheel of her car, but used luck to describe her escape on the roads.

James and Sally brought Eleanor some of her own clothes to wear for the journey home from hospital and amazingly even with the dimension change, the dress Eleanor wore was one of her favourites from the old dimension. It was as if most of her life was amazingly identical to the old dimension, apart from the pleasant issue of having a son on the scene.

As Callison still lay peacefully in his coma, Eleanor was in the summer sunshine in the hospital car park being helped into her son's car. Although medically sound, her body was still weak from 7 weeks of dormancy and she was wheel chaired out to the car.

'I could have walked you know,' said Eleanor as they approached the car.

That's my mum alright, thought James happily, 'Doctor's orders mother. You just relax, we'll be home soon, then you can rest up on the sofa.'

James drove Eleanor and Sally back to his parent's cottage where Eleanor's fateful experience began in the reality departed. As they pulled up on the driveway, the cottage was quiet and it reminded Eleanor of the night she got back from bingo, just before she met Heinrich Muller in the basement.

James hoped his mother would have her memory prompted by seeing the house again, 'Well Mum, here we are. This is where you live. Do you remember it?'

Eleanor didn't lie, 'Yes, dear...' she was vague, '...I remember.' She was apprehensive, as she gazed at the cottage from the car. It looked exactly the same.

James breathed a small sigh of relief. His mother had been missing pieces of information during her recovery in hospital and he was happy his mother was even alive, but if she could get her memory back it would serve as a full recovery to him.

James hopped out of the car, and gave the keys to Sally who went to open the front door. Eleanor followed, sitting in the wheelchair that James pushed. As James pushed his mother towards the front door Eleanor was amazed. Everything about the house was identical to the cottage she knew in the old dimension and it felt eerie, like a programmed simulation. The window frames were the same, the external walls were exactly the same colour and the small sprouts of ivy climbed in the exact same places on the wall as they did in her last reality.

'Here we are, home sweet home.' said James, as they got to the front door.

'Thank you dear.' She liked having a son and as she thought about it, James turned the wheelchair round and pulled it over the lip of the doorframe backwards.

When they were in the hall, Sally offered drinks, 'Can I get you anything Ellie? Tea, coffee?'

'A cup of tea please Sally.' she said gratefully from the wheelchair.

Sally looked at James, 'Tea? Coffee?'

'Coffee please.' James replied, and Sally walked off to the kitchen to prepare the drinks.

'Ok, time to get out of this thing.' said Eleanor as she hauled her upper body up and away from the wheelchair.

James was concerned, 'Are you sure mum?'

'Yes, I'm sure,' she said back. When she was on her feet she continued, 'I have to look about. Familiarise myself again. Can't do that in the wheelchair!'

James was unsure about how his mother's amnesia was adjusting, so hoped it would nudge her memory into gear. 'Ok. If you're sure you're strong enough.'

'Got to keep on walking.' she said back.

James watched his mother into the cottage lounge and followed to stand in the lounge doorframe. His mother was walking well.

Eleanor remained quiet, observing the room. Everything was the same. Same coloured walls, same coloured carpet. There was one thing that stood out to her that was different though, she was looking at a family painting they'd had done a few years ago. Callison was on the right, Eleanor to the left, and in lower centre was James. Callison looked just as Eleanor remembered and the family all looked very happy in the painting. A tear of unbridled happiness rolled down Eleanor's cheek.

Sally walked back from the kitchen and put her arm around James, 'How's she getting along?' she said softly into James' ear.

James asked, 'How's your memory getting on mum?'

'I remember,' It wasn't a lie, but she couldn't describe why she remembered, even to herself. '...but it's just vague.'

James and Sally smiled, 'You'll be right at home in a few days Eleanor.' said Sally, before walking back into the kitchen to pour tea.

'Sally's right, Mum. It will take time, but I'm sure you'll get a more detailed memory in time.'

He was a kind son she thought. Eleanor nodded, as she looked back towards her adult son, feeling like a dimensional intruder. She was unsure if she'd ever get the memories of James' young life. 'I need to look inside the basement.'

'It's only Dad's stuff down there. You've never been interested in that.'

'I need to, James.' She walked out of the lounge, and opened the basement door in the hallway. She still associated the door, and the steps with Heinrich, and the fateful night. This would affirm to her that it was definitely over.

James erred with caution, 'The stairs are steep mum, are you sure?'

'I have to go down there James.' She was adamant.

Eleanor was helped down the steep steps by her son, and when she saw the Trebla Eye standing in the centre stage of the basement, she was cast straight back to the night she met Heinrich down here. The portal was dormant and seemed to be a work in progress. It looked identical to the Trebla Eye she had witnessed in her departed reality though. As she found out more about this different life, she was uncovering mostly similarities.

'That's Callie's invention.' said Eleanor blankly.

James perked at his mother's recognition, 'Yes, it is. Do you remember?' He prompted more. 'Dad kept saying it would change the world.'

She remembered, 'Is it working?' she asked.

'I think Dad was nearly ready for a run, before he got electrocuted.' He still hoped his Dad would wake up.

She knew it was the strangest device in the world, 'Ok.'

They walked back upstairs and Sally had prepared some biscuits and tea. They sat down to watch TV and Eleanor was showing good recollection of the famous names and faces. It made James happy she could remember, but he worried about society. How could the TV be remembered, but not things close in one's life? He still didn't fully understand the situation.

Half an hour went by, when Eleanor remembered something. She sat bolt upright, and was amazed she had never had the thought before. She got the attention of James and Sally.

'What?' asked James.

'Memoirs.' she said aloud to herself. While watching TV, her mind was trying to piece together the reasons for things happening. There were things in this dimension that were identical to her old experience of reality, so she wondered about something else in the old dimension existing in this dimension; her memoirs.

'Of course!' James exclaimed, 'Mum's memoirs will tell her exactly who she is!'

* * * * * * *

36: Embarkation

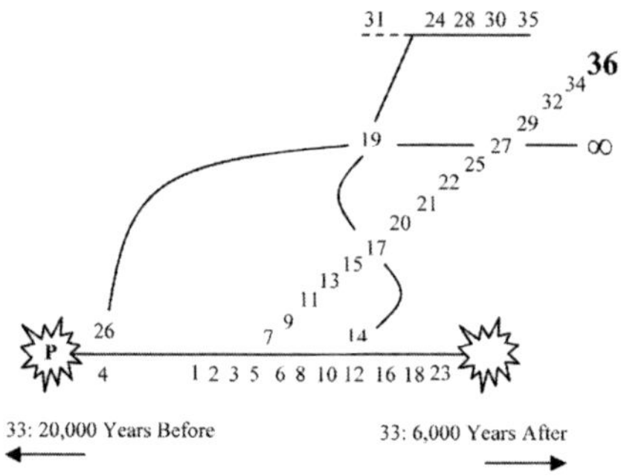

"We must walk consciously only part way towards our goal, and then leap in the dark to our success."
Henry David Thoreau, Philosopher and Transcendentalist (1817 - 1862)

36.1 –
Date not known:
Plus six says:

He'd made the ultimate leap of faith. The minute Callison's feet left the cliff's edge he felt gravity pulling him towards the ground faster and faster. His stomach felt like it was in his heart as the cliffs accelerated upward and the wind started to rush past his face faster still. The lagoon at the bottom was getting bigger and bigger. *This is only in my mind.* He thought. *I control my experience here.* He willed to fly like Liele as he continued to accelerate with gravity. He knew he had done the right thing in jumping, but didn't know exactly how to fly. *Pull up! Pull Up!* he willed. The cliffs were flying by at a tremendous rate now. *Pull up! Pull Up!*

As he willed, so experience reflected. He never needed to know how it was done; he just needed to trust it *could* be done.

Callison felt his head start to fall forward with G force as his body moved away from the cliffs and arced out of the fall like a plane pulling out of a dive, transforming the gravitational energy into the energy required for horizontal forward flight. He pulled his head back, fighting the acting force and looked where he wanted to fly. The wind rushed around his body with all of the speed he had gained from the fall. Before he knew it he was flying, and it was like nothing he had ever experienced. 'Yeeeeaaaahhhh!' Callison shrieked into the on coming air, as the tips of the treetops whistled past just below him.

He had conquered gravity. He arced backwards and started to climb again, just by willing it to happen. The trees became smaller as he continued to climb higher and higher into the sky. There seemed to be no physics anymore. No thrust force; just charged emotion and full empowerment. He was the most free he had ever been. Finally, as Callison Trebla, he knew his truth. Although it made little logic sense, it was his experience that *was* the truth.

'Woohoooo!' he shouted again as he levelled with the clouds in the sky. He flew through one of the fluffy white cotton wool wisps and emerged the other side, as free as a bird. From this height, he could see in the distance the Sukarmian skyscrapers and Noi Tu pyramid again. In an instant he was no longer lost. He wanted to go back and tell Liele of his fortune; and he would in time, but for now he was happy discovering his new aerial freedom.

He arced backward and upwards until he was upside down, then rotated back into upright flight. He arced forward and downwards and as he did he could feel the acceleration. He was travelling tremendously fast, he swooped down close to the trees again to fly just above them, turning right, then left. *How much fun is this?* he asked himself; the exhilaration not waning one bit.

As Callison flew over the green lands he took in the views and started contemplating his experience here. He had only been here for what felt like six days, but in that time he had made a good friend in Liele, who he realised now was Eleanor's dimensional version of consciousness during a life twenty thousand years away from Callison's time on Earth. Upon his return to the physical, he would be far away from Liele in linear time, but they were never far away at all through consciousness, he would just be in a different now. He still had much to think about on the topic and had many questions to ask Mystera also. Just how much did he know about the Trebla Eye and Callison's predicament?

The thoughts and musings came and went as he continued to soar around in the freedom of the sky. He called Liele telepathically. Hi Liele. I have learnt much in my intuitive integration. Thank you for looking after me the way you have. I leapt from the cliff you did and I'm flying like a bird!

After a short while, Liele replied giving Callison the sense that she was holding back, You're welcome Callison. It has been a pleasure looking after you! What did your intuitive integration reveal? You're flying? That's great! Liele smiled to herself. Her original intuitive integration to look after Callison in the mind and soul dimension had personal insight opportunities, and Callison falling from the cliff had affirmed Liele's future intentions for her ancient life on Earth. She would marry Togo, as she knew Callison represented Togo. Togo and Liele would go on to interconnect many other lives together, one such life being the life of Callison and Eleanor Trebla twenty thousand years along the wheel of time.

Callison told her directly as he flew towards Sukarmia. Amazed, It has revealed more than I ever thought possible. We know each other through dimensional consciousness. It's so obvious now. Where are you? I have to speak with you.

Liele was filled with an excited expectation. She knew Callison from the first day she saw him walking the undergrowth alone and naked. Come to the pyramid. I am waiting with Mystera. It is time for you to return to your life, in your time.

It was hard for him to work out how he felt about going back to the new reality. He knew he was ready however, and looked forward to the new challenge. I will be there shortly. I can see the pyramid in the distance.

Callison's heart started to race with anticipation as he made his way across the sky. Before long he made it to the Noi Tu outpost buildings and homed in on the top of the pyramid where two people were standing atop the monolith. As Callison descended further down toward it, he could see that it was Liele and Mystera waiting and waving.

He continued downward until he had to think about the landing. He had no idea how he was going to do it. He rotated his feet down ward, like an undercarriage of a jumbo jet and touched down on the ground. For his first flight, even he was impressed with the landing; and strangely, it felt an instinctive thing to do. He decelerated into a walk, and went to see his inter-dimensional friends. He had discovered much since they last saw him.

Mystera was smiling, happy that Callison was ready to go back to Earth. He understood the connection between Callison and Liele, and gave them time.

As Liele stood on the top of the pyramid looking back at Callison she smiled in the same way she had done throughout his experience in the mind and soul dimension. It was clear who she really was now. He walked to stand about half a metre away from her and looked into her eyes. He knew the Eyes from long before he first met her. They were Eleanor's eyes. He leaned in and kissed her on the forehead whispering, 'Thank you for helping me realise how positive our true nature is.'

She was modest but truthful, 'It's like you said, *you* did the realising, *I* couldn't do that for you. It was *all* you. But you're welcome all the same.' She looked back into his eyes, seeing the eyes of Togo, and thanked him in return. 'I have to thank you also for having the self-conviction to fall and fly.'

'Really?' he asked.

'Yes. Remember on your first day here you asked me what my intuitive integration mission was when we were at the lagoon, and I said I couldn't tell you?'

Callison recalled and nodded, 'Yes.'

'Well that's what it was.' she added, 'I couldn't tell you anything. You needed to fall into flight on your own conviction, and if you did, it would prove to me that Togo would be my true love back in my Earth experience.'

Callison knew he had made the choice intuitively, 'Well, you're welcome, I guess.' he said kindly. He was pleased he heard the intuitive voice that called to him, the voice that he now knew was the ultimate donator of his consciousness.

The dimensionally entangled lovers smiled at one another before embracing. They held each other for a few moments, feeling each other's true essence, knowing each other, and being each other.

'I'm not going to be here for much longer, am I?' pondered Callison into Liele's ear.

Liele remained quiet and semi-muted. She communicated by shaking her head as they continued to hold each other. A tear of happiness broke free from their eyes.

Mystera slowly started to walk forward toward the couple. He spoke softly, 'Give thanks for your experiences; you have both done extremely well.'

The pair slowly parted and both nodded wisely, choosing to give thanks for their meeting across time.

Mystera added, smiling, 'Besides, nothing really ever comes to an end, insomuch as something else always begins.'

Callison knew the master was right. He asked Mystera, knowing that he might not get another chance to, 'My higher self said that you could tell me more about the Trebla Eye?'

The Noi Tu master smiled, 'Yes,' he said, 'I have been speaking with my higher self also, and I have a character of inter-dimensional consciousness called Igor Popovic and I am living in the reality you will return to.'

Callison had never heard of Igor Popovic, 'Really?' he thought about why he didn't know the name, 'I would have heard of him surely, did his invention work?'

'Igor Popovic is dead relative to the dimension you have experienced on earth this far, so you won't have heard of him.'

Mystera answered his second question. 'And yes, his portal worked' said the Shaman. 'Igor Popovic had many journeys into the portal during the seventies, however, he would only spend a few minutes of unconsciousness before regaining it again, bringing with him his experiences in the dimension of mind and soul.' He explained Callison's situation, 'This is normally how the portal works when you don't have your body corrupted during your departure.' He looked at Callison, knowing that Callison knew this is what happened to him.

The Noi Tu master continued, 'Popovic discovered many things, but he eventually found something out.' Mystera warned, 'It had to do with the future of the planet and the existence of the human race,' he said. 'Popovic knew that his invention was too early for the people, who weren't psychologically ready and that if he carried on with his invention, the Eye would end up in the possession of people that would seek to keep it secret, and the world would never realise the truth. The collective ignorance would in turn lead the world into nuclear war and the loss of many lives on Earth.'

Callison and Liele were concerned, 'So what did he do?' asked Callison.

'Well that is part of the reason for your having this experience at all, and it is for him to tell you the rest. He will come and introduce himself to you when you wake up in your new reality.'

A smile appeared under Callison's silver moustache, as he thought about the future. Before long however, Callison realised he was changing. He was becoming sixty-five again. He'd lost more hair, he'd gone grey again and the golden paint was vanishing from his body.

He started to panic, 'What's happening to me?' he asked of his Sukarmian friends.

'It's time to go, Callison.' said his Noi Tu Shaman. Mystera gestured to Liele, 'Liele will guide you to the Alpine Stargate, the gateway to the physical experiences.' he looked back to Callison, 'When you go back through the gateway, you will be led through the corridors of time to the point at which you need to make the decision to give thanks for your son's loss. You will experience a frozen moment; this is where you enter your physical body again through your forehead. This is where the veil will be drawn, meaning you will play out a different history to the one you have experienced, completely unconscious as to your extra knowledge until you electrocute yourself while designing your invention. You will become conscious of all this extra knowledge in 2008 when you wake from the coma in the new reality. Your wife, Eleanor will be there waiting for you.'

Callison gave Mystera his honest thanks, 'Thank you Mystera, for everything you have done for me here.'

'You're welcome my eternal friend.' The master smiled. His student had been exceptional.

Callison turned to face his soul mate, who had been listening intently to the developments, 'Ok, I'm ready Liele,' he said, 'lead me home.'

36.2 –

Liele began hovering in the air, waiting to lead him to the Alpine Stargate. She had listened to the conversation about Callison's era and realised more why Callison was in the state he was when he first arrived. She remained playful though, 'Come on. I'll race you!' she said, throwing the gauntlet down.

'Race me?' questioned Callison. Before he could think more on the subject, Liele shot upwards and away from the pyramid like a bullet from a gun. She was gone. He looked at Mystera one last time, 'Thanks again, for everything.' He smiled graciously, and shot upward after Liele. He'd not forgotten how to fly.

Wait for me!

Callison chased Liele up and up, higher and higher until he reached her hovering high above the land and clouds.

'Not so slow Callison!' said Liele in a congratulatory manner from her suspended state.

Callison hovered next to her high above and looked down. All he saw was a green misty cloud. 'Where did the land go?' asked Callison, as he hovered in mid air with his soul mate.

She had seen this all before; her culture twenty thousand years ago willed everyone to experience his or her infinite nature. She replied, 'There was no land apart from that which you decoded as Sukarmia and the surrounds. We were not on Earth remember.'

He looked at what relatively appeared upward to him. It was a golden green colour that looked like an ether of some kind, 'Is that the mind and soul dimension?' he asked gesturing the rest of the 'sky'.

'That is the rest of the mind wisp we are in,' she said of the upward region, 'the dimension of mind and soul is further out there.'

'And the Alpine Stargate?' he added.

'Out there.' she repeated affirmatively.

Callison took one last glance at the green mist below him. *Sukarmia was in their somewhere*, he thought. *Thank you*. He thought about his experience there; the Kimeng Rat, the lagoon, the Noi Tu pyramid, the meditation, the ASI hover-racing simulation, the telekinesis, seeing Jack and the knowledge of meeting his higher self. He mentally said goodbye and left his adventure inside the mental wisp, but importantly took his memory and understanding with him. They would always be his. 'Ok.' He prompted, 'let's go.'

Liele explained more as she hovered next to him, 'In order to move away from this state and onward to the Alpine Stargate, you have to free your mind of who you think you are. This is what meditating and being soul conscious is all about. You are just the point of awareness, just the being. You will have no body as we make our way to the Alpine Stargate apart from that which you imagine, and you will feel me rather than hear me.'

Callison trusted his loving guide and wanted to explore with no fear; the leap off the cliff had smashed his fears into insignificance now anyway.

He followed Liele upward into the golden green ether and onward to the Alpine Stargate. As his guide floated into the ether, her appearance changed and she resembled a spark of light, looking much the same as Jack and himself had appeared to look in the reflection of the lake. *Magic Light.* He smiled, thinking of Jack with fondness.

As he followed Liele into the ether, Callison tried to relinquish thoughts of being a character, and concentrated on just being. He floated just behind the spark of light he knew to be Liele, and for some reason it was easier to tell who she was. Like she had her own beautiful frequency that distinguished her from the rest.

How long is the journey. How far away? projected Callison.

The journey just is, came a response from the lead spark, there is no time here.

I guess the journey is everything then thought Callison, as he followed Liele's spark onwards through the three-dimensional seas of experience and ethers of thought.

After a while, or what felt like a while of travelling, they reached a clearing of orange light that Liele said was a core structure of the dimension. It revealed a view high above and below them and it was as if they were in a vertical cylinder within the dimension and there were other white sparks; to start with maybe ten or twenty, but as their view opened up fully, other sparks of light floated about. There were *millions* of them that seemed to swim and travel through the dimension with them. As the clearing continued to recede, the scale of the dimension was hinted at. There must have been *billions* of other white sparks, towering high, high, high above them and way, way down below them.

There are loads of them! Callison broadcast to Liele, wrapped in awe. He could feel his brothers and sisters and the unbreakable nature of the bond between them all.

Welcome to your extended family! broadcast Liele as she continued into the orange light.

Soon, they were travelling away from the core structure again and the dimension darkened into the green ether again. Many feelings came and went for Callison on his journey to the Alpine Stargate, but none captured the imagination much like being in the orange light and seeing billions of other white sparks of energy. It hinted at a larger system; a much larger system; larger maybe, than he could even imagine.

They travelled onwards through more green non-physical surroundings before the surroundings seemed to dissipate altogether. It was not dark but not light either. They were in a silent clearing apart from one object of light ahead of them, looking just like a star shining bright.

That's the Alpine Stargate. transmitted Liele, gesturing with her mind to the yellow light ahead; It will act as the portal back to your experience on Earth.

Callison saw it. It looked like a sun, but as they drew nearer, Callison realised it was not globular in form. It was a two-dimensional plate shaped disc hovering in what he guessed was space. The Alpine Stargate shined brightly, but it didn't hurt to look directly at it.

The duo floated towards the bright light, but part of him wanted never to reach the gate; Callison knew he was going to have to say goodbye to his helpful steed soon. She had been the perfect host during his experience here and he would never forget her.

There was nothing passing them anymore and the space they were in was quiet, just the glow of the Alpine Stargate shone. 'It's not very busy here.' Callison said to Liele with surprise.

'That's because you are tuned only to yourself and me, I see everyone else on their journeys; they are everywhere, just like you saw at the core structure of the dimension.' She looked about and added, 'Everyone else has their own Alpine Stargate missions out in the universe, built from the energy of our creativity.'

Their journey continued as the yellow disc grew in size and Callison was mesmerised by what he saw. Around the outside of the round gate, light seemingly moved round at high speed. *It's a Trebla Eye.* Callison thought immediately, Do you know how the stargate works? he asked.

Liele knew enough from talking with Togo about it, I'm no expert on how the portals are made, but they function in much the same way as a hologram. When you go through the stargate you project yourself into a coded environment created by your consciousness.

'So life's definitely an illusion?' Callison said.

'It's as real as you want it to be.' she said. 'Don't forget that also coded into the programme is free will. You are always the master of your own destiny.'

They were now close to the surface of the portal, and zero hour for Callison. He was nervous. The pair arrived at the face of the portal and stopped. It was enormous, stretching out high above and below them, and to the left and right of them. The sheen of the surface looked similar to the sheen of the Trebla Eye portal, having a liquid-like quality to it.

'It's big!' Callison said as he looked at the horizon of light all around him.

'Or we're small.' said Liele.

The enquiring scientist started to look closely at the surface. It seemed to be built from incredibly small strands of light, each one intertwining with the next. 'Hard to imagine that these strands of light can make an entire Earth experience.' He was stalling.

Liele remained quiet and Callison knew he had to leave.

'Ok.' he said with certainty.

Liele smiled.

'I have to finish my life on Earth now. Thank you. Thank you for everything you've done for me during my stay, I'll always love you.'

'You're more than welcome; our souls have become stronger for it.' Liele imagined her body into view, and around her spark of essence materialised her body of light. She went forward to hug her soul mate.

Callison hugged Liele in return, 'Thank you again my darling, I will never forget you.' he said as they embraced next to the Stargate.

They parted from embrace and looked into each other's being; contented that their experience together had taken place.

'Goodbye Liele, and good luck.' Callison said, before turning and floating on through the Alpine sheen; his coded reality ride waiting within.

Liele spoke as Callison vanished through the curtain of light, 'Goodbye my Love.' Her assignment in the Mind and Soul dimension was over also. 'Good luck.' she said to herself as he barrelled back to his experience as Callison on Earth. She thought to herself for a moment, before she was ready. She broadcast remotely to Mystera from the Alpine Stargate. Mission Accomplished.

36.3 –

Liele waited at the Alpine Stargate and soon Togo and Mystera met her there.

Togo approached rapidly to Liele, pleased to see her. 'How was your intuitive integration my love? What did you learn?'

Liele knew that she was going to be with Togo for many lifetimes, and was happy about it, 'I learnt how important you are to me. And I learned that human spirit is built with Love.' she smiled. 'How about you? What did you learn?'

Togo smiled back, 'The same.'

They kissed, happy and confident in their successes.

Mystera was happy also. He was the Time Shaman, but his soul was one of the Engineers; one of the entities charged with constructing the collective Earth experience. The future timeline of awakening was about to come true for planet Earth, helped in part by Callison, Igor Popovic and an inter-dimensional gateway.

Mystera, Liele and Togo all left the dimension of the Mind and Soul via the Alpine Stargate, and made their way back to their physical bodies waiting in the physical Noi Tu Pyramid on Earth, twenty thousand years away from their inter-dimensional acquaintances from 2008.

Liele and Togo walked back to the city of Sukarmia, with a broader knowledge of who they were and ended up spending the rest of their lives together, happy forever after.

Mystera continued to host visitors from the future as part of an information bridge of light across time. Not only would Callison and Popovic prove humanities link with the light via the Eye, but the people would also have been primed enough to the very idea of it, triggering a planetary remembrance of the truth for those that would realise.

The Sukarmians went on to live in peace and light for another seven thousand years, until the thirteen-thousand-year galactic day ended and the Sukarmian way of life fell into the sea, along with the continents of Atlantis and Lemuria, taking with them the knowledge of the light. The Earth would fall into galactic night, where it would remain isolated from the light for another thirteen thousand years. These dark ages would continue up until the galactic dawn of the ages where humanity would eventually find the light again. The light would overpower the dark, the new galactic day would begin, and the wheel of time would roll on for another lap of eternity.

* * * * * * *

37: Waking into a New Now

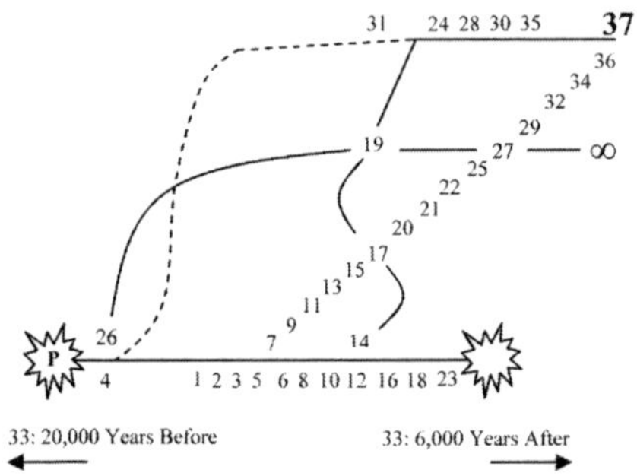

"There are two ways to live; you can
live as if nothing is a miracle,
or you can live as if everything is a miracle."
Albert Einstein, Physicist (1879 – 1955)

37.1 –
Current reality:
August 8th 2008:

It was hard to say how it came to be, but she was flying with Callison. It was night time, and the moon shone down its silvery streaks of light, illuminating the clouds and the ground below. They felt so free, soaring high above the drama.

'There's the pyramid I stayed at!' said her husband, pointing to the ground as he flew.

Eleanor looked down and saw a pyramid on a floor of greenery and rivers. She didn't know what he meant. She didn't know where they were. She followed silently, as her husband arced over to the right. The wind was rushing past her face, but it was as if it had been quietened; just a silent whooshing sensation was all she could detect. She was dreaming.

They arced over a moonlit cloud, and Callison had some more information, 'I stayed here also!'

As Eleanor emerged from above the cloud, she saw from above a city standing high with moonlit water surrounding the tall buildings. The skyscrapers looked not of the age she knew, but futuristic in design. She wanted to know more. She called back to her husband, 'Where have you been Callie?'

Callison called back as he flew, 'Sukarmia, I have realised my power!'

Eleanor had never heard of it. 'I... I don't know what you mean.'

'I have finished my tasks here now. I'm on my way home Ellie!'

Eleanor became excited. Just then, Callison popped out of existence. The abruptness shocked Eleanor and she woke up too. She was in her bed alone and it was nearly five in the morning. She contemplated the dream, thinking.

37.2 –
In Transit:

Callison's journey back to Earth looked different from his journey away from the planet. It was as if the information he received in the mind and soul dimension had altered what he saw. The moment he had passed through the light curtain of the Alpine Stargate he wasn't in a closed tunnel network this time; he was in the universe travelling through it at a tremendous rate. As the alternate galaxies and realities came by him he felt a tunnel effect in much the same way as driving into falling snow would create tunnel syndrome.

Before he arrived back into his own Milky Way galaxy, something, or more aptly some*one* caught his attention. It was another beam of light headed in the opposite direction to him. As the inter-dimensional travellers passed, they stopped next to one another and Callison knew exactly who it was just from the feeling he received from the being. He was confused to see his old nemesis Heinrich Muller as a corrupted being of light, partially disfigured by his own dark shadows.

'Hello Callison,' said the being that had animated Heinrich Muller in Callison's departed reality. His ex-boss seemed to be regretful, 'I think I owe you an apology...'

Callison heard the words of Heinrich from the being in front of him but also from everywhere around them too. It was like they were inside their own consciousness where their words here and now echoed throughout the entire non-space they occupied. Callison was stuck for words to say in return, but emitted an unconscious feeling of sorrow for Heinrich rather than anger.

Heinrich picked up on the sorrow that Callison emitted and felt it like a feeling of inward pain. As he spoke, the non-physical multiverse all around them echoed his words, 'I know I made some ill choices in my past life, but that was always the danger for me. I don't know how I could have been so blind.'

Callison was aware of the blindness sensation of Earth experience in the light of his recent experiences. 'It's ok I suppose,' he looked Heinrich in the eyes, 'being human can drag you into these places.' He thought, but remained silent.

After another pause, the disfigured light asked, 'Where are you going?'

'Back to Earth.' said Callison.

With remorse, he inquired, 'But how, did I not kill you?'

Callison was sure of his experience. 'I am going back to an alternate life; we don't die like we think when we are in the game. Earth is a part of an infinite time continuum that we visit for a lifetime to learn expression. It is like a school.'

Heinrich knew some of it, but was unsure of his future from here. 'Yes, I realised when I died that the surroundings were like a hologram. I couldn't touch anything, I would just move through the matter as if it were light from a projector.'

Callison nodded and stated for the record, 'I forgive you, you know, for your actions back on Earth, I have learned from the experience it forced upon me.'

Heinrich felt his pain ease, but knew he would find it harder to forgive himself. 'Thank you. You are kind. What do you think will become of me?'

Callison thought about the question, before articulating in a way that would ease his brother. 'The universe and everything else seems to me to be a nice place. It's our human fear that is the monster. The truth is I don't know what will become of you, I guess that will be down to you and what you learn from your experiences.'

Heinrich was eased, and knew that Callison was in actual fact a friend rather than an employee. They paused before Callison felt duty bound to depart for his Earth experience. 'Right, I must be off. I am working on another Trebla Eye in my alternate reality.'

Heinrich was obliged to tell him, whether it would make a difference he wasn't sure, 'For the record, before you go, everyone that was keeping your invention a secret is now dead. We all died in an explosion underneath the Quanta building. Good luck Callison it was a pleasure to have lived with you, and I'm sorry I was so blind.'

Callison felt no regrets as he prepared to depart. 'See you soon Heinrich, who knows one day when we are richer in experience we will laugh about these lessons.' Callison started to move away from Heinrich and onward towards his parallel Earth experience.

Heinrich hoped, but still had a lot of fear with in him. His friend's words had helped, but he still had work to do to forgive himself. The pulling sensation started to tug at him again and as Callison headed towards Earth, Heinrich started his journey to the Alpine Stargate and on to the realms of light. He would end up intact in the end and would realise that his experience being Heinrich Muller was more a nightmare than a reality. He owed a favour to his eternal friend that animated Callison however; this was Karma, the law of experience.

For Callison, the passing celestial structures whizzed by again as he raced towards his parallel life. His mind thought about Heinrich and why he had met him there and then of all places. What did Heinrich mean when he said everyone was dead that kept his invention a secret? As he continued to make his way across the universe he had a series of thoughts and visions about unveiling the Eye to the world. Callison's expectations built as he travelled.

He continued to pass galaxies and nebulae systems, until his trajectory lead him straight into the white dense mass in the middle of the Milky Way before everything went white and blank. After a disorientating sensation similar to being thrown about in a forceful breaking wave subsided, his vision came back. He sensed he was hovering in a frozen moment in his own history, not quite knowing how he had arrived in it. He remembered that Mystera had told him about this moment.

It was a scene Callison had hoped he would not see again: October 23rd 1980. In the scene, Jack was dying in his younger self's arms. Not an object moved, and the frozen snapshot of time in the high street seemed to be eternal. The driver of the car was suspended in frozen animation in the middle of the road on his knees with his head in his hands. Every detail from the scene was there and he could through the ambulance, the cars, the people and his own body. He understood what Heinrich had meant about the surroundings feeling like a hologram. Some white light shone out of Callison's younger forehead in the scene and it glistened, being the only thing that moved in the still snapshot of time.

His actions were instinctive; enter his body through the forehead. He didn't so much ignore the scene, as accept it. He had dealt with Jack's passing and he now thought it was always supposed to be. As he floated into the light in his forehead, the attractive forces pulled his pocket of awareness into the body, and time clicked into motion again. Callison would live out his new choice to give thanks for Jack's short life completely unconscious as to his movements in the parallel dimension and his experience in the Mind and Soul dimension until twenty-eight years later, when he would have a fated accident with electricity, and miraculously remember.

Justanother Town Hospital Coma Unit: (Current Reality)
August 8th 2008:
(Twelve weeks after Callison's accident)

The coma ward of the hospital was at its quietest in the non-stop twenty-four hour ebb of activity. It was four-thirty am and while the night staff at the hospital worked the tail end of their shifts, Callison Trebla started to come around.

He tried to open his eyes and slowly, tiny cracks of vision let the first photons through his lenses and onto his retinas. It was all blurry still. The information coming in through his eyes triggered him to open them more, but it was still too early. His mind kicked into action and he noticed his breathing again; it felt odd, but familiar.

Over the next few minutes, the sleep paralysis subsided and he could feel more of his body. He wiggled his toes. He felt them move as he rapidly regained consciousness. He itched his arm; it really itched. He continued to itch until he heard a beeping noise that tugged his consciousness into alerted action. Within twenty seconds he had company, a doctor and two nurses were dealing with Callison's re-entry into his own body.

'Doctor Trebla, can you hear me?' said the doctor. He took a light out and shone it in his eyes.

That's bright thought Callison. His eyes winced automatically in recoil to the light, 'Yes. I can hear you.' he called back to the voice that had just spoken and the light vanished.

The doctor pulled the stethoscope that dangled from his neck, and placed the cold metal receiver onto Callison's chest. He spoke with a professional tone, 'You have been in a coma for three months Doctor Trebla. You are in Hospital.' The doctor looked into space as he concentrated on listening to his patient's heartbeat.

The shock from the cold stethoscope on his chest quickened his awareness into his body. He breathed in deeply as the temperature registered cold in his nervous system. His neurons fired again, and a jolt went through his legs, his eyes opened fully and he could see the doctors and the beds to the left and to the right. His conscious mind awoke, and he processed the incoming information. *Three months* Callison thought. He had been away for what felt like just a week. Callison questioned, 'Three months? What is the date today?'

The doctor had a surprised look on his face and his attention was taken away from the machines, 'Pardon?' He looked at his patient in disbelief.

Callison looked back at the doctor, fully aware of his journey through the dimension of mind and soul. This place was supposed to be a parallel Earth reality to the one he left, 'Is this Earth? Who am I? Who is the prime minister now?' he asked the doctor. He fired off some more, 'Is it different? It's different isn't it?'

The doctor became even more intrigued. Patients upon wake up were never this inquisitive this early. He spoke back out of surprise rather than profession, 'Yes, it's Earth. You are Dr. Callison Trebla.' He added, 'The date today is the 8th August 2008, and the prime minister is Gordon Blair.'

Nothing new. 'How did I get here?' pressed Callison.

The doctor was even more intrigued; Callison's mind was quick, 'You electrocuted yourself in the basement of your house. Your son found you.'

My son? Callison thought. 'My son! Of course! Jack!'

'James. Your son is called James.' corrected the doctor, 'Jack was your first son. He passed away long ago now.'

He thought. 'What's my son like?' he asked the doctor.

The doctor wasn't sure how much he should say. He'd never been put on the spot so unexpectedly before, 'Err, he's nice? Following in your footsteps with the science and things, got a girlfriend called Sally.' He tried to bring back some professionalism, 'Anyway I think your first priority is rest, Dr Trebla, your mind seems to be doing well, but your body will be weak. You are weak. You need some rest.'

Rest? I have been resting for three months... he thought, 'Is Eleanor ok?'

The doctor answered again, 'Yes, she is fine.'

Callison smiled to himself, 'Can I speak with her?' he requested, 'You know, on the phone.'

'All in good time Dr Trebla. Visitors are allowed in at 9am, that is about four hours from now. I suggest resting up until the time comes, you're no spring chicken after all.' The doctor continued filling in a clipboard with charts and forms.

Callison remained quiet, remembering he was sixty-five again. He didn't mind at all though and rested his head in the pillow. Staring at the ceiling thinking, he couldn't bring himself to believe it; *I'm in a parallel universe to the one I was born in* he thought. *So was Eleanor.* He couldn't wait to talk to her.

The doctor smiled, and walked off with the chart, 'I'll be back shortly, Dr Trebla.'

Callison remained in the bed thinking like a freight train, while a nurse reattached the drip line into his arm that he had knocked out upon wake up. The winds of his mind changed, and he thought about the consequences of being here. It was freakily weird, but in a way exciting and kind of fun. It was like he was an infiltrator in this dimension, and his body was his camera and measuring equipment. He realised his two personas. There was his character, which everyone knew as his body and the name, and then there was the self; which no one knew but himself. It felt easier to notice being *in* his body but not *being* his body. The teachings that Mystera had given him on lessons of identity resonated more clearly now and he'd awakened more to consciousness.

The nurse finished attaching his drip, and asked if he felt ok. He was entranced in a world of thought and possibility. She asked again, 'Dr Trebla? Can you hear me still?'

Callison snapped back into the physical room, 'Yes. I can still hear you.' he answered.

'How are you feeling Dr Trebla?' She had tended to his body for three months and wondered often what his character would be like.

'You can call me Callison.' The nurse nodded. 'I'm feeling ok, considering. Just getting used to my body again I think.' He didn't tell her his true experience.

'Well, you get some rest. If you feel up to it you might have visitors in a few hours.' She added, 'Welcome back to Earth, Callison.' And with that the nurse walked up the ward to her tasks.

Callison's mind was falling back into semi sleep, when the doctor arrived again to snap him back into the "real" world, 'Dr Trebla?'

He stirred, 'Yes?'

The doctor continued the wake up procedure, 'Just some quick questions and I'll let you rest again.'

Callison nodded.

'Any pain in the head or chest?'

'No.' said Callison.

'Can you feel my fingers on your toe?' The doctor touched Callison's big toe.

'Yes.'

'Can you move your toes for me?'

Callison wiggled the toes on both feet, as the doctor ticked positive for left and right feet. He pulled his head up from the clipboard. 'Ok. You seem to be doing very well,' the doctor said, 'but please try and get some rest for now, and we will move you to a recovery ward later on this morning.' The doctor smiled. 'It's good to have you with us again Dr Trebla.'

'Ok,' Callison replied, 'Thank you doctor.'

'You're welcome.' The doctor nodded happily and walked off into the hospital ward network again as Callison dropped back into thought about his adventure. It felt like a vivid dream now, but one that was still fresh in his conscious memory.

As Callison lay thinking, the nurse was checking his medical records for the next of kin, 'Gemma, the form says to call any hour of day if Callison wakes up.' she said to her superior ward nurse, Gemma. She looked at the clock, and was detectably hesitant to ring. She queried, 'Five thirty in the morning? What do you think? A bit early?'

'I'll do it,' said the ward nurse helpfully, 'Eleanor has requested that we call her anytime if Callison wakes up, so we call no matter the time.'

The ward nurse made the call. She dialled Eleanor first, but after eight rings without answer she gave up. The other number on the form was James Trebla, Callison's son, so she dialled in the second contact number and it rang three times before someone picked up.

'Hello?' came a voice.

'Is this James Trebla?' said the nurse.

'Yes?' he confirmed.

'Hi, it's Gemma Smith here, I'm the ward nurse from Justanother Town hospital, sorry for calling you at this hour, but we have some good news about your father.'

Good news? 'Oh?' said James, perked but still semi-conscious.

'He has woken up again and is talking. He's doing really rather well. You can come and visit him at nine this morning if you would like?'

James was overjoyed by the news and woke up like he had been awake for hours. He replied happily, 'Yes, that would be great, thank you Gemma.'

The nurse continued, 'Ok. By the way we tried ringing your mother first, but we didn't get through, so could you let her know for me?'

'Yes, I will. Thank you.'

As the nurse put her phone down looking forward to the end of her day, James did the same, looking forward to the start of his.

37.3 –

The August sun was already well above the horizon and streamed down in shallow orange rays. Glimmers of doubt had started to creep into her consciousness during the drive to the hospital that maybe she was wrong; maybe he wasn't awake. But her dream had been so vivid. Eleanor and Callison would end up talking about their reunion as fated to be this way. It provided the perfect one-to-one for them to talk about their experiences without James present.

It was almost a quarter to six in the morning by the time Eleanor made it into the empty reception room of the hospital. The reception and indeed the whole hospital had become familiar grounds for her over the last two months. She walked up to the wooden framed reception window, where the receptionist was buried in paperwork, 'Hi there, I am here for visiting.' she said, realising she was too early, 'I'm Callison Trebla's wife, Eleanor. Has there been any news?'

The receptionist thought it strange. She had spoken with Eleanor many times before, 'Hi Eleanor, you do realise visiting starts at 9 a.m.?' she said in a patient-friendly manner.

'Yes.' She paused and told the truth, 'I just had a really vivid dream, and knew something had happened.' She sounded crazy, 'I wanted to be here. Do you know if anything has happened?' She looked solemnly and honestly at the receptionist.

The receptionist sensed her sincerity, 'I'll have a check for you,' she smiled re-assuring, 'take a seat.' She gestured with her hand to the seating area, before picking up the phone to find out about Callison. She, herself was now intrigued.

After a couple of minutes, the receptionist called Eleanor over to the desk again, 'It appears your dream was either well timed, or a miracle took place,' she said as her eyebrows gave away her surprise, 'Callison woke up about an hour ago. He has been talking, and the doctor says he is doing well!'

Eleanor was relieved. 'Oh, really?' She breathed deeply, 'That's great.'

The receptionist couldn't believe it either, but smiled for Eleanor.

Eleanor started to well up with tears of joy and relief, 'I knew my dream was correct. It felt different; it felt more real than normal, do you know what I mean?' She knew she wasn't mad, but she sure as hell felt it. She couldn't wait to hear if her husband had knowledge of being somewhere while he was comatosed. She had so much to tell him also, 'Can I see him now?' She'd forgotten about the current hour.

The receptionist felt awkward, but rules were rules, 'It's still too early I'm afraid.'

Eleanor seemed confused. She looked dejected, but walked back to her seat.

'I'll see what I can do.' said the receptionist sympathetically from her booth.

Eleanor perked up, and kept thinking about her husband as the morning sunlight continued to creep down the walls.

About five minutes passed, before a nurse walked into the reception through the swing doors next to the desk and walked up to the only person waiting in the seating area, 'Hi Eleanor? We were told you were here.'

She was excited, 'Yes?'

The nurse continued, 'I know visiting hours are not until nine, but Callison is awake and talking, and would love to see you.'

She stood up straight away, 'He is? That's great, I'm ready now.'

The nurse cautioned, 'It will only be for about half an hour and please be quiet. You can visit again at nine.'

'Yes that's fine.' said Eleanor.

The nurse was happy and started to lead the way. As they walked past the reception desk window, the receptionist smiled at Eleanor. Eleanor thanked her with an expression that said it a thousand times.

The pair walked into the ward system and the nurse spoke about the dream. 'I'm told you dreamt that Callison was awake?' she asked and questioned.

Eleanor nodded and explained, 'Yes, we were flying in the moonlight, and he said he was coming home. It was a very vivid dream.' she recalled. She had been waiting for this day for over two months.

'Hmm... Spooky.' wondered the nurse, but her response was automatic and unconsciously programmed, dreams weren't spooky; they were merely deliverers of information. If it weren't for dreams we wouldn't have AC current or the telephone.

They continued to walk the ward network, slowly homing in on Callison's bed.

As the pair walked around the last of the corners, Callison was there in bed waiting for his wife and smiling like he'd seen her for the first time. Their eyes locked and they both beamed at each other as Eleanor walked towards the bed. She looked relieved and glad to see him as a tear started to roll down her cheek. The nurse gave them some time alone.

She arrived at Callison's bedside, 'Callison my darling.' She leant down and put her arms around him, 'I've missed you so much!'

Callison was happy he was back on Earth. He had missed his wife during his journey and the feel of her unmistakable touch was blissful and emotional, 'I love you Elles.' he told her, 'You didn't think I'd stay away too long did you?' His body was still new to him, and it ached as he hugged his wife back.

Eleanor subtly wept tears of joy at their reuniting; they were together again. The nurse brought a chair over and Eleanor sat down next to her husband's bed. She held her husband's hand as they talked about their experience in comas.

Callison told Eleanor about his departure through the Trebla Eye as he rested in the hospital bed, 'You were out at the home wares exhibition, and I started the Eye up, and I was jumped by two men in suits, one of which helped us move into the cottage.' Eleanor remembered him. 'Then Heinrich turned up and demanded I see how fast it would go.' It was all still so clear. 'So we opened the portal, then Heinrich wanted it back. I thought he was going to kill me, so I jumped into the portal to escape.' He thought back on his time in Sukarmia. 'And then the rest was even more amazing!'

His wife reassured him and opened up too. She hadn't spoken about it to anyone yet, 'I jumped too. We went to the

Bingo after the home wares exhibition, and I got back from the Bingo with a strange feeling,' she continued, '...strange enough to make me phone the police ahead of arriving home. I got back to see Heinrich in the basement, staring at your invention. He pulled a gun, but it misfired twice. Then, while Heinrich went to speak with the police, I jumped...' she paused, '...and then had another experience...' She paused again, trying to make sense of where she went. 'I stayed in a village called Capee, with a man called Togo. He showed me things, about my mind and myself, and this will sound strange...' she hesitated almost in fear of her own madness, '...he was you?' she thought about it, worrying and questioning whether she had dreamt it. She continued to hold her husband's hand.

Callison saw a parallel between his wife's story, and his own experience of the mind and soul missions of Liele and Togo. He lifted his head, and turned to face her as best his body would allow. While propping up her sanity he explained, 'It *was* me Ellie,' he marvelled, 'it was just a dimensional aspect of me living a life as Togo in a land twenty thousand years away!' Had someone been overhearing their conversation they would assume insanity. 'I was looked after by someone called Liele, who turned out to be a dimensional aspect of *your* consciousness!'

'So, we've known each other before then,' Eleanor reaffirmed.'

'Yes.' He looked into her eyes thinking about how unique and beautiful they were to him. The information he'd acquired on his inter-dimensional trip was still fresh and he explained, 'I met a being of light, who said he was my higher self, who told me that Togo and Liele aren't really our *past* lives, they are parallel characters separated by the illusion of time in a dimension with a different now. Their choices affect us and our choices affect them.'

Eleanor smiled, she had similar memories, 'I met a being of light too. It was me, but it wasn't me,' she was confused, 'but it told me that I had retaken a choice in the past which created this new present?'

His wife's validation confirmed his own experiences further and the soul mates continued to discuss, Callison remembered, 'Yes, an intuitive integration. We decided to be give thanks for Jack's life, rather than regret the loss and we ended up having James, and a whole new history has been made.'

His wife smiled like she could help his understanding, 'Do you want to hear your new history?'

She surprised her husband, 'Yes? Why?' asked Callison.

Eleanor told him, 'Well it would appear that my memoirs weren't so useless after all.' She knew she had one over on him, and smiled like she could tell him so.

Callison gestured a rye grin as he remembered joking about why she wrote them in the last reality, 'Ok, I concede, they have their uses,' Callison joked, 'You were right, I was wrong!'

'As always!' Eleanor laughed. She was glad she had her Callie back and explained, 'Well in this reality I have read back what I've unconsciously written for nearly thirty years, placing the history together,' she added, 'it will help when it comes to friends and family, trust me.' She spoke from experience.

Callison was excited, 'Yes, please tell me what you know.'

She told him, 'Well, the first difference was that not only *I* wrote memoirs...'

He looked confused.

She finished, '... so did you.'

'Really?' he said, surprised.

'I haven't read yours, I have stuck to mine out of respect.' she said courteously.

'I wouldn't have minded, Elles.'

'Well, I just didn't; I wanted to make sure you were going to be ok.' she added. 'and I'm glad you are.' She smiled, stroking his forehead.

Callison learned that soon after Jack's death they had decided to write memoirs together exploring their feelings and thoughts. Callison was able to face his fear and grew from the experience. As a result, James was born two years after Jack died, and changed their known histories to this day. They moved into the fateful cottage soon after James was born in 1982, which Callison worked out was when the dreams about the cottage started for him all those years ago in the departed reality. Callison was now the managing director of a company called Quantum Attic Research, a leading research organisation into human consciousness and quantum effects.

'You'll have to read your memoirs.' Eleanor said, 'It was really fun and emotional learning of James' younger years. We have been quiet a happy family from the sounds of it.' She was relieved, and smiled peacefully.

As they talked, the nurse walked over. Callison looked healthy and it surprised the nurse, her patient was recovering quickly. The pair stopped talking as the nurse approached, 'Hi, it's getting on, we have to get ready for our morning shifts now, could we ask you wait outside, and let Callison get some rest?' She was kind in her tone.

Eleanor was about to concede, but Callison protested, 'Please, just a few minutes more?'

The nurse smiled, and caved, 'Ok,' she was serious again and wagged a finger in jest, 'but *then* it's rest time!'

Patient and visitor agreed.

The few minutes ended up being another fifteen, while Callison and Eleanor talked about the portal and what had happened more. He told her about seeing Heinrich on his way back, and remembering that everyone who wanted to keep the eye secret was dead. Callison told Eleanor about Igor Popovic also, 'Mystera, the time shaman that I met said that he had a dimensional aspect of his own consciousness living in this reality and he had built a Trebla Eye before me. He also said that this man, Popovic died in 1978 relative to the timeline we once knew but that he would be alive in this one!' The information still had him rapt with intrigue and excitement.

Eleanor fuelled the fire, 'Was his name *Igor* Popovic by any chance?'

Callison's eyes opened wider; 'Yes?' he said in astonishment, 'Why do you know him?'

Eleanor enlightened him, 'There is someone on your board of directors at work called Igor Popovic. I've met him.' Eleanor had been to the Quantum Attic Research buildings where Callison was now the semi-retired CEO. 'He was a nice man I thought, from what I saw of him.' she postulated.

Callison thought, wondering about the man and whether the man would remind him of Mystera, 'Well, I can't wait to meet him and I can't wait to meet our son.' He gave his beloved a look from the bed that said he was happy to be with her once again, 'We've had quite the adventure haven't we?'

His wife agreed wholeheartedly, 'It was certainly the strangest journey I've ever had,' she said, 'but here we are, a dimension away.'

The nurse came back over to hurry Eleanor along. She was pointing at her watch. Eleanor saw her and obliged, 'Yes, I'll get off now.'

Callison still tried to protest, but Eleanor insisted, 'You do need to get some rest. I'll head for a coffee and wait for James. Glad to have you back my darling.' She kissed him on the forehead.

'Good to be back,' said Callison, 'I love you so much.'

She smiled back at the love of many lifetimes; in this one his name was Callison, 'I love you too Callie.'

It had just turned seven am as Callison fell straight back into thought about his circumstances. *Popovic was already here!*

37.4 –

The clock on the waiting room wall had just ticked past nine O'clock. James, Sally and Eleanor all waited for the hospital's receptionist to turn the hanging sign around notifying the waiting people that visiting time was now. It didn't take long and they signed in, before making their way towards Callison's bed.

In the waiting room, James had been talking with his mother about the final third of their family. Eleanor told James that his dad was doing remarkably well, but gave Callison some wriggling space by saying he was amnesic still, just like she was when she woke up. James didn't mind; he was just relieved and excited to have his dad back. His mother had slowly adjusted to reality again after her bout of amnesia and he was convinced his dad would too.

They walked into Callison's ward and expected to see him, but he wasn't in his hospital bed. His name was still on the bed allocation plan, but his bed was vacant.

'Where is he?' asked James of his mother.

'I… I don't know…' She turned to find a nurse, thinking in horror that she had imagined her meeting earlier in the morning, and as she did so, James exclaimed.

'Dad!'

Eleanor looked back and Callison had rolled himself around the corner onto the ward in a wheelchair. He smiled at his family from his rolling seat.

James saw his dad up and conscious for the first time in four months. He had unshaven silvery cheeks and an over grown moustache, but he was conscious again.

Callison saw his son for the first time in his life, 'James,' he said, like he'd known him all his life. His son was exactly as he'd imagined he would be.

'Dad, we're so glad you're awake!' said James. He leant down to give his father a hug in the wheelchair, oblivious to his adventures in the dimensions.

Eleanor watched on knowing the emotional roller coaster Callison was currently riding.

Callison couldn't believe it, and shed a tear, 'I've missed you so much James.'

'I've missed you too, but we're here. You're ok. Are you going to think twice about playing with live wires now?' James joked sarcastically. He stood up again, and looked down on his seated father. He was just as James remembered before the accident.

Callison remembered that as his unconscious parallel self he had accidentally electrocuted himself. He chuckled, conceding

James' humour. 'Yes, I'll make sure the ring main is off in the future.' He decided to keep the change of reality and the different version of event history to himself for now; he would get his bearings first.

Sally hugged her future father-in-law to be, 'Glad you are well again Callison.' she smiled.

Sally was nice Callison thought. He liked the new additions to his family straight away, and sensing a wholeness to his life again he sighed with relief as he realised he'd made a journey of personal change.

James looked at his mum and as she smiled back, she subtly pinched herself; this was really happening.

After Callison had persuaded the hospital staff that he was well enough to be rolled around the hospital gardens, the four of them took to the morning sunshine. Callison's recovery was coming along fast.

The newly formed Trebla unit walked slowly around the hospital peace gardens. England was having a warm summer and despite the early hour of the day, it was pleasant and warm already. As James pushed his father forward on his wheelchair, Callison told James, Sally and his wife of his memories of being in the coma; about meeting himself as spirit, and the dimensional aspects of consciousness. Eleanor admitted to them also that she had a similar experience in a land of mind during her coma.

James listened to his parents as they all walked, talked and rolled through the gardens and was amazed at the information the out-of-body experiences had given them about spirit.

'Why didn't you tell me this before?' asked James to his mother.

His mother justified honestly, 'I didn't want to seem crazy,' she said, 'I wanted Callison to wake up first, to see if he experienced anything.'

'Well it's bizarre, the whole underlying mechanism I mean. It means...' James paused, 'Well, it's evidence for life after death isn't it?'

'It is for me.' said Callison, 'It's a truth of my experience. But for you, and everyone else that's not had my experience, it's a matter of trust. What if you explained this information away by believing I'm insane instead?'

The quartet arrived at a small pond that had a large wooden bench next to it. His son was sincere, 'I trust you. You're my father.'

Eleanor, James and Sally all sat on the bench as Callison sat in the wheelchair. They continued discussing Callison and Eleanor's coma experience.

'You shouldn't trust me,' said Callison talking to his family, 'You shouldn't trust anything except your own experience.'

'Why so?' asked Sally.

He answered, 'Because it's only *you* that can know *your* experience. Who we are lies *within*; and no one can realise for someone else. When we look within, we realise our physical outward experience is merely a reflection of what is within. We *are* the truth, every single one of us.'

'And what is that truth then?' James asked, as he kept up with the cryptic wisdom, 'Who are we?'

'The truth is that we are whatever we imagine ourselves to be.' He clarified, 'We are constantly inventing and reinventing concepts about ourselves every second of every day. We are the animator of our own character, but we're not the character. It's like driving a route, and thinking you're the car. We all choose where we drive; we are the driver.'

Suddenly, a duck flapped its wings in the pond behind them and took off. The noise startled them. James questioned, 'So what do you think death is then?'

His father pondered before answering, 'I now see death like a grand unveiling of everything to you once again, revealing the true consequences of the choices we made in the lives we acted out. And this,' he looked around the gardens as if to say *this physical experience*, 'this experience, here and now of being human, *this* is more like a collective stage onto which you are born and off of which you die.'

Sally had heard of a similar concept, 'I have read that the Aborigines in Australia see the physical world as the illusion, and the dreamtime as the reality.'

Callison agreed, 'I can believe it. Somewhere along the lines though, the knowledge has disappeared, leaving us lost to our true identities.'

'So can we get it back?' asked James, 'the knowledge I mean, how does it work?'

'I think somewhere deep inside every one of us there is a spark that transcends the mind. It is that spark that the very fabric of the mind is built from and it is that part that knows exactly how it all works. And quietness and intuition are the keys to listen to it.'

'Following hunches and gut feelings you mean?' said Sally.

Callison agreed, 'Essentially, yes, but if you turn down the volume and the frequency of your thoughts, your intuitive voice is louder. You are closer to yourself, your soul, and can make the choices you wanted to make instead of letting the character-blinkered choices make you.'

As the four of them talked about the subject, two sparrows flew and landed on the grass in front of them. It was strange to see the birds so close up. It was as if they had characters themselves. They were small birds and had streaks of subtle green plumage, nestling in amongst mousy brown feathers. They showed little shyness, staying on the ground for about thirty seconds and flicking their heads around to stare at the four human beings staring back at them. Then, as quickly as they had arrived they took flight and flew off into a nearby tree.

Callison was reminded of Nuridaga, the silhouette of light he met and his words, *I will be with you in the game also, but I will just be harder to spot.* He wondered if the light being was saying hello to him through the birds on the floor and decided to believe it was. It was a choice made by the experience he had; *everything is connected*, rather than a choice made from the information he'd been trained to believe; *everything is separate.*

After sitting and talking on the bench about more stories of infinity, the Treblas left Callison to get some rest in the hospital bed. The family unit went their own ways for the day ahead feeling happy and whole again.

As it would turn out, Callison would be discharged from hospital the very next day. But before that, he was to meet an old friend.

37.5 –

Callison lay on the hospital bed staring at the ceiling in quiet amazement. *I have a family now*, he thought as he traced the roof tiles with his eyes. He felt well enough to go home, but the hospital doctor was keeping him in to run some further tests. It had been about an hour since his family left and they would be back at three pm to see him again, but now it was just past noon and the ward was bright and airy.

The new arrival to the reality was deep in thought about what Heinrich had said about the people who tried to guard the Eye all being dead as one of the nurses walked up to his side and broke his thought.

'Hi Callison, are you feeling up to seeing another visitor?' she asked politely.

A visitor? 'Yes?' he questioned, 'Who is it?'

'Igor Popovic is here to see you, he said you would know who he was.'

The name rang through Callison's mind like a gong, but he portrayed calmness as his heart raced, 'Oh yes, ok. Send him in.'

She acknowledged and walked off to phone reception.

A few minutes had felt like an entire hour for the hospital's patient but Mystera's multi-dimensional consciousness through Igor Popovic finally arrived into Callison's life, mystifying him when he did.

'No way!' he spoke under his breath to himself as Popovic made his way toward him carrying a briefcase. Callison recognised him straight away, but couldn't believe it. It was the man in the cream suit that spoke to Callison on the bench of his former reality!

'Hello Callison,' said the man as he approached the bed smiling; he was obviously glad his friend was ok, but he smiled for another reason, 'did you have a good awakening?' He stood at the side of the bed staring down at Callison who was by now sitting up in disbelief. Popovic put his leather briefcase down beside him.

'You!' Callison exclaimed, 'How did you get here?' He observed the Popovic of this dimension; he was older than when they met on the bench and had a trimmed grey beard, and matching head of hair, but it was unmistakably the same man, the emerald green eyes piercing Callison's consciousness once again.

'I've been here for thirty years now,' Igor said in a slight Russian sounding English, 'the more relevant question is how did *you* get here?'

Callison thought as the nurse brought a chair for Popovic to sit on. He thanked her and took a seat next to Callison waiting for the answer.

The newly conscious Callison told him, 'This might sound strange, but I think I got here via a portal, which you helped me to re-design and it led me through a crazy experience in a dimension of mind and soul.'

The grinning Igor Popovic nodded and was in agreement, 'Yes, I did the same journey nearly thirty years ago...' And that was the start, or the continuation depending on the reality viewpoint, of their friendship. Callison and Popovic both sat with intrigue as the other explained their version of experience.

* * * * * * *

38: Making Time

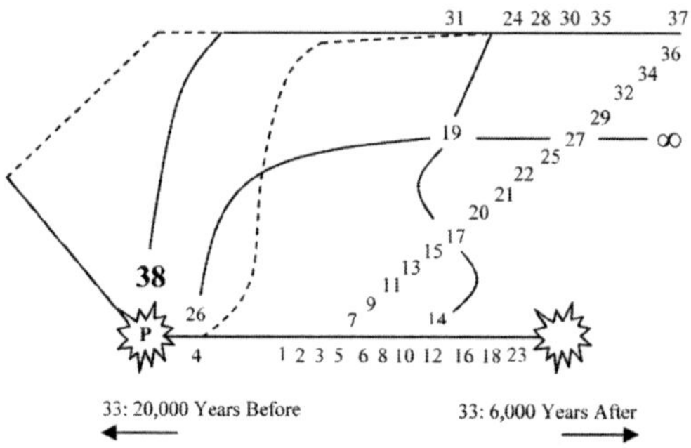

"He, who every morning plans the transaction of the day, and follows the plan, carries a thread that will guide him through the labyrinth of a most busy life."
Victor Hugo, Playwright and Novelist (1802 – 1885)

38.1 –
Flashback:
Siberia, March 10th 1978:

Igor Popovic was just thirty years old when he succeeded in his goal. His time travel idea had worked and now he stood in his solitary research quarters in the Siberian mountains staring at the open portal. The portal consisted of a two metre tall circle with matter whizzing around a tunnel within the circle at light speed. This created a rip in the space-time continuum and now an array of colours all built from light swirled around, mixing in the middle of his invention.

After more research and with excitement, he intrepidly went when no man had gone before and walked through the curtain of light. The experience changed him; it was nothing *like* he expected. It was more an awakening to selfhood than a visit in time. His body hadn't vanished from time and space, but his awareness had and he regained consciousness to find himself lying down on the other side of the portal. His location on the floor tied in perfectly with the lessons he had learned behind the veil of light, taught to him by a being of light over what felt like a few days, that he was conscious energy at his core, rather than body.

The experience was mesmerising for the young Popovic who wrote as much as he could into journals and diaries of his lessons and understandings. As he went back and forth into the realms behind the portal he learned many things. He learned that he wasn't time travelling in the body-limited sense of the term, he was experiencing a larger reality, from where Earth looked more like an illusion or a game of experience. His body on Earth was his vehicle and he was the driver, but in much the same way as we use cars to travel, there are some places that our cars can't go, like into shops and into offices. Similarly, there were some places, or dimensions, that the human body can't go, but the driver can. Igor's awakening was the realisation that he was the driver and had a life outside his vehicle.

Popovic's portal experience broadened as he continued to use the device and he went on to make friends in the realms of mind and soul, learning about the multi-dimensional nature of consciousness. He found out that he had another branch of his consciousness living an Earth life as a Time Shaman called Mystera twenty thousand years ago. Popovic learned directly from his alternate-consciousness new skills and one of which was how to look up and down Earth-based timelines.

Popovic used the skill to witness the looming future of Earth and received a vision of destruction in the future that horrified him; nuclear war. This war didn't last for days, weeks or months however; it lasted for *hours*, until when no nation was capable of launch. It was the last world war. The human race killed itself in an act of collective suicide. During the terrible vision of the future, he saw the worst scenes imaginable; within minutes of the first launch there were a hundred others all fired in mutual retaliation. An eye for an eye was the phrase, but blindness was the inevitable result. As the missiles came back down to the ground, it was like a raining hell. They scorched everything they exploded on without prejudice; houses, businesses, schools, forests, animals, and humans: life on Earth witnessed its darkest day.

Popovic traced back along the time line to see how civilisation had arrived at this doorstep of destiny, and what he learned shocked him. The release of Popovic's own invention would have averted the whole situation, but it would be eventually stolen from him by a ruthless and powerful cabal who sought to suppress the portal of origin and meaning, keeping it for themselves for their own gain over their fellow brothers and sisters. All the while the masses didn't *really* know who they were, or why they were *really* here on Earth, they ended up believing what they were told by the Elite through its mouthpieces of politics, of media, of law and of patriotic propaganda. The shaped and controlled minds of the masses would believe to the death that they were British, French, Iranian, Japanese, Chinese or Russian before they'd believe they were one inter-connected multi-dimensional consciousness observing itself through infinite perspectives. They would believe they were the best nation, region, religion or society and should judge their lesser-perceived counterparts in consciousness and even kill their fellows of opposing illusory division. It was this tendency to believe what they were told blindly that led the masses to the nuclear tragedy.

Mass knowledge of his device would have enlightened the people enough to realise the lie, and hence see the truth; that they were one force experiencing itself through many eyes. To kill another, was to kill a part of yourself.

Behind the portal, Popovic plotted with a being of spiritual light known as his higher self and they looked at changing the blueprints of time so that his portal *would* be revealed to the masses, enlightening the people to where they *really* came from and who they *really* were and waking the free spirits on earth up to the looming geo-political mass-suicide.

Popovic and his higher self noticed that within the blueprints of time someone else would invent a portal some thirty years after Popovic. His name was Callison Trebla, and as the future stood his portal too, would be captured by the world elite. So Popovic and his spiritual self, along with an unsuspecting Callison and his spiritual self sought to avert the future catastrophe.

Popovic woke from this portal nightmare in his usual position on the floor behind the portal and stood up, knowing that in order to avert the future nuclear apocalypse he had to change the current timeline by destroying his portal and all knowledge of it, including himself. Callison's portal would be the one that the world would end up seeing, with Popovic's help.

Popovic stood in front of the portal and breathed in. *This plan had better work* he thought, before entering the portal for the last time in this reality and while his empty human body lay on the floor behind the portal, the invention intentionally began to break up. The resulting explosion was enormous and left nothing but the smallest pieces of evidence strewn over the surrounding site. Popovic was dead. But he wasn't gone; he was in the portal; he was everywhere and everywhen all at once.

During this portal experience, he travelled forward along his departed timeline to the year 2008, ten years before the nuclear catastrophe. He materialised into a street scene on Earth and he walked to where a troubled Callison Trebla sat on a bench trying to work out what was happening to his consciousness. Popovic wore a white cream suit with a matching top hat and spoke with Callison, giving him the idea that he needed in order to realise his invention; the magnetised steam.

After Callison had the knowledge seed planted into his mind, Popovic departed for another moment on the hidden time line, this time a week after Callison had jumped. The dimensional traveller, Igor Popovic watched on as Baron

Braithwaite III spoke before his fraternity deep underneath the Quanta Research laboratories about Callison's portal. Popovic was non-physical in form, and found he could walk around the underground space undetected to its physical beings much like a secret ghost. Popovic even walked onto the main stage, but not a single crowd member noticed him.

After ten minutes of watching and listening to the Baron talk mainly about Popovic's prophesy, Popovic observed the Baron jump through the portal and emerge the other side in the form of a hovering being of light. With the Baron's physical body now slumped unconscious on a mattress, the Baron's conscious self could now see Popovic in light form also.

The two realised each other hovering right in front of the audience, but they were to all intents and purposes invisible from the physical dimension. And while the physical people waited with concern over the pile of atoms that was the Baron's body, Popovic told the Baron everything, about Callison, about himself and about the altered history coming to erase this present. The Baron's game and his secret society's time was up. Their portal was destined to explode and they were being erased.

The Baron eventually disappeared back out of the light spectrum and back into his body, where he came round on the mattress and knew that his time was fated to finish. Popovic witnessed the physical dimension carry on without anyone even seeing him, and after speaking telepathically with the universal mind, Popovic left the fated physical dimension a message they could not miss. He held a marker pen in his attention and grasped it mentally with his mind. The marker pen attracted the attention of the whole room and floated over to the whiteboard where it began to write the words: Karma is coming...

Soon after the secret Quanta audience had realised what was happening, the Eye started to break up. The time wave rippled through the whole room, overwriting the present with a different version. The Eye let go, sending streams and streams of white light out into the room. As the white light slowly subsided, Igor Popovic realised he was the only person around. It was eerily quiet again. His telepathic communication with the Universal Mind continued and he set about the rest of his tasks in the dimension of Mind and Soul.

As the young Siberian scientist's physical body was destroyed in the Siberian explosion in 1978 he could no longer return to it, and instead carried out an intuitive integration while behind the veil of light, to retake a past choice in his life and create an alternate timeline for himself to return to, one where there was no portal in 1978, and one into which Callison Trebla could emerge after his dimensional journey from 2008.

Popovic proceeded on his intuitive integration to a much-feared scene of his own memory. Ten years before he invented his portal, his house had burned down, cruelly taking his mother from him. The young Igor Popovic harboured resentment and guilt towards life at large and regretted deeply the loss of his mother, to the point that his negative outlook helped to create his negative life experiences. The memory was almost too hard to bear for Popovic a second time around, but he observed the scene again as a non-physical third person. He witnessed himself as a twenty-year-old crying in a ball of pain and loss outside his burning house but this time as the ambulance and fire service turned up, something magical happened.

His mother, who had just died in the fire walked amongst the emergency people and onlookers as the drama unfolded. She looked like an angel of white light as she walked towards the now non-physical Popovic. No one else could see them, including his former self but they could see each other. The non-physical dimensional Popovic learned from his mother's spirit that she was supposed to die in the fire; it was her departure from the game. She told him to give thanks for her life, rather than to regret her loss and that she would always love him. After talking about the bigger reality of light, the apparition of his mother floated into a hazy golden light source and for a second time, Popovic had to say goodbye to his mother. But this time he gave thanks, knowing now that she was waiting for him on the other side of life and that death was like a doorway back into higher reality rather than a scary outright end.

He passed the test, and created an alternate reality; one where he decided to give thanks for his mother's life. He eventually went travelling instead of enrolling on a physics course and the portal would be delayed until 2008.

Popovic departed the dimension of mind and soul via the Alpine Stargate and was born consciously into the alternate reality as a thirty-year-old waking from a coma. He had a completely new ten-year history to the one he had left, which had overwritten the time that already had been, but not his memory; Popovic would always remember his departed reality and the route from the portal through the intuitive integration and waking into the parallel life.

Callison would end up jumping into the portal from the old timeline in 2008, and have an experience that would mirror Popovic's, before waking into the parallel reality and finally meeting his friend in time, Igor Popovic.

Popovic lived his relative parallel life quietly, keeping the knowledge of the portal and the inter-dimensional reality behind consciousness to himself until eventually coming to England and getting employment at the Quantum Attic where he would meet a spiritually unconscious Callison Trebla; spiritually unconscious until 2008 that is when he would electrocute himself and fall into a coma.

38.2 –
August 8th 2008:
Current reality in the hospital:

'And that's how I met you. I've known you for nearly fifteen years.' said Popovic as he spoke with Callison about his experience, 'I've been a director at the Attic for six of them.'

Callison lay in the hospital bed stunned at the information

he received, 'You realise I don't remember any of this version of history?'

Popovic understood only too well, 'Of course you don't remember, your experience wasn't here, it was in the last reality, just like mine. You can place your unconscious history together retrospectively though to the point where you will eventually accept it as your actual memory, the human mind is really quite amazing.'

'It's certainly a strange feeling.' said Callison, still coming to terms with being in a parallel reality.

Popovic changed his tone as he spoke with his slightly Russian accented English, 'You want to know something really strange?'

Callison's intrigue was evident, 'Of course,' he curiously replied, 'what is it?'

Popovic spoke with mystery and moved in closer to keep the information between them, 'Well when I woke into this reality, I researched the date on which my portal exploded in the Siberian mountains, you know, to see if there was any evidence of my last timeline's explosion in this reality.'

'Ok.' Callison followed.

'Well...' Popovic was still baffled, 'there wasn't any explosion in the mountains...' he paused again, 'but there were however masses of reports saying that a UFO was seen above the Siberian mountain on the morning my research station exploded in the first reality.'

Callison was as confused as Popovic, 'A UFO? Like a flying saucer you mean?'

He nodded affirmatively, 'According to reports and eye witnesses, in this reality a bright white round disc, that appeared from nowhere, hovered above the location of the former reality's explosion and stayed in place for ten minutes, before vanishing into thin air again. There was no explosion, just a beam of light that reports say shone down as if scanning the site.'

Callison wondered, 'Weird. What do you think it was doing?'

'I don't know, erasing a previous future? Sweeping up an explosion from a parallel reality? Your guess is as good as mine.'

Callison continued to wonder as Popovic opened his briefcase. He handed Callison a newspaper, 'Now read this…' he said, seemingly upping the ante.

Callison's heart rate increased as the new arrival to the dimension scanned the date of the newspaper, it was dated May 23rd 2008; the Justanother Town Gazette. The title headline read: Local MP Jailed Over Expenses. Callison looked back at Popovic, 'What's so strange?' He continued scouring the page until a small column story caught his attention: UFO Sightings Over Justanother Town. He read the article with intense scrutiny, which was continued inside the paper.

According to the story, a strange disc of white light was seen in the sky over Justanother Town's business area on the evening of the 22nd May. The report was very similar to Popovic's UFO over Siberia.

Popovic spoke his thoughts, 'My time in the portal included a visit of your portal exploding. This is what happened in the old reality on the evening of the 22nd May 2008, a week after you jumped. Your portal was scheduled to explode in the hands of the manipulators. I think the UFO's were here again hiding the explosion from the mainstream reality.'

Callison knew that the sightings had been near his old work, Quanta and wondered about it. Now Heinrich's comments made more sense. He had told Callison that the manipulators of the Eye were all dead in an explosion at Quanta. He was in a coma when the UFO story was in the paper. 'I have no answers Igor, but I did see Heinrich on my way back into this reality,' said Callison who had no logic for the events, 'he said that everybody who tried to conceal the device was now dead. Do you think it was this explosion that killed them?'

Igor Popovic nodded, 'It must be. I think we have an Eye to get out into the public domain.'

Callison told him what he knew, 'I am informed by my family that I am still building one in this reality.'

Popovic knew all about it, 'Yes I know, I've been suggesting and helping you from the start. I was just waiting for you to wake up. We are now the only people on the planet, along with your wife that know this technology works.'

Callison tried to understand why all of this had to take place, 'Why did you not just release your invention? Why mine?'

Igor explained, 'My vision of the future showed me that if I had tried to release my findings I would have been easily censored and the authorities would have confiscated the device, and kept it to themselves. It's now 2008, and the rules have changed. The manipulators are gone, and the Internet will spread the news quicker than it can be stopped.'

'What makes you think no one else will seek to censor us?' asked Callison.

'Just a hunch.' Popovic said in his slight Russian English.

'A hunch?' questioned Callison. He thought about it, before realising his lessons on intuition. A smile broke out, 'Ok then, on a hunch it is…'

* * * * * * *

39: Terminus

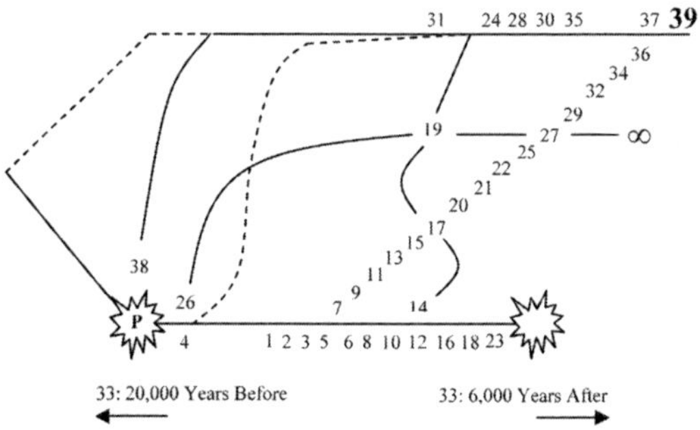

"The power of intuitive understanding will protect you from harm for the rest of your days."
Lao Tzu, Mystic Philosopher (c.600BC)

39.1 –
Current reality:
August 8th 2008:

Callison Trebla lay in his hospital bed as the evening of one of the strangest days of his life came around. His family had been back to visit in the afternoon and left him with the first volume of his memoirs. He sat, propping his back up with pillows reading it with imagined nostalgia, for they were still new memories to the man that only knew his ex-reality. His memoirs were impeccably dated and stretched back nearly thirty years into his unconscious past. He read his most early memoirs that he started writing to help him get through Jack's passing.

Next to his first entry in the old misshapen notebook was a newspaper cutting from the 24th October 1980. The paper had turned a deep yellow colour and was taped into the memoir book. The headline read: Tragedy on High Street. It was the newspaper report that articled Jack's fateful last experience. Reading the paper report again, he felt a tear wanting to break free as the memories came flooding back but the tear subsided as he realised that Jack left the game due to plan. Callison had let him go. His pen marks from nearly thirty years ago showed their age, and the notepaper too had turned a pale yellow colour from the elapsed years. He started to read his own words.

"2nd November 1980: I miss him so much. Every time I close my eyes, I see him laughing and being happy." Callison could feel the words stir his emotions, but continued reading, "It is like I am at a lake," it read, "I am lost. The lake is so still." *The lake of reflection* Callison thought, as he read on. "I see Jack's face telling me everything will be ok. Telling me to be strong, but I cry again. Am I strong or weak for that?" He looked up from the page as a feeling of memory came back to him from the lake of reflection; he understood his intuitive integration more now and seeing Jack at the lake was part of this realities' mental grieving process, it would seem.

He continued to read the memoirs, and slowly they moved away from feelings about Jack and started to detail his, as yet unknown life. Shortly after Callison had come to terms with Jack's death, he decided to hand in his resignation from the Quanta Research Corporation, to pursue a fascination with the nature behind the mind and mental healing. He took a research post doing studies into psychic phenomena and the nature of consciousness, before Eleanor fell pregnant for a second time with James, and the rest he guessed was history. He still had many of his memoirs to read, but the rest all still lay at his house.

A nurse came round encouraging the patients in the ward to turn lights out and get to sleep, so Callison put his memoir volume on the table at his side and closed his eyes; he'd been awake for the whole day and getting some sleep was just what his body needed and he easily floated off into the very unconscious process of entering the dream state.

Callison was asleep and relaxed, and as his memories and thoughts slowly spiralled into a dream, he could see and hear his first son, Jack talking to him, leading him out of the darkness of his sleep and into the light of a timeless dream.

'Follow me daddy...' Jack's little voice called.

Callison called back into the darkness, 'Where are you Jack?'

'I'm here daddy.' His voice sounded like it was captured in time and echoed all around Callison.

Callison couldn't see anything but a white dot emerge in the darkness and grow into a scene. The sun was out, it was green and they were by a lake. Jack stood next to the water's edge looking like he was as real as ever. He was naked, and painted in a golden colour as was Callison.

The dreamt wind blew across their faces as father and son smiled at each other from across the divides of time. Callison ran to Jack and held him in his arms again. Not even death could keep the characters apart.

'Jack, I'm so glad to see you. I have so much to tell you son.' said Callison as he crouched down to speak to his boy on his level.

Jack laughed, he was still five years old in Callison's image, 'I told you that you had to let me go daddy.'

'And you were right son, I am very happy again.' said the dad full of positive emotion, 'You are a very wise little man, do you know that?'

Jack smiled and looked into his dad's eyes, 'I like it when you are happy.'

Callison had forgotten he was dreaming. 'I like it when *you* are happy son - you are happy, right?' He was still a parent at heart.

'Yes, of course I am happy, daddy.'

Callison felt relief, 'That's good.' The dream moved on unconsciously and before long, father and son were flying through the clouds riding the wind.

'Weeeeee!' shrieked Jack with enjoyment as he flew high above the ground.

His dad was exhilarated with him, Wooooo hoooooo!' he shouted back.

They flew next to each other with the wind of imagination blasting their faces. Jack called to his dad, 'I like going fast daddy!'

It wasn't the first time Jack had used those words. Callison challenged him, 'Come on, I'll race you to the horizon!'

His dad started to accelerate away from him, but Jack put his hammer down, and caught up. Father and son raced faster and faster towards the infinite horizon, until they gave up, exhausted and exhilarated. 'That was fun son, you *are* fast!'

Jack was proud as he hovered in the dreamtime.

Callison was happy to be in a good dreamscape for the first time in as long as he could remember.

Suddenly Jack changed the subject. 'I'm still with you daddy. I'll always be with you.'

'What do you mean Jack?' said Callison, slightly confused.

Callison heard his voice, but things had changed. His awareness was pulled back into a quiet hospital ward. Jack was a memory and it was dark and quiet again.

He had been dreaming. Reality took over and he heard some footsteps at the end of the ward, he glanced in the vicinity of the footsteps and a clock on the wall read three-thirty in the morning.

Nice dream. Callison thought. The emotions were uplifting and exciting compared to the confusing nightmares he was used to. Jack was happy in the infinite mind somewhere and Callison could get on with living his life, guilt free. It had taken nearly thirty years, but he had finally accepted the loss and felt the weight lift from his weary shoulders. Alone in the hospital ward, Callison silently cried tears of happiness and sadness rolled into one, like he had been freed from his self-imposed chains of misery. He said a prayer to Jack, *Be free son. I am going to be ok. Daddy will always love you. See you in the infinite.*

His tears abated, but he continued to mentally dwell upon the dream and his situation in the current reality until dawn broke and the hospital geared up for the coming day again.

39.2 –
The next day:

He had been discharged just thirty hours after waking from a four-month coma. To say the doctors were impressed with his recovery was an understatement, Callison stubbornly walked out of the doors of the hospital.

James drove his father, along with Sally and Eleanor back home in Callison's larger car. Callison couldn't believe it when they approached the vehicle in the hospital car park; the car was identical to his car in the old dimension, the large German saloon, even the registration number was the same. *For all its differences this reality sure is similar*, he thought as he got into the front passenger seat with a confused smile.

Eleanor climbed into the back seat behind him, and Sally sat behind James who was in the driver's seat. Their ordeal was over and the family were in high spirits as they left the memory of the hospital behind them and continued their lives.

Callison was amazed to set eyes upon the parallel dimension at large. As his son drove him home, Callison sat and looked out the window at the surroundings of Justanother Town passing by. Although this dimension was a parallel one to the one he knew, it looked identical. Callison knew where they were travelling and remembered things he'd done in the old reality at the places they passed along the way.

Still, the major change of experience was *inside* the car. Callison pulled his gaze inside the cabin again, and looked at James, his son, driving. He smiled back at Eleanor in the back seat, who knew the profundity of the situation they found themselves in.

James approached the motorway slip lane and as he pulled onto it he accelerated the car and its occupants to eighty miles per hour.

Eleanor warned him in a mothering way, 'You be careful now James.'

Their son was adamant it was ok as he eased off the accelerator, 'There's no traffic about mum, I'm not going to break the sound barrier!'

Callison smiled. It was what he used to do.

'Still, better to be safe than sorry.' said Eleanor.

James protested to his mother, innocently joking, 'But I like going fast!'

Callison stopped smiling as the memory of his dream with Jack came back to him with a bang, *I'm still with you daddy. I'll always be with you.* Callison sat staring at his second son, James, realising who he was. His intuitive integration made more sense; *You need to let me come back daddy, by letting me go...*

'Are you ok Dad?' asked his new favourite son, concerned as he drove.

Callison smiled back at him; his new life was perfect, 'Yes son, I'm perfect.' he said, realising he'd changed everything. He added, smiling at Sally and Eleanor also, 'Everything is just perfect.'

THE END...

Well almost...

40: Choose Love...

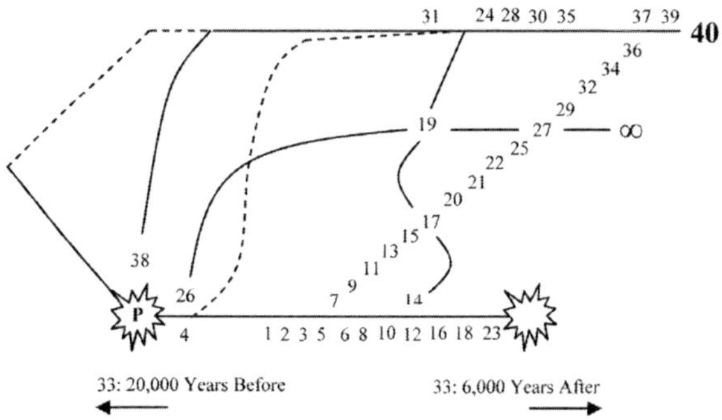

"Love is the lesson to learn in our time."
John Martyn, Songwriter and Guitarist (1948 – 2009)

40.1 –
Somewhere, somewhen:

'It has been said that we live in interesting times...' the grey haired and bald scientist paused, as his words were amplified and echoed around the press conference room. He hoped they would like his discovery, but didn't honestly know if they were ready for it.

Some camera flashes from the press flickered cyclically as the scientist continued; 'We live in a time for instance, where we can download vast amounts of information from all over the world to a mobile phone in a matter of seconds.' He paused for effect. 'We live in a time of space exploration and space rockets. We live in a time of gadgets and electronics,' he said before another pause, 'we say we are in the modern age, the technological era. We say we are an advanced species.' He paused, to give his words time to soak in. 'But are we *really*? *Are* we an advanced species?' He reasoned, 'We also invent money and nuclear weapons, yet when it comes to inventing money to feed and clothe the people of the world, we say there is not enough money and it's just the way the world is.' Another pause. '*Are* we really advanced?' he asked again.

The speech changed tack, 'The answer to that question, one might argue, would depend on the inbuilt nature of mankind and whether we are inherently violent or peaceful.' He let the words hang. 'What do you think?' The cameras continued to roll. 'Are we naturally peaceful, and tend to violence, or are we naturally violent and tend to peace? If we don't know the answer to that question, I suggest we are in the midst of a global identity crisis.' He paused for more effect. 'I read a quote from somewhere once, I forget where, or even who said it, but it was this: It is pointless to try and see the world the way it is, for we will only ever see the world the way we are.' He let the concept settle. 'How true do we think that is? Do we even understand it?' The presenter looked around the room.

He moved on. 'The scientific papers that I will be publishing today, along with Igor Popovic will outline a device, called "The Eye" and provide detailed analyses of subjects interfacing the device for a period of one year. The study has been classified secret until today and the findings reveal proof for the continuation of consciousness after death.'

Murmurs and talking rippled around the audience as the news sunk in. The speaker tried to assume order again, 'Now this day has been coming, science and spirit have been on a collision course for some years now.' His audience were listening again. 'The now infamous double slit experiment has proven that the very act of observing matter affects the matter we see. We see the matrix of matter all around us, thinking we're separate from it, but in actual fact we are part of it and it is part of us. Well, what if we could knowingly interact with that matrix? What if we could master it?'

And that was the start of the speech that changed the world.

Soon, Callison was demonstrating what the Trebla Eye was and how it was powered with some slides on the front facing projector. The audience were captivated, and hung on the scientist's every word while looking at the diagrams on the screen. He explained how the magnetised steam circumnavigated the outer periphery at light speed, opening the zero point field and pulling open the portal revealing a doorway to the infinite. He showed photographs of the white shimmering portal growing in size to take up the entire space in the portal area as the magnetised steam hit light speed.

He moved on to talk about how the portal was interfaced by the user. It was only the head that needed to penetrate the portal boundary, so The Eye had been modified to include a motorised bed that resembled an MRI scan machine. The subjects of the case studies lied down on the bed and were dipped, head first, through the portal, then one minute later, the bed was moved back through. As the head broke through the portal for the first time, the body jolted and the subjects were then to all intents and purposes, unconscious. When the bed moved back through the veil of light, the subject came back round to consciousness after a few minutes.

The subjects of the study were of most significance. In the year that the study had been running for, approximately one thousand people had agreed to experience the portal's effect. They included people from all walks of life, from businessmen, to students to housewives to scientists. All subjects were paid for their time, and all had seen Callison use his own machine. Psychiatric notes were taken, and peoples' experiences were all documented. All of the subjects said the experience felt at first like a vivid dream, but as they became more accustomed to it they could associate in more detail what was happening; it wasn't a dream, it was another reality they were experiencing; a reality that showed them insights about Earth and about being human; insights into another larger community outside the confines of planet Earth.

Many subjects started to report a complete awareness of leaving the body as they penetrated the light curtain and seeing themselves lying down on the Trebla Eye bed. Other experiences included walking through impossible geometric surroundings, communicating with telepathic beings of light, visiting whole cities of light, even meeting past life characters and deceased relatives. Even though the subjects were under for only one minute in earth time, they reported back having experiences that lasted for what felt like hours or days. A small proportion of the subjects reported feeling like they'd been away for years. Callison highlighted the obvious topic of reincarnation, but made no attempt to either confirm or deny the concept. He was a scientist; these were the findings.

Callison explained that as the study progressed, the subjects reported a building up of familiarisation in the realms beyond the portal. They met regulars, and became friends with the inter-dimensional entities they met. Inter-dimensional entities they knew even before they were born, who reminded them of events they had plans for during life. All subjects noticed their life situations start to change for the positive, as they followed more intuitively what they wanted to do in life. It seemed like all the logic in the world was not as good as conscience and intuition for guiding oneself through the matrix of life choices.

Some subjects learned skills while outside their bodies, and brought them to their physical existences on Earth in their human form. Telekinesis and telepathy were the most pronounced, but subjects also displayed newfound painting talent, memory improvement, remote seeing; that is seeing as another person, precognition, levitation and teleportation. The press conference room was stunned. All subjects portrayed an increased sense of empathy, and a decreased frequency in anger. Whatever was behind the portal was improving the life-quality and the knowledge of the test subjects.

Callison came on to the current research, 'Now, moving onto the latest research...' He looked at the clock. 12.30, '...and I'll try to be brief...' He checked with his press secretary, acknowledging a hurry-up signal. '...but this has to be said.'

'In the last month of the study, four of the test subjects are reporting that they can access the portal's realm through their own mind at will, which leads me to believe this,' he paused to sum up.

'The Eye is not the doorway; it is the path *to* the doorway.' His audience were lost momentarily. 'Now what I mean by saying that is I believe the doorway is in our own minds, and it's always been there. The Eye is merely the stimulant that propels one through that doorway. Every single one of us has the doorway, but very few of us find it, or are even aware of it, for in order to find it we need peaceful well built minds.' He added. 'Or as it would appear, a stimulant like The Eye.'

'This internal doorway within the mind has been called many things over the ages, The Third Eye, The Lantern of Osiris, The Minds Eye, The All Seeing Eye.' He paused again. 'Modern science would know the doorway as the pineal gland; a gland in the centre of our heads that secretes a chemical known as DMT, or Di Methyl Tryptamine to induce the dream state. Philosophers have called the Pineal gland the Seat of the Soul and religions have referred to it's effects as divine visions.'

'Now, the questions raised by this research study certainly make for strange bedfellows, and I certainly don't propose the answers. For instance, where did the knowledge go? What is the difference between history and what actually happened in our past?'

It got stranger for the audience. 'What if what *we* call reality, is actually a higher world simulation? What implications would this have to our experience of life? Does it mean life doesn't matter? Does it mean life is meaningless? No! It means life *has* a meaning.' He paused. 'It would mean the world is a stage and we are the actors, in a drama that will be retold throughout the eternity of our being. What is the story looking like so far? What do we want the story to be?' He paused.

'Before the questions, of which I'm sure they'll be some,' he smiled. 'I'd like to finish by coming back to that question of our identities: Who are we? Well, the answer to that when you truly understand yourself is: We are whatever we invent ourselves to be,' Callison stopped before completing his speech, 'we are the inventors of experience, and we can invent to the limit of our own imagination.' He smiled and nodded his head assertively, as if to say *end of presentation*.

After a standing ovation of applause, the audience knew it was time for their questions and the room sparked with competing press.

One of the questions prompted Callison to really cement the day in history. About halfway through the question time slot, someone asked. 'Telekinesis? What a load of rubbish. Are you serious or mad?'

Callison heard the question in amongst others fired to him, and something inside him flipped. His actions were automatic and he zeroed in on the press agent. 'Sorry I didn't hear you? What did you say?'

He asked again. 'Telekinesis? It's a load of bull.' He went quiet under the scrutiny of the other press agents.

'Sorry. Still didn't hear you. Here, have the microphone.' Callison didn't even look at the microphone in front of him, but it started to move towards the journalist, seemingly hovering through the air. Every eye and camera in the room focused on the hovering microphone. Callison continued when the microphone was in front of the man, where it hovered near the journalist's face. 'There, if you'd like to ask again? What was your question now?'

The journalist didn't know what to say. His eyes were telling him something his mind couldn't; all the while he had the attention of the whole room. He went red with embarrassment. He couldn't believe it was Telekinesis, and waved his hands around the voice transformer. There were no wires.

'Telekinesis isn't bull,' said Callison. 'It's just that you believe experience to be a certain way. Experience is only limited by your own imagination.'

All of the next mornings' papers carried the same picture on their front page; that hovering microphone.

* * * * * * *

Callison retired officially one year after he made the presentation, and five years after his first retirement episode in the last reality. He and Eleanor lived out the rest of their collective Earth dream blessed with their family, and grateful for their experiences. These life times would be talked about during their eternity to come.

As for humanity, it slowly woke up in time to avert the nuclear annihilation. As more and more people used The Eye to experience the larger reality, they realised that the information they needed was inside all along. The illusory pictures they had built in their minds of who they thought they were and what they thought they should do was like a default programme. It was society's programme on them. They had been unconsciously conditioned to make money, consume and compete, unknowingly causing a prison of character to form in their own minds, cutting them off from their true power to grow collectively.

As the pieces of default programme were taken down in their minds, the people of Earth opened themselves up to the universal truth: we were consciousness, not body. No longer was death the feared mystery it had been, and instead became the next chapter of an exciting experience in the amusement park of the eternal now.

Experience rolled on and the collective Earth drama had to reflect the newfound mental state of its actors. That was the rule. As people individually realised peace for themselves, their true nature revealed itself and the collective changed, peace by piece. A planet-wide party of love and unity swept the planet by storm and the planet was united in the galactic light of the new dawn.

A year after Callison's invention was released, a fair money system was created. The old, fraudulent interest-based system and its perpetrators were exposed and their flimsy houses of cards fell like giant towers. A new economy, based not on inventive financial grounds but on energy and population resources rose from the scandal. People were witnessing the evolution of ideas, and it seemed as if anything was possible. The new system freed the people. They still worked, but for two days a week for the running of services only. The extra time off allowed them to explore their own divine spirit in however which way they wanted.

Two years after the Trebla Eye was unveiled, all armies stood down globally and destroyed their nuclear arsenals. War was a forgotten nightmare of the dark ages. Terrorism, state sponsored and religious, ceased and crime vanished.

Three years after the eyes release, all country borders were dissolved and humans called themselves Earth beings. Starvation and poverty slowly became a thing of the past. One hundred million people signed up for the space project and one year later would travel the galaxy telling stories of the upheaval and collective emergence of the consciousness of peace on planet Earth. The star people came from all over the galaxy to congratulate the world on its rise to maturity and donated their technology to nurse the planet back to health again.

After the long, arduous, and twisting passage of time, the human race came to a new era of conscious thought and started to write the Earth story the way *they* wanted it. And, boy, *what* a story they would write....

JUST THE BEGINNING....

41: Or Choose Fear...

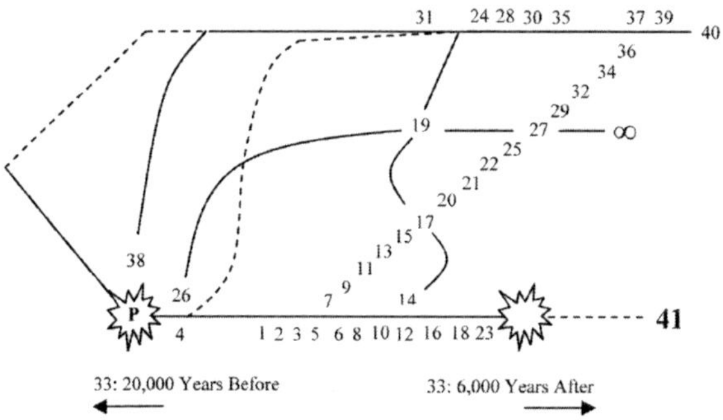

"It is not death or pain that is to
be dreaded, but the fear of death or pain."
Epictetus, Philosopher (55-135AD)

41.1 –
Somewhere, somewhen:

Meanwhile, in the reality departed, Callison was dead. Murdered by Heinrich as part of a top-secret corporate agenda. His wife too, had been murdered. The Portal was now consigned to secret history again, meaning it was as good as extinct. The dimension was far from over from the point of reference of its inhabitants though, and last night a huge explosion in the confines of the business district of Justanother Town had devastated the Quanta Research Corporation's headquarters.

After some modest media attention and misinformation over the mysterious explosion, the story was eclipsed by another breaking news story. Micha McDonnell the well-known popular music celebrity was found to be guilty in court of throwing her phone at a member of paparazzi. The world looked on in horror as she was sentenced to 200 hard hours of community service. Most normal people couldn't bear to leave the television alone, fixed and gripped by the shocking news that topped the bill of all the talk shows, chat shows, news broadcasts, web pod casts, interviews, that were all for the benefit of the people.

The guilty verdict had shocked, but this was not the first time a shocking news story had broken. They were seemingly breaking everyday in this mad and chaotic world, crashing in on the shores of the minds of the people as if a mental storm were brewing on the islands of the minds of humanity.

To leave the shores of one's mind now would be pure madness the people thought, you'd just not survive it, some of the economy waves and war waves were enormous and crashed in hard on the shores of many minds. No, they stayed on their mental islands instead, building walls to protect them from the incoming waves of information but in the process blinding them to their true position in the sea.

They were the sane ones they thought, because on the islands of their minds they had everything they imagined they wanted; a warm home, happiness, television, food, sex, money, a growing economy, and all they needed to do was work for someone else for it.

There was one thing however, that the island characters didn't have and had grown to forget: the knowledge of how they had arrived on their mental islands in the first place, and knowledge of what actually existed off their coastline of ideas. It scared them, and instead of setting sail into the stormy waves, and exploring the tranquil seas off the islands of their minds, they answered the questions of origin by inventing something called common sense. *Believe someone else.* Many other minds came forward and suggested what lay off the shores of their minds and why we were all on our mental islands in the first place. The people would never need to set sail again, they thought; the experts informing them owned many qualifications and had won many distinctive awards.

From what the people of this physical dimension and time could see, the war, the destruction, the poverty, the money worries, the financial unfairness, the unemployment, the stress - this was just the way their world was, they thought, but it wasn't; it was just the way *they* were. They had no intention of finding out what actually lay beyond the horizon of their minds because they believed in common sense; everyone knew that nothing lay off the shores, and those that thought different were deluded. So they craved infotainment and possessions while they were stranded on their self-imagined bubbles of stormy illusion.

Occasionally it would occur when a human being decided to brave the crashing waters around their psyche and advance past the emanation of the waves to find a stunning peace and tranquil sea. Occasionally a human might find other islands; taller islands, more peaceful islands, where they could see further and understand more. They travel back to the islands they once called home to tell the people and encourage the people to get out past the big scary waves coming in and see that reality is whatever they imagine it to be.

But the message fell upon deaf ears. Instead of listening, the islanders resisted out of fear. They would sooner fight each other for the survival of their illusions than explore themselves for the understanding of their truth.

And so the last world war drew ever closer...

THE END

Final Comment from the Author

I hope you enjoyed reading this story and that it took your imagination to places it maybe hasn't been for a while. Now I did have another thirty pages here, explaining how human beings interpret and process information. It included Tetris metaphors, identity metaphors, human learning metaphors, and metaphors within the story you've just read, but I've edited most of it, because I felt like I was attempting to file the information of this book in your mind for you. You are the only one that can see how this information sits upon the landscape of your mind and you are the only information handler on duty within you. So I leave it up to you what to think about Callison's journey and the Copernicus Effect.

Instead I will leave you with an anecdote about an ox, two more quotes and some of the inspirational seeds that eventually germinated into this story.

The anecdote about a cow concerns an implied collective intelligence, and goes like this; Francis Galton, scientist and cousin of Charles Darwin, made a discovery in 1906 of what is known as 'the wisdom of crowds'. He attended a farmer's fair in Plymouth where he was intrigued by a weight guessing competition. The goal was to guess the weight of an ox and the person who guessed closest won a prize. 800 people entered the contest by writing their guesses on tickets and after a winner was found, Galton asked to take the 800 individual guesses and run a statistical analysis on them. He discovered that the average guess of all the entrants was remarkably close to the actual weight of the ox. In fact the 800 people's average was under by only 1lb for an ox that weighed 1,198 lbs. This collective guess was not only better than the actual winner of the contest but also better than the guesses made by cattle experts at the fair! Is there a collective intelligence at work here? Or was it just coincidence? The mind boggles...

The penultimate quote is from the late, great, Bill Hicks. He was a stand-up comedian who has given me many hours of enjoyment and laughter. I also think that he realised something in his short but illuminated life, and it is summed up in this quote. It's how he used to close his shows and he called it his message. I agree with it; let's hear it:

> "No matter how scary life gets, and it does; it's just a ride. And when we choose to go on the ride we think it's real, because that's how powerful our minds are. It goes up and down and round and round; it's very brightly coloured and it's very loud, and it's fun for a while. A lot of people have been on the ride for a long time and they question, *is this real? Or is this just a ride?* And they remember, and come back to us and say hey, don't worry, ever, because it's just a ride... And we kill those people. *Shut him up, I've got a lot invested in this ride, shut him up, look at my furrows of worry, look at my big bank account, this just has to be real.* It's just a ride, but we always kill the good guys, don't we? But let the demons run amuck? Jesus; murdered. Ghandi; murdered. Lennon; murdered. Luther King; murdered. Reagan.... wounded. But it doesn't matter, coz it's just a ride. And we can change the ride any time we like. It's just a choice you can make right now, between love and fear. The eyes of fear want you to get bigger locks for your doors, buy guns and the eyes of love, instead see things as though we are all one. Here's how we could make the ride a better place right now: instead of spending the money we do on arms and weapons each year, why don't we spend it feeding, clothing and homing the poor of the world, which it would

many times over, not one human being left behind, and maybe we could explore space; inner and outer, together. For ever."

Bill Hicks, Comedian (1961 – 1994)

I hope you understand Bill's message, but if not, one day you might.

The last quote is by George Bernard Shaw and was highlighted to me by my father, just as I was closing out this section of the writing. Now people have often called me cynical in my assertions about the corporate ownership surrounding politics, media and our lives in general, so this quote kind of resonated with me:

"The power of accurate observation is commonly called cynicism by those who have not got it."

George Bernard Shaw, Author (1856 – 1950)

The timing of hearing this quote was perfect and it's as best-as-way as any to close this book out.

And so to the inspirational seeds I mentioned earlier. The inspiration for writing this story came from our innate interest to try and make sense of the world that we live in, and the internet is better than any other source when it comes to information on the subject. The weight guessing anecdote above shows just how much more accurate we are when we work together, and the internet is the embodiment of that effect. It has grown to the point where it could be considered a collective consciousness more than a computer program and I can't stress enough how important it is that we do not tolerate censorship of the internet in any way, shape or form. One can propose the case that the internet has helped warp people, but I can equally propose the case that it has helped enlighten people more.

So these seeds below particularly flourish in video internet search engines when words like 'interview', 'speech' or 'documentary' are added. If you want a balanced opinion, and to prove I'm not a misled paranoid freak in a tin foil hat trying to manipulate you, try adding the words 'Hoax' or 'fraud' to these seeds. They are not the truth and they are not the lie, for the truth and the lie can only ever exist within you. These seeds are raw information.

Who Are You? Spiritual Understanding, Primacy of Consciousness, Peter Russell, Ian R Crane, The Illusion of Reality, Universal Consciousness, Leonard Horowitz, Zeitgeist, Richard Gage, John Hagelin, Nicola Tesla, Ascension, Bob Dean, Bill Still, The Money Masters, The Economic Hit Man, Outfoxed, Loose Change, Paradigm Shift TV, Carl Jung, William Cooper, Bob Proctor, Jordan Maxwell, The Bonesmen of Yale, John James Harris, Freeman on the Land, Atlantis History, Lemuria History, Richard D. Hall, Richplanet TV, Prescott Bush the Union Oil Corporation and I. G. Farben, The Corporation, Joel Bakan, G. Edward Griffin, Fractional Reserve Banking, Modern Money Mechanics, Robin Cook, Fred Allen Wolf, The Club of Rome, The Committee of 300, Aaron Russo and the Rockefellers, America: Freedom to Fascism, Kymatica, Pull it, Building 7, David Icke, Problem-Reaction-Solution, Graham Hancock, Ayahuasca, Francis Crick LSD, James Gilliland, Michael Tsarion, Architects of Control, Dolores Cannon, The Secret, Bill Hicks, Doug Stanhope, George Carlin, Edgar Cayce, Jim Marrs, What the bleep do we know, Dean Radin, Dannion Brinkley, Stanislav Grof, Hank Wesselman, Lorraine Day, Lee Gerdes, Russell Targ, Robert Verkerk, Scott Tips, Leuren Moret, Lynne McTaggart, Clifford Stone, MK Ultra, Monarch, Rendlesham Forest,

The Reichstag Fire, False Flag Terrorism, Gulf of Tonkin Incident, JesseVentura, Democracy Now, PNAC and a new pearl harbour, Journey of Souls, Michael Newton, The Story of Stuff, Peter Power, Muad'Dib, Stan Meyer, Water engine, Robert Monroe, Soul travel, Astral projection, Lucid dreaming, Out-of-Body experiences, The Spirit Molecule, David Kelly, The double slit experiment, The observer effect, Quantum entanglement, Joe Vitale, Enlightenment, Secret History of the World, Illuminati, Bilderberg, History of banking, The Rothchild Story, Council on Foreign Relations, Chatham House, The Trilateral Commission, Dave Von Kleist, Michael Beckwith, The Awakening, George Kavassilas, The Corporatocracy, Brian Gerrish, Edge Media TV, Conscious Media Network, Regina Meredith, Jon King, The Forbidden Cures, Esther Hicks, Money as Debt, William Buhlman, Red Ice Creations, Rauni Leena Luukanen-Kilde, The British Constitution Group, Roger Hayes, Lawful Rebellion, Robert Arthur Menard, Andy Thomas, Quantum reality, The Field, Manjir Samanta-Laughton, David Bohm, The Montauk Project, MJ-12, Karl Pribram, Holographic reality, HAARP, Richard Hoagland, Rick Strassman, James Gleick, Jeremy Glick vs Bill O'Reilly, The Story of Stuff, David Noakes, Saxe-Coburg family history, Ancient wisdom, Time wave zero, and....... I think that's enough seeds. I know it takes time on the internet, what with work and everything, but plant them, or leave them; it's up to you.

So I bid you farewell. Happy trails reader, and remember, the difference between knowing something and thinking you know something... well, there is no difference.

Will Disdale, 2011.